Operation Origami

The Ire of Claudia

Book #5 Max & Olivia Series

Books In This Series

Operation Underpants (2016)

Claudia (2017)

Operation OBE - Over Bloody Eighty (2018)

St. Mary's Dating Agency (2020)

Operation Origami - The Ire of Claudia (2021)

Operation Snowflake (2021)

Other books by Mark A. Biggs

Above and Beyond: 2nd edition (2014)

Love Letters From Dresden: Book #1 Artōrius Series (2019)

Silent Trail: Book # 2 Artōrius Series (2024)

Operation Origami

The Ire of Claudia

A CIP catalogue record for this book is available from the National Library of Australia.

First published in Australia 2021.

mbkbooks

62 Sunnybrook Ave

Warragul Victoria 3820

Australia

www.markabiggs.com

Dedication

To Jack and Charlee

PROLOGUE

The explosion rattled the church hall windows and the entire building quivered as if struck by a magnitude six earthquake. Afterwards, the sound of the blast receded and, for a few seconds, not a noise could be heard, only deathly silence.

John's house in Pi-Ski, Cornwall, England, had been destroyed, and he was dead. The Crane would have killed them both, but John dying on his own was a bonus for the assassin. For such a creature, nothing was more satisfying than inflicting permanent emotional scars on an adversary. The CIA and MI6 believe that the Crane now worked exclusively for the Chinese Ministry of State Security, the MSS and, over the previous ten years, the assassin had systematically eliminated people who annoyed the Chinese State with brutal efficiency, including foreign agents. Their government kept the dirty work at arm's length, providing plausible deniability, though the international intelligence community knew who paid the bills.

By falling in love with John, Claudia had condemned him to death.

'You shouldn't have done that, Sweetie,' Claudia screamed in her raw pain and grief. She pictured Chen Li, the man who headed MSS intelligence operations in Britain plus his six colleagues she'd encountered at the prestigious Chinese Shark Fin restaurant in Soho London, knowing they were responsible for John's death. His murder was an act of retribution for her termination of Mr. Yáyī, one of the diners, who had been sent to take her life.

Claudia visualised the table of diners at the restaurant, her mind racing. *I will start with you, Sweeties, all of you! Then, Crane, whoever, and wherever you are, I am coming for you next. John, this is my solemn vow and promise in memory of you. I will show no mercy, Sweeties. Before you die, you will each beg me to end your suffering.*

Claudia crumpled the paper crane handed to her seconds before the explosion in her fist, letting it fall to the ground. In her mind she screamed, *Hell, hath been unleashed. Claudia is coming*, but on the outside, she appeared to those around, unmoved, stoic in the face of adversity. A brave woman, some who were there would later pronounce.

CHAPTER 1
The Ire of Claudia

John Moss had been an unwitting mule, recruited by the lure of love by a British secret agent, Claudia, to carry the "Quantum Cube", a national secret stolen from the Chinese government into the United Kingdom. Once Claudia retrieved the device, she was going to leave him stranded at the altar. Falling in love hadn't been part of her plan.

Following the explosion which killed John Moss, Claudia spoke with Stephen Walls, the head of MI6, over the phone and his instructions were for her to remain in Pi-Ski for a couple more days.

'It may look suspicious Claudia, if you up and leave in too much of a hurry,' he'd said. 'Although, I will want to see you.'

Because of Christmas, New Year and the attention the explosion garnished, the funeral for John Moss was delayed until January. A week before the interment, Claudia was summoned to London and a meeting with Stephen Walls at the MI6 top-secret facility underneath the St Ermin's Hotel in Westminster, London.

Stephen Walls was fifty-nine years of age with a crop of black hair, albeit dyed. He was a smart dresser, preferring a tasteful lounge suit and tie to the brightly coloured bow tie and scrunched-up handkerchief protruding from a breast pocket, as was the way of many of his peers. Claudia first met Stephen after the sinking of the yacht *Lelantos,* when he welcomed her into MI6. She considered him handsome for a man of his age and found his well-spoken English accent alluring.

'Come,' Stephen called when Claudia knocked on his office door.

Stephen was seated behind his antique carved oak pedestal desk and stood when Claudia entered before walking over to greet her. He smiled warmly, saying, 'Thank you for seeing me, and so quickly after the unfortunate incident.' Stephen extended his hand for Claudia to shake.

Claudia wanted to say, *Did I have a choice?* But she said, instead, 'It's okay Stephen, I knew you wanted to talk with me.'

Stephen nodded as he pointed towards one of the two vacant red Chesterfield armchairs in the room. They each took a seat, making themselves comfortable, as Stephen said, 'Can I get you something to drink?'

'Tea. English Breakfast.'

Stephen raised an eyebrow, thinking the beverage a strange choice for an ex-Russian spy, but Claudia ignored his reaction. Stephen pressed the intercom button on the elegant side table next to his chair, saying, 'James.'

'Yes Sir,' came the reply.

'Two teas, please. English Breakfast.' He paused and looked at Claudia. 'Milk?'

She shook her head, and he said, 'No milk.'

'Right away, Sir.'

Stephen looked at Claudia, and with his face and voice showing genuine concern, said, 'I was sorry to hear about John's death.'

'Collateral damage,' Claudia said dismissively. 'It's never a good look but, in our line of work, Stephen, sometimes an outcome like John's is inevitable. Given the circumstances, it could have been worse; the Church could have been the target of their retribution.'

Stephen pondered on what Claudia had said, ignoring her attempt to widen the conversation beyond John. He'd seen the footage taken during the filming of the Vienna Boys' Choir Christmas Special at St Mary's Church, Pi-Ski and watched, as Claudia and John nursed a baby, while Max Joseph, arguably the world's best boy soprano sang, *Away in a Manger*. Years of experience in the spy game told Stephen that Claudia had fallen for John Moss, intended as a pawn, manipulated into becoming a mule, and then a sexual partner; all part of Claudia's cover. If Stephen was correct, and he was sure that he was, Claudia was a loose cannon, a wounded revengeful animal, planning retribution against the Chinese. She was a risk to MI6 and Britain. She was also expendable, but he hoped it wouldn't come to that.

Moving his hand to his chin, a gesture of introspection, Stephen said, 'Yes, unfortunate but sometimes inevitable. Even so Claudia, John was an innocent bystander in this whole sordid affair. It would be understandable if part of you felt you had failed to protect him?'

'Is that what MI6 thinks?' Claudia said, maintaining her calm, knowing that she was playing cat and mouse with Stephen.

Stephen shook his head as he said, 'No, not at all. You did what was necessary to secure the quantum cube. We are grateful...' Their conversation was interrupted by a knock on the door and Stephen called, 'Come.'

James entered carrying a tray with a pot of tea and two bone china cups and saucers and after placing a cup in front of each of them and pouring the tea, asked, 'Is there anything else, Sir?'

'No, that will be all. Thank you, James.'

When the door closed, Stephen continued, 'We are indebted to you, Claudia. I ask because I watched the Christmas Special footage. You appeared...' he paused, seeking the right words, '...fond of John. Understandable, of course. Our practice is to support an agent who loses their partner in our service.'

Claudia was careful. She knew Stephen was fishing, wanting to discover if she'd become unhinged, a lone wolf desiring to strike back at those behind John's murder. She needed to deceive MI6 into tracking down those she thought were responsible. That would mean feigning detachment while acknowledging regret at his loss, a hard path to tread, striking the right balance.

Claudia thought: *I should, at the very least, use the word "sad" during the conversation, or is that too strong?*

'Thank you, Stephen, but I wouldn't describe the death of John Moss as losing a field partner; I appreciate the sentiment. It is true, I was fond of him, as we do of any person with which we spend time. He was a very pleasant man, genuinely nice. The Crane targeted him at the cruel behest of the Chinese Ministry of State Security,' Claudia said, sighing, 'What they did was wrong and I'm sad that the Crane believed killing John would make me suffer. I must have played my role as the doting girlfriend too well, and an innocent man paid the price of my Oscar-winning performance.'

Stephen considered asking Claudia about the Crane but, because he felt she was manipulating him into believing that she was unaffected by John's death, he decided to keep probing. There would be time enough for the Crane later.

'After John's death, you reverted to using your Russian Mafia name, Claudia. Is that a message to his killers?'

Careful, girl, he's trying to trip you up.

She took a sip of tea before saying, 'They targeted John because they thought it would affect me, inflict permanent emotional scars. They thought Lucy was vulnerable and, yes, I'm sending a message to them and to any who become my adversary in the future. What I do is a job. People like John are tools, nothing more, nothing less. It was criminal that he died and I'm frustrated that he was lost on my watch. Permanent emotional scars—no, not my style. By reverting to Claudia, I'm telling them that if they try to hurt me, they'll be wasting their time,' Claudia paused before continuing, 'Harsh, I know, but trust me. John being killed was tragic, but it doesn't sit heavily on my conscience. We two are professionals, Stephen, and we do not let our emotions interfere with our duty.'

Oh, that's a good line - duty. Stephen will like that.

Unconvinced of Claudia's detachment, Stephen thought he would try another tack. 'You were captured by the Chinese State Security Service in Germany, then freed by my German counterpart, Eric Storch of the BND. He insisted you leave Europe, fearing that you would seek revenge against your Chinese captives. What does that say?'

Claudia took a sip of her tea before she said, 'That's a good question, Stephen, and one I've thought a lot about.'

It's a ridiculous question. Stephen! As if I'm going to fall for that! I mean, "What does that say to you?" Almost as sickly as, "How do you feel?"

Hiding her real thoughts by maintaining a reflective and considered voice, Claudia continued. 'Given the circumstances, it was an understandable precaution but, as we both know, unnecessary. Not knowing me as you do, Stephen, their concern was unfounded.'

Stephen nodded, 'I see. Can I be honest with you, Claudia?'

Honest? Does he know how?

'Yes, I would expect nothing less.'

'I find myself in the same predicament as Eric.'

Claudia lifted an eyebrow, feigning surprise as she said with a curious inflexion in her voice, 'Why would that be, Stephen?'

'MI6 is concerned that you will seek personal justice for the death of John. If you do, you'll spark a tit-for-tat war between the Chinese and British intelligence services, something we couldn't sanction.'

We are at war, Sweetie; can't you see that? The Chinese Ministry of State Security wanted to torture me, remove my teeth without an anaesthetic, no less. They shut down your communication and computer systems and they assassinated an innocent person. They don't care about your stuffy diplomacy and are determined to interfere in your democracy. It's time that Britain pushed back against China. The major powers may lack the appetite for a traditional military war, but make no mistake Stephen, we are at war, only by more sophisticated means: espionage, cyber-attacks, propaganda, and fake news. If the Government won't do it; I will wage a private war.

Claudia hid her true feelings, exposing little in her facial expressions or tone of voice as she said, 'I think we should investigate this Crane, whoever he or she is. The Crain has killed our agents.'

Claudia hoped that, by introducing a subtle change of direction in the conversation, she could move the focus away from herself. Stephen spotted the ploy immediately. He thought for a moment, taking a sip of his tea before deciding to allow the deflection, although he was far from convinced Claudia was detached from the events at Pi-Ski. To ensure Claudia understood he recognised her tactics, he said,

'I see, Claudia, that you wish to move the conversation away from yourself.' Stephen paused, nodding his head as if considering the proposition, even though he had already made up his mind. After the moment of silence, Stephen said, 'Okay. Locating and terminating the Crane is a top priority, and it is true, historically, we, along with the CIA, have failed to identify this assassin. The task has once more become urgent; however, this time, we will try a different tack, old-fashioned policing rather than spy craft. I've asked your old friend Inspector Axel to help, as he is acquainted with both worlds.'

'A good choice,' Claudia agreed. 'I wonder, Stephen, if the local police noses will be out of joint, especially with Inspector Axel poking about?'

'I'm sure he can look after himself but, with the cause of the explosion that killed John identified as a faulty gas appliance, which is our lie, this isn't a murder inquiry. Someone has to prepare a report for the coroner, that's all. Because of the high-profile nature of the explosion, its international guests, and the filming of the choir Christmas special, the local constabulary was told Inspector Axel from Scotland Yard will prepare the report. They were pleased to stay well clear of the investigation.'

'Will I be working with him?' Claudia asked.

'No, not initially. I want you to go back to Pi-Ski to attend the funeral because that is what the locals and John's friends will be expecting.'

And so am I.

'When is the funeral?' Stephen asked.

'In five days', time.'

As if you didn't know!

'Right, go back and stay until then. After the funeral, say your goodbyes and that you're returning to Australia. Leave the work in Pi-Ski to Inspector Axel. Is that understood?'

Claudia nodded as she said, 'You don't think, is it possible, someone on the St Mary's Church Parish Council is the Crane?'

Stephen shook his head. 'Highly unlikely, but, as Inspector Axel said, they are all potential suspects, not merely witnesses. He wants to start the investigation in Pi-Ski and then work backwards. As part of the cover of the operation, he will interview you along with the others in Pi-Ski.'

Stephen's demeanour changed, a stern look appearing on his face. 'Speaking of Australia. Is it a coincidence that, when you were in Melbourne, sophisticated yet bogus terrorist attacks were perpetrated against the Melbourne International Airport and in the CBD?'

Claudia remained silent. When she didn't answer, Stephen continued.

'The attack caused the Australian stock market to plunge. A group with links to the Russian Mafia had short-sold shares, and they made a fortune because of the chaos. It has your fingerprints all over it.'

'Stephen!' Claudia said indignantly. 'I was visiting Penny, Max, and Olivia's granddaughter. If you remember, it was Eric Storch of German Intelligence who suggested that I leave Europe. An unfortunate coincidence, that's all.'

Stephen let out an audible sigh and then said, 'Let's agree to disagree, shall we, Claudia?'

Claudia laughed before saying, 'I appreciated the help of the BND and was surprised by their level of cooperation.'

Stephen smiled. 'Lucky for you and for us. Eric and I became friends during an operation known as "Operation Rubicon", code-breaking, in which we shared some secrets we unearthed.' Stephen paused. 'Enough of this. We're getting nowhere. Return to Pi-Ski where you and Inspector Axel are staying at the local pub, the Little People's Arms. The Inspector will ask you to introduce him to John's church associates, Edith Kelly, Catherine Hepburn, Josephine Carter and Vicar Charlotte Foster.'

Claudia knew that to enact her vengeance, she would need to identify the five colleagues of Mr Chen Li from the Shark Inn restaurant and to do that, she needed access to the MI6 database, all without arousing Stephen's suspicions. Claudia took a last sip of her tea and said, 'Thank you, Stephen. I am looking forward to seeing Inspector Axel again and can certainly introduce him to the church members. I am wondering, will he be investigating Chen Li and his associates from the Shark Fin restaurant?'

'Yes, I imagine so.'

'Would you like me to take him those details?'

Stephen thought for a second before saying, 'There was no CCTV footage from the restaurant. Do you know who they are?'

'No, Stephen. However, if the MI6 computer systems are up and running and the attendees are in the database, I'm sure I'll be able to identify them. I could do that before leaving for Pi-Ski. Although I imagine by now, they have fled to China.'

Claudia knew it was unlikely that they had left Britain because the World Health Organisation (WHO) had been notified by the Peoples Republic of China of a cluster of cases of pneumonia of unknown cause in Wuhan City, Hubei Province of China. SARS, severe acute respiratory syndrome, a virus that jumped from animals to humans, had previously elicited a slow response from the Chinese government and eventually saw eight thousand and ninety-six people, in twenty-six countries contract the viral illness, resulting in seven hundred and seventy-four deaths. It was unlikely that Chinese agents and their families operating in Britain would be in a rush to return to China until more was known about this mysterious illness. Claudia knew, as indeed her targets did, that the situation in Wuhan was dire, worse than was currently being reported to WHO. According to a source, a Chinese doctor, Li Wenliang, an ophthalmologist at Wuhan Central Hospital, had identified the existence of a contagious new virus that resembled SARS but had new characteristics. In December, he'd sent a message to former classmates on WeChat, a messaging app, warning them of fresh cases of SARS, later to confirm that the virus was a Novel Coronavirus. Claudia had learned that he was subsequently arrested for making falsehoods that had "severely disturbed the social order". Soon after the WeChat post, the Chinese government took things more seriously and notified the WHO of the presence of an unknown virus. The genie was out of the bottle but, if history was a guide, Claudia thought it would be weeks before Chinese health officials acknowledged the seriousness of the outbreak. There would be plenty of time for her to track down and execute the people responsible for murdering John.

The statement, *I imagine by now; they have fled to China,* was a ploy by Claudia, to impress upon Stephen that she had no interest, above that expected of justice, in identifying the men at the Shark Fin restaurant. Stephen hesitated, considering his response to Claudia's suggestion. He decided it was a reasonable request and said, 'The systems here weren't affected by the Chinese interference, so okay then, see if you can identify the Chinese agents before you leave. It would provide valuable intelligence for Inspector Axel.'

Claudia nodded; her face neutral.

'Then a day or two after John's funeral, time enough for you to make your goodbyes. I want you back here for a new assignment.'

'Here! Not to Rosie and Postbridge?' Claudia asked.

Stephen glanced at Claudia, his mien wary as he said, 'I want you here, Claudia, where I can keep an eye on you.'

Claudia chuckled, 'I didn't know that you cared, Stephen.'

Without a pause, Stephen retorted, 'I don't.' He placed his cup and saucer on the table next to the intercom and stood, indicating to Claudia that it was time for her to leave. She took the cue, rose, and passed Stephen her crockery.

'As always, Stephen, it's been a pleasure.'

'Claudia, you did an outstanding job securing the cube. I truly regret how the operation concluded. The government is grateful for your efforts, and I share that gratitude as well.'

'Thank you, Stephen.'

Claudia turned to leave and, as she approached the door, Stephen called out to her, saying, 'I almost forgot, James has replacements for the equipment you lost in the explosion.'

She hesitated, and a smile drifted across Claudia's face as she said, without turning around, 'My new car, that is part of the replacement of course.'

Stephen Walls' scorn was apparent as he replied, 'The government is grateful, but not that grateful.' He paused, adding, 'Before you go.'

Claudia stopped, turned, and faced Stephen.

'Yesterday, you dropped off our radar?'

'Are you tracking me, Stephen?'

'We like to know the whereabouts of all our agents, for their safety and wellbeing, you understand.'

Claudia shrugged, glancing at Stephen with a hint of uncertainty. 'I have no idea what went wrong, Stephen. But I'm sure the replacement equipment you're providing will fix the glitch in your system.'

'Okay, Claudia, that will be all.'

Claudia had been right to be cautious. Stephen had confirmed her suspicions; she was under electronic surveillance. Claudia was confident her precautions were sound and that the location of her safe house was not compromised. Her scheme was progressing to plan, and the next task was to find the home address of the Chinese agents, a closely guarded secret. Then she'd kidnap him to extract the intelligence needed for her revenge. With her replacement gear issued, Claudia logged into the MI6 database and set about identifying the people who were dining at the Shark Fin, she knew the names of two agents: Chen Li and the man the MSS called, "The Dentist", Mr Yáyī. He was the person who intended to torture her in Germany and who she later killed. Claudia started by searching for a list of those accused by the British government of spying for the People's Republic of China.

Chen Li was known to British intelligence, and his place of residence was recorded as the Chinese Embassy, which was unlikely. If searching for the other men delivered no results, she would enquire of Mr Yáyī, through Britain's "Five Eyes" intelligence partners. Claudia felt sure that Yáyī would be known to one of them. She would then cross-reference Yáyī's known associates, hoping for a positive ID on those from the Shark Fin.

The number of suspected Chinese Ministry of State Security agents recorded as operating in the UK wasn't extensive, probably a reflection of an intelligence failure rather than a statement of fact. Within a short time, Claudia had identified all but one person from the Shark Fin restaurant, four names but no addresses: Ying Lee Hong, Ji Zang, Wen Xu, and Chi Ye.

I need an address!

Having exhausted the MI6 database of known Chinese operatives, Claudia tried another approach. Using the agency's facial-composite software, from her memory, Claudia reconstructed the fifth person's face, hoping for a match with records held by an intelligence partner, or even an image on the World Wide Web. She created a near-perfect likeness, yet her searching came up short. He was unknown to any of the Five Eyes spy agencies, and a google image recognition search also drew a blank. The fifth man remained elusive.

Most disappointing; the algorithms aren't working for me. What is it that Stephen said? Good old-fashioned policing. If I want to find the mystery man, I will have to methodically sift through all the information MI6 holds on known Chinese operatives in Britain.

Claudia sighed.

Looking for what - I'm not sure? The fifth man is likely to be a sleeper agent, the kind that is dormant for years, building community and business links while secretly maintaining contact with his handlers.

Claudia knew the task would be a long and tedious process, so she decided to stretch her legs first. Outside, she found the cold winter air stimulating, and it brushed aside the mental cobwebs that had formed. After a brisk walk, she returned to the office, fetched a cup of coffee and settled in behind the computer screen. Claudia clicked on an icon and displayed the MI6 file on Ying Lee Hong and started reading. The plan was to work through the people of interest one at a time. Four hours later, while sifting through the reports on Wen Xu, Claudia noticed something. A freelance journalist, Richard Liew, had written newspaper articles on each of the men she had researched. His stories were not investigative but commentary pieces, positive reports about the men's work, philanthropic, and business activities. Knowing Liew was writing about suspected spies, Claudia believed the newspaper articles were propaganda, reinforcing the agents' cover. A search for Richard Liew on the World Wide Web matched, returning a picture of the fifth person she was seeking.

I've got you.

Claudia entered Richard Liew's name into the Police National Computer System. Unlike the others who were unrecorded, the search returned Richard Liew's driver's licence details, along with his home address and date of birth. The flood gates had opened and, with a little work, Claudia discovered that Richard Liew was married to Samantha and they had a seven-year-old daughter called Molly.

Chuckling to herself, Claudia said, *You're mine, Sweetie!*

James's voice disturbed her as he said, 'How is it going?'

With a click of the button, Richard Liew's dossier was replaced by that of Wen Xu on her computer screen. 'Almost done. I've found four of the five men for Inspector Axel's investigation.'

'Well done.'

'Thank you. Does Axel have access to our systems?'

'Yes, he does.'

'Good. I'll prepare a briefing note on each of the agents and take it with me for the Inspector. After that, James, I think I will call it a day.'

'What about the fifth man?'

Claudia shook her head. 'No luck, unfortunately. I'll leave him to Inspector Axel.'

James looked at his watch as he said, 'Do you intend to drive to Pi-Ski tonight or in the morning?'

Why? Are you asking me out on a date?

Claudia resisted the urge to indulge in sarcasm. Instead, she lifted her wrist to check the time, saying, 'My goodness, it's later than I thought. I'll drive down in the morning. Would you mind letting Inspector Axel know that I'm staying in London tonight, in case he is expecting me? We wouldn't want him to be worried.'

'Certainly Claudia. I'll call him right away, and would you also like me to book a room for you upstairs?'

'That would be perfect. Thank you, James.'

CHAPTER 2
Windsor Castle

One thing that attracted Claudia to Britain, and London in particular, was its history. The first time she had visited the secret MI6 headquarters underneath the St Ermin's hotel in Westminster, she had read online about St Ermin's past. According to the website, "St Ermin's was built on the site of a 15th century chapel dedicated to St Ermin. In the mid to late 19th century, Westminster underwent significant changes and expansion, resulting in the creation of St Ermin's Mansion by E.T Hall in 1889, the building that now forms the basis of St Ermin's hotel." It is said, according to Claudia's reading, that in 1940, following a meeting with Winston Churchill, Prime Minister of Britain during World War Two, the Special Operations Executive (SOE) was formed, a unit which carried out covert operations during the conflict. Its headquarters was an entire floor of St Ermin's Hotel, with MI6 stationed two levels above the SOE. The new MI6 facility that Claudia was visiting was below the hotel built in the old 15th century chapel crypt.

Only the British, with their unique sense of humour, would build a top-secret facility underneath a building famous for espionage. They love their irony.

Having booked into St Ermin's hotel and washed and changed in her room, Claudia told the concierge she was going out for dinner. In truth, Claudia was meeting her former Russian Mafia partner of four years, Linda Orr. Linda was forced to leave the Mafia when Claudia did, with the sinking of the *Lelantos*. Like Claudia, she was offered a job with MI6, but after a short stint, decided not to stay in the service of the British Government. The meeting was taking place at The Windsor Castle pub in Campden Hill Road, Kensington, one of Claudia's favourite haunts when staying in central London, a hidden gem amongst London's myriad of pubs. In particular, Claudia liked their steak and ale pie with mashed potatoes, quintessentially British food, necessitating however, a ten-kilometre run to ward off its effects on the waistline.

Linda was waiting at the pub when Claudia arrived. She was two years older than Claudia, and like Claudia, was slim and muscular and apart from their breast sizes, Claudia being well-endowed, the women were similar physically, but that was where the similarities ended. Linda could pass as a distinguished businesswoman, a smart dresser when she wished it. Unlike Claudia, however, Linda had no interest in the latest fashions. Linda was intelligent, cunning and clever but often played the blonde bimbo to deceive her adversaries. What Claudia had loved about working alongside Linda was their verbal jousting, especially when in a tight situation.

Yesterday, when Claudia phoned Linda to place an order and arrange the meeting, it was the first time the two of them had spoken since saving Max and Olivia from the sinking *Lelantos*. Linda had not intended to defect from the Russian Mafia to MI6, but when Claudia returned to the *Lelantos,* and she went back for Claudia, the die was cast. Linda could never go back to the Mafia, a place where she had been happy.

Seeing Claudia enter the pub, Linda stood and waved, not that she needed to, because Claudia had already observed where Linda was sitting, looking through the pub window when she had scanned the pub from the other side of the road. In the gameplay between the two women, Linda had chosen a seat where she could be seen.

They hugged as Linda said, smiling warmly, 'It's so good to see you again.'

'Likewise.'

'Can I buy you a drink?' Linda asked.

'Thanks. I'll have a pint of one of their organic wheat beers.'

Linda smiled. 'Phew, I thought you were going to ask for a glass of 1996 Dom Perignon.'

'The Rose Gold Methuselah at US $49,000 a bottle?'

'That's the one.'

Claudia shook her head as if serious and replied, 'I've been in here before; they don't stock it. The wheat beer will have to do.'

Linda laughed, 'I've missed you.'

'Likewise.'

For a while, the two women drank their beers and reminisced about old times. Secretly, Claudia was pleased that their friendship had been unaffected by her rash decision to help Max and Olivia and not kill them. After twenty minutes of catch-up, Claudia said, 'Let's get down to business.'

Linda nodded, picking up a small daypack that was on the floor next to her, and placing it on the table. Claudia took it and, without looking inside, put it next to her feet, saying, 'Thank you.'

'Service with a smile,' Linda said, giving a cheesy grin. 'I have most of what you wanted. However, some items on your wish list will take longer. A day's notice is cutting it fine, Claudia, even for me.'

Claudia raised an eyebrow, chuckled, and said, 'The Linda Orr I remember would need only half a day.'

'Ah, "Those were the days my friend",' Linda sang, using the English lyrics to the Russian romance song Dorogoi dlinnoyu. The English version was a number one hit for Mary Hopkins in 1968.

'The thing is Claudia, I need a photograph, a headshot, for the Passport you wanted.'

'Did you bring a camera?' Claudia asked.

'Of course, yes.'

'What about the prepay mobile phone?'

'In the daypack.'

Claudia nodded, adding, 'Excellent. And the surveillance equipment?'

'You've everything except the false identify documents, driver's licence, and passport. Even the replacement credit card is in there. You don't have to answer this my friend but, does this have something to do with the killing of John Moss?'

Claudia was surprised that Linda was aware of John's death, and she said, 'You've heard?'

'Oh, yes. The word on the street was that the "Cold, heartless bitch Claudia" had fallen in love. Your admiration of Shakespeare led them to call it "The taming of the Shrew". Harsh, I thought.'

'Linda, you're all heart.'

'Why, thank you, Claudia.' Linda's lips turned up at the corners as she paused for a moment, took a sip of her beer, and continued, 'Those who killed John could not have understood what I know. Some things are untouchable. Akin to attacking an American aircraft carrier, for instance; the consequences for any country attempting that would be catastrophic. The street noise suggests that the Chinese Ministry of State Security failed to appreciate the consequences of hitting on the Shrew's lover. They do now, Claudia, so be cautious. They will be waiting for you if you try to seek retribution.'

A smile on her face, Claudia said, 'I'm surprised that people consider me vindictive.'

Linda laughed as she said, 'I hear MI6 wants to keep you on a short leash.'

'I'm impressed, Linda. You are well informed. Obviously still a woman with good connections. I'm pleased that since leaving the Russian Mafia, then your short stint with MI6, you haven't been idle, and that begs the question,' Claudia paused, exhaling gently before continuing, 'without giving away trade secrets, what have you been doing since last we saw each other?'

'Freelancing mainly. Life got a lot easier when you squared things with Monya, and I've even done work for our old mafia colleagues since then. You must tell me what you did to have the hit removed from our heads?' When Claudia didn't respond, Linda kept speaking. 'It was a relief; I can tell you. I've become the go-to person when someone wants something stolen, artworks for insurance fraud, corporate secrets, that kind of thing. Trade has been brisk, and it's a luxury I know, but I've been selective in my choice of engagements. I have stayed away from the sinister side of our game.'

Claudia pondered for a moment before saying, 'I'm pleased you've landed on your feet. I never did thank you properly for returning to the *Lelantos* and sacrificing your career to help me, Max and Olivia. You truly are a great friend.'

Linda, in a mocking tone, said, 'That's what friends do.' She grinned, then said in a solemn voice, 'It is what friends do.'

Claudia bowed her head, acknowledging Linda's sacrifice.

'That's okay Claudia. I've wanted to ask, what happened to the old-timers, Max and Olivia? Where are they now?'

Claudia shrugged her shoulders. 'I don't know.'

'Are they dead?'

'I've spoken to them once; it must be close to a year ago now. Max and Olivia are a wonderful age; anything could have happened to them since.'

Linda nodded.

Claudia raised her glass. 'To old friends.'

'To old friends,' Linda repeated.

Looking at the day pack, Claudia said, 'I'm already indebted to you for coming back to the *Lelantos,* and here I am again, the recipient of your help.'

'That's okay.'

'Linda, I have one further favour to ask.'

'Another favour,' Linda said in feigned horror. 'That will cost you... um, let me see; it must be your turn to buy the next round of drinks.'

'I've heard you're cheap,' Claudia retorted, enjoying the banter they once regularly shared.

With fresh drinks in hand, Linda asked, 'What is it you wish of me?'

'You were right when you said that MI6 is keeping me on a short leash, and for the moment at least, they are tracking my movements via my phone.' Claudia removed her MI6 supplied phone from her pocket and placed it on the table in front of her.

'The favour I wish to ask of you, Linda, is to take my phone out on a date tonight. Perhaps you would like to visit a nightclub? Then, return it to my room, unseen of course, at the St Ermin hotel, say about eleven or eleven-thirty tonight. I won't be there, of course, but would like you to wait for my return.'

From her pocket, Claudia took her hotel room swipe card and handed it to Linda.

'I can do that,' Linda said, laughing as she added, 'Going out to a nightclub and being home by eleven o'clock? What's happening to us, Claudia?'

In a humorous tone, Claudia replied, 'I wouldn't want my employer thinking I'm reckless, now would? Tomorrow is a workday, after all.'

'As I know. You've always been a responsible woman. When will you be back?'

Claudia thought for a moment before saying, 'I'm not sure. It could be as late as two or three in the morning.'

'A long night. You won't mind if I have a kip on your bed?'

'Linda, I was hoping you would because it's best if the bed looks slept in, and while you're there, help yourself to the minibar. The company is paying.'

Linda took a sip of beer, then said, 'Are you confident that they're not following you?'

'Pretty sure, unless you've been engaged by MI6 to keep an eye on me.'

Linda smiled, 'Remember I said, I'm selective about the jobs I accept.'

'Ha, I thought Stephen would have asked you. Perhaps MI6 isn't as dim as it sometimes sim.'

Linda took Claudia's mobile phone from the table and placed it into her purse. 'I haven't heard the phrase "dim as it sometimes sim" in a long time. It's good to be working with you again. Is there anything else you need?'

Claudia moved her head from side to side, something she did while contemplating, before saying, 'You probably already know that we think the explosion that killed John was the work of the infamous assassin, the Crane. I was wondering if a well-connected woman like you had any thoughts on the identity of this Crane?'

Linda shook her head. 'I don't know, and it's a dangerous question to ask. Are you going after the Crane too?'

'I like to keep my options open.'

Linda finished her beer. 'I'll put the feelers out, but be careful, my friend. The Chinese will expect you, and so might the Crane.'

CHAPTER 3
Cat Got Your Tongue

After taking the photos for the false identification documents, Claudia and Linda remained at the Windsor Castle Pub reminiscing until Claudia looked at her watch, saying, 'It's about time I was going.

'Good hunting, my friend.'

Grabbing the day pack, Claudia left the warmth of the pub for the dark and cold of an English winter evening to search for Richard Liew's house.

If all goes to plan, she whispered to herself, *by the early hours, I will have broken into the house and installed the surveillance devices Linda so kindly acquired for me.*

Richard Liew lived with his family in Dalston, East London. Ordinarily, Claudia would refrain from breaking in without first conducting a reconnaissance; however, being under MI6 surveillance was forcing her to take the risk. For security reasons, she caught a taxi to the Dalston Junction Railway Station, walking the rest of the way to the house, familiarising herself with the area for a speedy exit if necessary. The temperature was close to freezing and, despite her warm attire, Claudia shivered as she left the main road and weaved her way through the back streets to where Richard Liew and his family lived.

Perch Street. Excellent, this is the one.

She peered down the quiet road, taking stock before entering to find the Liew residence. In the still of the night, Claudia's footsteps echoed on the deserted footpath as she walked. The sound of an approaching vehicle caused her to slow until it passed and vanished into the distance. Alone again, Claudia continued, searching for the house number of the Liew's. '*There you are,*' she said, and as she spoke, condensation drifted from her mouth, and she breathed out again to witness the phenomenon of vapour disappearing into the night air.

It's a frosty night.

The house of Richard Liew was a two-storey semi-detached residence, joined to its pair on one side by a shared wall and separated from the other party by a tall red gate, the entrance to a narrow alleyway running between the two houses and leading to the rear garden of the Liew residence. From her vantage spot, opposite the Liew's, Claudia checked her watch; nearly nine o'clock, not late yet. The Liew house was in darkness.

They're out. Perfect.

Taking off her daypack, Claudia removed an electronic scanning device, part of the equipment supplied by Linda, to see if the Liew's had an active alarm system. They did, and in keeping with modern trends, the Liew's alarm was a wireless type. *Easy,* Claudia whispered to herself, understanding the vulnerability of this type of security. It relied on high-frequency signals sent between door and window sensors to a control panel to trigger an alarm when one entry was breached. Many of the systems on the market failed to encrypt the signals sent by the sensors or to authenticate it before transmission. Professional criminals could gain ready access without these safeguards. The encryption of Richard Liew's signals was sophisticated, more so than an off-the-shelf system, but it was no match for the tools Claudia was carrying. To disarm the alarm, she would simply need to walk to the front door, where the signal was most reliable and push a button on her gadget. Her scanning also revealed multiple wireless devices, video cameras, motion detectors and smart home devices, collectively referred to as IoT (Internet of Things), connected to the network within the Liew house.

This should be a piece of cake.

The IoT made spying easy. Rather than installing her surveillance equipment, Claudia would hack into a smart home system and, once connected, have access to any device on the Liew network. Then, the Liew's would not be the only people monitoring their home. Claudia didn't need to break in now; however, spy craft was more than algorithms and data; it was knowing and understanding an opponent. Plus, when the time was right, Claudia wanted Richard Liew to realise that his home had been violated and the people he loved were vulnerable.

Before gaining entry, Claudia thought it wise to scout the house's perimeter in search of a safer entry point, one not as exposed to prying eyes from the road like the front door and also in case she needed to make a quick and unnoticed exit.

Let's do it.

A small LED torch in hand, Claudia crossed the road, stepping over the low front fence before trying the handle on the red gate. It was unlocked and pushed easily open. Before entering, Claudia glanced behind. The coast was clear, and she moved into the passageway between the two houses, closing the gate behind her. In the pitch-black she switched on the torch and began walking along the length of the pathway to the rear of the Liew house, switching the flashlight off again, to prevent a neighbour seeing a flickering of light, when she reached the backyard. The garden space was dimly lit by the residual glow of its urban surroundings, and Claudia noticed that the area was the width of the house and stretched back thirty metres away from the property. Needing to explore potential escape routes, Claudia hugged the fence line and followed it to the back fence and was disappointed to discover the rear garden of another house.

Not ideal. A laneway would have provided a better getaway. None-the-less, I won't be trapped, though it will be trickier.

Turning, Claudia looked back and studied the rear of the house, her eyes scanning from window to window. There was still no sign of life. She checked her electronic monitoring device and spotted that the Wi-Fi signal was as strong at the back as it had been at the front.

Excellent.

Claudia could deactivate the alarm and break in from the rear, hidden from the footpath and main road.

Right, Claudia, in you go.

Walking towards the back door, Claudia scanned for escape routes in case she was upstairs when the family returned. Looking up and next to an upstairs window, the bathroom, by frosting on the glazing, was a drainpipe that ran to the ground.

Excellent, if caught inside, I can climb down that.

BING!

The rear garden lit up, transformed from semi-darkness, to be bathed in a brilliant white light. Claudia's movement had triggered a motion sensor above the back door; she was a rabbit caught in a spotlight and, for a moment, motionless.

How annoying.

Claudia darted back to the safety of the passageway separating Richard Liew's house from that of his neighbours. Hidden in darkness, Claudia waited for the light to extinguish. Had it alerted a neighbour, she hoped that their curiosity was quenched when they spotted nothing. A cat, bird, or any moving creature could have triggered the spotlight. While she waited, Claudia pondered her options. The motion detector, one not connected to the internet, ruled out the rear of the house as a point of entry. She wondered,

Is there a light at the front?

Thinking, Claudia recalled what she had seen. The front door was set back from the footpath by a mere five metres, so it was unlikely, she considered, that a motion sensor would be at the front as it would be triggered continually by passers-by.

Okay. No sensor lights. On the downside, the front door is visible from the street and illuminated by the streetlights. Is there another way?

The front door was the only viable option, and Claudia knew that if she went in that way, she couldn't afford to linger in full view of the world. Her entry needed to be swift and fast. The rear sensor light clicked off, and the garden fell into semi-darkness again. She poked her head out, and all was quiet.

What do they say? If first you don't succeed, try, try again. Now, Claudia, where did that saying come from? That's it, Thomas H Palmer, Children of the New Forest. I'm impressed with you, girly.

Using her LED torch, Claudia made her way to the red gate, where she took out her electronic hacking device to disable the alarms and the IoT devices connected to the Wi-Fi router. It wasn't, however, as easy as she expected. Because she didn't want Richard Liew to receive "disruption of service" messages on his smartphone, alerting him to the existence of a hacker, it needed additional jamming measures, something she hadn't expected. A two-minute task took ten; ordinarily, that wouldn't have concerned her but, the later it became, the more likely it was the Liew's would return.

The job done, Claudia popped her head out from behind the gate, glancing up and down the road.

All clear. Now young Claudia, act as though you own the place.

Claudia slipped out from the alleyway and walked purposely towards the front door. As she approached, she removed a lock picking kit from her daypack and focused the beam of her LED torch on the lock.

Right, what do we have here? A simple pin tumbler, very primitive. I'll be in within seconds.

Placing the torch in her mouth, Claudia opened the break and enter kit and scanned the array of tools at her disposal.

You, and you, will do nicely.

Claudia withdrew a lock pick wrench and a wavy-edged pick, a Bogota rake, as it was called, with its three ridges. She planned to use a technique called Raking, involving many moves, including ripping and scrubbing. Raking was a quick and easy method for opening the type of lock in front of her. Still, Claudia knew that lock picking was an art, rather than a science, and was a matter of touch, necessitating a sensitivity to a lock and its tumblers. Taking the tension wrench, Claudia used her left hand and placed the tool in the bottom of the keyhole, applying slight pressure in the direction that the key would have turned. With her right hand, she inserted the rake pick, pulling it back while simultaneously lifting it, repeating the motion five times enough to set the lock pins. Nothing happened, and Claudia reckoned she had applied too much pressure with the wrench.

You're rusty young girl. Relax, let the pins reset, and start over again.

Moving the rake in and out at different speeds and angles, she increased and decreased the tension on the wrench, but the second attempt also failed.

Well, young Claudia, it's not you. I would surmise this tumbler lock has pins of different sizes—a little more complicated than usual.

Conscious of the time she was spending at the front door, Claudia thought she could afford one further attempt before she would be likely spotted and reported to the police.

It's back to the old tried and tested single pin picking method.

Without rushing, Claudia changed from using her raking instrument to a pick. Probing the pins of the lock with her new tool, adjusting the pressure exerted on the wrench as she did so, the lock clicked open. She was in.

That wasn't so difficult, was it, young Claudia?

On the far side of the door and out of sight of prying eyes, Claudia placed the lock breaking implements inside their wallet and returned the kit to her daypack. Not wanting to alert passers-by or neighbours, seeing a light beam flashing about in a darkened house, Claudia held her figures across the lens of the torch to muffle its light.

It's time to take a look.

Claudia walked through the downstairs rooms, and as this was a reconnaissance mission rather than a search, she used the time to familiarise herself with the layout, leaving the family's possessions untouched.

This is better than I hoped.

In each room she visited, there were voice-controlled speakers, similar to Google Home, used to play music or control smart home gadgets. They were ready-made listening devices for her to hack.

He's a geek!

Moving upstairs, Claudia checked her watch and decided that her priority was to find the bathroom she'd seen from outside. Claudia wanted to be sure of an escape route, should it be needed. It was behind the third door she checked.

There you are.

Inside, Claudia opened a window above the bath and looked outside, and it was as she hoped. The drainage pipe was adjacent. Next, Claudia ran her fingers around the edge of the window frame, checking for wires or a sensor. If there was and she re-armed the home security system while the window was open, her gig was up.

Excellent, no sensors. I'll leave you slightly ajar and ready for a quick exit, just in case I need it.

Leaving the bathroom, Claudia retraced her steps out on to the second storey landing. Pausing, she thought,

I might as well start with the first room I checked, the one with the soft pink feature wall, Molly's bedroom, I'd bet.

From the doorway, Claudia's torch revealed a bedroom, and there was no doubt in her mind that it was Molly's. She remembered reading once, in a glossy décor magazine she'd seen while waiting for an appointment at the dentist, that in the modern well-heeled family, children's rooms are more than a place to sleep. They are cool, comfortable environments, places of beauty where a child can thrive, be creative and imaginative. In the torchlight, this room was picture perfect, a replica from the exotic designer magazine. Examining what she saw, Claudia said to herself,

The room is beautiful, but it's also sterile and austere. It feels... I don't know - unlived in?

As Claudia pushed the door wider, it creaked in protest. Inside, the polished timber floor was immaculate, free of discarded toys or clothing. A large pink mat lay at the centre of the room, and against the pink feature wall stood Molly's bed, its headboard flush against the vibrant surface. Above it hung a cheerful picture of a unicorn. To one side, a bedside mirror and the other, under the windowsill, was a brilliant white writing desk on which Claudia spotted neatly stacked paper and an elegant wooden box, its lid open. Inside were colouring pencils, used but returned to their correct position ordered by colour tone. "Derwent Fine Art Pencils", the gold writing on the lid read. Resting against a pastel-coloured wall was a multi-storey doll's house. Like the desk, its contents and the miniature occupants were neatly arranged. The only sign that Molly's room was lived in was a white cat, curled up, asleep on the coffee-coloured bedspread atop the bed.

There was something about this room that troubled Claudia, and then it struck her: She shuddered, then sighed. It reminded her of her room as a child when she'd been kidnapped and imprisoned. Although she was older than Molly was now, a memory came to her, the same one from the time when she had stared into Max's old green eyes and squeezed on the trigger that would have ended his life. Her mind drifted into the past.

'You're my favourite, Lucia,' she'd heard Tamara say as Tamara caressed her fine blonde hair. She could sense the sweeping motion of the brush as it had pulled against her scalp. In the mirror, a young Lucia saw Tamara smiling, standing behind her chair, her body pushing against her back. 'We have some special guests tonight, Lucia,' Tamara said. 'They will want to take some pictures. Remember to be a good girl. You don't want Ivankov to send you away like the other girls.'

'Just pictures?' Lucia asked.

'These are special guests, Sweetie. You know I'm always outside and wouldn't let anything bad happen to you.'

Tamara stopped her brushing and, in the mirror, Lucia watched as Tamara leaned over and kissed the top of her head. Tamara smiled as she said, 'Now get dressed, my little mouse, and make yourself beautiful.'

Tamara placed the hairbrush on the dressing table beside Lucia and turned to leave the room. When she reached the door, she paused. With her beautiful blue eyes and flowing brown hair, Tamara was the only mother Lucia could remember. She raised her hand to her mouth and, in the reflection, Lucia watched her blow a parting kiss.

Lucia had been living there for so long that she no longer remembered arriving, or when she was given her own room. Unlike the other children, locked in their rooms, Lucia could roam about the big house, the house in Macinec, Yugoslavia, on a large estate, surrounded by a high stone wall. Where they were was immaterial because Lucia was a prisoner and her room, the cell.

To survive, Lucia had learned to smile, please, and be pleasing. She had seen what happened to girls when a guest complained, so had become a special gift, earning privileges in return. But, when she was alone in her room at night, she cried herself to sleep, wishing someone would come and save her.

At first, the tears were because she'd been taken from her family and wanted to return home, until one day, she could no longer remember them. The tears became habitual, not because of what was being done to her, for she had become numb to their abuse. She cried for the rescue that never came.

'Please save me. Take me away from this place,' Lucia whispered as Tamara pushed the bedroom door closed behind her. The memory from her childhood faded, and Claudia returned to the present and Molly's bedroom.

I wonder if her life is as sad?

Curious, Claudia went to the writing desk and looked at the neat stack of paper. The torchlight revealed a drawing on the pile, a colour picture, a house with a mum, dad, and a little girl, all smiling, a happy family. Lifting it, Claudia saw the beginnings of a simple story accompanied by a similarly cheerful hand-drawn picture, a vibrant unicorn and rainbow. Claudia started reading.

"One foggy day there was a mysterious village of unicorns and Pegasus' in all shapes, sizes and colours. One was called Frosty, and she had a BFF...", Claudia hesitated,

What in the name of hell is a BFF?

Using her phone, she searched for the term, the result: "Best Friend Forever".

'LOL,' Claudia uttered to herself and continued reading.

"One was called Frosty; she had a BFF named Snowflake. Snowflake had a BFF named Flora. Flora had a BFF called Brownie. One day, a girl named Molly was flying through the air in a helicopter. She saw Frosty and thought, what a beautiful unicorn."

Claudia exhaled, saying aloud to herself. 'Lots of best friends forever. This place isn't at all like my childhood bedroom. No, it's a room of happiness. Someone, perhaps a nanny, is routinely restoring this room to its pristine state. It's not a prison but a wonderland.'

The momentary sense of solidarity that she had felt for Molly passed and was replaced by bitterness, bordering on jealousy.

Young Molly, you're precious to your parents, and so will do nicely, very nicely indeed. Through you, your father will suffer.

Claudia had read that, for a parent who lost a child, the pain was indescribable. They suffer a mixture of depression, anger, guilt, despair, and loneliness, the grief varying depending on how the child died. Claudia smiled to herself.

The painful death of Molly, because of your involvement with the Chinese Ministry of State Security, Mr Richard Liew, will be a hard pain for you to bear. Before this is over, you will beg me to take your life and end the suffering.

Claudia returned Molly's drawings to the desk and arranged them to appear as if nothing was touched. As she turned to leave the room, Claudia spotted a child monitoring camera fixed to the wall.

Oh, that's perfect. I'll be able to watch Molly through you.

The cat on Molly's bed opened an eye and sleepily looked at Claudia. She paused and stroked the kitty, and when she stopped, it gently nudged her hand to continue, purring rhythmically.

You're a cute little thing.

Drifting back to the landing, Claudia paused, deciding where to go next.

Let's find the master bedroom.

THUMP!

The sound of something hitting the front door. Molly, running ahead of her parents had smacked the door playfully with both hands, the impact echoing inside the house. Any second and a key would be in the lock, and the house occupants would return home.

How annoying, and I'm having such fun.

Calmly, Claudia removed her daypack and retrieved the electronic device to reactivate the alarm system and reconnect the IoT devices to the Wi-Fi network. The security system needed to be back online before the family entered; otherwise, Richard Liew would know that someone had been inside the house; however, Claudia had to wait until she was exiting.

Time to go.

Claudia moved towards the bathroom and the escape route down the drainpipe when she stopped in her tracks. She recalled she intended to take something from the house to show Richard Liew when the time was right. His home wasn't a castle, and all of its occupants were within her reach.

That would be cruel. Claudia thought, giggling to herself. *Imagine flaunting that in his face.*

To the sound of a key placed inside the front door lock, Claudia swivelled on her heels and took two strides back into Molly's room. Sweeping the sleeping cat from its comfortable refuge, she stuffed it into her daypack and zipped the bag closed, a smile adorning her face as she thought.

The family will search the house up and down for you, my furry feline friend, and when they can't find you, assume pussy has somehow escaped outside. They will never reckon on you vanishing from Molly's bed. Who would do such a terrible thing? Who could perpetrate such an outrage?

Claudia's musing was interrupted by the sounds of a child's footsteps running along the floor of the hallway below. The parents would be seconds behind. Time was running out. Stepping out of the bedroom, Claudia swung the daypack over her shoulder and crept towards the bathroom. In her mind's eye, she saw Richard Liew walking towards the control board of the home alarm system, open the alarm panel, ready to enter the deactivation code.

Click.

Pushing a button on her electronic hacking device, Claudia brought the system back online. For a millisecond, Richard Liew thought he saw the flicker of a red LED, showing the system was off but, in the time, it took him to blink, three green LEDs were flashing. Subconsciously, the changing of the colours disturbed him, and Richard hesitated, not understanding his unease. He shook his head and entered the code; the keypad beeping with each number he pushed.

'Daddy, daddy,' Molly called, and his momentary disquiet was forgotten.

Upstairs, trying not to make a sound, Claudia manoeuvred herself through the bathroom window and once outside, hanging from the drainpipe with one hand, she pulled the window closed behind her and gently lowered herself down the wall to the ground. With the family at home, light shone from the downstairs windows, illuminating the garden. Not wanting to trigger the outdoor sensor light, nor be seen through the windows, Claudia pushed her back hard against the brick wall, causing the cat to meow loudly, squashed between Claudia and the house.

Sorry kitty, I forgot you were there. Patience, Claudia. Anytime soon and they will close the curtains.

As if on command, the light seeping from the house dimmed.

Thank you.

Trying not to squash the cat again, Claudia hugged the house, moving towards the cover of the side fence. Having made it unseen, she followed its length to the rear of the property and the boundary fence separating the Liew's from their neighbours. Placing her hand on top of the fence, Claudia leapt, heaving herself over, landing safely on the other side.

One down.

After scaling the fences of two further properties, Claudia reached the street. She transitioned from wearing the daypack on her back to her front, partially unzipping it, allowing the cat to push its head through the opening.

'Hello Moggie,' she said, stroking its head.

'I wonder what your name is?' The cat purred, unfazed by the evening's events.

Claudia checked her watch. She'd expected to have to wait for the Liew household to be asleep before breaking in, and so the mission was over earlier than expected. Setting off towards the railway station and a taxi, Claudia whispered to herself,

The night is yet young, and so there is no need for Linda to wait in my hotel room.

As she walked, Claudia called her friend, and the phone answered after the third ring. 'City Morgue, you kill'em we chill'em' came Linda's cheerful voice.

Claudia laughed as she said, 'I'm on my way back, and I'll meet you at Castle, which is short for the Windsor Castle Pub, in case you didn't know.'

'No snags I hope?' Linda said, conscious that she hadn't been expecting Claudia to return until two or three in the morning.

'It seems I become more efficient with age because everything went perfectly. I'll meet you in - say, an hour?'

'Yep, an hour is fine.'

'By the way, Linda, you do like cats?'

Linda laughed. 'You haven't, have you?'

Hanging up the phone, Claudia felt pleased with her night's antics and, stroking the cat as she walked, her mind filled with visions of what would happen when she kidnapped Mr Richard Liew.

He is held in the basement of my Safehouse and wakes to find himself tied to a chair. I'm sitting in front of him, Molly's cat on my lap.

Claudia roused herself from the daydream.

'Kitty, you need a name.'

She pondered for a moment, imagining eavesdropping in on the Liew household as they searched for Molly's missing pet.

'What do they call you?'

'I know, Snowflake, from Molly's story.'

Scratching Snowflake on the head as she continued to walk, Claudia returned to her fantasy: The cat was contentedly on her knee, purring with each stroke.

'Look Snowflake, he's waking up.'

Through Richard Liew's groggy eyes, I will come slowly into focus. He will recognise me from the Shark Fin restaurant, and his attention will be drawn to my lap. A surge of panic will ripple through his body when he sees Snowflake, his beautiful daughter's precious cat. He will know that Molly's life is in danger. With all the strength he can muster, he will launch himself at me, but tied to the chair, he cannot move. He will try again.

I'll watch his vain attempts in silence, all the while stroking the cat in a rhythmic motion.

When he stops thrashing, I'll say, speaking to the cat in a sympathetic voice.

'Ah Snowflake, poor Mr Liew is all tied up.'

'What do you want?' Richard Liew will snarl.

'I want information in exchange for the way you die.'

'Leave Molly out of this,' he will spit while looking at the cat.

'You should have thought about that before you killed John.'

'Please, you know children are off-limits.'

Looking at the cat, I'll say, 'Do you hear that Snowflake? Children are off-limits!'

Claudia sees herself lifting her gaze and staring menacingly at Richard Liew.

'Sweetie, are you telling me there are rules? When I suggested that to your boss, Chen Li, I think, I said something like: Operating in the United Kingdom requires that you adhere to rules of etiquette. Some behaviours are expected of you, long established conventions observed by the spy agencies and their personnel ...' I'll pause and put my hand to my chin. *'What else did I say, Snowflake? Yes, now, I remember. Operatives are required to act differently to the Triads, Mafia, or Yakuza. Intelligence agencies*

are not savages. You were at the table, Mr Liew. You must remember me saying that?'

He will nod, eager to agree to what I sat, to save Molly.

'Do you recall how Chen Li replied?'

Richard Liew will remain silent.

'No, has the cat got your tongue?' Looking at Snowflake and then back to Richard Liew, I'll continue.

'Let me remind you, Sweetie.' Imitating Chen Li's accent, I will say, *"Your Western conventions came about to maintain balance because each had spies operating in the other's country. I have heard it described as, if you don't kill one of mine, I won't kill one of yours. Your agreements are pathetic and weak. The difference between the Chinese Ministry of State Security and other foreign parties with which you deal is that your western agencies' presence in China is insignificant. You bring nothing to the negotiation table. The consequences for you meddling in Chinese affairs will be severe, uncompromising, and merciless".*

'Sweetie, do you remember what he said next?' I won't wait for him to answer because it isn't a question: *"How is John Moss, by the way?"*

Richard Liew may drop his eyes in shame before regaining his composure. I'll continue to stroke the cat while I say,

'You see, Snowflake, the naughty Mr Liew is quite content, for there to be no rules until it affects him personally. Now, he's grown a conscience. Children are off-limits. Are they? I think not!'

As the scene plays out in Claudia's mind, she sees him throwing up a smokescreen of denials.

'I was invited as a journalist to have dinner with Chen Li at the Shark Fin. I knew nothing of his connections to spy agencies. Not until you appeared.'

'You're lying,' I will say calmly.

Claudia imagines him pleading that he's not connected to the death of John Moss. *'It wasn't me; I wasn't there.'* He might even say, *'I was only following orders.'*

When the real time comes, Claudia would not engage Richard Liew with pointless debate because she'd found him guilty already.

Claudia smiled as she imagined herself intimidatingly saying, *'Would you like to see Molly?'*

Richard Liew's heart will sink in despair when he believes Molly is also held captive.

I'll wait a few seconds to allow the hopelessness of his situation to engulf him before dangling the smallest prospect of salvation. I will take him to the edge of anguish before bringing him back again. A cat playing with a mouse.

I will turn my computer screen to face Richard Liew and it will display a live feed from Molly's bedroom where his daughter is sleeping peacefully. He will think there is still a chance to save his beloved daughter. He may even try his denials again.

'I swear I had nothing to do with the killing of John.'

'Sweetie, you may not have pulled the trigger, but your guilt is the same. You took from me the one person I have ever loved. I will do the same for you.'

I'll pause and allow pain to seep into his consciousness before saying,

'Unless?' giving him another glimmer of hope.

Richard Liew will stare directly into my eyes and say hopelessly. *'Unless what?'*

'As I've said, I want information in exchange for how you die. If you prove helpful, Molly will learn of the tragic death of her father, killed in a car accident. The psychology books say, the death of a parent during one's childhood is difficult but, depending upon the circumstances of the death, such as an accident, children adapt and move on with their lives. They are such resilient little buggers.'

'You're not going to hurt her?'

'Sweetie, kill her? No. Hurt her! Well, that will depend on you, won't it, Snowflake? Mr Liew, if you prove yourself unhelpful, then I will traumatise Molly, f..k up the rest of her life.'

Claudia suddenly stopped walking as a devious thought brought her back to the present. A revelation. She knew what was needed. 'Cruel, Claudia, very cruel.' While Richard Liew is watching Molly through the child monitor in her room, I'll call, 'Molly... Molly... wake up Molly. The boogie man is here.'

Can you imagine his face?

She laughed and continued her journey towards the station.

Where was I? Oh, that's right.

'Sweetie, if you prove yourself unhelpful, then I will traumatise Molly, f..k up the rest of her life. Do you remember the classic scene in the film The Godfather, when Jack Woltz wakes up with a horse's head in his bed, a gift from the Mafia boss, Don Corleone? It won't be a horse's head Molly wakes up to, but yours, and that's just the beginning.'

Richard Liew will fight back the tears and plead, *'What is it you want to know?'*

'Simple Sweetie, how do I find the men you were dining with, Chen Li, Ying Lee Hong, Ji Zang, Wen Xu, and Chi Ye?

Claudia stopped at a set of traffic lights, ready to cross the main road to the railway station and the taxi rank.

No, that's too easy on him. He will tell me what he knows and then go to his death willingly, a martyr. He needs to suffer. I want him to understand my hurt. To know and feel pure loss and pain.

The lights changed, and Claudia walked across the road.

You could always kidnap them all, Molly and Samantha, his wife. Make Richard Liew watch as you torture his wife to a slow and agonising death. Yes. You could start with what the Ministry of State Security was going to do to you, pull Samantha's teeth out one by one.

Claudia shivered in delighted anticipation.

With Samantha barely alive, still conscious, she needs to be awake; I'll bring Molly into the room and say, *'Samantha, I am going to ask your husband some questions. If he doesn't answer or he tells me a lie, I will do to Molly as I have done to you. Richard has a single opportunity: information for Molly's life.'*

'Where to, Madam?' asked the taxi driver. Claudia wakes from her daydream.

'The Windsor Castle Pub, Westminster. Francis Street. Do you know it?'

'It's number 23 Francis Street, Madam.'

'Indeed, it is Sweetie.'

Seated in the back seat of the taxi, the rhythmic movement of the car returned Claudia's thoughts to her plans for Richard Liew.

Where was I?... You could always kidnap all of them, Molly and his wife, Samantha.

As the scenario played out again in her mind, she stopped herself.

No, Claudia, not even you are that perverted. Children *are* off-limits; the threat will be enough. If Richard Liew or any of his family died in gruesome circumstances, the other Chinese agents would be alerted, whereas a tragic car accident will go unnoticed. There is no need to indulge yourself in Mr Liew's gruesome execution. There is cumulative pleasure in tracking down and terminating the others, five killings to savour and enjoy. Revenge is a dish best served slowly.

Claudia let out an unconscious laugh.

'Madam?' said the taxi driver.

'Sorry nothing, I was just thinking of something.'

***

Linda occupied the same table they'd used before and smiled at the sight of a cat's head sticking from the top of Claudia's daypack. She shook her head from side to side as she said,

'Where did you find the Moggie?'

'Cat rescue. I heard you wanted to become a foster carer, providing a haven to catnapped felines.'

Playacting, Linda shook her head in disbelief. 'You're kidnapping animals now, are you? You know, this wouldn't have happened when you were with the Mafia. It must be an English thing, perhaps it's the weather. What is the world coming to?'

Claudia shrugged her shoulders, smiled, and said, 'The cat is kind of cute.'

'I suppose.' Linda said, changing her voice to a more serious tone. 'How long will I be operating a cat sitting sanctuary?'

'Oh, not long. Snowflake here ...'

'Snowflake?' interrupted Linda. 'You know its name?'

'Nah, that's what I'm calling it.'

Claudia took a sip of the beer Linda had waiting for her, buying time to formulate the lie she would spin.

'Snowflake here is a motivational tool, and a means to encourage cooperation. Once the Moggie has served its purpose, it will miraculously reappear at the family home. Hopefully, you won't be a furry carer for long.'

'Oh, that's okay. I'm not planning on being away anytime soon.' Linda sneezed. *Achoo, Achoo.*

'Are you alright?' Claudia asked.

'I forgot to tell you. I'm allergic to cats.'

'Really?'

'Yes, whenever I'm in the company of a cat, and my beer glass becomes empty, I can't stop sneezing until my glass is full again. It must be your round.'

Claudia smiled. 'I'll be right back. Why don't you and Snowflake become acquainted?'

Claudia returned to the table carrying two glasses of Champagne.

'I thought we would celebrate again,' she said, handing a flute to Linda. 'To old friends.'

'We've done that one. How about, to best friends,' Linda replied. They clinked glasses and then took a sip.

Linda smiled. 'Very agreeable. The 1996 Dom Perignon?'

'I wish. Now, what did you get up to while I was out rescuing cats?'

'While you were "stealing" a cat, I went to a nightclub.'

'Nice.'

'It was. You'd know it. We used to frequent it back in the day, with our Russian Mafia colleagues. They were friendly enough, but not overly helpful.'

'Our old friends don't like people snooping about.'

'Nah, it was fine. They knew who I was, but what I found interesting was that some of the younger ones had never heard of the Crane.'

'We are showing our age, Linda?'

'Speak for yourself. It was Carlos who said something interesting.'

'Carlos?'

'He's been around a while, an ex-Russian Alpha group commando, about fifty-five, balding, from Serbia. He took over some of your duties when you left. Works for another Oligarch now, a man called Sergey Rutskoy.'

Claudia nodded and said, 'I remember Carlos. A nice man for a thug. Ex-Alpha group, and nasty.'

'Yep, that's the one. Anyway, Carlos said that the Crane retired a few years back. If that were true, the Chinese must have offered a very lucrative contract.'

Claudia lifted an eyebrow and said, 'That is interesting. The Brits think the Crane is still active.' She gave a half-laugh. 'Activating the Crane for me shows how vindictive the Chinese are.'

From her handbag, Linda took Claudia's MI6 mobile phone and held it towards her. 'You'll be wanting this.'

'I'll swap you for a cat.'

CHAPTER 4
Axel

Claudia left Linda at the Windsor Castle Pub and returned to the hotel room, only to find that sleep evaded her. Looking at the bedside table clock for the umpteenth time, she gave up trying to rest and decided to drive to Cornwall and Pi-Ski instead. On the threshold of leaving, her bags packed and hand turning the doorknob, she stopped, angry with herself.

What are you doing? You know MI6 is tracking you? What will the Psychologist say to Stephen if you leave for Cornwall at four in the morning? That you're having difficulties in sleeping, a warning sign of stress, depression or anxiety. At the very least, they'll tell Stephen that you are unsettled. No, we can't have that. You must wait until six o'clock when leaving early seems like a rational decision to miss the traffic.

Dropping her bags at the door, Claudia plonked herself onto the bed in frustration.

Now what?

After thirty seconds, she got up from the bed.

Up and down, up and down, you are worse than a cat on a hot tin roof.

Claudia opened her suitcase and retrieved the smartphone Linda acquired for her and plonking herself back on the bed, logged into the camera live streaming from the monitor in Molly's bedroom. Richard Liew's daughter was sleeping peacefully, the blankets gently rising and falling as the child breathed, the rhythm light and smooth. The serene vision was accompanied by the meditative whisper of Molly inhaling and then exhaling in a regular pattern. The sound was hypnotic. Claudia found herself drawn into an imaginative journey: Molly was crying when Snowflake couldn't be found and there was pain etched on the child's face. Looking at the bedside mirror, Claudia saw herself in the reflection, tears streaming down her face.

There was a tap-tap-tap on the door, followed by Tamara's voice. 'Don't be too long, Lucia. Sweetie, come downstairs when you finish dressing.'

Tamara's footsteps faded as she walked away down the corridor.

Suddenly there were gunshots and yelling coming from outside.

Claudia's head jolts and her nightmare fades as she wakes. On the phone screen, Molly is still sleeping and Claudia, looking at her watch, huffs in annoyance.

That would be right. Now it is six-thirty in the morning, and I'm late.

Claudia glanced again at the peacefully sleeping child and, betrayed by her feelings of tranquillity, she conjured up dark thoughts to suppress them.

You should call to her through the monitor. Molly, Molly, wake up Molly. That would scare her. I could be a ghost that haunts her slumber, calling to her in her dreams. Oh, that would be wicked. Yes, I could do that. Do you know what's even better, Claudia? Her parents wouldn't believe Molly when she said, 'Mummy, mummy, there's someone in my room calling my name.' They would think their child was afraid of the dark. Fearful of the boogie man. You should start the cruelty right now.

Claudia hesitated.

No, you're already running late. Tomorrow? Yes, definitely tomorrow. I'll scare her then.

Leaving London, Claudia would follow the M4 before joining the M5 and then the A30 for the run down to Cornwall and Pi-Ski. She expected to complete the trip in a little over five hours, meaning that the Little People's Arms would still be serving lunch when she arrived. Having rung Inspector Axel as she was driving, they'd agreed to meet at the pub. Although they knew each other well, he would play a deception, acting as the investigating police officer meeting Claudia anew, the grieving girlfriend of deceased John Moss.

Inspector Axel stood when he saw Claudia enter the Little People's Arms and Claudia, acting her part, scanned the room, seemingly meeting someone, but unsure of his identity. When her eyes moved to where Inspector Axel was waiting, he raised his hand. Pretending to be speaking to herself, but in a voice loud enough for others to hear, Claudia said. 'That must be the Inspector.' To the man behind the bar, it appeared Claudia's comment was meant for herself and not for general consumption. Her deception was perfect.

Claudia approached the Inspector. He held out his hand in a formal greeting.

'Good afternoon, Lucy,' Axel said, using the name the people of Pi-Ski knew her by. 'I'm Inspector Axel from Scotland Yard. Thank you for agreeing to meet with me today.'

Claudia nodded and shook his hand. He gestured towards a vacant chair at the table. Waiting for Claudia to be seated, he said, 'May I get you something to drink, a glass of wine or beer, perhaps?'

'Oh, that would be most kind of you, Inspector. A white wine, Sauvignon Blanc please.'

As Inspector Axel rose to go to the bar, Claudia added, 'Perhaps something to eat as well? They do a nice ham and salad sandwich. It was a long drive from London.'

Inspector Axel laughed to himself, then mimed, 'You're enjoying this, aren't you?'

Ignoring Axel, Claudia said, 'They will make the sandwich while you wait.'

At the bar, Inspector Axel ordered the same for himself as Claudia had requested and as he returned to the table, balancing two plates of sandwiches and two glasses of wine, a feat worthy of Cirque du Soleil, he scanned the dining room. Most of its guests had left and they could talk freely.

Placing the lunch and wine in front of Claudia, Inspector Axel said, 'I was sorry to hear what happened.'

Claudia intended to maintain the pretence of emotional disconnection, implying that her attachment was nothing more than a job. 'Thank you, Inspector. It's always disappointing when an innocent person dies. What's your plan?'

Inspector Axel studied Claudia for a moment, not deceived by her words, and wondering how to respond.

If she wanted to talk with me, she would. Perhaps she needs to speak with me, but won't. I hope she confides in someone.

He gave a small sigh, an indication that he didn't believe her story, before saying, 'I have a copy of the invitation list and the footage taken inside the church on the day of the incident. My elves back in London are cross-referencing the two, searching for anyone in the church not invited.' Claudia nodded, saying nothing, so the Inspector continued, 'Here in Pi-Ski, I plan to interview your parish council friends, which is where your inside knowledge comes into play. Who do you think I should start with?'

'Josephine Carter is a person of interest. Her husband once worked for the British Government, and he was also a Russian spy; ended up being murdered in Italy, and not by the Russians.'

'Yes, Stephen told me about him. He also told me that Josephine recognised you as the person following them in Italy prior to her husband's death.'

Claudia objected. 'That's a little unfair. "Prior" makes it sound like I was following twenty seconds behind. In fact, Inspector, it was a day, at least.'

Holding out the palms of his hands, Inspector Axel said, grinning, 'I'm not here to judge you, Claudia.'

'Good job that I like you, Axel, or I'd be tempted to punch you on that Gallic nose. And Inspector, you must call me Lucy while in Pi-Ski.'

'Yes, of course. The punch in the nose, Lucy, that might be reasonable but luckily for me, you do like me. Besides, I bought you lunch, and that must buy me a few insults. Now, where were we before descending into rudeness? Josephine Carter. I will talk to her last.'

'Last?'

'It's best to gather as much information as you can before interviewing a potential suspect. It helps me spot inconsistencies and provides a better idea of when they are liberal with the truth.'

'The more you know, Inspector, the harder you will find it is to make up your mind.'

Inspector Axel was tempted to say, *I also enjoy Tim Minchin*, the person accredited with the quotation. Instead, he ignored Claudia's comment, continuing his original line of thought as he said, 'If, as Stephen suspects, Josephine Carter has, or had, some links to the spy game, she is undoubtedly well versed in the ways of deception.'

That's interesting. Stephen didn't mention to me that Josephine may have links to the intelligence community.

Claudia nodded before saying,

'I'm catching up with Edith Kelly at three this afternoon. If you like, I'll introduce you.'

'Yes, she would be a perfect place to start. Where are you meeting?'

'At her place. We can go straight from here.'

Inspector Axel agreed.

A comfortable silence descended, and they each sipped their wine and ate their lunch before Inspector Axel asked, 'Have you heard from Max and Olivia?'

'I've had one phone call since New Zealand. The woman from the CIA...' Claudia hesitated, trying to recall the person's name.

'Bronwyn,' Inspector Axel said. 'America's secret weapon, a woman capable of destroying a building with a single stare.'

'Yes, that's her. Bronwyn was pretty furious when Max didn't kill Monya. Olivia and Max thought it best to keep a safe distance from the intelligence community and the people they care for, fearing retribution. They asked me to keep an eye on Penny, their granddaughter, which I have been doing, and I even spent some time with her in Australia. Penny thought her grandparents might be in Spain.'

Inspector Axel smiled as he said, sighing, 'They are a wicked couple. I wish I could see them before...'

Claudia finished the sentence, 'Before they die.'

'Yes, they've both had good innings. How old are they now?'

Claudia thought for a moment before saying, 'If they are not yet ninety, they must be getting close. Somewhere in their eighties.'

Inspector Axel looked around and, comfortable that they were still alone, lifted his wineglass and said, 'To Max and Olivia, our remarkable friends.'

They clinked glasses.

***

Edith Kelly was looking forward to seeing Lucy again, yet she felt awkward, unsure of what to say about John.

Do you pretend it never happened and wait for Lucy to raise the topic, or do I offer my condolences? Can I ask how she is, or will that offend her? She might reply, "How do you think I am?" Oh, dear, I'm not sure what I should say. I should have invited Josephine; she would know what to do.

A knock at the front door startled Edith and shattered her daydreaming. Glancing at her watch, she noted it was just after three o'clock.

It has to be Lucy. Oh, dear!

Walking down the hallway to answer the door, Edith stopped and looked at herself in the mirror. Straightening her dress in the reflection, she said to herself, 'Are you ready, Edith? Yes - Oh dear, now I'm answering myself.'

'Hi Edith,' Lucy said.

Her ruminating forgotten, Edith instinctively threw her arms around Lucy, embracing her while whispering, 'I'm so sorry, Lucy.'

'Thank you, Edith.'

Stepped back from the embrace, Edith's eyes lifted, taking in the man accompanying Lucy. She hadn't seen him when she opened the door and now felt anxious. Sensing her friend's apprehension, Lucy said reassuringly, 'Edith, this is Inspector Axel from Scotland Yard. He was interviewing me earlier today and, when he said he was going to make a time to speak with you, I offered to do the introductions. I hope you don't mind me bringing him along?'

Edith smiled, trying to hide her unease.

Claudia touched Edith reassuringly on her arm, saying, 'I thought it better I bring him than a strange man appearing unannounced on your doorstep; that can be disconcerting.' Changing to a light-hearted tone, Claudia continued, 'Not that I'm calling you strange, Inspector. You don't think he looks strange, do you, Edith?'

Claudia's attempt at humour to ease Edith's fears only worsened her friend's anxiety. Inspector Axel, seeing the awkwardness, coughed, and said, 'Do you mind if we come in?'

'No ... No, not at all. Please, both of you, come inside.'

'Thank you,' replied Inspector Axel. 'I won't disturb you for long.'

Edith led them down the hall and into the sitting room, then gestured towards the couch, saying, 'Please have a seat. Would you like a cup of tea?'

Claudia smiled in amusement at Edith's formality, extended only because of Inspector Axel's presence. Trying again to ease her friend's discomfort, she said. 'They've identified the cause of the explosion as a gas leak, but the police must still prepare a report for the Coroner. That's why Inspector Axel is here.'

'I see,' Edith acknowledged and glanced at Inspector Axel, 'Will you be speaking to everybody who was in the church that day?'

He shook his head as he said thoughtfully, 'No, not at all, only the Vicar and Parish Council members. It helps paint a picture of who John was, for the Coroner and me. I understand that St Mary's was an important part of his life. He was a member of the Parish Council.'

'Oh yes, Inspector, St Mary's was.'

Inspector Axel wanted to speak to Edith about the paper crane she had given Lucy, but to avoid the crane appearing significant, he needed to be patient and introduce the topic carefully.

'Edith. I may call you Edith?'

'Yes, of course.'

'Can I take you back to the day of the filming in St Mary's?' Edith nodded. 'Tell me, what do you recall? Start from the moment you arrived at the Church until you heard the explosion.'

With occasional prompting from Claudia, Edith recounted the events of the fateful day. As the Inspector hoped she would, Edith told of being given a paper crane to pass on to Lucy.

'I would like to explore the paper crane, if I may, to satisfy my curiosity. If I were to show you some pictures of the choir, do you think you could identify the person who gave it to you?'

'Like a photo line up from TV, you mean? Where the police show photographs to a witness to confirm the identity of a suspect?'

The creases on Inspector Axel's face relaxed as he smiled warmly and said, 'Similar, but that's not the analogy I have in my mind. None of the choir, Edith, are suspects. As I said, it's to satisfy my curiosity. Would you recognise him?'

'Oh, dear, I don't think so. I didn't take any notice although now perhaps I think I should have.'

'Why is that, Edith?'

Well, Vicar Charlotte found a paper crane on the Church altar, the same as the one handed to me.

'When was that?' Claudia said, trying to hide the surprise from her voice.

'The day of your party.'

'The day of the party?' repeated Inspector Axel, before adding, 'How do you know she found one?'

Edith looked to Claudia as she said, her voice betraying her surprise, 'She told us, the Vicar, you were there Lucy, weren't you? I also told you, well, I think I did - Oh dear, now I'm not certain. Was it when I gave you the crane at the church, before the explosion?'

Claudia shrugged her shoulders dismissively and said, 'I'm sure you did Edith, I must have forgotten.' Outwardly calm, inside, Claudia's mind was racing. Had she known of the paper crane on the altar, she would have handled events differently, and John would still be alive. Another revelation occurred to her, one with dire consequences: the choir boy who gave Edith the paper crane. Did he see the assassin and was his life at risk?

Surely the Inspector has thought of that too?

Claudia resisted the urge to ask a question, and as the scenario played out in her mind, she dismissed the thought.

Don't be silly, Claudia. The Crane's identity has remained a mystery all this time because they are astute—a master of murder, subterfuge, and deception. The assassin didn't just walk up to the choir boy and hand him the origami crane. The go-between isn't at risk, but he is a clue, no matter how small.

'Is the paper crane important?' Edith asked.

'I doubt it,' said the Inspector, 'Never-the-less, I like to be thorough. If you don't mind, I would like to show you the photographs of the choir anyway, in case it prompts your memory. Is that alright, Edith?'

'Oh dear, I'm not sure I'll be able to recall ... I'm sorry, this must be so important to you.'

'Edith,' Inspector Axel said, 'there's no need to concern yourself. We know who the boy is. The photographs are a prompt, a technique for triggering memories that can be otherwise hidden. Would it be better if I were to come back tomorrow, say eleven o'clock?'

Edith nodded, 'Will Lucy be coming with you?'

'No.' *Whoops, that was too dismissive.*

'Oh.' Edith said, disappointed.

Inspector Axel's voice took on a tone of reassurance as he said, 'Edith, you are most welcome to ask her. I would not object. Do whatever makes you feel comfortable. Perhaps a discussion for when I'm gone, which is the perfect segue. I've taken enough of your time today so, if you ladies will excuse me, I will leave you alone. Thank you for your time, Edith, and I'll see you again tomorrow.'

As he stood, Claudia and Edith rose to their feet, preparing to accompany the Inspector to the door, when Claudia said, 'I might see you later this evening, Inspector.' Edith was surprised by Claudia's comment until Claudia added, 'We are both staying at the pub, Edith.'

Edith swallowed a gulp of air as she said, her voice flavoured with regret, 'I'm so sorry, Lucy, how thoughtless of me, I should have invited you to stay with me. What sort of friend am I?'

Claudia touched Edith's arm reassuringly. 'Not at all. The pub is perfect.'

Edith sighed with relief.

Staying at the pub with Inspector Axel provided Claudia with the perfect alibi. She could slip out at night, wreak havoc on the Chinese agents, and be back in Pi-Ski before morning. MI6 may suspect her of orchestrating, perhaps even executing, retribution. They couldn't, however, be sure. The more time she spent with Inspector Axel, someone who undoubtedly had been instructed by MI6 to keep a close eye on her, the more likely MI6 were to give her the benefit of the doubt when the Chinese agents started dropping like flies.

Who me? I was with Inspector Axel in Pi-Ski.

'Besides,' Claudia said to Edith, 'It means that I can keep a close eye on the Inspector, to ensure he doing John's legacy justice.' Glancing at Inspector Axel, she said. 'Tonight, let's have dinner together, and you can update me on your progress.'

Inspector Axel shifted his weight, swaying a little, a sign for Edith's benefit, that he was uncomfortable with the suggestion and said, 'Maybe.'

'Perfect, Inspector, then it's agreed. I will meet you in the lounge at seven-thirty; and tell me! Who else are you to see this afternoon?'

'Vicar Charlotte,' Inspector Axel said and coughed, suggesting annoyance. 'Now, if you ladies would kindly excuse me.'

'Certainly Inspector,' Claudia said stridently, before adding. 'I'll see you at seven-thirty.'

'Um,' was all that the Inspector said.

Edith smiled.

I wish I had that kind of gumption. I can't wait to tell my Parish Council friends Lucy is on the job.

***

Unlike their lunchtime meeting, the Little People's Arms was humming with patrons when Claudia descended from her upstairs room to join Inspector Axel. She had to duck as she passed through the low door frame separating the bar from the dining room, a reminder that in the 1600s when the pub was built, people were shorter than the current generation. Inspector Axel was waiting for her, seated at one of the antique, dark wooden tables. He'd chosen one near the open roaring fire and beneath one of the exposed, bent ceiling beams. The room, with its historical character, was cosy, full of pleasant company and, for a moment, Claudia was engrossed in its atmospheric charm. She imagined Charles Dickens, Shakespeare, Oscar Wilde, C. S. Lewis, even Tolkien, drinking here, although none of them ever did.

There are some things that I hope time will never change, and this place is one of them.

Their lunchtime conversation had been private because they were alone, but now their words would be lost in a pot-pourri of vibrant chatter that filled the room. 'Hello Lucy,' greeted Inspector Axel, standing as she approached.

Claudia lifted her right leg and shook it from side to side in acknowledgement. Inspector Axel did a double-take, confounded by the gesture, so Claudia said, her voice serious, 'I would shake your hand as I did at lunchtime but, because of the Coronavirus, that's no longer etiquette. I can give you an elbow bump or a leg shake. Which would you prefer?'

'Really?'

Claudia took out her smartphone and scrolled through images and stories on its screen before saying, 'You haven't been keeping up with the news, have you, Inspector? Let me read this to you:

'As authorities around the world scramble to contain the Novel Coronavirus which has infected more than 90,000 and spread to more than 70 countries, people are facing a dilemma: How should I greet someone?'

Claudia stopped reading and added, 'They go on to list a range of alternatives to handshaking and cheek kissing. You can bump elbows, wave, bow with palms together, and my favourite, the leg tap. The dilemma is–is it one leg tap or two? A video has emerged from Iran of people tapping their feet on the ground.'

Inspector Axel questioned with a smile, 'I see Lucy, and do you neigh or whinny like a horse as you tap your feet?' Without waiting for a reply, he continued in a more serious tone. 'I know we're both trying to make light of what is becoming a dire situation.'

Claudia nodded her agreement.

Gesturing with his hand to the empty seat, Inspector Axel said, 'Please, Lucy, join me.' When they were both seated, he added, 'Do you know what the current death toll is?'

'Three thousand and there are now three countries outside of China, with more than one thousand reported cases. Within weeks, I fear it will become hundreds of thousands, if not millions, spread across the world who are infected. I am sure of it, Inspector. As for the eventual death toll? I think we can pick a number and multiply it. Whatever happens, it is not going to be pretty and the UK won't be exempt. I fear Britain will be hard hit. From what I'm reading, there's a sense of complacency at senior levels, which the virus will inevitably exploit. Only time will tell.'

Inspector Axel nodded and said, his tone sombre, 'We are in uncharted territory; a matter of watching this space. In the meantime, I guess that handshaking and kissing are out, although I can't see leg shaking or foot-tapping catching on.'

'Oh, I don't know. I thought the foot-stamping was catchy. The best advice I've read comes from a Health Minister in Australia. He recommends a degree of caution with whom you decide to kiss. And here I was puckering my lips for any Tom, Dick or Harriette.'

Inspector Axel smiled.

Claudia continued, 'Can I buy you a drink, Inspector? I seem to recall that it's my turn.'

'A red,' he said and paused before adding, 'After that conversation, best make it a bottle.'

'That's my theory,' Claudia said.

Taking the bait, the Inspector Axel asked, 'What would that be?'

'Because of the Coronavirus, people are panic buying. Supermarkets are running out of non-perishable items, like tissues and toilet paper. It will be bottles of wine for me. A good bottle is practically a non-perishable item. I'll join the herd and become a doomsday prepper, but my bunker will be a cellar.'

Inspector Axel laughed, saying, 'A glass will suffice. The thought of becoming a doomsday prepper is enough–well, almost enough, for me to become a teetotaller.'

'A teetotaller! That would be catastrophic. I'll be right back.'

Walking to the bar, Claudia glanced at her watch. She wasn't planning a clandestine mission tonight. Still, Claudia wanted to be in her room at a reasonable hour for intelligence gathering: listening in on conversations taking place at the Liew residence. Part of her also wanted to see Molly again, although she wasn't sure why. Returning and placing the drinks on the table, Claudia yawned and said, taking a sip from her wineglass, 'Oh, excuse me, it's been a big day. I won't be long from my bed. Did you learn anything of interest from the Vicar?'

'No, although she is very personable, which I suppose goes with the territory. My elves in London tell me she was present throughout the filming in the church, as were Edith Kelly, Josephine Carter and Catherine Hepburn. I'm still to interview Catherine and Josephine but, at this stage, it appears we can place them all in the church, and then the church hall after the concert. It is unlikely that any of them could have placed the explosives that killed John.'

Claudia thought a moment before responding. 'You are working on the assumption the explosives were put in the house after we left for the concert?'

'It is possible, I suppose, that the explosives were in place while you were there, but I would think that is unlikely. They would have to conceal them, so you didn't find them. Second, there's the trigger mechanism. They tell me it wasn't remotely activated and we know that there was no timing device. The preliminary findings point to a motion detector plus a delayed trigger, to ensure that the victim was entirely in the house before the detonation occurred. If that hypothesis holds, the device was placed in the house after you left for the church. I doubt the would-be assassin ...'

'The Crane,' interrupted Claudia.

Inspector Axel tilted his head to one side and then back up again, a gesture indicating he didn't agree, before saying, 'What was it that Sherlock Holmes said? *There's nothing more deceptive than an obvious fact.* It pays to keep an open mind on these matters. Nothing blinds you more than certainty. I doubt the assassin would have anticipated John returning to the house without you, and therefore, you were the likely intended target and John dying on his own was an unfortunate accident. This raises some interesting questions.' He paused and stared at Claudia, inviting her comment; he wanted her to examine the killing from a different perspective.

'Am I still a target? That's what you're saying, right?'

'It is a possibility. If the Crane has a contract to eliminate you, then there is unfinished business. What bothers me are two things. John's death was untidy, by which I mean that whoever walked into that house was going to killed by the explosion. It feels scrappy. The Crane's career has been scrupulously professional, killing innocent people while eliminating a target is anathema to someone like that. A motion sensor bomb seems a poor choice given...'

Claudia interrupted, 'Unless John was also a target. If those who hired the Crane believed me to be emotionally attached to John, his death might have been desirable to them? They may not have cared which of us the Crane killed.'

Too messy, Inspector Axel thought before saying,

'Possible, yes. Regardless, we shouldn't dismiss the prospect that there's still a price on your head–a contract unfilled.'

'The second thing that troubles me, Lucy, is the paper crane, the one Vicar Charlotte found on the altar in St Mary's church before the day of the fateful explosion. She told me you were in the kitchen when she showed the others the piece of origami. Had you seen the paper crane, you would have been alerted. Why would the Crane signal intention? That makes no sense, not to me.'

Claudia shrugged her shoulders, apparently unmoved by the Inspector's speculation. 'Torment, mockery, arrogance, who knows what goes through an assassin's mind? Confident of their ability, perhaps they wished to tease me, make me aware that my demise was imminent. I've done it myself. It's a powerful and cruel psychological weapon.'

Inspector Axel considered Claudia's response and, hoping to challenge her perspective, asked, 'Would you have foreshadowed your move to the Crane?'

'No.'

'That's interesting; why not?'

'The Crane is a formidable opponent. I know where you are going with this and what you are suggesting, Inspector. What you may not realise is this: since my move to MI6, in the "World of Ruthlessness" I'm being considered weak. Baiting or humiliating me is what I would have expected. I am no longer feared, which ...' Claudia stopped herself from adding, *which is their mistake.* Instead, she gave Inspector Axel a reassuring but deceptive smile before continuing, 'I'm pleased that you are challenging my thinking. I agree with you; It is best to keep an open mind.'

Inspector Axel drained his wineglass and then said, 'Would you like another?'

'Why not?'

As Inspector Axel stood to go to the bar, he said, 'What you're telling me is all legitimate, I mean in terms of explanations but, as a police officer, I use a null hypothesis approach to my investigations. Here, for example, that would mean I'd test that the Crane wasn't responsible for John's death until evidence proves otherwise. It's like a defendant in a jury trial, presumed innocent until found guilty.' He paused before adding, 'I've found our discussions enlightening.'

Claudia smiled, regretting having told the Inspector a white lie about having her views challenged, as she said, 'Thank you

Inspector, and that does help me understand your approach.' As the Inspector turned to leave, Claudia called after him, 'Wait a moment, I'll come with you. We might as well order something to eat, and I think it is my shout too.'

'I think it is,' the Inspector said, a grin on his face as the tension between them eased. Over dinner, cautious not to be overheard, Inspector Axel and Claudia continued their discussions.

'Any news from... how did you describe them, Inspector ... "your elves back in London"? They were looking at the invitation list, were they not?'

'It is still early days. As I said already, we have looked at the Parish Council members. Apart from them, there were more than a hundred people to examine. We're checking who's who in the zoo and also accounting for their movements. For instance, we want to know if anyone arrived late or left during the concert. There were a hundred and four people at St Mary's, to be exact, and we will interview each of them.'

'Your minions will be busy, Inspector. What of the choir boy given the paper crane? You're not concerned about his safety?'

'That's a good question, Claudia. I don't believe he's in any danger.'

'It's Lucy, Inspector! The choir boy, is he not a loose end?'

'No, I wouldn't think so. At the time, the boy was in a group and in my mind, that makes too many loose ends.'

'You've spoken to him?'

'Only by phone, and he couldn't recall much. Said he couldn't identify the person who gave him the crane; however, he did remember the man was wearing a jumper under his suit with a small flag embroidered on it. He only glimpsed it, but it stuck in his mind because he was from Denmark originally. The flag was a Scandinavian cross, like that of Denmark, but without its red background. Green, he thought, but wasn't sure. It's a lead of some sort and, for the moment, it's the only one we have.'

'The other boys?'

Inspector Axel laughed as he said, 'Typical teenage boys, lucky if they could remember their names.'

'I would have thought that their memories would be extraordinary, having to learn all of those musical pieces, often in foreign languages.'

'There's no doubt of that, Lucy, but only when they switch their minds into gear and unfortunately, after the concert, perhaps the relief of completing it without a hitch, it wasn't one of those times.'

Claudia nodded her head in agreement. 'How's the salmon?' she asked, while eating a piece of her plate.

Grinning, Inspector Axel said, 'I didn't realise your shout meant you would also choose my meal. I was looking forward to a Parmigiana and chips.'

'Inspector, someone has to look after your waistline. Besides, salmon is healthy.'

'I was going to have a salad with the Parmigiana. The salad is healthy!'

In comfortable silence, they ate the last of their meal together, surrounded by the laughter and chatter of the other patrons. Putting her knife and fork down when she'd finished, Claudia said, 'I've been wondering, Inspector, how did the choir boy explain to Edith who to pass the origami crane on to? None of them knew me.'

Inspector Axel, wine approaching his mouth, replaced the glass on the table and said, 'That was easy. It was for the woman in the front row holding the baby. There was only you.'

Feeling a twinge of sentiment, Claudia sighed, and annoyed with her emotional response, said, 'That there was. Please, forgive my use of colloquial English. Now, Inspector, if you would kindly excuse me, I think I will retire for the evening and thank you for being open with me.'

'That's okay, Lucy; we are partners, after all. If you hear of anything, please let me know.'

Claudia stood and said, 'I will. Good night Inspector. Oh, I forgot to ask, when are you seeing Josephine Carter?'

'Tomorrow afternoon. I'm talking with Catherine Hepburn and Edith in the morning, then meeting Josephine in Truro at three, at the Cathedral of all places. She's the last of the Parish Council.'

'That's interesting,' Claudia said. 'Why the Cathedral?'

'Heaven knows.'

Claudia shook her head and smiled.

'Excuse the pun,' Inspector Axel said before adding, 'My Elves organised the meeting. Something about flower arranging?'

'You haven't met her yet?'

'No, although I am very much looking forward to it. It may prove interesting.'

'I do like her Inspector, even if she killed her husband.'

Raising his glass to Claudia, Inspector Axel said, 'There's no accounting for taste.'

'It's the company I keep,' Claudia said chuckling. 'I bid you goodnight and will see you for dinner here again tomorrow. Same time, don't be late.'

With a grin decorating his face, Inspector Axel said, 'It will be my turn to pay, meaning I choose the menu.'

'Not all things are "equal" Inspector.'

'My apologies Lucy, I should have asked earlier. Before you go, will you share your insights into Catherine and Josephine?'

Claudia sat down again.

***

Upstairs in her room, Claudia logged into Richard's Liew's house by hacking into their Wi-Fi router. First, she checked the camera in Molly's room and found the seven-year-old fast asleep. Once more, the tranquillity of the peacefully sleeping child touched her and, rather than fighting the reaction, she allowed herself to be immersed in the vision, feeling immediately at ease. She gazed at the image for a couple of minutes.

Okay, Claudia, that's your nightly dose of indulgence. Now it is time for work.

Scrolling through the other live feeds coming from the house, Claudia found Richard and Samantha Liew talking together in the lounge room. It was audio-only. Annoyed, Claudia said to herself, 'That's not good enough. I like to see what is happening because body language can reveal more than words.' With a little extra effort, she hacked into the camera on their smart TV.

Ah, now I can watch and listen.

It was a mundane conversation, the truth of married life. They were discussing having the car serviced.

I wonder if Samantha knows her husband is a spy?

Claudia pondered the thought for a moment before asking herself,

Had you married John; would you have told him?... That's a difficult one. No, I suppose I wouldn't or is it, couldn't?

She had answered her question. Samantha was unaware, she was sure of it.

CHAPTER 5
Parkour

New Zealand–Twelve Months Earlier

Olivia didn't ask the question in her mind because it didn't matter. Instead, she caressed the cyanide capsule in her pocket as she strolled beside Max, the man she had always loved. As the light faded, they found a bench seat near the water's edge which looked out over The Bay of Islands.

'It's the end of a beautiful day,' Max whispered to Olivia.

Instead of answering, Olivia let her weary head rest against his shoulder and as the daylight drifted away, the moon and the twinkle of the stars taking the baton from their friend the sun, their eyes adjusted to the dimming light. In comfortable silence, they listened to the lapping of the water on the shore.

Lifting her head, Olivia said, 'Where shall we go?'

Max considered the question before he said, sighing, 'I've upset a lot of important people, so we will need to find a hideaway, vanish for a time. I thought A Coruña, in Spain, would be nice.'

Olivia gave Max a sideways glance as she said, 'Dare I ask why A Coruña?'

'It tickles my sense of humour. It's where the Spanish Armada set sail in May 1588 to invade England.'

Smiling, Olivia replied, 'Was it now? And here I thought it was because of its climate: winds and rain and often overcast. Miserable, like you, my love, and England.'

Standing, Max offered his hand to Olivia, saying, a grin on his face, 'I resemble that remark. It takes hard work and practice to become as miserable as me. Not everyone can master it.'

Olivia didn't respond immediately, allowing the banter to fade, breaking the emerging silence with, 'You know, Max, living in Spain has always been on my bucket list. I'm such a lucky woman and who would have thought at my age I would have the chance to brush up on my Spanish?'

'Por qué, gracias m'lady. Why thank you, m'lady,' Max said while pulling Olivia carefully to her feet. 'Do you think we should tell Penny?'

Olivia dropped her head a touch, moving it from side to side as she spoke, 'No, my love, everyone we care about is at risk, perhaps when the dust has settled, and we are safe in A Coruña. Maybe then.'

Max nodded in agreement, adding in a serious tone, 'That sounds like a plan. If I have regrets, it's how the career we chose affected the lives of the people close to us and those we loved. A lifetime of lies and deception has had its consequences, even if our intent was for the greater good. Maybe our children would have turned out to be nicer people if ...'

Olivia interrupted, 'We made a promise to ourselves a long time ago, Max. No looking back.' Olivia lightened her tone. 'I have one question?'

Max's melancholy mood left him, as he glanced at his wife and asked, 'And what would that be, my love?'

'A Coruña is over 19,000 km away. How on earth do we get there?'

'I have a plan,' Max said, as a smile spread across a face adorned with lines betraying his years.

***

WEEKS (AND A SWASHBUCKLING ADVENTURE) LATER

A Coruña Spain

'Max, you must read this.'

Max, enjoying poached eggs on toast for breakfast, peered over the top rim of his glasses. Olivia was holding up the morning newspaper, allowing him to scan the headline before doing what he thought Olivia wanted of him, reading it aloud:

'BRITAIN'S SECURITY AT RISK AS THE UK DIALS UP.'

It was another story about the brewing geopolitical storm concerning the Chinese firm Huawei, he thought, something he'd been following closely. The United Kingdom's Five Eye Partners, including Australia and the United States, had banned Huawei Technologies from their broadband and 5G infrastructure, fearing that the company was a risk to their national security as an untrustworthy vendor. Meanwhile, Britain was considering allowing the company to supply some of the equipment for its network.

'I think Olivia, that the UK should push back against China and adopt a more forward-leaning posture.'

Olivia glanced at Max, a confused expression decorating her face as she said, 'What are you talking about?'

'Huawei.'

'Huawei? No!' Olivia waved the newspaper at Max, expecting him to see the article she had been reading. 'This is what I wanted to show you.' Max mumbled something inaudible before skimming the page from top to bottom, assessing the headlines, trying to guess which of the many articles, other than Huawei, had caught Olivia's attention. Nothing stood out, so he shrugged his shoulders and said, 'The next clue, please.'

Olivia shook her head in disbelief and with irritation in her voice, 'It's right here.' She turned the paper back towards herself and, having identified its position on the page, rotated the newspaper back towards Max, this time with her finger pointing at the article.

> '*AT 82, ARLENE FINDS PARKOUR IS NO OBSTACLE, SOPHIE AUBREY.*'

Max read the headline out loud. Olivia smiled and, flipping the page over; she began reading the rest of the story to Max.

> '*Arlene Advocat used to watch in awe videos of people doing Parkour, a sport known for its gravity-defying jumps from city buildings. But, never at the time, did she consider that she, at the age of 82, would be able to try it for herself.*'

> '*It was fascinating to me. It looked so beautiful,' Ms Advocat says. "I even watched a class on Southbank, and I thought I couldn't do that. It was all young people.*'

'That all changed with her discovery that senior Parkour classes were available in the US, prompting the West Footscray woman to ask local trainer Ms Kel Glaister, of Melbourne in Motion, to start teaching her last year.'

Olivia stopped, skimming the last of the article, wanting to find and read out the part she'd found so appealing. 'Here it is. Now, listen to this Max.

Ms Glaister says. Everything we do can be scaled to any level of ability. Ms Advocat has already learned about Parkour "vaults", techniques for passing over obstacles.'

'Vaulting over obstacles, Max, and Arlene is over eighty. That's a mighty achievement and I think we should enrol, don't you?'

Max, who had been thoroughly enjoying his breakfast of poached eggs on toast, now faced a dilemma, knowing that rejecting Olivia's suggestion of Parkour lessons outright wasn't an option. He knew, from a lifetime of marriage, that Olivia's words *I think we should,* was code for: *We will.*

He could try to ignore the statement with a dismissive, 'Yes, dear.' That strategy was risky, only attempted in circumstances that permitted the use of self-deprecating humour. Equally, there was little to be gained from raising objections or pointing to the flaws he could see in Olivia's suggestion.

No, I need to agree and then deflect. It's the only way.

'Parkour, I've seen it on TV. It's where they jump from heights, doing 4-point landings rolling from one shoulder to the opposite hip to dissipate the force before bounding from wall to wall to climb a building, like in a James Bond movie?'

'That's it.'

'Good. I've always wanted to do that...' Max said and paused, unintentionally signalling to Olivia that he was searching for a way out. Olivia bit her lip, trying to suppress a smile while waiting for the deflection that she knew was coming. Max placed his hand on his chin, a sign that the man was about to speak words of wisdom.

'Do you remember last year, when we left the Queen Mary 2, and we were at the airport? We struggled to carry our luggage and, if you recall, I fell onto the luggage carousel, trying to lift our case off. I'm not opposed to activities to improve our fitness, but I wonder if Pilates or Yoga might be better? If, while learning to roll to dissipate the force, we were to break a hip, well, that would be a death sentence.'

Olivia loved Max but knew his techniques well, and she smiled as she said, 'We made it from New Zealand to A Coruña. Along the way, we fought pirates, were kidnapped, robbed a bank, stole planes, trains and automobiles, yet here we are. The last thing I want is for us to slip into our old lazy ways of the nursing home, or QM2. Now, Max, that would be the ultimate death sentence. If we have to go, let it be by jumping from a height. Once we sign up, it's something we have to do, a commitment that will pull us from our bed every day. Consider it training because you never know, the British or America may call upon our services again.'

Talking of their spy days had the desired effect, and Max nodded in agreement. He took a sip of his coffee and, when he spoke next, the resistance to Parkour had melted like chocolate in hot milk. Instead, his thoughts drifted to the CIA and MI6.

'Bronwyn and Stephen would have our guts for garters because we didn't kill Monya, despite World War Three not breaking out, as they wrongly predicted. It wouldn't surprise me if they've put a price on our heads, so I doubt they will call us back into service, even if Hell were to freeze over. We went swiftly from celebrated national heroes to outcasts, our only allies now being the Russian Mafia—a twist of fate as strange as it is unsettling. Here in A Coruña, Spain, we live out our days in seclusion, hiding like rats. Isolated, friendless, and devoid of visitors, we exist in a state of exile. Unnecessary and unwelcome, a painful reality we can't escape.'

Olivia reached across the table and said, touching Max lightly on the hand, 'You made the right decision despite the impact on us. Killing Monya would have been morally indefensible, plain wrong. We both know that. If the penance for your wisdom is to spend our remaining time on earth living in this luxury hotel apartment, with unparalleled views of the sea, then we have little to complain about.' Without taking a breath, preventing Max from responding, Olivia added. 'And our Parkour classes start tomorrow morning.' Max tried to hide his surprise, but failed. 'I rang while you were in the shower.'

'As you would,' he mumbled to himself.

'Are you grumbling, Max?'

Max smiled cheekily, 'Who, me, the curmudgeonly king? Why no? Do we have any incontinence pads?'

Olivia shook her head in mild disbelief, wondering where this line was going. 'No. Why?'

'I thought I could put one on in the morning, to cushion my bum for when I fall on it during the training.'

'Ha, the drop might knock some sense into you.'

'Do you think?'

'No, or I would have given you a kick up the bum a long time ago.'

Max and Olivia exchanged smiles before Max returned to eating his breakfast and Olivia reading the newspaper. They both understood that a new chapter in their lives was about to begin, probably their last. A Coruña, Spain, was a far cry from the nursing home in Australia or the luxury life onboard the Queen Mary 2.

CHAPTER 6
Truro Cathedral

Driving towards Truro and his meeting with Josephine Carter, Inspector Axel mused on the session he'd completed with sixty-four-year-old Catherine Hepburn. He knew it was unwise to have preconceived notions of someone before meeting them because it can affect one's behaviour. Regardless, Catherine Hepburn had not been what he had expected, especially from Claudia's description. She'd used words like Attila the Hun, forceful, unafraid of expressing her opinions, a no-nonsense alpha woman lacking in empathy. It was unsurprising then that Claudia had told him that Catherine was, in so many ways, like her.

'What you see is what you get,' Claudia had said. 'I respect a woman who is not afraid to speak her mind.'

At the time, Inspector Axel had wanted to say, 'Reason without emotion is nothing,' but held his tongue because he knew Claudia was not in as tight control of her emotions as she would have liked.

Catherine Hepburn appeared older than Inspector Axel had envisaged, but what surprised him was that he found her alluring, not sexually. He wasn't sexually attracted to her, but she possessed charisma, a captivating charm. To him, Claudia's description was wide of the mark. Catherine Hepburn had an intangible power that influenced how others saw her and, subconsciously, he found her warm and trustworthy. There was a possibility that his perceptions were inaccurate; Catherine Hepburn may have been a woman who was well versed in manipulating people, ensuring that she achieved her objectives. Claudia knew Catherine better, and her assessment may have been more accurate than Inspector Axel's immediate impression. As their meeting had progressed, Inspector Axel cultivated the inkling that he was being taken in by her act, finding himself smiling and laughing at the right moments. Self-aware, he had concentrated on extracting the facts, filtering out spurious emotions.

Humans are a complex entity. With Catherine, we have two contradicting personas. Or do we? The problem, Inspector, is that you are trying to align the assumptions you had about Catherine Hepburn with the reality you saw. Your expectations colour the experience. Different paradigms can exist concurrently. She wasn't presenting a different persona at all, merely tailoring one to fit her target. Me in this case. Control, that's what it was. Catherine Hepburn likes to control her audience.

His analysis of the character of Catherine Hepburn caused Inspector Axel to further examine his session with her; nothing she said had raised alarm bells, yet he couldn't shake off the niggling feeling that there was more to her than met the eye. He decided he should meet up with her again. Inspector Axel came back to the present and the upcoming interview with Josephine Carter when the satellite navigation system spoke.

"You're over the speed limit," said Jenny, his mistress, the voice of the GPS.

'No, I'm not.'

"In thirty yards, at the roundabout, take the first exit onto St Austell Street."

I wonder what Josephine is like. How will my perception of her differ from Claudia's?

"You're over the speed limit."

'I'm on a roundabout! How can I be over the speed limit?'

"In forty yards, turn left onto Old Bridge Street."

Inspector Axel could see the road. Following the GPS commands, he slowed and turned.

"Arrive at your destination on the left."

Inspector Axel signalled, then turned into the Old Bridge Street Car Park in Truro.

"Traffic jam ahead."

'Oh, be quiet.'

Inspector Axel manoeuvred into a vacant parking spot.

"You have arrived at your destination."

He turned off the engine, and Jenny fell silent.

Truro was the only place in Cornwall designated as a city, despite there being larger towns in the county. The Cathedral, where Inspector Axel was to meet Josephine, with its Gothic appearance, was the most striking feature of the city, its spires dominating the skyline, making it easy to find.

'The Cathedral of the Blessed Virgin Mary,' Inspector Axel said to himself, reading the name on the signage aloud as he walked towards the front entrance, up a couple of steps and then into the church. He had been in many of the great Cathedrals of Europe and the United Kingdom. Even so, each time, he marvelled at their captivating architecture, and Truro was no exception. A rose window dominated a wall, and its stone vaults were a sight to behold, making his body tingle. Finding himself alone in the church, he walked down the central nave towards the altar, the sound of his footsteps disturbing the tranquillity of the holy space. As he strolled, he wondered whether Josephine was elsewhere in the building, somewhere he couldn't see, or if she was late for the appointment. Churches from this period had secret spaces and hundreds of claustrophobic, poorly lit stairs; she could be nearby, and the Inspector wouldn't know. He wasn't a religious man, but these magnificent buildings awoke a spirituality from deep within him; the structures were impressive and invoked humility and, whether it was the presence of God or the grandeur of the architecture and art that influenced his emotions, didn't matter. He was moved regardless. His eyes were drawn to the ornately carved wooden choir stalls, and he paused to study the intricate craftsmanship. Had he not been examining the timbered surface; he would have missed the flicker of the red dot of a laser sight. He flung himself into the cover of the stalls as the sharp crack of wood splintering from a bullet's impact reverberated through the church, soon accompanied by a series of muffled gunshots.

Thoop! Thoop! Thoop!

As the projectiles smashed into the choir stalls above the Inspector's head, still concealed, he rolled onto his back, attempting to determine the direction from which the gunfire was coming. Moving his eyes from side to side, he scanned around the Cathedral seeking the red dot, the telltale sign of a laser sight so that he could trace it back to its origins.

Where are you?

After the shots, the Cathedral returned to its holy silence. Nothing stirred, and Inspector Axel hid like a startled mouse. The shooter, concealed in the church, was a stalking cat, its senses primed, waiting for its prey to move before it pounced.

The silence was broken. 'Inspector Axel,' a female voice called.

From the tone, the inflexion in the voice suggested a greeting, and the direction from which it came, the main entrance, Inspector Axel assessed that this was not the hunter taunting him.

'Hello, Inspector Axel,' the voice called out again.

If he didn't respond and warn the person, Josephine Carter, he guessed, to the presence of an assassin, Josephine would be at risk. If he called out, the hunter would know of his hiding place.

'Don't come in,' Inspector Axel called loudly. 'Someone is shooting in the church, and I've called for an armed response unit.'

It wasn't the truth; he had not had time for that, however, he wanted to alarm his pursuer, and his ploy was successful. Moments later there was the sound of a side door of the Cathedral opening then slamming shut.

They are making a run for it. Here I go. I hope this isn't a trap.

Jumping to his feet, Inspector Axel ran the length of the central nave towards the main entrance, where he expected to find Josephine Carter. Instead, Vicar Charlotte Foster was waiting, confused by the commotion and Inspector Axel's alarm. With no time to ask the Vicar why she was at the Church, he called out, panting as he sped towards her, 'Call the police. Tell them; an officer requires urgent assistance; he's chasing an armed offender. Do it now!'

'Oh my goodness, an armed offender!'

Whether the Vicar would understand his instructions he didn't know for, within an instant, he had passed her and was outside the Cathedral door before she could reach for her phone. Outside, he hesitated on the church steps, glancing over the paved street surrounded by shops, in search of his assailant. A slim hooded person appeared from nowhere, running down High Cross Street, a road that ran beside the Church. The person slowed, glancing toward the Inspector, face hidden. The Inspector felt a twinge of recognition; a wisp of blond hair, perhaps, or did he imagine it? Claudia flashed through his mind.

No, it can't be.

He dismissed the thought, sending it to a recess in his mind. The figure lingered, as if baiting Inspector Axel to follow, and, a moment later, turned towards King Street and started running again. Inspector Axel descended the church steps and started sprinting in the same direction but, in the time it had taken him to go down the steps, possibly less than five seconds, the hooded character had vanished. He slowed to a walking pace and muttered to himself, 'Where are you?'

He could see the entire one-hundred-metre length of King Street.

Nobody.

He glanced left to right while moving down the road, all the while searching for clues. On his right was a narrow alleyway running between the buildings. Inspector Axel moved towards it and looked along its length. Thirty metres inside, he spotted the back of a figure walking away from where he was standing.

It's walking casually, too casually?

Unsure if this was the person he was pursuing, the Inspector decided to risk calling out, expecting an innocent person to halt or his target to flee. Either way, he would know if he should abandon his search of King Street for the alley.

'Hay! Police. Stop!' he yelled; the person kept walking.

'Police!' he called again; this time louder.

'It has to be you,' Inspector Axel said to himself as he entered the alleyway. The suspect took flight without looking back.

Bugger, here we go again. I'm too old for this.

Taking a deep breath, Inspector Axel started running. The end of the alleyway joined The Leats, the unusual name of a Cul-de-sac in Truro. Reaching it, Inspector Axel's assailant turned right, heading towards one of the main roads running through the city. Not wanting to lose sight of the figure again, the Inspector began sprinting to catch up, running as fast as his legs would take him. He reached the Cul-de-sac in time to see the target disappear around a corner, once more out of sight.

'Come on Axel, you can do it,' he panted, trying to catch his breath before breaking into another sprint.

Inspector Axel sensed he was closing in on his target. With a surge of determination, he quickened his pace, propelling himself forward, swinging his arms furiously, adding to his momentum.

Rounding the bend, he saw the figure again, jogging, slower than before, towards the Castle Street Intersection, one hundred and fifty metres away. With each stride, the Inspector closed the gap; he wanted to catch the assailant before they left the Cul-de-sac. His lungs burned as he gasped for air, perspiration dripping from his forehead. The person glanced back, gauging the space between them, surprisingly they maintaining their measured pace. Gulping for air, Inspector Axel knew that even though he was closing in, he couldn't continue, his body forcing him to slow. At first, the gap between him and the assailant was even, but as the Inspector slowed further, the pursuant began pulling away. The tortoise and the hare came to Axel's mind, with him not being the victorious character of the story.

Exhausted, Inspector Axel stopped and, panting, slumped over, resting hands on his knees, he tried to regulate his breath by breathing in and out deeply. As if sensing the chaser was beaten, his suspect glanced back, too quickly, for the Inspector to have a good look. Yet again, he felt an uneasy sense of recognition. The suspect slowed and stopped running, walking briskly instead. The person raised an arm and gave a mocking wave of goodbye.

Vroom! Vroom!

The rattling sound of a two-stroke motor caught Inspector Axel's attention. To his left was the back entrance to the clothing store, "Trevails", along with a small car park. A woman in her thirties, he guessed, wearing black leathers, long blond hair tied back by a pink ribbon, had kicked the engine of a vintage orange Vespa motor scooter into life. The woman, bright red helmet in hand, threw one leg over the bike and, in a dignified manner, made herself comfortable on its seat by wriggling her bottom from side to side. Taking out his police badge, Inspector Axel straightened and holding so she could see it, he called, his voice betraying his exhaustion, 'Police!' She paid no attention, so he called again, walking in her direction, 'Madam, police!'

'Oh, hello darling.' she said, leaving the engine running as she dismounted the Vespa, moving towards him, curious why a police officer would hail her.

Digging deep, Inspector Axel filled his lungs with air, ready for one more spurt of exertion as he said, 'Sorry Madam, but I need your bike.'

The Inspector rushed past the woman and before she could object; he mounted her trusty steed and, in a halo of blue smoke from the Vespa's exhaust, surged from the car park out onto The Leats, once more in pursuit of his prey, this time with a mechanical advantage. Hearing the vroom, vroom of an approaching motor scooter, the hooded offender swivelled and looked behind. Seeing Inspector Axel zooming forward in a cloud of oily smoke, the suspect broke into a run, turning left into Castle Street, a one-way road. In front, forty metres away, were stationary cars waiting at a stop sign for the traffic to clear on Frances Street. The assailant glanced back once more and was relieved to see that the scooter hadn't yet turned the corner.

I should have known that Inspector Axel wouldn't have given up that easily. Now, what do I do?

A plan formed in the suspect's mind and they crossed to the right-hand side of Castle Street while continuing to run towards the intersection and the waiting cars.

Even for the underpowered 50cc Vespa, Inspector Axel approached the corner carrying too much speed. Turing his head in the direction he wanted to go, he leaned into the corner by pressing smoothly down on the grip and rolling on the throttle.

Smooth equals control.

He flung the bike into Castle Street and it bucked on the uneven surface, wobbling, almost dislodging him from the seat as it negotiated the curve.

Come on, Inspector, concentrate.

He lifted the Vespa from its lean, straightening and settling the bike before pushing it back over. In control again, Inspector Axel felt the jerk of the automatic gearbox as he raced forward.

I've got you now.

Within seconds Inspector Axel would be upon the target. Loosening his grip on the Vespa's handlebars, Axel prepared to launch himself from the bike to rugby-tackle the fleeing person to the ground. There was no need for the shooter to turn around because, from the sound of the approaching Vespa, the assailant knew that Inspector Axel was moments away. A green wheelie bin was in a driveway coming up on the right. Reaching for it, the suspect grabbed hold and pulled it onto the road behind them.

Inspector Axel had no time to swerve. All he could do was hit the brakes. The rear of the Vespa slid first to the right and then to the left in a fishtailing motion. Holding on to the handlebars as tight as he could, the bike smashed headlong into the bin. The rubbish must have been collected recently because the bin was empty. Rather than the impact sending him flying over the handlebars, the bin skidded along the road, washing speed from the scooter. Inspector Axel's heart pounded as he came to a halt. Exhaling loudly, he said to himself, 'That was close!' He took stock, trying to regain his composure, and saw the offender rip open the driver's side door of a green Fiat 500 that was facing the Frances Street Stop sign. The hooded person pulled the driver out from behind the steering wheel and threw him to the ground. Stopping and facing the Inspector, the suspect gave an exaggerated bow before getting in the car.

Better luck next time, Inspector.

Without waiting for a break in the traffic, the Fiat's motor screamed and its front wheels spun as it turned right, launching itself into Frances Street. Horns tooted, and car brakes squealed as the other road users tried to avoid colliding with the fleeing Fiat.

'I'm not done yet!' whispered Inspector Axel defiantly.

Taking a deep breath, Inspector Axel negotiated the scooter around the prostrate rubbish bin before twisting the accelerator grip on the Vespa to unleash its 50cc of power. With a cough and splutter, it surged forward once more in pursuit. The road users on Frances Street, who had narrowly avoided crashing into each other as they took evasive action to miss the erratic driving of the Fiat, now choked the intersection that Inspector Axel approached. He slowed, his brain calculating whether he could manoeuvre the Vespa safely through the vehicle obstacle course he faced.

If I weave in and out, I'll lose too much time, and the offender will get away scot free.

The scene erupted into chaos as vehicles attempting turns in both directions from Frances Street grid locked the road, halting oncoming traffic in its tracks. The fleeing perpetrator had turned Truro into a chaotic mess akin to Times Square during rush hour.

However, the assailant's carefully laid escape strategy fell apart when a bus halted abruptly to load and unload passengers, blocking the path ahead. Stationary vehicles in the opposite lane further thwarted any chance for the Fiat to manoeuvre around the bus. Inspector Axel spotted his opening, yet found himself ensnared in the traffic jam as well.

Come on, Inspector, think.

On his right was a narrow footpath, devoid of pedestrians. Spurred on by the sight of the stationary Fiat, Inspector Axel gunned the Vespa, mounting the pavement with a thud and raced to close the gap between himself and the offender. Looking in the rear-view mirror of the Fiat 500, the pursuant saw the approaching Vespa on the footpath.

Inspector, you are a persistent little insect.

Hand firmly planted on the Fiat's horn, warning pedestrians to flee, the assailant yelled, 'Get out of my way,' before following the Inspector's lead and bumping the car onto the opposite footpath to that of the Vespa. Even for a compact car like the Fiat 500, the gap between the bus and buildings was too narrow for it to fit without scraping panels.

What is it they say? Pedal to the metal.

The screeching of metal on metal was like the sound of fingernails dragging down a chalkboard as the car forced its way through the narrow space. Once clear of the bus, the open road remained elusive as four stationary cars blocked the route forward. The Fiat would have to stay on the footpath.

'Things are going from bad to worse,' the assailant mumbled.

Keeping their foot planted on the accelerator, the Fiat ricocheted left and right, like the metallic ball in a pinball machine, as it rebounded off cars and buildings. On the far side of the road, Inspector Axel was unimpeded and, as he glanced to his left, he noticed he was now narrowly in front of the Fiat. However, a wall of vehicles prevented him from crossing the road.

In front of the battered Fiat, the shooter could see that Frances Street arced to the left and became Ferris Town Road, while straight ahead was St George's Road, which the assailant knew led out of town. Having cleared the last of the four cars, a narrow gap, the width of the Fiat, existed between it and the next vehicle. Seizing the opportunity, the hooded driver drove the camel through the eye of a needle, crossing the street and onto St George's Road, albeit on the wrong side of the road, with two wheels on the footpath to manoeuvre around the cars choking the intersection. The shooter laughed aloud, spotting Inspector Axel, seated astride the vintage Vespa motor scooter, only ten metres in front of them. The tables had turned, and placing the Fiat 500, lining it up with the rear of the scooter, the assailant was once more the hunter.

Have you seen the movie "Duel", Inspector?

The reference was to a 1971 American film where a businessman, driving a Plymouth Valiant, is chased by an unseen driver of a rusty truck. In the Vespa's side mirror, Inspector Axel watched the Fiat cross the road and place itself behind him. He opened the throttle, hoping to keep some distance between them, but the vintage Vespa was no match for a modern car. The Fiat closed, accelerating to ram him. Inspector Axel knew that his timing would be everything. Juggling watching the path ahead and with the approaching Fiat 500 filling his mirrors, he prepared an evasive move, straight-lining a left turn from St George's Road into John Street. At the last moment, a second before the Fiat would hit him, Inspector Axel leaned hard left, jumping the Vespa off the footpath and onto the road. He raced across to the opposite side, his angle of entry perfect for a left-hand turn into John Street at full throttle, requiring all the road for the manoeuvre. It caught the green Fiat 500 off guard. The driver, foot planted on the accelerator, aiming to make the same tricky turn as had the Inspector, wrenched on the steering wheel, veering hard to the left. The Fiat leapt from the footpath and, landing hard, bounced a couple of times onto the road, but it was carrying too much speed. Rather than entering John Street, its trajectory was straight for a building opposite. Standing on the brakes and swerving to the right, the assailant attempted to avoid an impending collision. Unsettled, the Fiat wobbled from side to side before straightening, disaster averted. Having missed the turn, the pilot of the Fiat 500 followed St George's Road out of town, abandoning the pursuit.

Until next time, Inspector.

Checking in his mirror, the Inspector could no longer see the Green Fiat, so he slowed the Vespa before bringing to a complete standstill.

Inspector Axel laughed aloud, saying, 'I'm getting too old for this.' He thought for a moment, then said, 'I'm sure you've said that today already.'

He made a U-turn and rode the short distance back to the St. Georges Road intersection where he glanced to his left. In the distance, he spotted the back of the Green Fiat 500 as it sped away. He watched it pass under the railway line viaduct and out of sight.

BEEP!

The sound of a car horn from behind startled Inspector Axel.

'F..ken move, mate,' yelled an abusive, impatient male voice out of a car window.

With the events that had just occurred, Inspector Axel felt his blood pressure rise. 'Some people are so inconsiderate,' he muttered and, unhurried, he flipped the bike stand down and dismounted the vintage orange scooter.

BEEP! BEEP!

Inspector Axel smiled at the driver, removed his police warrant card and badge from a pocket, and held it for him to see.

***

Claudia, at the Little People's Arms, was waiting for Inspector Axel when he arrived and had a glass of red wine on the table ready for him. Looking at his watch, it was ten past six in the evening, and Inspector Axel wondered how Claudia knew he would arrive now? He shrugged his shoulders, dismissing the thought.

Seeing Inspector Axel enter the lounge, maintaining their charade, Claudia stood up and called, 'Inspector. Oh, Inspector.' She waved her arms to gain his attention and, as he approached, said, 'Would you mind joining me?' Before Inspector Axel could answer, Claudia added, 'I took the liberty of buying you a drink. It was wine, red, yes?'

He gave a shallow nod, a sign of reluctant agreement to any onlooker. Whether any of their fellow patrons had taken any notice was impossible to tell. Perhaps, he pondered, the masquerade was for his and Claudia's benefit only.

'Good evening Ms Lucy,' the Inspector said, as he pulled back the vacant chair to join her at the table.

Do I tell her about the events at the Truro Cathedral? He mused.

I wonder if she's connected to the shooting and chase? Claudia knew I was going there. Does it make any sense, does any of this? Why would Claudia want to kill me? Then if she did, I would already be dead if that was the case. Claudia is a friend, isn't she?

Inspector Axel picked up the glass of wine and, lifting it slightly in the air, said, 'Thank you for the drink. Cheers.'

'Cheers,' Claudia repeated, although they didn't chink their glasses together. After taking a sip, Claudia studied Inspector Axel's face and added, 'You're a little flushed; red around the gills.'

'Really,' the Inspector answered, a surprise decorating his face. 'Don't you mean green around the gills?'

'No, you don't look ill or nauseous. What I can see are the telltale remnants of an adrenaline rush. You could have been in your room bonking your heart out with the maid. That would be one explanation, however unlikely. So, that leaves. What was it that Winston Churchill said? "This is no time for ease and comfort. It is time to dare and endure". You look like a man who's done just that: dared and endured.'

Inspector Axel tilted his head to one side while smiling at Claudia. 'Perhaps it is you who should be the detective.'

'How so?'

'It wasn't your friend, Josephine Carter, who was waiting for me at Truro Cathedral. No, I was welcomed by a would-be assassin. A shooter no less.'

'They missed, obviously,' Claudia said, without a trace of compassion in her voice.

'Your concern is noted.'

Claudia smiled, saying dismissively. 'That's what happens when you have a sociopath as a friend. Did you ID the hired gun?'

'What makes you think I didn't apprehend them?'

'My dear Inspector, paperwork, paperwork, paperwork. Had you arrested someone for attempting to kill a police officer, I wouldn't see you for a month of Sundays. I'd be eating alone tonight.'

Inspector Axel considered his friend's response and, unable to shake off a niggle of suspicion, decided that the observation was sound as he said, 'They escaped.'

Claudia took a sip of her wine. 'Was it Josephine?'

'I think not. It would be too obvious unless it's a double bluff?' He paused and added, 'These things are rarely that complicated.'

'Are they not, Inspector?'

'No, but what was interesting was that Vicar Charlotte was at the Cathedral.'

'That is curious. Have you spoken to the Vicar, Inspector?'

'No, not since yesterday. It can wait.'

'What about Josephine?'

'I'll see her at her home.'

Claudia thought for a moment before saying, 'Josephine will be at John's funeral. You could wait until then?'

'Um, I might do that. Have you ordered dinner?'

'No, I thought I would wait for you, besides it's your turn to pay.'

Inspector Axel laughed and said, 'So, you're only a sociopath when you want to be?'

'Sometimes, I forget. Call it a "Max senior moment".'

'Now Claudia, you're fishing for compliments. You're too young for a senior moment.'

A comfortable blanket of silence descended like snow in the countryside before Claudia said, 'Do you think it was the Crane waiting for you?'

'I have no idea.' Inspector Axel said, biting his lip, pondering whether he should tell Claudia of his nagging feeling of recognition.

'Is something worrying you?'

'Yes, if I'm paying, I get to choose, and you're not going to like the parmigiana and chips.'

CHAPTER 7
Ashes to Ashes

When a younger person dies in tragic circumstances, the gathering at the funeral is often larger, partly because of a young life ended before its time, and also because the deceased usually has a wider circle of connections: work, family, friends, sport, hobbies, and more. Often this is in stark contrast to those who live to a ripe old age, even when that person made a worthwhile contribution to the community, living a good and fruitful life. Those gatherings can be modest, and the celebration of their legacy diminished, if not lost, to the passing of time. On this occasion, the day of John Moss's funeral, St Mary's Church is bursting at the seams, a celebration for a man with so much more to give. With mourners unable to find a seat inside, the undertakers piped the church service to those standing solemnly outside in the cold. Hidden amongst those gathered were MI6 agents observing, on the lookout for clues, watching for anyone who didn't belong. After the church service, the funeral continued to the Pi-Ski cemetery to lay John Moss to rest.

'Blessed are those that mourn, for they shall be comforted,' said Vicar Charlotte Foster.

As the Vicar spoke, Inspector Axel moved to stand beside Josephine Carter who, with her head bowed, was listening to the words of the Vicar. Josephine glanced at the Inspector as he arrived and, although they hadn't yet met, she whispered, before returning her focus to the service, 'Hello Inspector.'

Inspector Axel shifted from one foot to the other, trying to keep warm while scanning those gathered at the graveside. As the Vicar spoke, most leaned forward in prayer or from respect for the deceased. The Inspector's eyes settled on Claudia, and he tried to read her emotions. Her expression was of a grieving woman, occasionally wiping a tear from her cheek. For Claudia's sake, he hoped that what he saw was a truthful representation; when it came to Claudia, nothing was as it seemed, unless, of course, it was.

Vicar Charlotte Foster lifted her voice as she said, 'In sure and certain hope of the resurrection to eternal life through our Lord Jesus Christ, we commend to Almighty God our brother John Moss, and we commit his body to the ground, earth to earth, ashes to ashes, dust to dust. The Lord bless him and keep him, the Lord make his face to shine upon him and be gracious to him, the Lord lift up his countenance upon him and give him peace. Amen.'

Those gathered repeated the word, 'Amen.'

With the service nearing its end, Josephine Carter lifted her head and turned to look at the Inspector saying, 'I hear you want to speak to me.'

'If I may.'

'Certainly, I'm going to the church hall for the refreshments. Why don't you walk with me and we can chat?'

Inspector Axel nodded. The graveside service finished and, before leaving, those gathered filed past Claudia to give their condolences. Inspector Axel followed Josephine. After throwing a handful of rose petals on the coffin, Josephine led the Inspector out of the cemetery, and as they walked, she asked, 'What is it you wish to talk to me about?'

'My staff spoke to you on the phone and arranged for us to meet?' Inspector Axel paused; his statement intended as a question.

Josephine turned toward him with a look of surprise as she said, 'I have been expecting a call, Inspector. Nobody has spoken to me. Is this about what happened at Truro Cathedral?'

Josephine's reply didn't surprise Inspector Axel. 'May I ask how you know about the Cathedral?'

Josephine laughed and said, 'My dear Inspector, this is a small Cornish village. There are no secrets.'

'Vicar Charlotte?'

'Yes, Vicar Charlotte. She was quite excited about the whole affair. She mentioned something about having to call an armed response unit. Regardless, what I say is true. Pi-Ski is a small village, and there are few secrets.'

'Really? Perhaps you can tell me who left the Origami Cranes. Both of them?'

'That I don't know, Inspector.'

Josephine Carter saw the Inspector curl his lip, and she wondered what he was going to say.

'I don't think that's true, Josephine.'

Josephine remained quiet, neither ignoring the question nor replying. Inspector Axel let the silence linger, like a parent scolding a child, before he said, 'I think it was you who left the origami crane on St Mary's church altar.'

Axel thought he observed a trace of a smile drift across Josephine's face. 'My good Inspector, why on earth would I do that?'

Inspector Axel took his notebook from his pocket and flicked through it as they walked. When he located the page he was seeking, Inspector Axel found that the motion from his walking made it challenging to read, so he stopped, as did Josephine. 'You said to Lucy, at the reception in the church hall after the performance, *Does he know you are leaving?* Then you said, *Oh my goodness. You're thinking of staying, aren't you?*'

Inspector Axel waited for Josephine to comment, but she started walking, and he fell in beside her. 'Josephine, this tells me t you knew that there was more to Lucy than met the eye. You had access to the church, too. Logic tells me it was you who left the folded paper.'

Josephine's voice scoffed at him as she said, 'What a vivid imagination you have, Inspector. I suppose it comes with the territory.' She stopped walking and stood in front of the St Mary's message board, and staring at it said, 'I will miss John.' Inspector Axel gave a questioning look, so Josephine added, 'The sign, Inspector.'

'What about it?'

'Precisely. The Pi-Ski pesky pixie hasn't changed the wording.'

'The prankster was John Moss?'

'I just make the observation, Inspector, and it's your job to work that out. You are the detective, after all.'

Inspector Axel nodded, and together they moved off toward the church hall. 'Josephine, you haven't asked me why I think it was you who placed the Origami Crane on the altar.'

Josephine shrugged her shoulders. 'Why would I?'

Inspector Axel thought for a moment before saying, 'Josephine, where were you when I was at Truro Cathedral?'

'At home, Inspector.'

'Is there anybody who can confirm that?'

Dismissively, Josephine responded, 'I live alone Inspector, and that's one reason we created The Saint Mary's Dating Agency. You must take my word for it.' As they approached the church hall, they heard mourners talking inside. 'If you will excuse me, Inspector, as a Parish Council member, I have duties to which I need to attend.'

'I may need to speak with you again.'

'Are you saying, don't leave the country, Inspector?'

'Are you intending to?'

Josephine smiled and walked on.

CHAPTER 8
Oligarch

James, who was working behind his desk at MI6 headquarters, looked up when the office door opened.

'Good morning, Claudia.'

'James,' Claudia replied as she walked in. She was to meet with Stephen Walls and expected to be under further scrutiny. If Claudia was to exact revenge for the murder of John Moss, she needed to pull the wool over the eyes of MI6 by being patient, the route to success in any deception. She expected now John had been buried, and she'd left Pi-Ski, MI6 would find a suitable task to keep her occupied, out of harm's way, perhaps overseas, and away from the UK based Chinese agents. Whatever happened at today's meeting, Claudia was determined not to snap if Stephen baited her; she was being tested and intended to pass.

'It's good to have you back, Claudia.'

Claudia smiled warmly and said, 'James, it's a pleasure to be here.'

'You're always so positive.'

'Thank you, James, and I'll take that as a compliment.'

'Stephen is expecting you. He is on a call at the moment so, if you wouldn't mind taking a seat, I'll let him know you're here as soon as he is free.'

'Thank you, James.'

Stephen Walls was in his office talking on the phone to Inspector Axel, preparing for his session with Claudia. With frustration creeping into his voice, he asked, 'Inspector, I need your recommendation. Should Claudia return to work, or not?'

'I'm not a psychologist, Stephen.'

Softening his manner, his voice suggesting empathy, Stephen said, 'Inspector, you know full well what I'm asking. Is she planning anything that would be an embarrassment to the British government? Is she up to something?'

'Candidly Sir, I find myself unable to provide a definitive answer. It appears someone is deliberately complicating matters, yet their identity and motives remain elusive to me. I asked Vicar Charlotte why she had travelled to Truro Cathedral, and she told me that a member of my staff had called and asked her to meet me there. Nobody from my office called the Vicar, as I'm sure you are aware. Both the Vicar and Josephine Carter could be lying, but I'm inclined to believe them. The shooting and Vicar Charlotte's presence at the Cathedral is the consequence of mischief; that's what I think.'

'By Claudia, you mean?'

'Who can tell? It could be the Chinese State Security Service.'

'I understand your hesitancy to speculate Inspector, however, tell me, what does your instinct tell you about Claudia?'

Inspector Axel felt trapped. Claudia, Max and Olivia and he himself had been a team. Trusting partners, watching each other's back, keeps one alive in the murky world of espionage, a place of few friends, especially ones that you can rely on. He sighed, knowing that he had his doubts, questioning Claudia's motives and wondering whether she'd been the assailant in the Cathedral. After a pause, he said, 'Stephen, take her out of circulation in the UK, not for too long, perhaps until the water clears? Is there an overseas operation to occupy her?'

I've just betrayed a friend. She'd not forgive me if she knew.

'Thank you, Inspector, I agree with you. That would be a prudent decision.'

'My fear, Stephen, is that this is precisely what our adversaries want, to cast doubt on one of our own. I can't tell you why I feel that way, but there's an itch, one I need to scratch; my senses are tingling. These feelings have a habit of becoming clearer with time, often after the damage is done. A decision that looks wise today may prove unsound with hindsight.'

'I understand Inspector, but we must act prudently. We will give Claudia enough rope for an each-way bet.'

Another surge of disloyalty rippled through Inspector Axel; Claudia wouldn't let him down, he was sure, yet he'd snitched on her. Raw logic told him that Claudia would settle for nothing less than for revenge against those who'd taken John's life. Asked point-blank, she would deny it, just as she had hidden her feelings for the man. He was no psychologist, as he'd told Stephen, but his years of policing had exposed a truth: people who suppress traumatic emotions sometimes behave in ways they later regret; love makes people act irrationally. Even at the best of times, Claudia was not always prudent. Inspector Axel's musings were interrupted by another question from Stephen Walls.

'Do you have any leads on the murder of John Moss or the identity of the Crane?'

'Its early days, Sir.'

Inspector Axel wasn't sure how to address his MI6 master. Stephen had told the Inspector to call him by name, but old habits caused him to revert to "Sir," the title with which he felt most comfortable. In their conversations, he often used a mixture of both, sometimes Sir and Stephen together. 'We've completed matching the invitation list to the photos and video of attendees. No one was at Saint Mary's Church who was not on the invitation list, or that's the way it looks. The choir boy who gave Edith Carter, the origami crane, recalled that the man who left him the folded paper had a flag embroidered on his jumper, a Scandinavian cross, similar to the Danish flag. However, he's positive that the background colour of the flag wasn't the red of Denmark. He's not ....'

Stephen Walls interrupted, 'Good. You'll be able to identify him in the images you now have, yes?'

'He was wearing the jumper under his suit, so perhaps not. We have made a list of the countries and places that incorporate the Nordic Cross in their flag, and are running checks to see if any of the guests travelled from one of those locations. You would be surprised how many places incorporate the Nordic Cross; it's common amongst the islands of Scotland.'

'Any luck?'

'As I've said, it's still early days. We are also methodically studying the images and footage we have from the performance, hoping to glimpse the flag.'

'A tedious task, Inspector. Does Claudia know what you're looking for?'

'Yes.'

'Perhaps you need to be circumspect in what you share with Claudia, at least for the time being.'

'As you wish, Sir.'

'Thank you, Inspector. Keep me informed.'

Ten seconds after ending the call, Stephen's office intercom buzzed. 'Yes.'

'I have Claudia for you, Sir.'

'Send her in.'

'Good morning, Stephen,' Claudia said in greeting, her smile appearing natural.

'Ah, welcome Claudia. Please take a seat. May I get you anything? A cup of tea, perhaps?'

'No, thank you, Stephen.'

'How are you after John's funeral?'

'The Vicar did a fine job; a fitting tribute for a decent man.'

As Stephen expected, Claudia revealed nothing of her own emotions, and he gave a slight bow of his head in acknowledgement of her loss and accepted that Claudia had slammed the door on that discussion. He moved on to the reason she had been summoned to

MI6 headquarters. 'We have a job for you. Something you're likely to be familiar with.' Pausing, expecting Claudia to speak, he continued when she remained silent. 'Are you familiar with the term "Reverse Money Laundering?"'

Claudia laughed without intending to, as she said, 'A Russian Mafia speciality, along with traditional money laundering. As it was sometimes crudely put when I worked for the Mafia, "We like it both ways".'

'Yes, thank you, Claudia. That's why I thought of you,' Stephen stopped speaking and gave a nervous cough, 'I mean the Russian Mafia and not, because... Well, I think you know what I mean.'

I think you're embarrassed, Stephen.

Stephen recovered from his fleeting awkwardness as he said, 'If you wouldn't mind sharing your wisdom on reverse money laundering, Claudia.'

The victory that Claudia felt for embarrassing Stephen turned to one of irritation, although she nodded politely while thinking,

Don't patronise me, Stephen. Do you think me stupid?

'Reverse money laundering is where you disguise an otherwise legitimate source of funds so that it can be used for illegal purposes. Say, a criminal organisation invests in a legal business, withdraws cash to finance tax evasion, bribery or terrorism. It shifts the money supply balance in favour of cash, a shadow economy. Such matters are for the police, Stephen. Why would MI6 be interested?'

'The international nature of the footprint makes it difficult for law enforcement agencies to trace the source of funds. Most of our modern criminal syndicates operate across jurisdictions, unhampered by boundaries or protocols. The person who has captured our interest is a Russian Oligarch living in London, Sergey Rutskoy. Do you know of him?'

'He's number five on the Report to the US Congress Pursuant to Section 241 of the Countering America's Adversaries, Through Sanctions Act ...'

Stephen interrupted, 'Yes, thank you, Claudia. It's good to see an agent keeping up with their departmental reading. Sergey Rutskoy, amongst his other criminal activities, is engaged in illegal arms trading and funding terrorist groups through his business operations in Italy and the UK, hence our interest. MI6 and law enforcement have been waiting for an opportunity to disrupt his endeavours for some time. A person calling themselves Saint Vladimir contacted me.' As Stephen mentioned the name, he watched Claudia for a sign of recognition, but there was none. 'This individual is offering information regarding Sergey Rutskoy's operations for legal immunity, protection, and a new identity. The preview, a teaser to whet our interest, proved to be substantial. Saint Vladimir, also alluded to a crime group calling itself "The Firm". Have you heard of it?'

'No.'

Stephen curled his lips as he said, 'That's unfortunate because neither have we. What about Davros or Cosy Bear?'

'Cosy Bear is a joke, or it's Russian. As for Davos, that's where the annual world economic forum takes place.'

'Different spelling, but I suppose Davos could have been what Saint Vladimir intended. Were this group, The Firm, to attack the world economic forum, it would represent a disastrous failure of the intelligence community. No matter. The Minister has agreed to Saint Vladimir's terms and only I, the Minister, and now you will know the true identity of the informer, a man named Daniel Tinkov. He's the Chief Financial Officer of the Sergey Rutskoy business empire.'

Claudia raised an eyebrow and said, 'Impressive.'

'Yes, this is the breakthrough we've been seeking.'

'If you can keep him alive.'

'Precisely if we can keep him alive,' Stephen said, hesitating before continuing. 'Do you know Daniel Tinkov from your time with the Russian Mafia?'

Claudia glared at Stephen, unwilling to commit.

'I understand the past is your secret, and I don't ask out of curiosity. It is essential Claudia that witnesses, the cornerstone of successful investigations and prosecution, have confidence that they will receive support and protection from intimidation and the harm criminal groups may seek to inflict upon them in attempts to discourage or punish them from cooperating. I do not wish to break confidences, but MI6 doesn't want you protecting Daniel Tinkov if you've had dealings with him previously. He must feel safe under our protection.'

Claudia nodded. 'I understand Stephen. I am aware of Sergey Rutskoy's operations and his involvement in serious and complex forms of organised crime; regardless, I've had no direct dealings with him nor heard of Daniel Tinkov.'

'That is as we hoped, Claudia. Now, our Gibraltar office has been placed on standby, ready to pick him up when I give the order. He will go to our safe house on the Canary Islands, where you will keep him safe until he's moved to the UK and then handed over to Scotland Yard.'

'How long will I babysit him?'

'Two and a half weeks.'

That's a long time, she thought secretly.

'Why the Canary Islands?' Claudia asked.

'In witness protection, there are no simple solutions, particularly when dealing with a powerful man like Sergey Rutskoy who has a global reach. Extraordinary measures for Daniel Tinkov's safety are needed, and with Sergey Rutskoy expecting the UK to be the hiding place, the Canary Islands is a good choice.'

Claudia didn't like textbook answers, as it implied the truth was elsewhere. She repeated her question, 'Why the Canary Islands?'

Stephen let out a gentle sigh as he said, 'We have to work with what we have, Claudia.'

'You do, or I do, Stephen?'

'We both do. Regardless, a stay on the Canary Islands will buy time to allow law enforcement to make the necessary preparations. The shroud of secrecy has caught them unawares.'

'You haven't told them?'

'Not yet. We want Daniel Tinkov to spend as little time as we can manage in the UK.'

'Far be it from me to question why you are embracing inter-agency cooperation, Stephen. I take it that MI6... how do you British say it - will want the first bite of the cherry?'

'Naturally. Once we've had our chat, Daniel Tinkov will be handed over. Afterwards, he'll receive a new identity and resettlement to an undisclosed place and country. I expect one of our Five Eye Partner countries as usual, but that will be a matter for law enforcement.'

'Will MI6 be "chatting" to him while he's at the safe house?'

'No. That would risk drawing attention to the location. The situation calls for extraordinary measures.'

Claudia thought for a moment before she said, 'How many people will be protecting him?'

'Extraordinary measures, Claudia. Just you.'

Claudia raised her eyebrows, surprised by the revelation.

'Outside of us. Only those retrieving Saint Vladimir know where he's being taken, and they don't know his true identity.'

Claudia bit her lip, fighting back the urge to scoff at Stephen's statement. The noise, however, still slipped out, and Stephen gave her a disapproving glare.

What the heck, go for it, Claudia thought, as she said, 'The British Secret Service is notorious for leaking like a sieve. Your communications and computers have already been compromised.'

'Well Claudia,' Stephen said sternly, 'you'd better be on your game. You leave this afternoon.'

Claudia knew that John's revenge had been put on hold as she said, her passion betraying her inner thoughts, 'This afternoon!'

'Yes, you will need time to make preparations before the package arrives. Do you have a problem?'

Don't bite, Claudia.

Claudia brushed back her hair, saying, 'Not at all, Stephen. I was hoping to have my hair styled, nothing more.

'I see. That will have to wait. MI6 needs Tinkov secure before his ex-employer takes him out the loop and puts a price on his head.'

Wanting to divert the attention away from her faux pas, Claudia said, her voice light, 'I thought you wanted to keep an eye on me, Stephen?'

Stephen smiled, 'Needs must, Claudia. Times change. You'll find a dossier on Daniel Tinkov waiting for you at the safe house. It contains the extraction date, but not the means. For security reasons, that won't happen until the day he leaves.'

'Who will provide that information?'

'Me. You will talk only to me and nobody else.'

'That's good, Stephen.'

'Okay. Do you have questions?' When Claudia shook her head no, Stephen said, 'That will be all,' followed by, 'I'll be in touch before you board the flight.'

Walking from Stephen's office, Claudia's mind drifted to her lover, John Moss. She'd been watching the growing Coronavirus news reports coming from China and other parts of the world as the infection rate and death toll gained momentum. She was confident that even with this overseas assignment, her foe would remain in Britain until she returned.

What is it I keep saying? Revenge is a dish best served up slowly! I can wait. With the delay, the Chinese will believe that they are safe, and that will make my reprisal sweeter.

'Bye, Claudia,' said James as she walked past, heading out of the office.

Claudia lifted a hand in recognition and said, 'James.'

I'd better let Linda know she is cat-sitting for a little while longer.

CHAPTER 9
Max & Olivia

A Coruña Spain–Many Months Earlier

'It's your lucky day, Max,' Olivia said, as he joined her at the table for breakfast.

'If I'm breathing, it's a lucky day,' Max mumbled to himself loud enough for Olivia to hear, while picking up the morning paper Olivia had put on the table for him.

Ignoring her husband's grumbling, Olivia smiled enthusiastically and said, 'Remember, today is our first Parkour lesson.'

As if I could forget.

Olivia looked her husband up and down, saying, 'You know I don't like being critical, my love, but I was wondering if business shoes, suit, and tie is the most appropriate dress for this morning's activities? I admit you look handsome, though.'

Speaking with a cheekiness in his voice and a smile that Olivia couldn't see, as his face was hidden by the newspaper, Max said, 'Only this morning?'

Olivia knew Max was angling for the response, "You always look handsome," but decided this morning not to oblige and instead said, 'No, no, Max. Parkour lessons are four times a week.'

Max took the bait, exclaiming in alarm, 'Four times a week!' Then he realised he had duped and added, 'I only have three suits!'

'That's alright, my love, I exaggerated. They are on three days a week.' Olivia picked up her cup and took a sip of coffee before saying, 'I know I'm going to regret asking, but why the suit and tie?'

Max dropped the newspaper a smidgen so that he could peer over the top and, in a solemn voice, said, 'I expect to die and thought they could drop me straight into the coffin.'

Olivia placed the cup back on its saucer and replied, 'Oh dear, that would be such a waste of a good suit.'

The Parkour lessons were at ten o'clock, near the main entrance to the Casa das Ciencias, a dome-shaped science museum and planetarium in a park close to where Max and Olivia lived. If Olivia expected Max to change clothes before they left, she was to be disappointed; he also carried a black umbrella to add to his attire. The only thing missing, Olivia thought, apart from common sense, was a bowler hat, with which he would have genuinely been the eccentric Englishman. She hoped their Spanish instructors would appreciate his wacky sense of humour, or maybe they would think that he was in the early stages of dementia. Max and Olivia arrived at the museum early, at seven minutes to ten.

'What are these old people doing here?' Max said, spotting seniors similar to themselves milling about.

Olivia was struggling to contain her laughter as she said. 'You didn't think we were special, did you? Lots of older people use Parkour for exercise. We're part of a senior's class.'

Max huffed as he said, 'You should have told me that before we left. I look like a right old pillock.'

'And whose fault might that be?'

Grumbling, Max answered, 'You're enjoying this, aren't you?' Adding as he changed the tone of his voice to that of a naughty schoolboy, 'You'd better watch out because, when you're practising your balance on a beam, you might feel a poke of my brolly on your bottom.'

'Just don't mistake me for someone else, okay? Being arrested isn't part of the lesson.'

Max beamed radiantly at Olivia, saying, 'Oh, that's a good idea, a way of getting out of Parkour.'

'Yes, my love, and if you did, it would be in that coffin you mentioned.'

Max and Olivia's attention was attracted by the sound of someone clapping. A slim young man, probably in his mid-twenties Olivia thought, with shoulder-length black hair tied back in a ponytail, stood in front of the building, trying to gain the notice of the gathered group of seniors.

'Venga, acérquese–Come closer,' he shouted. Standing on either side of him, dressed in matching red tracksuits, were two slim, fit-looking women, a good match for the young man.

'Our instructors,' Olivia whispered.

Max counted the oldies present as they huddled together to hear what the young man was saying. He leaned towards Olivia and whispered, 'There's sixteen of us.'

'Eighteen,' she replied.

Max counted again and said, 'No, my love, definitely sixteen. I think you spread a little too much dementia on your toast this morning.'

Mouthing the words so that only Max could see, she pushed her finger gently into his chest, *seventeen,* and turned her hand so that her finger pointed toward herself. *Eighteen*. Max mumbled something to himself, although Olivia wasn't sure what it was.

'Bienvenido!–Welcome,' called the man, his ponytail swinging from side to side as he glanced at those present. 'My name is Felipe,' he said, pointing first to the woman on his right and then to his left. 'This is Sara and Zoe. We are your coaches, or instructors, if you prefer that term. Parkour is a functional movement discipline with an empowering philosophy to overcome physical and mental obstacles to allow us to be as capable as we can be.'

Max turned to Olivia whispering, 'I think eighty plus is what we in the real-world call an immovable obstacle.'

Olivia whispered back, 'And you're married to an unstoppable force. There's your paradox. Now shush, I want to listen.'

Felipe continued, 'Through Parkour, we will build and adapt our levels of strength, mobility, flexibility, coordination, balance, special awareness and more. We will work on techniques such as fall prevention...'

When Felipe had finished describing Parkour and explained what they, as a group, would achieve over the next six months, he said. 'Right then, are there questions?'

As Max went to raise his hand, Olivia pushed it back down.

'If there are no questions, we are going to break into three groups of six.

Ignoring Felipe's instructions, Max returned to an earlier musing he'd shared with Olivia. 'I wonder, what does happen when an unstoppable force meets an immovable object?'

Olivia put her hands on her hips and, in good humour, shook her head in disbelief, saying, 'Look about you, Max, count the number of men.'

Exaggerating the mathematics, Max lifted his hand, raising a finger each time he saw a man. Excluding Felipe and including himself, there were three.

'That, my love, is what happens when an unstoppable force meets an immovable object. Now, unless you want to be in a different group, you'd better follow me.'

Max, went from using his hand as an abacus to resting it under his chin, mimicking the famous bronze sculpture by Auguste Rodin, The Thinker, 'Did I tell you, my love, what a wonderful idea you had, signing us up to Parkour? Lead on, come, let's join a group.' Thrusting his English brolly out in front, he strode forward, a man with a purpose. When the umbrella's tip clipped the pavement, and his legs had caught up, he thrust it forward again. 'Hola–Hello,' he said, as he reached a group of four ladies. 'Do you mind if we join you?' Max had readied himself to be the source of amusement, an eccentric English expat, wearing inappropriate clothing for the activity at hand. They didn't give him a second look, and Max was disappointed.

Their group's instructor was Felipe and, seeing that Max was holding an umbrella, said as he took the brolly, 'May I? This umbrella is fantastic, but we suggest that it not used as a walking stick because the most fundamental aspect of good Parkour is attaining balance, proper balance at all times. All aspects of Parkour include it. Balance is essential to preventing falls and, with it, all other movements become easier. Parkour practitioners learn equilibrium and move on objects, like these walls around us here.' Felipe pointed the umbrella at the knee-high walls that were on either side of the walkway leading up to the museum. 'Yes, Senoras, in the days ahead we will have you walking on top of those walls. Even you.' He looked at Max, inviting him to say his name.

'Max.'

'Max will be learning what we call the "Cat Balance".' Felipe said, moving towards the wall closest to him and, with the brolly held in one hand, leapt on top. 'Cat Balance is a technique where we centralise our weight and equally distribute it between our arms and legs. We use our whole body to maintain balance and poise.' Felipe leaned one way and then the other, adjusting his body weight to regain balance. 'It's a matter of practice.' Using Max's umbrella, he held the brolly in both hands in front of him. 'The wonderful thing about being a senior class is we allow cheating. As Tightrope Walkers know, carrying a pole helps increase your rotational inertia, which maintains stability.' Felipe moved from demonstrating Cat Balance to imitating a Tightrope Walker using the umbrella as the pole. 'Then, of course, we can combine the two. What's your name?'

'Olivia.'

'Well then Olivia, this is what I hope to achieve from your husband within a month.' Felipe held the umbrella as if it were a fencing foil, mimicking an advance and lunge. He jumped down from the wall, handing Max his brolly while saying, 'Please, bring it with you again next time because I will do the same.' Max raised an eyebrow as if to say, "What for?" Felipe smiled and turned away from Max as he called out enthusiastically to the other gathered seniors, 'Are you ready?'

'Si,' they each replied in a cacophony.

It was week three of the Parkour classes, a week earlier than Felipe had estimated, that participants were allowed to practice their balancing skills by stepping up onto the walls. Most were hesitant until the instructors told them that each would have a classmate standing on either side of them for support; they could use each classmate's shoulder for balance. Olivia helped steady Max when it was his turn to climb onto the wall. As he straightened to stand tall, he wobbled and placed his hand on Olivia's shoulder to steady himself.

'You're too rigid Max,' Felipe said, watching from beside Olivia, 'As, during our practise sessions, I want you to flex those knees. Shift your weight.'

Max's immediate reaction was to say, "well that's easy for you to say," but he'd come to like Felipe, a lot. Instead, he tried to put into practice what they had learnt.

'Excellent. Now, Max, this is for you,' Felipe said and handed Max his umbrella, while holding another in his own hand. As he jumped onto the wall in front of Max, he added, 'I've been looking forward to this.' He adopted a fencing stance and, in a voice loud enough to be heard by the other Parkour participants called, 'En garde!'

Max, eager to accept the challenge, lifted his hand from Olivia's shoulder, placed it slightly behind him for balance, and then readied his brolly for the bout. With a catcher positioned either side of him in case he toppled, Max engaged Felipe to the cheers and claps of his Parkour classmates, the commotion attracting other park users to come and see what all the noise was. As Felipe had hoped, with Max's focus shifted from falling off the wall to the game at hand. Smiling like a Cheshire cat, Max unconsciously put into practice all he'd learned in the prior weeks. Fencing, especially using umbrellas, had nothing to do with Parkour but, for Felipe, it was a tool. He aimed to improve the strength, balance, and confidence of his class of seniors and, if using an umbrella achieved it, then so-be-it.

'Does anyone else want a go?' Felipe asked, as Max climbed down from the wall, still grinning. When each of the hands of his Parkour participants reached for the sky, he said. 'Well, I suggest you bring a brolly with you next time.'

'It has to be black,' Max chimed in.

From that moment on, three times a week, eighteen elderly people, led by a man in a bowler hat would gather and then march, black English umbrellas in hand, to the museum for Parkour lessons, including the new sport of "wall brolly fencing". To Olivia's dismay, Max had purchased his hat. The notoriety of eighty years plus seniors, balancing precariously atop a wall, blocking and lunging with their rainy-day sabres, grew. People gathered to watch, cheering the participants, dazzled by the possibilities afforded by the process of ageing. Their fame grew, so it should have been no surprise when a national newspaper came to take photographs.

'Olivia,' Max said, with alarm, 'We can't have our pictures taken. Imagine if our photographs were to appear in a newspaper or online? We could be recognised, and by the wrong people, our hiding place compromised.'

Max's recalcitrance, masquerading as humour, had caused this problem in the first place, and Olivia wanted to say, "And, whose brilliant idea was it to carry an umbrella to Parkour classes in the first place?" She kept her thoughts private and, instead, said, 'We can't refuse, my love. I suggest we shuffle to the rear and hide in the back row. With any luck, when the picture is published, we won't be seen.' Olivia gave Max a thoughtful frown. 'My love, can I suggest that this may be the opportune moment to discard the hat?'

Max sighed, speaking to his bowler hat as he removed it. 'Goodbye, goodbye. Parting is such sweet sorrow.'

'You mean good night, good night, dear. It's "goodnight, good night, parting is such sweet sorrow", act 2, scene II,' Olivia said, as they found a place to stand behind the other participants ready for the group photograph to be taken.

'When Juliet is saying the words to Romeo, they are thinking about the next time they meet, Max. In your case, it is time for the hat to depart, for good.'

Oh, Olivia, I couldn't do that, for I feel my friend may yet have a part to play.

Hiding his thoughts, Max asked, 'You, quoting Shakespeare, takes my mind to Claudia. I wonder how she is and if she thinks of us?'

The newspaper photographer climbed atop the wall the Parkour class had used for its practice and yelled, 'Can you spread out a little at the back? I want to see your faces.'

'I'm sure we're in Claudia's thoughts if not her heart, Max. Did we tell her we were in Spain?'

Max thought for a moment before he said, 'I think so, or was that Penny?'

'Please,' the photographer called again, 'Just a little more ... That's perfect. Now, if you would all look this way, up towards the camera, that's it. Now, smile - perfect. Just a couple more - thank you, everyone. The last task, then we're done. I just need your names.'

Max flinched as he whispered, 'What about our names, Olivia? If our pictures escape recognition in the article, our names will be a dead giveaway. If we use false names, our Parkour classmates will be suspicious.'

Olivia chuckled while touching Max gently on the arm as she said, 'Perhaps a "dead" giveaway isn't the phrase I'd have chosen, but I share your concern. We do as we have always done, Max; stay as close to the truth as possible. You can be Maxwell, and I'll be Olive. Our Parkour friends will assume that Max is short for Maxwell and that the paper misspelt my name. Our cover shouldn't be blown - this time. Might I suggest, my love, that you keep a cap on your English eccentricities next time?'

'What a brilliant idea! A flat tweed cap to replace my bowler?'

Olivia glanced at Max, and it was enough; he knew it was time to be quiet.

***

The Octogenarian Army article appeared in El Pais, the bestselling National Newspaper in Spain. Six months later and with no adverse outcomes, Max and Olivia's fear that their hideaway would be compromised faded, forgotten altogether. A lifetime of covert training, however, was not easily forgotten so, it was no surprise to Olivia when, as they were leaving the park after their morning Parkour workout, Max whispered, 'Someone is following us, my love.'

Olivia exhaled and said, 'I've had a niggling sense of being watched for a couple of days now, and it's no coincidence, I fear. Is it the woman standing over there?'

A sophisticated dark-haired woman, late fifties, black trousers, wearing a camel coloured front fastening tailored woollen coat with notched lapels and a black leather bag over her shoulder, was lingering near the sculpture of two bent-over figures, one leaning on the other.

'Yes,' Max said as they approached the statue.

Claudia nodded. 'I'd noticed her too, except today she's more obvious, as if she wants to be spotted.'

Max, umbrella in hand, gave its tip a couple of taps on the ground saying, 'I suggest m'lady, that we go for coffee at La Cantera café, as we usually do on the way home and if, as I suspect, she follows, we invite her to join us. I always think, m'lady, that it's best to confront these things head-on.'

Olivia swung the black umbrella she was carrying in an arc, copying Max by giving its tip three quick taps on the ground, before saying, 'Parker,' a reference to a 1960s British TV series called Thunderbirds, 'I'm getting too old for this.'

'Nonsense, m'lady,' Max replied. 'She looks mostly harmless.'

'Ha,' Olivia said, while giving Max an affectionate tap on the bottom with her umbrella. 'Mostly harmless. That's exactly what they said about us.'

'True.'

The La Cantera café, with its six outdoor tables, was on the ground floor of an older style blue coloured six-storey residential apartment block. It was similar to an elegant neighbourhood café of Paris overlooking a historic square, the primary difference being that the La Cantera café vista was a brick roundabout, and the buildings surrounding the square didn't have the architectural charm of those in Paris. Other than that, with an active imagination, the similarities were remarkable. Max and Olivia occupied their usual seats outside under the black and red awning. They had expected their tail to sit inside the café or a place nearby that would allow her to overhear their conversation. Instead, she meandered up to their table, catching them both by surprise.

'Olivia and Max,' she said, greeting them in a Spanish accent as she pointed to the vacant chair, 'May I join you?'

'Please do,' Olivia replied.

'My name is Sofia,' she said, hesitating as she spotted the waiter approaching to take their orders. 'What would you both like?' When they didn't answer, Sofia spoke to the waiter, 'Three café con leche's please, extra hot. Oh, and in takeaway cups, please.'

The order was Olivia and Max's usual. When the waiter left, Olivia asked, 'To what do we owe this pleasure, Sofia?'

'Monya, he sent me.'

A look of surprise flashed across Max's face. 'Really? Why would he do that?'

'He heard rumours that some unfavourable people were looking for you and that they have offered a contract on your lives, a substantial contract, I might add.'

'Who?' Olivia asked.

'A new player, it seems. Not any of the spy agencies, state-sponsored groups or criminal gangs that he's aware of. In short, he doesn't know, but perhaps you've heard of them: Davros?'

Olivia shook her head. 'Davros, it doesn't ring any bells.' She looked at Max.

'Me neither,' he said.

Sofia nodded as she continued. 'No one knows the group. Regardless, Monya has spread the word that you're protected by Russian Mafia although, he fears that this wouldn't prevent a fringe player from accepting the contract. That's why I'm here.'

Olivia gave Sofia a looked that said clearly, "And why is that?"

'Your photographs appeared in a newspaper, which was careless of you, and if Monya could find you, others will too.'

Olivia pondered the observation before saying, 'That was a while ago, so I wonder, why are you here now?'

'The word on the street is, the contract is live. You're in danger.'

Max glanced at Olivia, half expecting her to remark that "this is your doing Max" but her eyes stayed firmly focused on Sofia.

'Undoubtedly, you've seen me watching you over the last week. My obvious presence was intended as a message to your assassins that we have your back. That was until yesterday. The rumour circulating is that a team of mercenaries, one with no connection to Monya's circles, has accepted the kill and this makes it more difficult to protect you. Monya has offered you the shelter of a safe house in Barcelona.' Sofia handed Olivia a business card with an address and a series of five numbers, the entry code for an electronic lock on the front door. After studying it, Olivia passed it to Max, and Sofia continued, 'If these mercenaries fail, others will follow. Monya thinks it best if you go into lockdown for a short time while we work this through.'

The waiter returned, carrying their coffees, and said, 'Will there be anything else?'

'No, thank you,' replied Olivia and, when the waiter left, she took a sip of her drink and asked, 'Is it possible that Davros is connected to an intelligence agency?'

Sofia shrugged her shoulders as she said, 'We don't think so, although we can't rule anything out. We need to understand why you are both targets, as that would help us in determining who is involved. May I inform Monya you will be accepting his hospitality in Barcelona?'

Max and Olivia stared at each other, Max raising an eyebrow, asking without speaking, "What do you think?" Olivia replied by tilting her head to one side and gently biting her bottom lip. "Let's think about it."

'Sofia,' Max said. 'We'll let you know tomorrow.'

'Okay,' Sofia nodded. 'I understand you both need time to think this over; regardless, we don't have long. We'll have coffee here again tomorrow, and you can give me your answer then.' Sofia placed her black shoulder bag on the table and opened it before continuing, 'In the meantime, I have gifts, a little something for each of you from Monya.'

Sofia removed a chocolate leather carry purse and handed it to Olivia.

'Inside you will find a Glock 42. It's small, light and very dangerous. Max, for you a single stack, 9mm, Glock 43 pistol, ultra-concealable.'

Sofia handed Max what, to any passerby, looked like a large handkerchief, the Glock neatly wrapped inside. 'It will fit in your pocket, Max.' After a brief pause, while Max and Olivia held their items, weighing the concealed guns in their hands, Sofia added, 'This is purely a precaution, and I don't expect you will need them. They are locked and loaded, should I be wrong.' Sofia stood, preparing to leave.

'Thank you, Sofia,' Olivia said, 'but before you go, I was wondering if you knew how Claudia is?'

'My apologies. Monya thought you might ask, and I was supposed to tell you. She's been on a skiing trip to Saint Moritz and then to Cornwall...'

Max interrupted and, with humour in his voice, said, 'Nice for some.'

Sofia picked up her black bag from the table and, throwing it over her shoulder as she stood, said, 'MI6 sent her.'

'Not so nice then,' Max added.

Sofia gave a wry smile while retrieving her coffee from the table. 'No, not so nice. However, between Saint Moritz and Cornwall, Claudia had a chance to visit Penny, your granddaughter, in Australia.'

Olivia wanted to ask Sofia about Penny, but said, 'Is Claudia still in Cornwall?'

Sofia shrugged her shoulders. 'She's dropped off the radar. Until tomorrow.'

Max and Olivia watched Sofia leave and, with their new weapons concealed, they finished their drinks in silence until Olivia said, 'What do you think?'

'A toasted ham and cheese sandwich would be nice.'

Olivia gave Max a disapproving glare.

'Sorry, do you mean about Claudia visiting Penny or Monya's offer?'

'Monya.'

'This is what I think. Life can change on a dime and who would have thought that the Russian Mafia would become our ally, especially Monya, with his close ties to the Kremlin? My love, if he's gone to the trouble of tracking us and sending Sofia to warn us, then there's something serious is afoot. I fear we are pawns in a much larger game, the rules of which we are yet to learn.'

'Whose game?' Olivia asked, although it was a rhetorical question and was surprised when Max answered.

'If Monya is correct, then the game will be played under the auspices of this new organisation, Davros.'

'Which means what, Max?'

'Deadly and Vicious, really Outrageously Sinister.'

With a tone of surprise decorating her voice, Olivia said, 'Does it?'

A wicked smile drifted across Max's face as he said, 'I just made that up.'

Rising to her feet, Olivia replied, 'Very funny. Let's go home young Max.'

'Lead on, my love.' Max stood and prepared to follow.

The abduction was quick and professional.

Max and Olivia had walked only two hundred yards from the café and were waiting at the curb to cross the road with no reason to suspect an approaching white van of anything untoward–until it was two metres away. It slammed on its brakes, nose-diving to a halt directly in front of them. A car they hadn't noticed, driving behind the van, had slowed the traffic to prevent the kidnap vehicle from being rammed as it performed its emergency stop. The side door of the van slid open, and two men, both in their thirties, jumped out. Max and Olivia dropped their umbrellas in unison when, with no respect for their age or likelihood of serious injuries, they were hurled onto the floor of the vehicle. Their Parkour training allowed the couple to use the momentum of the manoeuvre to their advantage as they rolled on impact, dissipating the energy and transferring the force. They were unhurt but lay motionless, eyes partially closed, assessing their opposition as the van sped away.

Olivia peeked through her semi-closed eyes.

We have a driver and two men in the back with us. There's likely to be a car behind, riding shotgun with another two men inside. That makes five in total.

Because she and Max had been a team since well before the assailants were born, she knew Max was performing the same calculations as she was. Closing her eyes, Olivia listened to the two men speaking, waiting for the right opportunity to strike.

'I told you this would be an easy six.'

What nationality is that the accent? South African, yes. Mercenaries, soldiers of fortune. Sofia had been right; they are not spies. I suppose that's a plus as they won't know of our past and hence underestimate the threat we pose, especially at our age. It's not much of an advantage, Olivia, but an advantage none-the-less.

The other man said, 'Yeah, it's an easy six million dollars, but only if they're alive.'

'They're not dead,' the first man replied. 'A broken hip perhaps, or a knock on the head. They'll survive long enough. Besides, the boss didn't say bring them back uninjured, just don't kill them. She knew our plan, Sweetie.'

Both men laughed before the first man spoke again. 'We should get some life back into them before we get there. Sit them up.'

From the tone in the first man's voice, Olivia knew he was giving the second man an order.

He will need to die first.

Max felt an arm placed under his shoulder, followed by the sensation of being lifted.

'Come on, old man, wakey-wakey. Let's see if we can't sit you up.'

Max opened his eyes and, while groaning, pretending to be in agony, he shifted his weight to help the mercenary move him.

'You are still with us, then?' the man said.

Max nodded, thinking.

They're not frightened of us, and that is good, very good.

A weak "thank you" escaped from Max's lips.

Once he was in a sitting position, Max let his eyes and body droop, not the sag of unconsciousness, more that of a frail old man. Glancing slyly to the side, he caught Olivia's eye.

Soon my love. We strike soon.

Max waited for his captor to position Olivia next to him before saying, in a thin, wheezy voice, characteristic of an old person, 'What do you want with us?'

The man who had moved him said, 'It's nothing personal mate, we're doing our job. Why don't you just sit there quietly and enjoy the ride?'

Looking at the two men and what he could see of the driver, Max reached the same conclusion as Olivia; the men were nothing less than mercenary scum. As the men talked amongst themselves, Max scanned them from head to toe, formulating his plan of attack.

Three white males, all of solid muscular build, sporting short-cropped hair and wearing black mirrored sunglasses. Why do the baddies always have sunglasses with a reflective optical coating? Who knows? I've always found it very unbecoming. The person giving commands has a horseshoe moustache, whereas the others are clean-shaven. They are all wearing black short-sleeved T-shirts with bone coloured cargo pants. The two men in the back have HK45s, Heckler and Koch semi-automatic pistols stuffed in the top of their pants. I'm guessing the driver has the same weaponry. What else?

Max, like Olivia, thought a car was riding shotgun.

Those in the car would be heavily armed, probably two people, no more. Max had reached the same conclusion as Olivia: *a team of five.*

'Are you alright?' Max said to Olivia, wheezing, pretending to have shortness of breath.

Olivia croaked back, 'I think so, dear. My arm is a little sore. Do you think it's broken?'

While taking Olivia's arm in his hands, Max surveyed his captors from the corner of his eye, expecting they would say, "Keep still and shut up". The man with the shoe moustache watched as Max examined Olivia's arm, seemingly unconcerned by his movements.

'It might be my love,' Max replied. 'We should get it looked at *soon*.'

The man who had moved the couple chuckled as he heard Max's concern for Olivia. He knew they would soon be dead, so diverted his attention back to his partner, resuming their muttered conversation.

Max's signal, understood by his wife and espionage partner, told her he was about to act and that she should be ready. Through the front windscreen, he noticed they were approaching a set of traffic lights, currently red.

It's now or never, Max thought.

'You're crying, my love,' Max said. 'You need to be brave... wipe your eyes.'

Olivia sniffled and apologised as she opened her purse, which was resting on her lap, seeming to take out a tissue, but she grasped the Glock.

'Let me get my handkerchief and dry your eyes, my love,' Max said, a sympathetic tone filling his speech, code for "follow my lead, I will shoot first". With his hand in his pocket, Max held the Glock, finger poised on the trigger. They were both primed and ready.

The van came to a halt.

Bang! Bang!

Two shots rang out from Max's pistol, the bullets now embedded into the chest of the man in command.

Bang! Bang!

Olivia targeted the driver, who slumped dead over the steering wheel. Before the second man in the back of the van could react, Max put two shots into his chest: dead. Scrambling over the bodies and climbing into the front of the vehicle, Olivia reached the driver. She unbuckled his seat belt and tried to drag him out of the way; he was too heavy and she couldn't move him.

'I need help here, Max.'

Max reached over from behind the driver and grabbed his shoulders as he said, 'On the count of three: One, two, heave. Even with their combined force, the dead man remained wedged in the driver's seat.'

'Damn!' Max said. 'Escaping on foot will be too much of a challenge. We're not as agile as we used to be.'

'Wait!' Olivia instructed and reached across the body to open the van door. 'Now, push,' she ordered. The body toppled from the van onto the road. Olivia positioned herself behind the steering wheel and then said, 'Climb over and hold on, my love, and... seat belt!'

'Is that necessary?'

Finding reverse gear, Olivia revved the motor and dropped the clutch. The van rocked backwards, striking the car behind as its occupants, two heavily armed men, were in the process of alighting. The impact knocked both men off their feet and onto the ground. As one man landed, his finger inadvertently squeezed the trigger on the automatic rifle he was carrying, and a spurt of gunfire erupted into the air.

Rat-a-tat-tat!

Olivia was hoping the impact on the car behind would trigger its airbags, disabling the vehicle.

Max, positioned in the passenger seat, said coolly, 'The lights have turned green, my love. You can go if you wish.'

'Sometimes you're insufferable,' Olivia grumbled and selected first gear, accelerating through the intersection. In the side mirrors, she saw the men climb back into their damaged car and start following them. Olivia groaned loudly.

'Is something wrong, my love?'

'Yes, they must have deactivated the car's airbags. They're still with us.'

'What did you expect, Olivia? They are professionals, but perhaps your wicked move has damaged their radiator. I predict it will billow stream shortly but, in the meantime, may I suggest you put your foot down. What's the expression? Shake a leg!'

Olivia swung the van hard to the left and then violently right again, as she forced her way past a slower car that was impeding their progress. Max, with nothing to hang onto, was flung about, first sliding toward Olivia and then hitting the passenger door as he cried, 'Ouch!' He reached for the seat belt and secured himself in position and, rather than admitting that he should have followed Olivia's guidance earlier, he peered out of the window, saying. 'I find the harbour is always pleasant at this time of day, don't you?'

Olivia ignored him as she prepared to overtake another vehicle.

'Damn!' Max said.

Olivia looked across, concerned. 'What is it?'

'My umbrella. I dropped it when the mercenaries threw us in the back of this van. It was my favourite...' His attempted humour came to an abrupt stop as he let out a sign of distress: *'Oh, my goodness!'* Up ahead, Max had spotted a truck reversing out of a side street directly in front of them. Olivia jumped on the brakes and, even though his seat belt restrained him, Max was pushed forward as the van wiped off speed. He gasped, taking a deep breath, knowing that they wouldn't be able to stop in time. Olivia's foot came off the brakes as she flung the van to the right, then stomped on the accelerator, sending Max's head from right to left like a rag doll. They squeezed past and Olivia glanced in her side mirror, watching as the mercenary's car also narrowly avoided the truck.

'Damn!' she called, seeing the car preparing to pull up alongside them, followed by, 'What on earth were you talking about, Max?'

'My umbrella, dear. Do you think it will still be there?'

'I'm rather busy at the moment,' Olivia answered as she jerked on the steering wheel, sending the van careering into the side of the mercenary's car. The vehicles collided with a thud and Olivia said, 'Why don't you make yourself useful and, instead of whining about your umbrella, have a look at the card Sofia gave us and see if her phone number is on it? We could do with a little help. A lot actually!'

Rat-a-tat-tat! Rat-a-tat-tat!

The twang of bullets accompanied the sound of gunshots as they struck the van. Max fiddled in his pocket, trying to find the business card; his task made difficult as Olivia swerved the van from side to side to avoid the gunfire.

'I think I've found it. Yes, look what do we have here, a card, and with a phone number on it.'

'Well?'

'Well! If you could hold the van steady, my dear, I could read Sofia's phone number? It's all rather a blur at the moment.'

'First, the umbrella and now you want me to drive in a straight line! You can be so demanding sometimes. If you wait just a second.'

Max gulped.

'You're not going to, are you?'

'I suggest you brace yourself, my love.'

In front, Max noticed that the traffic was stationary at road works. On the opposite side of the road, driving towards them was a tip-truck dropping stones. If they stopped, they would be the fifth car in a queue but, from their approaching speed and Olivia's warning, he knew that stopping wasn't on Olivia's mind. A narrowing gap existed between the first car in the queue and the approaching truck as Olivia swung onto the wrong side of the road and sped towards a head-on collision. The tip-truck continued crawling towards them, its driver's attention focused on his mirrors, watching the dropping stones. Olivia could have tooted the van's horn and alerted the driver but calculated that, if she did and the truck stopped, not only would her van fit through the narrowing gap, but so would the mercenaries. She took a deep breath, held it, and accelerated harder. With only feet before a head-on crash, Olivia flung the steering wheel to the right, the van clipped the driver's side-front fender of the first car in the queue as it raced past. The truck driver alerted to her presence by the impact, hit the brakes. The van made it through the gap, and as Olivia hoped, the truck plugged the hole behind her. Olivia had bought them some time. First, checking in her mirrors, Olivia slowed the van and said, 'Max, if you wouldn't mind calling Sofia?'

Max was surprised at the tremble in his hands as he entered the number into his phone. The bravado and gameplay between him and Olivia had always served them well–calm banter, developing into composed behaviour. It was a trick to control the fear. Fear led to anxiety and bad choices. His hands betrayed him and he hoped Olivia hadn't seen them. Within two rings, Sofia answered.

'Hello.'

Max was determined to come across as calm and controlled. Clenching his fist, he stopped his hand shaking and, in a composed voice, said, 'Sofia, this is Max.'

'Max,' Sofia repeated inquisitively.

'We seem to have run into your mercenary friends. Olivia and I were wondering if we might call upon you for some... assistance?'

Misinterpreting Max's tone, Sofia relaxed and said, 'When will you need me?'

'It would seem soon. We have three dead bodies in the van with us, and there are two other men in a car giving chase; and they have machine guns!'

An air of urgency edged Sofia's voice as she replied, 'Where are you?'

Max looked out the windscreen, searching for a well-known landmark. 'We're approaching the aquarium. Did I say? We're driving a white van and our mercenary friends are not far behind.'

'Okay,' Sofia said, followed by a brief pause while she gathered her thoughts, 'I want you to go to the aquarium and I'll meet you inside. You will be safer in a public space, somewhere with lots of people. How many assailants did you say there were?'

'Five, but only two are left.'

'I'm on my way.'

'What did she say? Oliva asked.'

'That she'd meet us in the aquarium. The turn is coming up on your right.' Max pointed towards the exit.

Olivia checked her mirrors and said while making the turn, 'I can't see them.' Easing back on the accelerator, Olivia guided the van into the nearly full car park of the aquarium. 'There are lots of people about, Max. Are you sure we're doing the right thing, putting innocent lives at risk to save our skins?'

'Ha, says you, who's been driving like an eighty-year-old grandma. Oh dear, my sarcasm doesn't work because you are an eighty-year-old grandmother!' Max released the clench of his hand. It had stopped shaking.

Olivia crawled along, looking left and right for a place to park. Max, sensing her indecision, said, 'Drive right up to the entrance, my love. There's bound to be a loading bay or disabled parking. We can dump the van there.'

Olivia nodded.

'See, I told you,' Max said, pointing to the vacant spot as Olivia pulled in.

Switching off the engine, Olivia looked at her husband. 'If you're ready, my love. Let's go.' She took in a deep breath.

Disembarking from the van and walking towards the main entrance, Max and Olivia scanned the car park, checking if the mercenaries had followed them, or if they could see any other signs of danger.

So far, so good, they both thought.

Despite the almost full car park, they didn't queue long for a ticket, regardless they were hyperalert of their surroundings, continually watching. Inside, as they walked, Max mused it was like entering a gigantic fish tank with many fish species gliding past behind large panes of glass. At one point, they walked through a transparent tunnel, sea creatures swirling all around them, even swimming over their heads. Had their circumstances not been so dire, Max would have enjoyed the outing and he wondered, as a manta ray drifted over his head, why they hadn't visited previously.

Come on, Max, keep your mind on the job at hand.

Refocusing, he said, 'Olivia, what do they look like?'

She gave a small chuckle as she said, 'What do you think?'

Max thought for a moment before saying, his tone sarcastic, 'Let me guess. Caucasian, black t-shirts, sunglasses, and wearing bone coloured cargo pants.' He paused. 'You don't think they would wear their sunglasses in here, too? Surely not.' Before Olivia could answer Max's question, two burly men swaggered into the building, dark reflective sunglasses covering their eyes.

'They're here,' he said, glancing towards the entrance. 'If they are armed, their weapons are well concealed.'

'As are ours, Max.'

They watched the mercenaries scan their surroundings.

'Do you think the tank glass is bulletproof?' Max asked, as a shark swam past.

'It would have to be,' Olivia answered. 'Wouldn't it?'

Max shrugged his shoulders.

'In the van, did you hear them say, "Sweetie"? That's Claudia's tag line. I'm sure they were referring to their boss.'

Max nodded. 'Maybe, but we know Claudia is in Cornwall. If there's subterfuge afoot, we're not the intended audience.'

'Didn't Sofia say that Claudia's dropped off the radar?'

'Yes. But it is subterfuge, believe me.'

Olivia pondered Max's words before saying, 'Shouldn't we keep an open mind?'

'I have faith and trust in Claudia, my love.'

'I agree,' Olivia said. 'Someone is being deliberately misleading. Damn! They've seen us.'

A sadistic smile flashed across the mercenaries' faces as they spotted Max and Olivia and started walking towards them.

'What now?' Max asked.

'We lead them away from these people because they won't care who they kill, but we certainly do.'

Max nodded as they made their way to the edge of the aquarium, occasionally checking to see that they were still being followed. When their backs were against a concrete wall, rather than the glass holding back the water, they stopped.

'This is it,' Olivia said, 'our last stand.'

A door with a sign above it saying "Staff Only" opened nearby. A woman stepped out and called, 'Max, Olivia! In here, quickly!'

They followed the woman, and once inside, she locked the door behind them. 'Sofia called me and told me to take you around the back where she'll be waiting for you. If you would, please follow me.'

The woman turned on her heels and strode away, leaving Max and Olivia staring at each other, wondering what was happening. 'Come along, please. We haven't got all day.'

CHAPTER 10
Barra Island

Before leaving for the Canary Islands, Claudia wanted to speak with Inspector Axel, both to let him know she was going overseas on a temporary assignment and to keep abreast of his enquiries. Their conversation was pleasant enough, yet Claudia felt he was holding back, withholding information from her. She chose to be straightforward, her gaze steady as she asked, 'Inspector, is there anything you haven't told me?'

Earlier that morning, after his phone conversation with Stephen Walls, Inspector Axel had learned the identity of the man with the embroidered flag on his jumper, the person they were seeking from the Pi-Ski concert. His name was Charles Scott, and the flag was of Barra Island, Scotland. According to a preliminary background check, before moving to Barra Island three years earlier, Charles Scott worked in the media and marketing department of H1 Technologies, an information and communications company, known for its leadership in 4G and now 5G wireless networks. It wasn't clear why he was on the Pi-Ski invitation list, although Inspector Axel surmised it had been because of his media connections. Nothing suspicious had emerged from the Inspector's scrutiny of Charles Scott. Still, the Inspector wondered why a man would leave a comfortable London lifestyle and isolate himself on a remote island. He had mused that perhaps he was writing a book and needed solitude.

Inspector Axel felt disloyal to Claudia as he considered answering her question in the negative, so, despite intending to keep Claudia in the dark, he changed his mind. 'The flag on the mule's jumper was from a place called Barra Island off the coast of

Scotland, and it belongs to a man by the name of Charles Scott.' He shared with Claudia what little he knew.

'Thank you, Inspector, and I appreciate your openness.' Claudia said, surmising that Inspector Axel was under Stephen's instructions to keep her out of the loop.

He's a good friend.

'No problem, Claudia. Stay safe while on assignment, and I hope to see you in a few weeks.'

As he finished the call with Claudia, Inspector Axel wondered if he was right to tell her about Barra Island. *It's done now*, he said to himself, trying to push the thought to the back of his mind.

Using his smartphone, Inspector Axel typed into the search engine, "Barra Island". From the screen he read: Barra, famed for its beauty, is the most southerly inhabited island in the Outer Hebrides, Scotland. It has a population of 1,174.

He noticed that the population figures quoted were ten-years out of date. As he scrolled the page, the location of the airport tickled his fancy as scheduled flights used the beach at Cockle Strand between tides as the runway. Many people had written accounts of their approach and landing; from the descriptions, it seemed a novel experience.

Initially tempted to fly into Barra, Inspector Axel chose the five-hour CalMac car ferry crossing instead. It was a long drive from Cornwall, so he booked a night at the picturesque port town of Oban from where he would catch the ferry the next morning. After dinner at his hotel, using Google Earth on his phone, Inspector Axel examined photos of Charles Scott's house.

Very pleasant, with a beautiful view of the sea. Inspector Axel laughed at himself. *It's incredible. With the free resources available on the internet, anyone can be a spy now.*

Closing the app and opening a search engine, he looked up the ferry crossing, reading the search results aloud to himself:

'After leaving Oban bay, around the north end of Kerrera you pass by the southern end of the island of Lismore and sail the length of the Sound of Mull, with Mull on your left and Morvern, and later the Ardnamurchan Peninsular, on your right.'

'Highlights include Duart Castle, perched atop a rock overlooking the sea, Tobermory, glimpsed sheltering in its bay; and the lighthouse at Ardnamurchan Point. Further out, you pass the north end of the island of Coll before coming into sight of Barra and docking at Castlebay.'

'I'm looking forward to this trip. It feels more of a holiday adventure than a spy mission. Sometimes this line of work has its compensations.'

Inspector Axel was at the ferry terminal with plenty of time to spare and, despite heavy skies and light rain, was looking forward to the crossing. Following the boarding instructions, he drove onto the ship and, after parking, left the car and walked up on deck. He rubbed his hands together to ward off the cold as he planned to spend much of the trip outside, enjoying the crisp air and scenery. His dream of a perfect journey was forgotten when the boat struck adverse weather with noticeable sea swells as it left the harbour. He started feeling unwell within minutes, followed by cold sweats, dizziness and nausea. The pleasant five-hour journey became the trip from hell and, by the time he arrived on Barra Island, he felt as though he'd been in eternal purgatory. Driving off the boat, he murmured 'never again' to himself, but he soon recovered and the memory of the trip faded like a terrible nightmare. That was until he remembered there was the return trip to the mainland.

Ordinarily, a police inspector arriving on Barra Island from the Scotland Yard would notify the local constabulary. However, this was to be a discreet visit on behalf of the British Secret Service, who were not known for flagging their presence. Inspector Axel planned to talk to Charles Scott and catch the morning ferry back to the mainland in two days. He'd booked accommodation at the Castlebay Hotel, described on its website as a quaint 19th-century building, plus an extra night in case his plan went awry. The additional night made him resemble one of the many tourists who visited the island each year. Axel wasn't expecting any ground-breaking revelations from Charles Scott but hoped that an insignificant observation might represent a piece in the jigsaw puzzle to help him find the Crane. Every contact leaves a trace, and he planned to turn over each stone until he found tracks.

According to MI6 intelligence, Charles Scott lived three and a half kilometres north-east of Castlebay, in Brevig Bay. The drive from the ferry to the stone cottage wouldn't take long, so Inspector Axel decided to complete a twenty-one-kilometre circuit of the island, driving clockwise, as a way of reaching Scott's home. The journey, despite its narrow sections, was completed in thirty minutes and, as he drove, Inspector Axel made a mental note of the sights he would return to, keeping up the guise of a tourist once the interview was over. Charles Scott's stone cottage, like many of the houses he had seen on the drive, stood alone, the closest house two-hundred metres away. The landscape, a lush cove with the sea on one side surrounded by a hilly green backdrop, was punctuated by rocky outcrops and, though barren of trees, was beautiful in a raw manner. Scattered around the cove were other dwellings, and

Inspector Axel assumed on Barra Island, this classified as a small hamlet or town.

Parking in front of the cottage, Inspector Axel studied the building before going inside. Smoke was spiralling skywards from the chimney and he wondered where the wood for the fire came from on a virtually treeless island. Charles Scott's car was in the driveway and his mobile phone, which was being tracked by MI6, showed that Scott was home. Before leaving his vehicle, Inspector Axel sent a text to let his London elves know he was going inside. He finished the message with, 'I'll check in again in 30 minutes. Axel.'

'Okay,' came the reply.

Inspector Axel set the alarm on his smartphone for thirty minutes. The last thing he wanted was to overstay and for the elves to send in a rescue mission and blow his cover.

Let's do it.

His senses were telling him that everything was too quiet as he walked up to the front door. *Surely, he's seen me arrive.* Inspector Axel knocked, then stood to one side while he waited, a practice from a lifetime of working on the street: A bullet fired through the door would miss him. While he waited, he listened for the sound of movement, but the house was still. Inspector Axel knocked again. No reply. He began moving around the house, peering through the windows. From what the Inspector could see, everything was tranquil, nothing disturbed. Regardless, he felt it was eerily quiet. Returning to the front door, Axel tried the handle, which turned. He pushed it gently open, while calling, 'This is the police. Hello.' The front door opened onto the main sitting room, which also served as the kitchen. Stepping inside, Inspector Axel called out again. 'Police!'

Silence.

Inspector Axel hesitated as he listened for signs of life, or of danger. The eeriness continued, the room noiseless, not even the sound of a ticking clock. With smoke drifting from the chimney, he'd expected to hear the crackling of the fire, but that was hushed, burning inside a wood heater.

'Charles... Charles Scott, are you in here?' Inspector Axel called.

An open laptop computer was on the kitchen table, next to a mobile phone and an empty cup. The phone was the one being tracked by MI6, which showed Charles Scott at home. The cup was a half full, and Inspector Axel placed his hand around it; it was cold.

Perhaps he was disturbed?

He explored the room, but nothing seemed out of place, no signs of a struggle. Other than the empty cup, there were no other dirty dishes. Inspector Axel opened the cupboards; crockery tidied away, and the cabinets filled with the food expected for a lived-in house: cereal for breakfast, an assortment of non-perishable tins of this and that, herbs, spices, flour, and pasta. Next, Inspector Axel checked in the fridge, removed the milk, and smelt it. It was still fresh.

Maybe he's gone for a walk?

Room by room, Inspector Axel moved through the house. The double bed in the master bedroom showed the signs of being recently slept in. There were clothes neatly folded in drawers, and men's shirts hung in the wardrobe. There were no women's garments. Inspector Axel flicked through the dirty attire in the laundry basket, looking for something hidden underneath. There was nothing.

Did he get wind of my arrival and do a runner? I wouldn't think so. Why would he leave his car, mobile phone and lap-top behind?

As he headed back towards the kitchen, he decided that the house feeling, as though someone had popped out for a few minutes, was an illusion. Nobody was returning, of that, he was sure.

Someone has been here before me.

At the kitchen table, Inspector Axel hit the enter button on the laptop and it whirled into life. On the screen, an image of an origami Crane appeared. Despite having checked the house, Inspector Axel scanned about him. The laptop screen was a message telling him that Charles Scott was dead or about to die. The LED next to the laptop's built-in camera lit up, showing that somebody was watching while the screen continued to display the Crane.

Speaking into the laptop, Inspector Axel said, 'Hello.'

A digitally altered synthesised voice replied, 'Hello, Inspector Axel. I've been expecting you.'

Axel felt vulnerable, but he also didn't like being toyed with and said, his voice taking on a commanding tone, 'Where's Charles Scott?'

'He was a loose end.'

'You killed him?'

'Let's say he went for a long swim and won't be coming back...' There was a brief pause and, when the Inspector didn't reply, the voice continued. 'I know what you're thinking, Inspector. You will check the passenger records for anyone who has come and gone from the island in the last week, thinking that you will find me. I can assure you it will be a waste of your time.' The voice was correct; that's what the Inspector would do.

Maybe, Inspector Axel thought, *this is the mistake I've been waiting for:* 'Was it you who tried to kill me at the Cathedral in Truro?'

'If I wanted you dead, Inspector, you would not be here now. You're not asking the right question.'

What's the right question? He bit his bottom lip, trying to thinking. *If the Crane wanted me dead, I would be.* He couldn't shake the feeling that he was a pawn in some macabre game.

What is the right question? It's not, was it you who tried to kill me, but why didn't you kill me at Truro?

The enormity of the revelation struck him like a ton of bricks. He'd walked straight into a trap. The hunter was playing with its prey.

'Is the house booby-trapped?' The Inspector sighed as if bored with the conversation.

'Bravo Inspector, now you're asking the right questions. Of course, it's booby-trapped.'

'Do I get a clue?'

The sound a clapping came from the laptop as the voice said, 'Excellent Inspector, you *do* understand. You and I are going to have some fun. Do you remember the notorious two-door puzzle from the film the Labyrinth? For your sake, I hope you do.'

The screen on the laptop changed. Gone was the image of the Crane, replaced by two medieval knights, one standing in front of a blue door, the other a red one. Between the guards was the text which read:

INSPECTOR AXEL, YOU HAVE TWO DOORS. ONE LEADS TO YOUR DEATH, THE OTHER TO YOUR SAFETY. YOU DON'T KNOW WHICH DOOR IS WHICH.

A GUARD SHIELDS EACH DOOR. ONE GUARD ALWAYS TELLS THE TRUTH, AND THE OTHER GUARD ALWAYS LIES.

YOU ARE ONLY ALLOWED TO ASK ONE QUESTION TO ONE GUARD TO FIGURE OUT WHICH DOOR IS THE ONE THAT LEADS TO SAFETY.

Under each guard was a text box in which Inspector Axel could type his question.

The puzzle, this is ridiculously simple. Everybody knows the answer to this.

If you ask the truth-guard, he would tell you that the liar-guard would point to the door that leads to death. If you ask the liar-guard, he would say to you that the truth-guard would point to the door that leads to death. Therefore, no matter who you ask, the guard tells you which door leads to death, and consequently, you pick the other door. The ease of the task made him uncomfortable.

Too simple; I must be missing something.

'What happens if I get it wrong?' Inspector Axel asked.

'You die, Inspector, which, may I add, would be a disappointment, as our fun is just beginning.'

'May I ask how?'

'Indeed, the clock is already ticking. The Enter key on the laptop you pressed. It was dusted with a biological toxin, a cousin of the Novichok nerve agent used by Russia, and it is the deadliest ever made. It's already inside your system and, if you don't inject yourself with the antidote within thirty minutes, you'll be dead. If you solve the puzzle, I'll tell you where the antidote is, and you live. Nothing could be simpler, or could it?'

"Or could it" Was that a clue?

The words of caution rang in the Inspector Axel's ears. With no choice, he typed in the text box under the knight protecting the blue door, "WHAT DOOR WOULD THE OTHER GUARD POINT TO?"

"BLUE."

Inspector Axel opened his mouth to say, QED (Quite Easily Done) but closed it again promptly.

What am I missing? There has to be more, another clue embedded within the instructions.

He sat back in the chair to contemplate the problem.

'Time is running out, Inspector; you're dying as the toxin spreads through your body!'

He coughed and glanced at his hand, expecting to see blood, but there was none.

Don't be rushed, Axel. You have plenty of time to think this through. Why mention the Labyrinth when the Crane could have simply posed the conundrum?

Axel had seen the film although a long time ago. The character Sarah, he recalled, solved the riddle, yet her success was short-lived. 'What happened?' he asked aloud to himself. 'She fell through a trapdoor. Why? After solving the riddle, had she dropped into the Shaft of Hands? Then it hit him.

She'd said something like - "This is a piece of cake"—a mistake of Labyrinth law. My "QED" is the same. The secret is to be humble in success.

Inspector Axel typed the answer: RED.

On the screen appeared the words: CORRECT!

Axel held his tongue and waited and a minute passed before the voice spoke. 'Well done, Inspector, you haven't disappointed, for your premature demise would have been most unfortunate. In keeping with the spirit of the game, you will find, in the microwave, a syringe filled with the antidote. Inject it, as if it were an EpiPen, into the middle of your outer thigh–upper leg. It takes effect immediately and you won't even know that you were ever sick. I suggest you bag and dispose of the laptop carefully. I can assure you Inspector; my little game hasn't been a hoax. Until we meet again.'

The light surrounding the laptop camera extinguished and the Crane was gone. The Inspector closed its lid and washed his hands thoroughly before injecting himself; he could ill afford to be infected again once he'd use the antidote. Slumping in a chair, emotionally drained, Inspector Axel wondered if the puzzle was as simple as it appeared, or perhaps there was a second-string to it. He'd made the right decision and would never know.

Speaking to himself, the Inspector sighed, *'I had better ring this one in because MI6 will have to roll out the hazmat suits and with it, there goes the low-key visit to Barra Island. Stephen is going to be displeased, especially when he likes his operations to stay in the shadows. Plus, there is our missing person, Charles Scott, possibly murdered. The local Constabulary is going to be peeved and angry. All-in-all, not your finest day's work, Inspector.'*

***

MI6 Headquarters London England

James was working at his desk when Inspector Axel entered. He glanced up and said, 'Good afternoon Inspector, please go straight in. Stephen is expecting you. Oh, by the way, Inspector, he's not in a good mood.'

Inspector Axel nodded before courteously knocking twice on Stephen's door and opening it.

'Come in Inspector. Please have a seat,' Stephen said, pointing to the vacant chair in front of his desk. 'A nasty occurrence, Barra Island?'

'Yes, the use of a nerve agent and the disappearance of Charles Scott.'

'The use of a chemical weapon on UK soil is unforgivable, Inspector.' Stephen sighed before continuing. 'I hear that you have been given a clean bill of health?'

'Yes, fortunately, there are no ill effects, although I'm told traces of the toxin are still in my system.'

Stephen sighed again, and Inspector Axel knew his grilling was about to start as he said, 'Inspector, this happened because of a failure of intelligence and now our private business is all over the front page of the newspapers. I want to know why. What went wrong?'

Inspector Axel pondered for a moment before he said, 'We...'

Stephen immediately interrupted, 'We, Inspector?'

'I ... I didn't anticipate Charles Scott being at risk, or the Crane making an attempt on my life, or more to the point, playing chicken with me. Before I left, I checked. There was no chatter from the intelligence community, state-sponsored groups or any of the terrorist cells we monitor. The attack came out of left field, Stephen.'

'Did it indeed, Inspector? You were shot at in Truro, and Charles Scott was a potential witness to the identity of the Crane. I'm not sure I would call that Left Field.'

Inspector Axel did not agree with the conclusions Stephen was reaching. He remained silent. When Axel didn't respond, Stephen continued, 'This is serious, you understand, Inspector. There will be an inquiry.'

'Yes, I see. Do you wish to replace me while the inquiry undertakes its work?'

Stephen shook his head. 'No Inspector, we need to get to the bottom of this' Stephen hesitated, before saying, 'With the disappearance of Charles Scott, have the leads gone cold?'

'For the moment.'

'Nothing at the house?'

'No.'

'Anything that might suggest why Charles Scott was involved?'

'Nothing at this juncture.'

Stephen thought for a second before he said, 'The voice on the other end of the laptop, was it the Crane?'

'It would seem so,' said the Inspector, though he had his doubts.

'Why that game, the puzzle for you to solve? That's not how the Crane operates.'

Inspector Axel shrugged his shoulders. 'I assume that I'm not a target.'

Stephen twisted his face as he said, 'The Crane is going to extraordinary lengths if you're not a target, Inspector.'

Inspector Axel raised an eyebrow, saying, 'It makes no sense, unless that's the point.'

'What do you mean?'

'Red herrings, diverting our attention away from the main game, whatever that is?'

'Muddying the waters, I see. Yes, that makes sense.' Stephen opened a file sitting on his desk, removing a photograph before handing it to Axel. 'This is Wen Xu. Do you recognise the name?'

'He is a person Claudia identified from the Shark Fin restaurant.'

'He is, or should I say was. Chen Li, my counterpart in the People's Republic of China, Ministry of State Security, tells me he has been found dead. Murdered, and quite brutally.'

'When?'

'The day before John's funeral.'

'Any suspects?'

'Chen Li told me they discovered a lemon sherbet sweet next to the body. Does that mean anything to you?'

'Should it?'

'Come now, Inspector, you know precisely what this suggests. A "sweetie" left at the scene.'

'Meant to suggest what, Stephen? Claudia was in Cornwall with me.'

'Yes, Inspector, but Wen Xu was killed two hours' drive away from where she was staying. Well, it's a simple enough task to slip out and be back by morning.'

'You are tracking her movements?'

'Yes, via her mobile phone, but it wouldn't be unlike her to leave it behind.'

'Are you suggesting Claudia murdered Wen Xu, Stephen?'

'Ignoring the question, Stephen said, 'This is happening at a difficult time for the British Government. What do you know about Huawei?'

Inspector Axel shifted in his seat, buying a few seconds while he recalled the information. 'Huawei Technologies is a Chinese multinational technology company providing telecommunication equipment and consumer electronics. In recent times, our allies, the United States and Australia in particular, have declared Huawei a security risk and banned it from supplying equipment for their 5G networks. This has angered China. Britain, on the other hand, has incensed its Five Eye Partners by agreeing to let Huawei supply equipment for the UK's 5G roll-out. The decision was labelled as the worst decision any British government has made in many years, and that's' quite an insult.'

'That's right, Inspector. The government has approved Huawei's involvement capped at 35% of the network. The Prime Minister is facing a Commons rebellion as several of his senior party members are set to back an amendment that would seek to end the Chinese firm's participation in the UK's 5G mobile internet network completely. The Government, in response, has given assurances that Huawei will be excluded from the most sensitive parts of the 5G network and that its market share will decline as new players emerge. China's most senior diplomat in the UK has attacked the Prime Minister over the cap on Huawei's involvement, calling it a Huawei witch hunt. The United States has attacked the

UK Government saying that it was wrong to allow Huawei into the 5G network at all and is urging the UK to rethink. Downing Street insists that its leading cybersecurity advisers are satisfied that the government's approach will not affect the UK's national security adversely. With Wuhan being the epicentre for the Coronavirus pandemic, anti-Chinese sentiment is running high in the UK. The disease may force the government to take a more robust line against China.'

'What's MI6's position?'

'We have remained consistent, Inspector. There is a clear and continuing danger from significant and sustained foreign interference in our affairs. Understandably, in this environment, the Minister doesn't want a tit-for-tat spat developing between British and Chinese intelligence agencies. Especially if something were to spill over into the media.'

'What are you suggesting, Stephen? That my run-in with the Crane may have been a shot across the bow, a "cease and desist" warning from the Chinese Secret Service following the death of Wen Xu?'

'We need to keep an open mind, Inspector. Behind the UK's Huawei talks, the British Government is in secret discussion with an alternative telecommunications supplier, one who would replace Huawei, an Indian company called H1 Technologies.' Stephen paused and looked at Inspector Axel, awaiting a response.

'That's who Charles Scott worked for before he moved to Barra.'

'Indeed, it was Inspector.'

'A coincidence?'

Stephen didn't answer the question but said, 'We believe the Kremlin is behind the misinformation concerning conspiracy theories linking the 5G network to the Coronavirus. Anti-5G arsonists have already set ablaze telecommunication towers across Britain. Russia is doing its best to stoke up fear within the UK and exploit the friction between London and Beijing.'

Inspector Axel weighed what Stephen had told him before saying, 'What's in it for Russia?'

'Economic warfare, Inspector. Economic warfare.'

'These are murky waters, Stephen!'

'Murky, no. The world is a complicated place, and we have multi-layer relationships with countries, often driven by fear and greed, or both. Espionage has always been an ingredient, as are the players, watching, waiting to exploit a situation. Inspector, this is par for the course. What I don't like is being kept in the dark and played like a fiddle.'

'What is it you want me to do?'

'For the time being, Inspector, stay the course with your investigations into John Moss and the Crane. Let's see where it leads. What's your next step?'

'The assumption is that Charles Scott was murdered and, unless his killer came by submarine, it's near impossible to travel to and from a small island like Barra without being noticed. There were no signs of a struggle at the cottage, so it's likely Charles Scott knew his killer. My hunch is that he picked up his assassin from wherever he or she came ashore and transported them back to the cottage, or the assailant killed Charles Scott on the way to the cottage. If the murderer drove the car, someone would have seen them; travel by ferry or airline would have left passenger records and CCTV footage. A journey by small boat, light plane, or helicopter would have alerted the locals. Sir, with your permission, I would like to involve the Barra Island and Scottish police?'

'Under what guise?'

'I suggest we tell them the truth that this is a matter of national security. My cover as a detective from Scotland Yard won't cut it, not if I want their cooperation and trust, particularly after my last visit to the island.'

'You know I don't like civilians being involved. Inevitably it goes pear-shaped.'

Inspector Axel remained silent, thinking, *It's a bit late for that, Stephen.*

After a brief pause, Stephen replied, 'Okay, and we need their resources anyway. Is there anything else?'

'Yes, there is. If the assassin had travelled by aircraft, the plane would have flown below the radar. RAF Lossiemouth in Scotland operates five Wedgetail early warning and control aircraft, always one in the air, tracking and coordinating intercepts of Russian bombers heading towards British airspace. They would have seen a low-flying aircraft, though it would be of little interest to them. I've asked them but was politely told to go away. You might be more fortunate.'

Stephen stared at Inspector Axel while he mulled over the request and then said, 'I'll see what I can do.'

Inspector Axel nodded as he said, 'I don't like coincidences, Sir, so I think, after what you have said, I would like to nose around H1 Technologies.'

Stephen hesitated before speaking, his instinct screaming that H1 Technologies was off-limits. Inspector Axel could see his reluctance. After a moment, Stephen sighed and said,

'Inspector, you must tread carefully with your inquiries into H1 Technologies. The growing unpredictability in US foreign policy has Britain seeking to strengthen its defence ties with Commonwealth countries like India. The government is at a crucial stage, identifying mutual defence and security opportunities, with the UK Defence Minister set to announce the signing of a Memorandum of Understanding between the UK and India. He will say,'

"it underpins the collaboration between our two nations, building on our defence ties, and ensuring our nations can combat emerging threats for generations to come."

'Economics and defence, are inseparable, Inspector, they go hand in hand. H1 Technologies has connections that reach to the top of Indian leadership. The defence agreement and the 5G discussions are at a critical stage; step on the wrong toes and I may not be able to protect you. Do we understand each other, Inspector?'

'Yes.'

Stephen softened his tone as he said, 'Keep this contained, Axel. These are all politically sensitive issues.'

'As you wish, Sir.' Inspector Axel rose and turned to leave.

'Inspector. After what happened on Barra Island, I shouldn't need to remind you to be careful.'

CHAPTER 11
Canary Islands

It was a four-hour flight from London to the Canary Islands, touching down at nine o'clock in the evening. The office had arranged for Claudia to spend the night at a hotel, picking up a hire car the following morning for the drive to the safe house. Once there, she had five days to prepare for Daniel Tinkov's arrival.

She rose early, taking in an early morning run before catching a taxi and picking up her hire car, a Volvo XC 90. Driving to the safe house, Claudia found the views on the rugged volcanic island were stunning as she zigzagged her way up a narrow mountain road with an ancient knee-high stone wall being the only barrier that separated the car from the sheer drops below. Twice she met oncoming cars and their mirrors almost touched as they passed. With a couple of kilometres to go, Claudia pulled over at a lookout, taking in the distant coastline. After stepping out of the car, she glanced back at the road she had travelled before turning her gaze toward her destination. It wasn't the tricky turns that occupied her thoughts as she shook her head from side to side, muttering to herself, 'This is all wrong. So very, very wrong.'

Rules governing the choice of a defensive safe house were straightforward. They needed to be easy to access and even easier to escape, avoiding capture in the event of a mishap. Access to transport was essential, and cars or public transport were speedier when escaping than was being on foot. Simplicity too, as a smaller space was easier to defend, although a building with hiding spaces, like basements, attics or places to crawl into, was an advantage. Most important was the ability to observe approaches, to detect suspicious activities. Leaving the lookout, Claudia drove another two kilometres, her emotion drifting from apprehension to anger as she turned off the mountain road, passed through the wrought iron security gates of the safe house and navigated the meandering gravel driveway.

A traditional two-storey Mediterranean style whitewashed grand villa came into view and easing the Volvo to a standstill, she got out, slamming the door behind her in frustration. The villa was set back onto the hill, surrounded on two sides by rocky, sparsely vegetated high ground and an undulating plateau that overlooked the valley below. Claudia placed her hands on her hips in exasperation. 'This is impossible to defend,' she said, sighing. 'What are they thinking?'

Shaking her head from side to side, annoyed but resolved to her situation, Claudia removed her luggage from the boot and began walking towards the front door. As she strode, she searched for surveillance cameras.

Either they don't have any, or they are well concealed. I pray that it's the latter!

Dropping her bags on the front porch, she looked for the house keys in her pockets.

I suppose it could be worse. Imagine if it were one of the newer villas, the ones with enormous glass windows. You might as well paint a target on your back.

The front door opened into a large entrance; a lobby dominated by a grand stone staircase leading to the second level.

Okay, Claudia, you might as well look around before settling in.

Leaving her bags near the staircase, Claudia set about exploring the ground floor. On the lower level, she discovered a sitting room with a massive fireplace, a cafe style dining area, opening onto a vast terrace that led down to a swimming pool, a powder room, sizeable butler's pantry, study and reading room. Each was furnished in a country style, befitting the age of the building. Collecting her bags, she climbed the stairs. Upstairs were four large bedrooms, each with an en-suite bathroom. The master bedroom came with double sliding glass doors leading onto a balcony with unparalleled views over the grounds and the valley beyond. Opening the sliding doors, Claudia stepped out, hoping to see the road carved into the mountainside, the one that she had driven up earlier. However, it was obscured from sight. She spread her arms out wide and spun around in a circle, shouting, 'You might as well shoot me now. I won't see you coming.' Moving back inside, she pulled the curtains closed behind her and locked the doors, though there was little point. For a holiday, the building was brimming with character; as a safe house, it was bristling with danger.

Before leaving Britain, Stephen Walls had told Claudia that, hidden in the butler's pantry, was the secret entrance to a weapons room. He had assured her that the armoury was well equipped, more than adequate to meet her needs. Cleverly concealed in the shelving was the trigger and as Claudia pushed a button to gain access to the arsenal, she feared the worst, grumbling,

If the safe house is anything to go by, the arsenal is likely to hold a child's cap gun and a water pistol!

To the whirr of an electric motor, the wall at the end of the pantry slid open where Claudia expected to see a rack of weaponry. Instead, she was greeted by a staircase leading down and out of sight. Going inside, Claudia turned and examined the slider, looking for the mechanism to close the door behind her, there positioned next to the opening, were two buttons, one green, and one red. Claudia pushed red, and the door shut, the lights coming on. Descending the spiral stairs carved into the volcanic rock, Claudia found a steel door at the bottom.

Stephen, you didn't tell me about this. Now what?

The door had a keyhole, the size of a domestic lock, but no handle.

Okay, there's a place for a key, but Stephen didn't supply one, except for the front door key. Perhaps?

Claudia was expecting an electronic mechanism to be triggered as she inserted the key. She waited - nothing happened. Claudia tried turning it to the right, then to the left, however still nothing. She breathed out loudly in frustration.

Try again.

To Claudia's astonishment, withdrawing the key caused the door to open, and it slid into the rock face with a hum. As she walked through and into the control room, she was surprised by the thickness of the steel door, saying, 'Blast-proof, now that is interesting.' Inside, against one wall, was an array of electronic equipment. CCTV displayed images from the outside and each of the rooms inside the villa. Other screens were monitors for a tactical radar system, designed to maintain a secure zone and provide early warning of attack.

This property is more sophisticated than Stephen made out.

'I see you found us,' came Stephen's voice over an intercom system.

Looking around for the source, Claudia said, 'I thought I was operating on my own?'

'You are.'

'Then who's monitoring the screens I can see in front of me?'

'No one, unless you request it.'

Claudia didn't respond, so, after a brief pause, Stephen said, 'In front of you, on the control bench, is a dossier concerning Daniel Tinkov.'

Claudia spotted the file next to the radar monitor, and she picked it up, flicking through its pages, intending to read it thoroughly later.

'You will also see a handheld display unit next to where the dossier was.'

Claudia replaced the file and picked up the device.

'That will receive signals from the remote ground sensors, microwave Doppler radar and passive infrared detectors, part of the house's perimeter security system. It shows the type of target and its direction.'

'A tactical radar system, Stephen.'

'Yes. You will notice the main monitor on the wall; you have the handheld unit which compliments it, so keep it with you at all times. If the house security is compromised, the MI6 control room is on twenty-four-hour standby and can monitor all the systems; however, this won't happen unless you request it. You have the phone number and activation code.'

'If someone attacks us, Stephen, they will hack into the CCTV system and use it against me.'

As I did to Richard Liew, Claudia thought privately.

'Not here, Claudia. We know better. The cameras are well hidden, disguised and hard-wired, no wireless at all. They could knock them out if they discovered them, but use them against you, no. The comms from where you are to our centre is via underground optic fibre. It's as secure as we can make it in this confounded digital age.'

'Far be it from me to be critical, Stephen.' Claudia said and paused, choosing her words carefully, 'While I will congratulate you on the perimeter security, the house is... well, it's positioned for a turkey shoot; far from ideal.'

'We didn't want a building perched on top of a mountain, able to repel an armoured division; it was bought as a discrete hideaway and fitted out with a couple of additional features. In today's budget, Claudia, as with all things, compromise is everything. If you're concerned, I suggest you keep Daniel Tinkov inside.'

'Inside and away from the windows too!'

Stephen ignored Claudia's sarcasm, saying instead, 'On the far wall you will see a keypad, and I'll text you the entry number. Inside is the Armoury, and I assure you, it is more than adequate.'

'I will need to place weapons around the area I am protecting; the armoury needs to be well supplied.'

'As I said Claudia, you will find it more than adequate. Now then, in five days' time, before Daniel Tinkov arrives at the driveway, I'll alert you via a text message. I want no accidents.'

Claudia knew it was scorned upon to ask about another agent's operation, so she hesitated, knowing Stephen Walls wanted to keep her in the dark.

What the heck.

'Is there news from Inspector Axel?'

Stephen's answer was blunt, his tone registering his displeasure. 'I'm sure he has told you anyway, though I suggested he shouldn't. He's going to Barra Island in Scotland.'

Claudia chuckled to herself. *There is something maliciously rewarding when antagonising Stephen Walls. Perhaps it's a hangover from when I worked for the other side?*

'I'll leave you to settle in, Claudia.'

Within seconds of the radio going quiet, Claudia's phone buzzed. Checking the screen, she read the encrypted message promised by Stephen before entering 57263# into the keypad. The armoury door slid open, and Claudia's face lit up with delight.

Oh Stephen, very lovely. Very nice indeed. Let's see, what do we have? Arwen 37 Tear gas canister launchers, SAS issue. An M72 LAW compact anti-tank rocket launcher. I'm sure I can use you. Two HK417 medium-range sniper rifles. One, two, three, four, five, HK G36 assault rifles, an excellent 5.56mm weapon, capable of firing 750 rounds per minute. Handguns. Ah, yes, five Glock 17's and the same for the more compact 19's.

Below the racks of weaponry was a series of drawers.

What surprises do we have in these? That's good, plenty of clips and ammunition. Looky here. Ten 230g tubes of P.E.4. plastic explosives with detonators, next to which are G-60, stun grenades, tear gas, anti-tank rockets, and five command-detonated mines. For once, Stephen, you're right - I'm not disappointed. This is a nice assortment of goodies.

Claudia slid the drawers closed and turned her attention to the tactical utility belts, lightweight body armour, and night-vision goggles, which were next to the guns and rifles. Satisfied, she closed the armoury.

The only problem with weaponry is that it can give you a false sense of security. You must never forget; your opponents are equally well equipped.

Claudia knew it was a matter of when—not if–a kill team came for Daniel Tinkov. They would be ex-special services soldiers and, in the ensuing firefight, she would be outmanned and outgunned. Ordinarily, Claudia could rely on her agility and speed, but in this operation, because of the civilian she was protecting, her abilities were compromised. When the fight came, proper preparation was her primary advantage. The ground sensors would help her know the position and direction of her targets, but on its own, it wouldn't be enough.

Even though Claudia believed a fight was inevitable, she still wished it wouldn't happen.

Let's hope that you're right, Stephen, and that no one knows where to look for Daniel Tinkov. If he is to live, he needs to vanish from the face of the earth, become the man who could be anywhere, and nowhere.

After enjoying a healthy lunch, Claudia began her preparations, the first task, a thorough mapping of the house and grounds. Pen and paper in hand, Claudia roamed room by room, plotting their layout, charting the position of furniture, light switches, or anything else she deemed necessary. When she looked at her watch, Claudia was surprised that it was late and she had yet to start on the outside.

There's just enough time to fit in some exercise before night settles in. The outside can wait until the morning. Don't rush the planning, Claudia; remember the adage, fail to plan, plan to fail.

That evening, a glass of wine in hand, laptop open in front of her, Claudia hacked into Richard Liew's house. Molly, their daughter, was asleep and Claudia watched the child as she'd done on prior occasions, finding her smooth rhythmic breathing mesmerising, unsure why it beguiled her. Claudia sighed before searching the other camera feeds, seeking Richard Liew. She found him in the dining room, speaking to his wife Samantha, who was saying,

'I think, darling, we should cancel the cruise. We don't want to find ourselves quarantined on the ship like those people who docked in Yokohama, Japan. They've tested 300 of the 3,700 people on the Diamond Princess; so far ten have the virus and authorities are expecting the number of infections to rise. Someone on TV described a cruise ship as a Petri dish.'

'I did as you asked Samantha and checked the cruise company website today. Both our trips are operating to schedule. Honey, if the cruise companies were concerned about the spread of the virus, they would cancel the voyage, I'm sure of it. I don't think we have anything to fear. We are going to have a wonderful–no–most wonderful family holiday.'

'I'm not sure Richard. COVID-19 has been declared a pandemic now.'

'Honey, the first cruise is only from Southampton to Barcelona, and then we have five days in the city before the next cruise to the Mediterranean and Greek Islands. If the situation deteriorates while we're in Spain, we'll fly straight home, and that's a promise.'

'I'm not sure!'

'Samantha, there's plenty of time before we depart; and what is it they say in the movies? - we will monitor the situation.' Richard chortled before his tone became more serious. 'The cruise web sites say that they have increased passenger screening before embarkation, so I'm sure we will be fine. They know what they are doing, Samantha.'

'I hope you're right, Richard.'

'Come over here and see what I booked for us today,' Richard Liew said, and beckoned his wife to look at his computer screen.

'Where's that? It's beautiful.'

'Montserrat. It's an Abbey forty-eight kilometres out of Barcelona, and I've booked us a private guide, Roxanna. We could have gone by car, but I thought the train and the cable car were more exciting. Roxanna will meet us at the Plaça España railway station, from where we'll take the R5 line to Aeri de Montserrat, a journey of about an hour. Once there, we take a cable car to the top. The article I read said the monastery was founded in the 11ᵗʰ century and still functions to this day. What's exciting about our trip is Roxanna can show us some secrets of Montserrat, places other tourists don't get to see. Do you remember when we were in Rome before Molly was born and we saw the tomb of Saint Peter and the Necropolis under the Vatican Basilica?

'Yes, I do.'

'I imagine that the secrets of Montserrat are similar.'

Claudia zoomed in on Richard Liew's computer screen, which was displaying the tickets he had booked. As he scrolled down, Claudia saw the date and time for their tour.

Well, well, well. That will work out nicely. Thank you, Richard.

Claudia chuckled as a devious thought flowed into her mind.

Imagine if, while walking in the dark and narrow catacombs deep below the Abbey, they stumble upon Molly's cat? That will give them a scare. I will ask Linda to bring Snowflake to Barcelona. This plan is so cruel that I love it.

Claudia returned her focus to the conversation between Richard and Samantha. Richard was still speaking. 'We catch the Funicular de Sant Joan, a rack railway, up the side of the mountain from Montserrat Monastery for a birds-eye view. From what I've read, Montserrat Mountain is spectacular.'

'That sounds wonderful, darling.' Samantha said and paused for a moment before continuing, 'A funicular Richard. Isn't a rack railway?'

'It's not?' Richard replied, surprise present in his voice.

'No darling, it's cable.'

'There you go, Samantha; I learn something new every day. Which is why I married you.'

How sickeningly sweet, Claudia thought, closing her computer screen with a thump.

The next morning, after a vigorous workout, a ten-kilometre run followed by a hundred push-ups and the same in sit-ups, Claudia showered before embarking on mapping the grounds. Off to one side, the side facing the mountain, was a large detached garage and, stepping it out, Claudia calculated it was ten metres from the house. Trying the four closed roller doors, Claudia discovered they were each locked.

How inconvenient.

Built into the side of the garage and closest to the house was a wooden door and it swung easily open when Claudia turned the doorknob. Once inside, she took notes of the position of the light switches; they were in easy reach on the left-hand side of the entry. Turning them on, the inside space lit up and Claudia said herself, 'My, my, what do we have here?' Searching the garage, she found a trail bike, a set of golf clubs, abseiling gear, fishing rod and reel, tandem hang glider, and an array of other recreational equipment. Claudia sneered as she said, 'This place is an aristocratic resort, not a safe house. No wonder the British empire collapsed in a heap.'

A white Range Rover Sport, supercharged 5.0 litre V8, was sitting in the second parking bay. Peering inside, Claudia saw the fob key for the ignition and the remote control for the roller doors were on the console. A sticky note was fixed to the steering wheel, which read: *PLEASE DON'T SCRATCH ME.*

Recalling all the MI6 cars she had destroyed, Claudia laughed heartily, 'Thank you, Stephen. What I love about you British is your sense of humour.'

After dropping the car keys in her pocket, Claudia clicked the button on the remote and the roller door in front of the Range Rover opened effortlessly to the hum of an electric motor. Stepping outside, Claudia closed the roller behind her. The rest of the day was spent strolling the grounds, charting, memorising and creating a mental picture of how she would deploy her defences. With the work complete, Claudia started back towards the house, reaching the Volvo, the car she'd hired at the airport. Claudia paused, and resting her arm on its bonnet, mused.

Now then, how best do I deploy you?

After dinner, a glass of red wine in hand, Claudia opened her computer, typing into the search engine, "How do you travel from the UK to Spain with your pet?", assuming someone had written an article for the pet-crazed nutters, as she considered them. She shook her head in disbelief when she read about the "Pet Passport".

"When you apply for a Pet Passport," the article told her, *"You will need to take your pet along with its identity forms, vaccinations and other medical records, to the issuing vet. Your pet will be microchipped if it isn't already, to identify it easily."*

'I wonder if Linda has ever been asked for a forged pet passport before?' Claudia read on,

"Dogs and cats flying into Spain can travel only as cargo, not in the cabin or as check-in baggage. It's easy to cross the English Channel with your cat in your car."

'Asking Linda to drive to Spain is too big a favour to ask of a friend. I'll have to engage her services; she is a freelancer after all.'

Claudia picked up her phone and dialled her buddy. Registering the caller ID, Linda answered, 'City Morgue, you kill'em we chill'em.'

'How's Snowflake?'

'Is that the way you greet your friend?' teased Linda. 'Not even a hello Linda. And who's Snowflake, anyway?'

'The cat! Don't tell me you've forgotten?'

'Ha, she misses the cat, but not her best friend. What can I say but, Hello Claudia!'

'Hello, Linda. I know this is a loaded question. Do you have much on in the way of work? Are your services currently for hire?'

'Um, I see that this is a business call rather than social. Well, that all depends on who's asking and, at present, I'm cat-sitting a moggy called Snowflake, as it turns out.'

In a humorous tone, Claudia retorted, 'I told you its name.'

'I forgot, and when I asked the kitty, it didn't say.'

'The job, it's a paid gig, Linda.'

'Go on, I'm all ears.'

'You will work for me. It's a delivery job.'

'A delivery job, is that all?'

'Not quite. I also need a passport, an unusual one.'

'Unusual, in what way?'

'It's for a furry friend of mine. A Pet Passport for Snowflake.'

'A Pet Passport! Is there's such a thing?'

'Believe it or not Linda, yes, there is.'

'We live in a strange world, Claudia. I can't decide what's worse, having children or pets?'

Claudia laughed, 'Who knows?'

'Okay, once Snowflake here has her passport, I'm to deliver the pussy to where?'

'Spain and you have to drive.'

'Snowflake is afraid of flying?'

'Something like that.'

'Ordinarily, Claudia, I wouldn't ask, but knowing kitty belongs to an agent of the Chinese government, I need to exercise some caution. Why do you want Snowflake brought to Spain?'

'Being the kind-hearted woman that I am, it's reuniting Snowflake with its owners. Richard Liew and his family are going to Barcelona on holiday.'

'No one can say that you don't have a wicked sense of humour. I'll do the delivery, but I can't help with whatever you have planned. Is that okay?'

'That would be perfect, Linda. I'll send you through the details.'

'Good. Now, that's enough talk of work, Claudia. Without giving away any national secrets, what else have you been up to?'

The two friends chatted warmly for half an hour.

***

The remainder of the time leading up to Daniel Tinkov arrived at the safe house, Claudia spent diligently checking her preparations, then double-checking them, until the day her phone finally beeped.

Here we go.

She checked the message; it was from Stephen Walls saying that Saint Vladimir was about to be driven up to the house. After replying with a confirmation code, Claudia ascended the stairs to the sniper rifle she'd positioned to cover the driveway.

Beep! Beep! Beep! The perimeter alarm on Claudia's handheld monitor, having detected one moving object, a vehicle, activated. Through the telescopic sight of her rifle, Claudia watched a Volvo, similar to the one she'd hired from the airport, come into view. At one hundred and fifty metres from the house, the car slowed before coming to a standstill. Knowing that Claudia would be watching, the driver lifted his hands from the steering wheel, inviting her to scan the car. From her vantage point, Claudia had a clear view inside: two occupants. Twenty seconds later, the car started moving again, continuing its journey towards the villa. It stopped close to Claudia's vehicle. Passenger and driver doors opened, and the occupants disembarked. She heard the driver tell his passenger,

'Stand very still while I fetch your luggage from the boot. It would be unwise to move, as we are both in the crosshairs.'

Through the telescopic sight, Claudia followed the driver as the boot opened and he removed a suitcase, placing it on the ground next to him while he slammed shut the trunk. He carried the luggage to where his passenger was waiting and, after putting it next to him, he said. 'I hope you enjoy your stay, Saint Vladimir.'

'What happens now?' Saint Vladimir asked.

'I leave, and you wait right here. Claudia will let you know when she's ready.'

As the car headed back down the driveway, Claudia turned her attention to the perimeter monitor. After a few moments, the car vanished from its radar. As best she could tell, the outside was secure. Assault rifle in hand, she dashed down the stairs to the front door, opened it, and called, 'Don't stand around. Come inside before you get yourself shot.'

'By you or the Russians?' Saint Vladimir retorted.

Forty-two-year-old Daniel Tinkov appeared fitter than Claudia had expected an accountant to be. He was short for a man, 175cm, or five feet nine inches in the old scale, and was carrying a little weight around the middle, though it wasn't fat. He had the look of a man who'd trimmed down, lost some weight as a walker, not a runner. If his appearance matched some of her prejudices, that was where it finished. He had a full crop of medium length free-formed blond hair, unruly, sticking out in an array of different directions. It represented a hairstylist's masterpiece if commissioned in a barber's shop, or a messy crop otherwise. Clothes maketh the man, Claudia believed, or they did before she met John Moss. If the adage was true, Daniel Tinkov made a great first impression in his blue wool blend tailored two-piece suit that cut a powerful figure. Rather than a business shirt and tie, he wore a casual red striped polo shirt, and his shoes were Valentino Garavani Backnet white slip-on sneakers. He hadn't the appearance of a man who'd made a dramatic escape.

The clothes have Stephen's fingerprints all over them. Either Daniel ordered the suit, or it's a welcome gift from MI6. What does it matter?

'From me,' Claudia replied.

'Well, that's okay. For a moment, you had me worried.' Daniel picked up his suitcase and walked towards the front door.

Humour. I may like this man, Claudia thought.

In the early days of her career, when providing personal protection, Claudia had adhered to the dictum of keeping a professional distance; that became counterproductive because if you liked someone, you were more likely to protect them. The reverse applied in kidnap and killings where empathy was cancer. Daniel paused at the threshold, waiting for an invitation to come inside.

Well-mannered too.

Silently, with a flick of her head, Claudia invited him inside and, once indoors, Daniel asked, 'Where would you like me?'

'Leave your bag there,' Claudia said, pointing to the bottom of the staircase. 'Have you eaten?'

Daniel patted his stomach. 'Unfortunately, I'm always partial to food.'

Claudia had been planning on saying dismissively, 'Well then, you better make yourself something.' That was until she met her target. Instead, she replied, 'I'll make us a snack, then show you around.'

Contrary to his apparent relaxed demeanour, inside, Daniel Tinkov was an anxious man. He knew he was in peril, and as Claudia gave him a guided tour of the safe house, he fought the urge to ask about the security arrangements. He hoped she would be more forthcoming when the time was right.

'This is your room,' Claudia said while opening the curtains. 'As you can see, Daniel, you have a lovely view out over the grounds and valley. Likewise, those outside have a perfect sight of you; if you want to live, I would suggest that you deprive yourself of the vista and never open the curtains. A single shot is all it takes.'

'I will keep that in mind.'

Daniel Tinkov was from Kyiv, the capital of Ukraine. He'd grown up in a criminal family and, from a young age, was groomed to follow in his father's footsteps, not as a thug but as an educated person exploiting criminal opportunities. Despite a life of crime, Daniel was a man of firm conviction; for those he cared about, making a mistake caused remorse, but he ignored the harm done to those anonymous people that his wrongdoing touched. If the threat of blood wasn't a sufficient incentive for his silence and loyalty, then greed, the trappings of wealth, made his activities worthwhile. Daniel Tinkov desired the more beautiful things of life, envying those with more than him: a bigger yacht, prettier girlfriends, faster cars, or a nicer house. He worked long work hours to achieve his goals, so he liked to party hard whenever the opportunity presented itself. As the Chief Financial Officer for Sergey Rutskoy's criminal empire, he viewed success through the prism of the company's profits, never considering the injustices that made them. He turned a blind eye to the wrongs about him. Daniel Tinkov's role as an accountant was civilised, but he was not naïve to the violence nor the brief careers of some of his colleagues who failed. Loyalty was demanded by the company, and those who erred were subject to brutal consequences. It was unconditional.

Before defecting, Daniel had heard stories of criminals testifying as a witness against their associates in exchange for leniency; no moral element involved in their motivation, merely self-interest. In his case, he hadn't been arrested and nor had he been on a watch list. His journey to become a justice collaborator was different and started three years previously in the summer, while in Milan, Italy, on business.

Daniel had driven up from his office in Rome and was staying for two days at his regular hotel in Milan, the Park Hyatt. On the last night of the business trip, rather than dining in at the hotel as he had done the previous evening, he'd taken a walk to eat at one of the many nearby restaurants. It had been a busy day of meetings, so to help himself relax, Daniel chose an elegant cosmopolitan establishment, attracted by its intimate atmosphere. He wasn't in the mood for a dynamic Michelin-starred restaurant, his usual choice.

She was seated at the table next to him, a woman in her mid-thirties tastefully dressed, wearing a black A-line sleeveless solid, knee-length casual summer dress. A glance told him that the clothes she was wearing weren't designer brand and probably purchased through an online retail store; he thought she was elegant anyway. He was used to women wearing bright lipstick to accentuate their botoxed lips, but her colouring was muted, classy. The women he wined and dined would be called "dolly birds", or trophy brides when attached to the arm of an older man. He liked them young, attractive, vibrant, and obedient. It was a partnership, he providing power and wealth and she the sex and glamour. Ordinarily, he wouldn't have given the woman on the table next to him a second look, but it was the book she was reading that caught his attention: Burial Rites by an Australian author, Hanna Kent. The title had encouraged him to read the story a year earlier; a ripping yarn cemented it in his memory.

With only curiosity in his mind at that point, he said, 'I enjoyed that book.'

She raised her eyes from the table, drawn to the voice, and replied, 'You've read it?'

'Yes. I believe it was Hanna Kent's first novel, a story that stays with you, or perhaps it's the unusual title that's memorable.'

The woman closed the book and studied its cover before saying, 'I am enjoying the read and surprised to be falling for Agnes Magnúsdóttir, the woman condemned to death for her part in the brutal murder of two men.'

'It's a moving story, and I remember myself not wanting Agnes to be executed, but as it's based on a true story, there's no changing history. What part are you up to?'

Before the woman could answer, the waiter arrived and asked Daniel, 'Water, Sir?'

'Yes, please.'

'Sparkling or still?'

'Still.'

'Excellent. Would Sir like to order a drink, a glass of wine, or beer perhaps?'

Daniel opened the drinks menu and ran his figure down over the offerings. 'I'll have a glass of the...' He paused and, turning to the woman, said. 'This is presumptuous of me but, would you share a glass of wine while you wait for your company? I would enjoy hearing your thoughts on the story.'

The lady reflected for a moment before saying, 'Yes, why not?' She joined him at his table.

'Would you prefer a red or white?' Daniel asked, surprised that she had agreed.

'As it's a warm day, I'll have a glass of white.'

Daniel held his finger on the name of a bottle in the menu, showing it to the waiter, saying, 'That would do nicely. Thank you.'

Looking at the lady, he said, 'Do you have a favourite passage or line from the book so far?'

The lady smiled and said, 'It so happens that I do.' She flicked through the book to a page she'd marked by folding down its corner and read, her voice captivating.

"They said I must die. They said that I stole the breath from men, and now they must steal mine. I imagine, then, that we are all candle flames, greasy-bright, fluttering in the darkness and the howl of the wind, and in the stillness of the room I hear footsteps, awful coming footsteps, coming to blow me out and send my life up away from me in a grey wreath of smoke."

With no alternative motive, other than being genuinely interested, Daniel Tinkov listened to the woman. They chatted about Burial Rites, and he learned her name, Mia Bella, and that she was an Architectural Historian and, like him, lived in Rome. The conversation flowed smoothly between them and, when Daniel Tinkov offered to buy her dinner, she politely declined but remained to eat with him at the same table. They talked long into the evening until the waiter, full of apologies, told them they were closing for the night. As they were standing to leave, Daniel Tinkov asked, 'I wonder if I might see you again in Rome?'

'I would like that.'

Meeting Mia Bella was the beginning of a new chapter of Daniel Tinkov's life. Instead of going to rave parties in darkened rooms, filled with laser lights, strobes, ecstasy and electronic music that lasted all night, Mia took Daniel on visits to less known historical sites of Rome, secret gems she called them. Drives in the country and picnics at beautiful locations replaced sailing trips on board his luxury yacht, accompanied by champagne, caviar, and scantily clad women. Falling deeply in love, Daniel went with Mia Bella to Sunday church and afterwards lunch with her parents, a table of fun and laughs. She stopped short of putting him on a diet, encouraging him instead to take daily walks with her. For his birthday, she brought him a GZDL Bluetooth smartwatch for tracking his fitness, relegating his Omega Speed Master to special occasions. Even now, Daniel Tinkov wasn't a hundred percent sure how Mia Bella discovered he worked for organised crime. It may have been as simple as putting the name of his boss, Sergey Rutskoy, into a search engine, or perhaps it was his wealth and the friends he kept. For Mia Bella, what Daniel did was at odds with her sense of what was right. They were deeply in love, but their worlds were on a collision course.

They were seated in the lounge at Daniel's home, listening to music and drinking a glass of wine. Now, whenever he hears the haunting melody, an instrumental by James Last, The Lonely Shepherd, it evokes memories of Mia, his Mia Bella.

Mia had lifted her head from her book and said, 'Do you know of Saint Vladimir of Kyiv, the city where you are from?'

Daniel shook his head and replied, 'No.'

'He was a sinner who became a saint.'

Daniel put down his drink, and Mia looked at him, giving him an ambivalent smile. He felt a sense of dread as she said, 'I don't ask about your work Daniel, and you don't tell... but I suspect many of the activities are not legal and...' Mia's voice began to choke as she fought back the tears. '... you make money from the misery of others.' She paused, waiting to see if Daniel would respond. Daniel remained silent; inside, his heart was racing, pounding, fearful that he would lose the woman with whom he wanted to spend the rest of his life. She continued, 'I love you, Daniel, truly I do, and I've fought my conscience, pretending not to know, trying to accept the indefensible, the inconvenient truth about you. Morally significant differences exist between us. If we married and had children, well, it wouldn't be right.'

Daniel tilted his head in shame and his eyes closed. Across his face drifted an expression of guilt. There was no denying the truth. Sadness filled his voice as he said, 'Do you want me to leave Sergey Rutskoy's company?'

'No Daniel, I'm not asking you to choose between your life and me. I wouldn't ask you to do that. It is I who must choose, and

I have chosen. Living off the suffering of others is something I can't accept.'

'Please, Mia, I'll leave, I promise. We can start again. Please!'

Mia broke into a sob and said, 'You can't leave. From what I know of your world, which is little enough, they won't let you.'

'Nonsense, Mia. I've known Sergey all my life, and he's been like a second father to me. Let me talk to him, please?'

She stared at Daniel for what seemed like minutes before saying, simply, 'Okay.'

Daniel Tinkov went to Mia, took her hand in his, and going down on one knee, said, 'There is only one way I can leave. Mia Bella, will you marry me?'

With tears filling her eyes, she said, 'Do you promise to repent of your life of crime?'

'I want our children to grow up in an honest and loving family. I promise with all my heart.'

'Yes ... Oh, Daniel, to marry you is what I want, more than anything else in the world.'

'I will tell Sergey tomorrow,' Daniel said. 'You know we won't be able to stay in Rome?'

'Anywhere, Daniel, as long as we are together and free.'

Daniel had a restless night, awake tossing and turning, thinking of what he would say to Sergey Rutskoy and how he would safeguard his wealth and belongings. He knew Mia was right; you didn't walk away from the mob.

His worry seemed in vain as the following morning Sergey Rutskoy pronounced himself delighted that Daniel and Mia Bella were to be married. Leaving his desk and putting his arm around Daniel's shoulder, he said, 'Daniel, my boy, I understand why you want to leave and find a new job with fewer responsibilities. It's the modern way to spend more time with your wife and the children when they come along. I'm old school, like your father. Work has been our life, our mistress. As with all things, Daniel, there will be compromises. You understand, your lifestyle will be different.'

'Yes.'

'In that case, congratulations on your engagement. You and Mia must join me at home tonight to celebrate. You know how excited Tina will be. She's seen herself as your second mother for a long time. I'll be sad to see you go, but I want nothing but the best for you both. Tell me you're free for dinner?'

'We would love to come.'

Sergey returned to his desk. 'Ordinarily Daniel, we like four weeks' notice before you leave. I was wondering because we must fill your position carefully. Would you consider granting us eight weeks?'

'Of course, Sergey. Eight weeks would be perfect. A little longer if you needed it.'

***

It was five weeks later, while Daniel was in London on company business, that he received the call. Mia Bella had been involved in a serious accident, run off the road, and killed when the car she was driving struck a tree. The police later told him she had been driving in wet conditions and had lost control of the vehicle, with no other cars involved. A tragic accident, they said to Daniel. His world fell apart and, when he told Sergey Rutskoy that he couldn't make it into work, Sergey had said, 'My friend, you may not want to come to work, but you need to come for your wellbeing. Now is not the time for you to be on your own. Take some time out in a few weeks.'

Sergey had been right. The routine of being at work with its responsibilities helped distract Daniel from his loss, yet the grief he felt for Mia was just below the surface. Slowly, as he buried himself in his work, the pain eased and, bit by bit, he settled into his old routine. He didn't tell Sergey that he no longer wished to leave the company, and the eight weeks' notice came and went. Neither spoke of it again.

With billions of dollars of illegal money flowing through the company, Daniel Tinkov was always on the lookout for fraud from within their own business, especially employees helping themselves. Eva Caprio was one of his senior colleagues, responsible for laundering dirty money and making it clean. She was good at her job using methods that included adding cash revenues to their legitimate business enterprises, manipulating electronic funds transfers and wired transmissions, smurfing, real estate transactions, securities and gambling, to name but a few. Each option came with its fee. What caught Daniel's attention was that the cost of laundering had grown over the preceding twelve months by four percentage points. It was only slightly above the inflation rate, a negligible margin, except the increase was an additional four million dollars for every billion dollars cleaned. Daniel inspected a few transactions surreptitiously before selecting ten million dollars and following its path through the web of trades created by Eva. He considered his audit a matter of good governance, not expecting to uncover dishonour among thieves.

Tapping his figures on the desk, Daniel said aloud, '*This doesn't add up, Eva. I know you've done something; I just can't see it yet.*'

With files spread across his kitchen table, his computer logged into the company's accounting software and spreadsheets open on his lap-top, he slowly unpicked the money trail. It took six weeks, and so that Eva Caprio didn't get wind of his forensic audit, long hours working from home at nights. In the beginning, Eva was skimming off two per cent and had she kept it at that amount, the discrepancy would not have been discovered. Her greed was her undoing; Eva's take rose to three and then four per cent, opening her up to his scrutiny. As he closed a manilla folder, one of many he'd brought home, Daniel Tinkov said, shaking his head, 'Silly girl.' Over the years, she'd siphoned thirty million dollars into a Cayman Islands bank account. The next morning, Daniel reported his findings to Sergey Rutskoy.

'Are you sure?' Sergey asked.

'There's no question.'

Naïvely, Daniel hadn't considered the consequences of his investigation, though he knew that, in organised crime, there was only rough justice. Eva Caprio was summoned to Sergey's office and not seen again.

By chance, during a weekend drive to the Alpine town of Klausen, Daniel read in a local newspaper about a woman, Eva Caprio from Rome, killed in a car accident. According to the article, the police had said, "She had been driving in wet conditions when she lost control of the vehicle".

Daniel reread the article and bile rose from his stomach, and he felt sick. The similarities between Eva and Mia's death were obvious. At that moment, Daniel Tinkov knew that Mia's death had been no accident; she'd been brutally murdered by Sergey Rutskoy to stop him leaving.

You may not have forced her off the road yourself, Sergey, but I know it was you who ordered her killed. I swear on the grave of my precious Mia Bella that I'll bring you down.

Vengeful thoughts flooded Daniel's mind, and he knew that taking on Sergey Rutskoy would be dangerous. Regardless, he was determined that Mia's death should be avenged.

How do I do this? Walk and think, Daniel.

He'd maintained the walking routine that Mia had introduced him to, even after her death. He changed into his sports shoes and strode the streets of Klausen to think. His mind went into overdrive as memories of Mia clouded his judgement. Stopping, he looked out over the picturesque landscape and the medieval town with its Gothic churches. Taking a deep breath, the charm of the spectacle began settling his anger, and it was replaced by an overwhelmed sense of regret.

'Forgive me,' he whispered as a tear escaped from his left eye.

You died because of the dishonest life I live, a man making a livelihood from the pain and suffering of others. That's what you said about me, and I'm sorry. Mia, this is my promise to you, my darling Mia Bella. I will become your Saint Vladimir and turn on Sergey, not from revenge or out of anger, but because it's the right and just thing to do, even if it costs me my life. I promise you I will do the right thing.

Breathing deeply, Daniel Tinkov began planning the dangerous road which lay ahead. As he walked, it occurred to him that Sergey would have put him under surveillance when he said that he wanted to leave; perhaps the scrutiny would be less after all of this time, but cameras and listening devices would be in use, of that, he was sure.

If I'm to do this, I need Sergey to believe that I'm returning to the life I led before Mia came along. He must remain oblivious, his trust in me unshaken. My betrayal should land like a lightning strike, unexpected, leaving him reeling in disbelief.

At a recent social event, Sergey Rutskoy had introduced Daniel to Laura D'Amore, a thirty-five-year-old brunette. They gelled, and he'd seen her two weeks later at another function. At the time, Daniel Tinkov had little interest in pursuing a relationship, and Laura showed no signs of wanting one either. Yet, as he walked and reflected, he couldn't shake the certainty that if he had truly desired a connection, it would have blossomed effortlessly.

Is there a more effective way for Sergey Rutskoy to keep tabs on me than to place a woman in my home? I suspect Laura D'Amore is a plant—a corporate spy. I'll bring her into my life as a cover; keep your enemies close, after all. But what's the next step? You'll need to compile a compelling dossier, one powerful enough to blow this organisation wide open. But how?

Daniel remembered that the file he'd put together on Eva Caprio remained at his home.

That will be a start. Assuming I'm right and Sergey is watching my house, there will be surveillance cameras. How do I copy the Eva Caprio files without being seen?

Bing!

His smartwatch beeped. He lifted his wrist and glanced at the display; he'd scored sixty-three heart points with activities at a brisk pace. Dropping his arm, he continued walking. Stopping, Daniel looked at his wrist again. The GZDL Bluetooth smartwatch, the one Mia Bella brought for him, and he wore to work every day, had an inbuilt camera.

That's it, that's how I photograph the files and information on the computer in my office with the watch. Mia Bella, you're a genius.

On the final two kilometres of his walk, he mused on how he could contact the authorities and then who. Sergey Rutskoy was involved in funding terrorist groups and in illegal arms dealing.

That will interest the intelligence community. The CIA, Mossad, and MI6. Britain is the closest. MI6 it is.

Laura didn't move in with Daniel, but she stayed over frequently. In keeping with his routine, Daniel Tinkov woke at six for his morning constitutional, a seven-kilometre walk. The first time Laura slept over, she failed to join him on his morning stroll as he'd hoped, which provided her with the opportunity to search the house. To test his mole theory, he'd laid a couple of traps. Wanting peace while on his morning saunter, Daniel Tinkov rarely carried his mobile phone, leaving it on the bedside table. Before going to sleep, he'd placed a speck of white fluff on the edge of the black wallet that housed the phone; the dust wouldn't move unless the wallet was opened. He also stuck a hair near the screen hinge of his lap-top. He wanted to know if Laura examined his essential possession. When he returned, both items were disturbed.

Perfect, I have Laura just where I wanted her!

Daniel started amassing evidence to expose Sergey Rutskoy's criminal activities. Despite his anxiety, he knew that rushing ahead would be a death sentence. Slowly, Daniel accumulated material while giving the impression of a man dedicated to his job. He showered Laura with gifts, a luxury she adored. His escape plan was a surprise romantic weekend away with Laura at a place of her choosing, and she had excitedly chosen Essaouira, a location she'd read about in one of Daniel's magazines. The article told of an enchanting port city on Morocco's Atlantic coast with 18th century seafront ramparts, spice-scented lanes, and palm-lined avenues. For a place to sleep, she had chosen the Heure Bleue Palais, a classy five-star hotel.

'Why don't we stay three nights?' Daniel had said.

Sunday, his phone left on the bedside table and Laura D'Amore sleeping in the king-sized bed, Daniel started his regular morning constitutional but, instead of returning to the hotel, he rendezvoused with MI6 and a high-speed boat ride. He hoped that his unexpected disappearance would buy him time before the underworld knew the truth and the hunt began.

CHAPTER 12
Alpha Group

It was with trepidation, wondering if the "Principal" knew of Daniel Tinkov's disappearance and betrayal, that Sergey Rutskoy logged into his fortnightly secure video conference with The Firm. Sergey was the last to join the meeting, his avatar image, and name, "Jasper", appearing alongside the other participants as a thumbnail across the top of his computer screen. He had chosen the name Jasper himself from the Latin "Gasper", meaning treasurer, reflecting his role in The Firm. His business empire acted as The Firm's treasury, laundering criminal profits to flow seamlessly into the financial system, or doing the reverse, releasing clean money so that it could be used for illegal purposes. At the centre of Sergey Rutskoy's computer screen, the avatar of a hooded figure without a face, the Principal, the meeting host and leader of The Firm.

Sergey Rutskoy was one of the seven, and unbeknownst to him, the only Russian oligarch in The Firm. The other six were heads of legitimate multinational enterprises or influential figures occupying senior positions in the United Nations and various governments. The Firm's mantra, enshrined in its charter, revolved around power, control, and wealth gained through bribery, extortion, and influence. Engaged in a myriad of illicit activities, they dabbled in arms trading, cybercrime, stolen art, piracy, and smuggling. The Principal ruled with an iron fist, and occasionally, one avatar would vanish only to be replaced by another; each member knew the unspoken implications of this shift. As the treasurer, Sergey held valuable insights into the members of The Firm, even if he remained unaware of the identities behind the avatars. Knowledge was power, but it was also perilous. Jasper, as the treasurer, stood as number two to the Principal.

'Jasper, I'm glad you could join us,' the Principal said, a remark made in a sarcastic tone, rebuking him for being late. Sergey knew better than to apologise. He remained silent.

'Davros report,' commanded the Principal.

The avatar depicting Davros, the creator of the Daleks from the long-running British science fiction series Doctor Who, illuminated as a voice spoke, 'The negotiations are proceeding as planned, Principal.'

'Any difficulties?'

'None.'

'What of Max and Olivia?'

There was a hesitation before Davros replied, 'They escaped, Principal, but we will find them.'

Anger resonated in the Principal's voice as he said, 'Davros, were you not warned not to underestimate them? It...'

Davros interrupted the Principal saying, 'We have it under...'

'Silence,' snapped the Principal. 'It's too late, and if our plan fails, the responsibility will be yours. Do I make myself clear?'

'Yes, Principal.'

'Tomoe?' The avatar of a female Samurai warrior lit up and its owner made a report. Cosy Bear followed Tomoe, the Principal wanting to know if they were successful in stealing the COVID-19 vaccine research.

Each of the seven spoke one after the other, and were meticulously questioned by the Principal. As the video conference neared its conclusion, the Principal's voice echoed through the line. 'Jasper, you're to stay online. The rest of you can log off.'

Sergey Rutskoy fought to control his pounding heart as his fellow members left, leaving him and the Principal on line. 'You have something to tell me, Jasper?'

'Yes, Principal. My Chief Financial Officer, Daniel Tinkov, is missing. I didn't include that in my report because I believed it was best discussed privately between us. We have been working to understand the circumstances of his disappearance and whether he poses a threat.'

'Have you reached a decision?'

'Yes, Principal.' Jasper coughed before he said, 'He's turned collaborator, working with the authorities... The British Secret Service, MI6. I've recently learned of his betrayal and was waiting until after today's conference call before informing you.'

'Does Daniel Tinkov know of The Firm's existence?'

'No, Principal, but he poses a serious threat. He understands my organisation's structure, operations, activities, and connections with both local and foreign groups. If the police or security services were to conduct a forensic examination of my records, the money trail could lead directly to the members of The Firm, placing them squarely on the radar.'

'So, he may know of The Firm?'

'Perhaps, Principal, but I've made the necessary arrangements. He will be eliminated. I'll report back once it's done.'

'You know where MI6 is hiding him?'

Sergey had hoped the Principal wouldn't ask that question. 'No, Principal. But I will; it's only a matter of time.'

The Principal snapped, 'You try my patience Jasper, and I don't have time for your incompetence. Daniel Tinkov is at an MI6 house on the Canary Islands and from there will be transferred to the United Kingdom. You will eliminate him before they move him to the UK. I will send you the details of the safe house. Do not fail, Jasper.'

'I won't, Principal.'

'Good. MI6 has assigned only one person to protect him—a woman named Claudia. Are you familiar with her?'

'By reputation, Principal. Claudia was the mistress of Monya Mogilevick, a billionaire property tycoon and head of the "Brotherhood," the Russian Mafia. Now she works for the British Secret Service. I assure you Principal, she is no match for the people I will send.'

'I want her unharmed, Jasper.'

Unharmed? That's ridiculous. A grenade thrown into their midst would eliminate Daniel Tinkov, Claudia, and everyone else nearby. An easy kill. Why would the Principal want Claudia unharmed? On all accounts, she's a nasty piece of work.

Questioning the Principal's motives meant death and registering an objection required care. Using the phrase "With respect, Principal" would provoke a rebuke. With Jasper's organisation threatening The Firm, he couldn't afford to offend the Principal further. In a passive voice, Jasper said, 'A targeted killing may prove difficult, Principal. She's a formidable opponent.'

'You told me she's no match for the people you will send. Make up your mid, Jasper.'

'I did, Principal, and that is true. However, surgically removing Daniel Tinkov from his protector is,' Sergey hesitated, carefully choosing his words, 'a far more challenging proposition. It requires planning time that may not permit.'

'You will send the resources needed to carry out my wishes. Your tardiness, Jasper, is interfering with another of our operations in which Claudia has a part to play.' The Principal softened his tone as he continued, 'If you could track her movements, would that assist your assassination team?'

'Yes, Principal, then greatly. That Intel would make the task easier.'

There was a pause in the conversation, and Sergey took a deep breath as he listened to the white noise from the speaker. The Principal's tone hardened, his voice accusing as he said, 'You're disappointing me, Jasper. If Daniel Tinkov makes it to the United Kingdom, The Firm's future is in jeopardy. He is to be removed and speedily. If you fail, your services will no longer be required and you understand what that means, I am sure.'

'I understand, Principal.'

'Good, I'm glad that we understand each other. With the spread of the COVID-19 virus, countries are preparing to close their borders, so you must dispatch your team immediately. Are you ready to depart?'

Sergey had already met with Carlos Gorelov, the man who would command the assassination operation. Their plan, once they knew the whereabouts of Daniel Tinkov, was to insert a three-person surveillance team to scout the location and direct activities when the kill team of five arrived. Both groups were to be Ex-Russian Alpha ground commandos, trained to accept orders without question, and known for executing some of Russia's most brutal operations. They were feared–and were entirely terrifying. Formally KGB, now operating under the auspice of the FSB, they were part spy network, part counter-terrorism team, and part general-purpose commando squad. Their orders were to have been– kill everyone, but with the Principal's directive that Claudia was to be left unharmed and the escalating COVID-19 environment threatening travel restrictions, the plan was in disarray. Jasper would keep this from the Principal.

'By the end of the week, Principal.'

'What exactly does that mean, Jasper?'

'In seven days, Principal.' Jasper repeated, 'They will leave in seven days.'

'You don't have seven days because MI6 will move him in five. You will contact me the moment Daniel Tinkov has been eliminated. Is that clear?'

'Yes.'

'That means Jasper, any time, day or night.'

Jasper wanted to ask the Principal if he knew how Daniel Tinkov was going to be moved to the UK, but he held his tongue, not wanting to betray his lack of intelligence and said, 'He will be killed, Principal.'

'Good, and I'm sending you the intel we have on the MI6 security arrangements for Daniel Tinkov and what you need to track Claudia's movements. On your life, do not fail Jasper!'

The teleconference screen went blank as the Principal left the meeting.

Before calling Carlos Gorelov into his office, Sergey Rutskoy studied the information the Principal had sent and, after making a hard copy, summoned Carlos.

'The plans have changed, Carlos.'

'As they do.'

Carlos Gorelov listened as Sergey outlined the new operational parameters for the mission, his face remaining blank throughout, a man accustomed to taking orders.

'Will there be a problem?' Sergey asked.

'There will be no time for ground surveillance, which is the most crucial part of a surgical strike. I know Claudia, and given the time she's had to prepare, it will be difficult to subdue her without inflicting injury.'

'She must be unharmed.'

Carlos nodded his understanding as he said, 'Three assault teams will be required if I'm to overpower her.'

'Use whatever resources you need. MI6 is moving Daniel Tinkov in five days and he's not to leave the island alive. When will you be ready?'

'My men are always ready!'

'Good. That is what I want to hear.'

CHAPTER 13
The Safe House

'This is your room,' Claudia said while opening the curtains. 'As you can see Daniel, you have a lovely view out over the grounds and valley. Likewise, those outside have a perfect sight of you; if you want to live, I would suggest that you deprive yourself of the vista and never open the curtains. A single shot is all it takes.'

In a nervous tone, Daniel replied, 'Is there a room that's not as exposed?'

'No, not really, and besides, I like this one.'

Claudia's answer piqued Daniel Tinkov's curiosity as he said, 'Where will you be sleeping?'

'Right there,' Claudia said, pointing to a couch in the corner of the room.

'You're expecting trouble? I was hoping MI6 would put me somewhere out of Ser...' He started saying Sergey Rutskoy's name but stopped himself, unsure of what Claudia knew, saying instead, 'Out of harm's way.'

'Before MI6, I worked for the Russian Mafia run by an Oligarch not dissimilar to your Sergey Rutskoy. I know your friends are dangerous people with connections and reach equal to those of the security services. For the moment, there is no "out of harm's way." It would be unwise for either of us to underestimate your former employer.' Daniel nodded as Claudia continued, 'If I were leading an attack, I would want to know where our weaknesses were, so I'd carry out surveillance. I'd hit us either in the early hours of the morning or just before dawn when our sleep is at its heaviest, and we're vulnerable. As there's only me to protect you, there are three rules which you must follow. First, we retire to this room at nine o'clock every night where you can read or do whatever you like, as long as you're quiet because I will be sleeping. At 2.00 AM, I'll awake and keep watch until seven, then return to bed until 9.00 AM, which is when you're free to leave the room. Second, you will never venture outside without me. Don't worry about staying fit because you will get plenty of exercise on patrol with me.'

'Patrol?' Daniel said, giving Claudia a sideways glance.

'If I were the assailant, I would want to know where we're vulnerable. I expect they will deploy a surveillance team before making a move against us, which Daniel plays to our advantage.'

'How?'

'I've set some traps to detect any signs of activity—people prowling the high ground around us—that will provide a warning of an impending strike. Our task, Daniel, is to inspect them together; this will also serve as your daily exercise. And remember, you must keep this two-way radio with you at all times. You asked if I'm expecting trouble. The answer is I'm expecting the worst, while hoping for the best.'

'I don't wish to be critical Claudia but, if you're expecting a confrontation, shouldn't there be more agents here? Not just you.'

'You might think that pitting strength against strength is preferred. That approach involves many people, increasing the risk of exposure, loose lips, if you understand my meaning. Sergey Rutskoy has tentacles that reach everywhere, as you know; the chances of him having a mole inside MI6 are high. Stephen Walls - I assume you know Stephen Walls, the head of MI6?'

'Yes. Well, I know of him.'

'For once, I agree with Stephen. Less is best and besides, you have me.'

Daniel Tinkov smiled, saying, 'That's a good thing?'

'Oh, yes. This Daniel is what I do.' She paused and, changing the topic said, 'Can you cook?'

The question took him by surprise, and he answered, 'Well, yes, very well, in fact.'

'Rule number three, I'll keep you alive as long as you cook because I'm bloody hopeless at it.'

'Wouldn't that be rule number four?'

Claudia shrugged her shoulders. 'Who's counting? Nice suit, by the way.'

Daniel Tinkov brushed his hands down his suit before saying, 'Thank you. I'm glad you like it. It's a copy of what I'd normally wear and Stephen had it waiting for me, both generous and a message that they, MI6, had been watching me.'

Claudia bit her lip, trying to hide the anger rising inside. If MI6 had been conducting surveillance on Daniel Tinkov, the gig was up already; his name would undoubtedly have leaked.

***

Despite her initial fears, Daniel Tinkov's time at the safe house had passed without incident as he neared the end of his stay. While on morning parameter patrol, checking for signs of activity, Daniel Tinkov's curiosity got the better of him. Having watched Claudia every morning study what appeared to be compressed dust, he whispered, 'What are you looking for?' The moment the words left his lips, he regretted them because Claudia's stare could have killed a man at a hundred metres, her message unmistakable: keep quiet. Afterwards, as they approached the house, Daniel felt uncomfortable, knowing that a reprimand was coming. Claudia's sympathetic tone came as a surprise.

'Daniel, Daniel, Daniel, what did I say about speaking on patrol?'

'Sorry.'

'The reason for the silence is not for stealth because, if we are under surveillance, they know we are there. The reason, Daniel, is so that we don't divulge secrets. Secrets like, *"What are you looking for?"* Got it!'

'I know, I'm sorry.'

Claudia sighed, 'No harm done. I'll explain. A surveillance team, Daniel, wouldn't leave obvious signs of their presence. Apart from my little traps, tiny twigs that will break when stepped on, I'm looking for minute signs of activity that are difficult to discern, including compressions and dust or grit left on the surface of an object. With my head low to the ground, tilted to one side, I can spot compression patterns not visible from above. Our patrol is first thing in the morning because I'm also looking for "dulling", where dew has been wiped from a surface by someone passing. I'm also looking for leaf depressions. You've seen me move leaves?' Daniel nodded. 'Footsteps leave an outline of the leaf in the soil below. The leaf springs back, but not always to their original position. Again, when my head is low to the ground, I can detect that.'

'If I promise not to speak, will you show me, point out a compression? I'd like to learn.'

'It's too late Daniel, because you're leaving tomorrow, so there won't be another morning patrol. If Sergey Rutskoy were sending in a surveillance team, they would already be here.'

Daniel smiled broadly, sighing in relief, as he said, 'He didn't find me?'

'It's not over until the fat lady sings, as the expression goes. We need to stay on our guard until you're safely on your way to the UK.'

'Do you know how I'm getting there?'

'Not yet. Stephen will tell me tomorrow. Now, your penance for speaking on patrol is that you can cook dinner.'

'I always cook.'

With a light tone, Claudia said, 'Well, you'd better make it something special.' As she uttered the words, Claudia realised that, for the first time since John's death, she had shed her fake façade of happiness. The smile was genuine, and the constant pain in the pit of her stomach was missing. She felt a flash of guilt for betraying John's memory and bit her lip, pondering the conflicting emotions.

Watching Claudia's smile morph into a look of concern, Daniel said, 'Are you alright?'

'Who me? Yes, I was thinking about tomorrow.'

You're a sociopath, Claudia. Since when did you worry about conflicting emotions? Bloody Max and Olivia, it's all your fault.

Daniel's sense of euphoria lasted the rest of the day and, when at dinner he wanted to celebrate his deliverance with a second glass of wine, Claudia reminded him, saying, 'Tut, tut, tut. You know the rules, Daniel. One glass only. We don't want to impede our abilities, especially this close to the end.'

He chuckled, knowing Claudia was right. Even without a top-up, the conversation flowed smoothly between them, as it had done since he'd arrived at the safe house. Although Daniel wanted to be in the UK and on his way to a new identity, he was also going to miss his guardian angel and felt sad when, at nine o'clock on the dot, Claudia told him it was time that they retired upstairs. He knew talking would cease because Claudia was a consummate professional and would go straight to bed, waking again at two in the morning to keep watch while he slept.

For the first time since arriving at the safe house, Daniel roused himself. As Claudia kept her vigil, he opened his heavy eyes and searched for her in the dim light. Daniel was surprised to see Claudia had positioned a chair near the head of his bed and was dressed in body armour and had an assault weapon in hand. She was seated right next to him and, on her lap, was the monitor for the ground surveillance radar system plus another panel he didn't recognise. Daniel's body armour was laid out neatly on the floor next to her. By the time he woke up, it was all packed away.

'You're awake,' she said, without looking at him.

'I've wondered what you do while I'm sleeping?'

'It's always the same, Daniel. Watch and wait and hope nothing happens.'

Sitting up in bed, he said, while pointing to the panel containing an array of switches and buttons, 'What's that?'

'It controls the command-detonated mines I've placed around the perimeter and the plastic explosives hidden in the house in case they make it inside.'

'Um ...' He said, hesitating before adding, 'Do you like what you do?'

Claudia thought for a moment. It wasn't she didn't want to respond; she didn't know the answer. Instead, Claudia asked, 'Did you enjoy what you did?'

Daniel sighed, 'It shames me to admit it, but yes, I enjoyed my work and the lifestyle that went with it, though I knew it was based on the misery of others. Mostly, you don't think about the impact of your actions. It was Mia who reminded me I wasn't free from the consequences of my behaviour. My work cost Mia her life.'

'By turning on Sergey Rutskoy, are you seeking revenge?'

Daniel Tinkov shook his head, emphatically, 'Not revenge, Claudia. Revenge, retribution, anger, hatred, whatever words describe it, drove me initially before I realised, evil intent only served to perpetuate my wrongdoing and was...' Daniel hesitated, searching for the right words before continuing, '... an insult, disrespectful even. I'm not sure how to express it, Claudia. Revenge would be contrary to Mia's wishes. Sounds confusing, I know, but do you understand what I'm trying to say?'

'I think so, Daniel. It's because Mia was a religious woman.' Quoting from the bible, Claudia said, 'Never avenge yourself, but leave it to the wrath of God, for it is written, "Vengeance is mine, I will repay, says the Lord." Romans 12:19.'

Daniel nodded. 'Yes, revenge was contrary to Mia's beliefs. No longer am I driven by hatred; I have turned on Sergey because it's the right thing to do.' He hesitated before adding, 'I didn't suspect that you were a religious woman.'

Claudia's eyes brightened as she said, 'I'm not,' and was about to add, 'it's a party trick,' but out of respect for Mia, stopped herself and added, 'Saint Vladimir, was that Mia's idea?'

Daniel laughed, 'Yes. I use the name to remind me to be a better person.'

'A sinner who becomes a Saint?'

Shaking his head as he spoke, Daniel said, 'I'm no Saint, but it helps me to unshackle the past and become the man Mia knew I could be.' He sighed, 'Or wanted me to be.'

Claudia was surprised at the similarities between herself and Daniel Tinkov and the different paths they were choosing to take: Sweetie vs Saint Vladimir. In two days, while Daniel was seeking justice, she would slaughter Richard Liew, his wife Samantha, and possibly their daughter, Molly. Seeds of doubt were creeping in and, for the first time, Claudia dropped her shields, allowing herself to think–what would John want? The answer was straightforward.

He'd want me to forgive, but not forget. Snowflake and I to go to Montserrat, not as an assassin, but as Jacob Marley from Charles Dickens in A Christmas Carol, to show Richard Liew that his behaviour has consequences for those he loves and that his future doesn't have to continue the same way.

Claudia threw up her guard again.

HA! If you did that Sweetie, the Chinese would be right; you've become weak! Leave the social compass rubbish to the Saint Vladimir's of the world.

Wishing to change tack, Claudia said, 'The news from Italy and your home, Rome in particular, isn't good. Over a thousand people died last night from COVID-19, and the entire country is in lockdown.' Before Daniel could respond, the screen on the perimeter surveillance monitor lit up, accompanied by an audible alarm.

BEEP! BEEP! BEEP!

Daniel swallowed hard as fear washed over him. He glanced at Claudia, who calmly raised her wrist and, after studying her watch, said, 'Five thirty. It will be dawn soon and the feral cat is on its way home from a night's hunting. You can set your watch by it.'

Daniel felt his anxiety ease as he said, 'How do you know it's a cat?'

'By analysing and tracking the behaviour of the target. We call these nuisance alarms.' Daniel nodded his head, acknowledging that he was suitably impressed by her skills, as Claudia smiled, adding, 'It also helped that, after the second night, I set up an infrared camera to see what was happening. It's a big cat, an ugly critter. Even so, I still watch the screen closely in case an unwanted visitor tries to use the opportunity to sneak in under my guard.' The dot on the radar screen vanished. Claudia showing Daniel the handheld monitor said, 'All good.'

'Have you named it?' Claudia looked at Daniel in an expression that said, *what on earth are you talking about?* 'The cat.'

Trying to think of a witty response, Claudia said, but didn't have time to finish: 'The name of the feral cat is...'

The beeping of the audible alarm on the radar monitor interrupted her mid-sentence. Across the top of the screen in red letters were the words: *INTRUDER ALERT.* Six red triangles with white circles around appeared on the screen, accompanied by arrows that showed the direction of travel. They were heading towards the house.

Daniel looked at Claudia, unsure if this was another nuisance alarm, however from the focused expression on her face, he knew it wasn't.

'We have company,' Claudia said calmly, punctuating her instructions. 'You need to get dressed, put on your body armour, gear up as we've practised and then stay here; wait for my call. You better take this.' Claudia passed him a pistol and added, 'Try not to shoot me.'

Daniel's voice trembled. 'Will we be okay?'

With an air of confidence that concealed her trepidation, Claudia replied, 'With the reception I've prepared, six will be a piece of cake. I've got to go.'

Automatic assault weapon in hand, studying the radar screen to determine where best to position herself, Claudia left the bedroom. As she did, the red triangles on the screen halted and Claudia hesitated.

It's as if they know I'm onto them. No, that can't be possible.

The targets moved again, heading towards the front of the house, although they had a distance to go.

It was dark when Claudia slipped out the back door, manoeuvred around the side of the house that separated it from the garage, and positioned herself behind the rental car—the Volvo she had parked for this very purpose. Glancing at the monitor, she noticed the targets had split into two groups. The first group, which she dubbed the A-Team, remained stationary, positioned to cover her, while the B-Team was poised to approach from the other side of the house.

They know where I am. How?

Claudia's plan was to engage the boogies as soon as she had visual contact; however, the attackers were staying out of her line of sight; she had to force a change in their strategy. On the screen, the B-Team was approaching a concealed mine. Claudia flicked up the missile cover, protecting the toggle switch that would detonate the mine.

Lighten up, girly!

BOOM!

What was left of the dark and still pre-dawn, evaporated in a brilliant flash of bright red and yellow, the aftermath of the explosion, dust and dirt showering the area. Immediately, automatic gunfire opened up on her position, the shots coming from the A-Team so that the B-Team, were they still alive, could advance on the house. Claudia dropped to the ground and, lying flat, returned fire from under the Volvo, expending a magazine toward the A-Team. Glancing at the radar monitor, Claudia noticed that the three red triangles of the B-Team were present, moving towards the house. Rolling around to the side of the Volvo, Claudia opened fire on them but was forced back because of the volume of covering fire coming from the A-Team. She was pinned to the spot, and the house would soon be breached.

'Daniel,' she said into the two-way radio. Another volley of shots peppered the Volvo. The radio remained silent. Claudia said desperately, 'For God's sake, John, put in your earpiece.'

The radio crackled back. 'Who's John?'

Did I just call Daniel, John? I'm slipping.

'That's irrelevant, Daniel. As we practised, now's the time for action. Over the balcony, around to the back of the house and into the garage. To encourage our intruders to enter through the front door, I'm about to set off another explosion on your side of the house. Don't worry; you'll be quite safe. Wait for the explosion, then go over the balcony and once on the ground, keep moving and don't look back. Do you hear me? Don't look back!'

Upstairs, Daniel Tinkov, already in an abseiling harness, clipped himself into the rope as Claudia had taught him. Down below, Claudia flipped up another missile cover, protecting a detonation switch.

BOOM!

Hearing the explosion, Daniel prepared to launch himself from the balcony and then stopped, remembering what had happened last time. He put his hand down his pants, making sure that his testicles were clear of the crotch strap. On one of his practices; while dangling from the balcony with his full body weight supported by the harness, the crotch strap had pinched a testicle. He'd screamed in agony and Claudia had laughed, letting him down with a series of jerks when he told her about his problem.

Coinciding with the explosion, Claudia concentrated her fire on the A-Team, allowing the B-Team to cross no-man's-land to make for the front door. The B-Team opened up on her position with automatic gunfire as they ran towards the house, bullets shattering the Volvo SUV windows above Claudia's head, sending shards of glass in all directions.

I should have put the helmet on.

Another volley of bullets came in at her, forcing Claudia to take cover.

That's interesting, they're suppressing me, rather than going for a kill–what is going on?

Lying flat on the ground, Claudia watched the B-Team reach the front door and enter the house. From their practice, Claudia knew it would take Daniel thirty-five seconds to travel from the bedroom balcony to the garage side door. Although she couldn't see him, she laid down a clip of covering fire for his benefit before falling back to join him. Going inside the garage, Claudia found Daniel waiting for her. He shook with fear as he stammered, 'What now?'

Claudia flicked the cover off another toggle switch, saying, 'We wait ten more seconds to give the soldiers inside the house time to be climbing the stairs, then we blow it.'

'You're going to destroy the house?'

Claudia didn't respond; instead, she yelled, 'Close the garage door. Now.'

'Oh heck,' Daniel said, pushing the door shut.

BOOM! BOOM! BOOM!

The plastic explosives inside the house erupted one after another, sending up balls of bright flame into the air, rubble scattering in all directions, some smashing into the garage with a thud. Claudia knew that anyone inside was dead and that there would be little left of the house.

Three to go.

'Quick, inside the Range Rover.'

'What now?'

'Didn't you just ask me that?' Claudia said but didn't wait for an answer before continuing, smugness present in her voice, 'Light them up and drive through. Now, get in.' Ditching her body armour, Claudia glanced at Daniel, who remained next to the passenger's door. She demanded angrily. 'What are you waiting for?'

'It's locked.'

'Oh, that would do it,' Claudia said, reaching into her pocket to retrieve the keys and unlock the doors. 'Go on. Now what are you waiting for?' Daniel shook his head in disbelief as he climbed in, wondering how Claudia found time for humour when their lives hung in the balance. After starting the SUV, instead of joining him, Claudia retrieved an M72 LAW Compact anti-tank rocket launcher she'd hidden under the car. The weapon in hand, she pressed the remote controller to open the roller door in front of the Ranger Rover. When it reached her head height, Claudia pulled the trigger, firing a rocket, aiming for where the A-Team had staked out. The area was lit up by the detonation and ensuing flames. Throwing the launcher away, Claudia climbed into the Range Rover and, pushing the accelerator to the floor, raced out of the garage. With the steering wheel in one hand and the trigger for the three remaining mines in the other, two of which were next to drums of petrol, she detonated the munitions. A scene that would have made the Apocalypse look tame erupted in front of them as they sped towards the fire, smoke and debris that accompanied the blasts. Discarding the trigger device, Claudia said, pointing to one of two assault rifles that shared Daniel's half of the car, 'Give me that.' Poking it out of the driver's side window, Claudia opened fire as they sped past the spot the A-Team had been, the deafening noise causing Daniel to push his figures into his ears. Fifty metres later, their escape meeting no resistance, Claudia slowed the car before coming to a complete standstill. 'Lock the doors and close the windows,' she said. 'You drive, and I'll ride shotgun.' When Daniel reached for the door handle, she added, 'Just slide across.'

Swapping of sides was challenging, with Daniel still dressed in his armour, their bodies locked together in a contortionist knot. As Daniel was about to oil the situation with humour, there was a THUD, the sound of someone trying the door handles, then hitting the Range Rover in frustration.

'Move!' Claudia commanded.

How Daniel was able to untangle himself from Claudia and position himself in the driver's seat, all within in a matter of seconds, wasn't clear to him later. The urgency lubricated the situation. As soon as his hands were on the wheel, not waiting for instructions, he prepared to punch the accelerator.

BANG!

A gunshot rang out, and a bullet punched through the driver's door, hitting the side plate on the body armour Daniel was wearing. He let out a groan of anguish, saying, 'I've been shot!'

'Drive!' Claudia commanded.

The car rocketed forward and–THUD–a fist struck the rear quarter panel as they sped away. Daniel muttered again, 'I've been shot.'

'Any blood?' Claudia asked, her voice dry of empathy.

Daniel placed his hand on his side, feeling the spot where the bullet had impacted. He raised it again, inspecting his fingers. 'No.'

'Good. The body armour did its job.'

'It still hurt.'

'Better than being dead.'

Daniel agreed with Claudia's observation and went quiet for a moment before saying, 'I thought we'd killed them?'

'We did. These are another team. You're a popular man!'

As they approached the end of the driveway, Claudia turned to look through the rear window. A vehicle was following and, in the early light of dawn, she identified it as a Volvo XC 90 SUV.

Claudia chuckled. *The poor hire company, this is not their day. They're about to lose another one.*

'Which way?' Daniel asked, panic punctuating his voice.

'Turn left and Daniel, keep your head down.'

As Claudia spoke, automatic weapons fire peppered the back of the Range Rover. Daniel swung the car onto the main road, headed down the mountain and, for a moment, they were out of range of their pursuers. Claudia waited for the Volvo to leave the driveway and, as soon as it came into view, she opened fire, the noise deafening inside the cabin. The back window shattered as a hail of bullets left the Range Rover. The Volvo behind dropped back, and Claudia stopped shooting. A moment later, Claudia was flung hard against the passenger door as Daniel, driving too fast, threw the Range Rover into a corner while hitting the brakes, pushing the car's anti-lock braking system to its limits to avoid a crash.

'Slow down,' Claudia said in a level voice. 'Let's not kill ourselves.'

'Sorry,' Daniel stammered. 'Are we safe?'

'No, they're sending us into a trap.'

'A trap! How do you know that?'

'Because that's what I'd do.' Claudia's said, accompanied by a hail of bullets from behind, 'They're keeping us moving, a little poke with a cattle prod.'

'What now?'

'You like that expression.'

'How can you be so ... composed?'

'It's what I do, John.'

'That's the second time you've called me John. When this is over, you need to tell me about him.'

Ignoring Daniel, Claudia said, 'There's a lookout coming up, it is on your right after the next bend. When you reach it, I want you to drive in.'

Daniel replied, his voice rising a pitch, 'Drive in?'

'Yes. Then stop!'

'Then stop?'

'There's an echo in the car,' Claudia said and, seeing the lookout, added, 'There it is, Daniel. Don't miss it.' As he turned in, she continued, 'A little further, okay, perfect, stop here. If I were you, Daniel, I'd get out.'

'Why? What are you going to do?'

From the back seat, Claudia took the second of the M72 LAW Compact anti-tank rocket launchers and aimed it at the Volvo through the rear window.

'Jeez, give me a second,' Daniel said, panic in his voice as he scrambled to evacuate the Range Rover. Before he had time to close the driver's door behind him, there was the sound of the rocket leaving the launcher and flames from its propulsion engulfed the front windscreen. He watched the projectile exit the rear of the

Range Rover and, following its track, saw it home in on the approaching Volvo. The rocket's speed was too fast for the pursuers to evade.

BOOM!

In a ball of flames, the SUV was lifted off its wheels, flipping upside down mid-air, before crashing down on its roof in a smouldering wreck. Daniel stood motionless, stunned by the experience, saying, his voice a whisper, 'Is it over?'

Rat-a-tat-tat - Rat-a-tat-tat. Claudia was firing.

Daniel's emotions numbed as he saw another SUV driving up the mountain road, a gun pointing from its passenger's side window and a plume of smoke coming from its barrel. He was being shot at again. Claudia stopped firing. 'Quick, start the car and point it downhill towards them.' When Daniel didn't respond, she yelled, 'Daniel!'

He stared back at her with a half-dazed look.

Speaking slowly but forcefully, Claudia said, 'Don't do this to me now, Daniel! Start the car and point it down the hill - Now!'

The haze lifted, and Daniel did as Claudia had directed.

'Get out of the car, Daniel.'

A gun flung over her shoulder, Claudia dashed around to the driver's side, putting the Range Rover into in neutral. 'Help me push this beast.' Remembering Stephen's note: PLEASE DON'T SCRATCH ME, Claudia laughed to herself–*Sorry Stephen*.

Together, they launched the car towards the approaching SUV.

Rat-a-tat-tat - Rat-a-tat-tat.

The two ex-alpha group commandos driving up the hill were firing when they noticed the Range Rover careering towards them. They swerved to the wrong side of the road expecting the car to miss them and pass harmlessly. However, at the last moment, as if guided, the Range Rover switched direction and smashed head-on into the Volvo with a mighty crunch.

'Hold this,' Claudia said, handing Daniel her assault rifle. Taking it, he watched as she darted across the road, alarm twitching his muscles.

Where's she going?

Moments later, she called, 'Help me, Daniel.' Claudia was dragging something Daniel couldn't recognise back across the road.

Rushing to her, he said, 'What is it?'

'A hang glider.'

'A hang glider?'

She smiled at him. 'I see we still have our echo.'

Together, they pulled the hang glider to the edge of the lookout. Taking the assault rifle back from Daniel, she threw it over her shoulder while giving him one of her pistols, saying, her eyes twinkling, 'Point and shoot.'

'At what? There's nobody there.'

Claudia, while beginning to assemble the sailcloth triangle-shaped wing glider, with its simple tubing, aluminium struts and wire bracing, said, 'At the moment Daniel, nobody is there, so let's try to keep it that way while I put the glider together. What I want you to do is keep shooting at the Range Rover until it explodes. Like you see in the movies.'

'How long do you need?'

'To assemble the glider takes three minutes and thirty seconds exactly.'

'Okay,' he said, sounding almost confident as he pointed Claudia's pistol towards the SUV and pulled the trigger.

BANG! BANG! BANG!

He kept shooting until the clip was empty.

'It's empty.'

'Now use your gun and, while you're at it, dump the body armour.'

Daniel let off two rounds.

BANG, BANG.

He stopped as he tried to undo his armour.

'Multitask, Daniel, multitask,' Claudia said as she glanced towards the Volvo to watch one of the Alpha group commandos extract himself from the wreck. 'You're supposed to shoot and undress at the same time.'

'That's easy for you to say. I'm a man. Everyone knows we can't multitask.'

Claudia stopped assembling the glider, took the rifle from her back and, aiming at the man leaving the Volvo, began firing while saying, 'Get that body armour off.' By the time she'd emptied the assault rifle clip, Daniel's armour was on the ground. She dropped her gun and took the pistols from him, inserting new ammunition clips, before handing them back.

'Keep shooting at the car.'

BANG! BANG! BANG!

On Daniel's third shot, BOOM! The petrol leaking from the stricken Range Rover ignited in an impressive explosion. The heat of the flames easily felt from where they were standing.

'Ready? Let's go,' Claudia said, taking Daniel by the arm and strapping him into one of the hang glider's harnesses, fastening her own next to him. With the glider in hand, Claudia manoeuvred it to the edge, the coast visible beyond in the early morning light and a sheer drop below.

Daniel said, his voice quivering, 'You're not going to, are you?' He paused before adding, 'Of course you are.'

Rat-a-tat-tat - Rat-a-tat-tat, the sound of automatic weapons fire coming from behind them.

'Unless you've got a better option, I'd start running if I were you.' Before Daniel could object, Claudia sprinted towards the edge. Strapped in next to her, Daniel's feet followed Claudia's lead.

Rat-a-tat-tat - Rat-a-tat-tat.

Leaping off the lookout, Daniel became aware of his weight hanging in the harness and, for a split second, felt as though he was about to fall to his death. The coolness of the air on his face replaced the sensation, but not the panic. Claudia, knowing that Daniels's heart was pounding with terror, said,

'I remember my first flight. I had watched the birds soaring in the sky, wondering and dreaming what it would be like to see the world from their point of view. It is always as wonderful as the first time.' Claudia shifted her body weight, changing the position of the glider, as she continued, 'Daniel, what I'm doing is searching for an updraught where the air is being forced vertically upwards by the cliff. If we find it, we'll be able to fly along without losing height. That should take us to the coast.'

Daniel, whose temperament was sounding calm for the first time since the shooting started, said, 'You can make it to the coast, it's a long way...' He was interrupted by the sound of gunfire.

Rat-a-tat-tat - Rat-a-tat-tat.

Claudia tried to twist her head to find the shooters, but the harness prevented her. She groaned as she said, 'You would have thought they would have given up by now. Hang on; I'm going to move my weight forward in the control frame, so we speed up to put us out of their range.'

Claudia dropped the craft's altitude and increased their ground speed, and within seconds, they were out of reach. She eased back in the frame to slow their descent and searched for an updraught to increase their height again. The glider wasn't responding as she expected. Examining the sail material, Claudia saw it peppered with bullet holes, and beginning to tear.

How inconvenient.

'Daniel, I'm going to have to put us down.'

Seeing the damaged glider, Daniel's heart pounded. He doubted the decision to become Mia's Saint Vladimir. Deep down, however, he knew he'd made the right choice and there was no turning back.

Claudia banked the glider tightly, trying to catch channelled thermals in an attempt to slow their descent. At a 45-degree angle, she fought against the centrifugal force as she tried to keep her vision clear. The nose of the glider suddenly dropped, sending it into a spiral dive, and the best that Claudia could do to maintain control was to set it into 360-degree turns while extending the arc. As the speed of descent slowed, Claudia forced the glider's nose up again, reducing the velocity of their fall further as she scanned for a soft place to land, wanting to avoid the nearby town. The sound of material ripping coincided with the glider veering to the right and rapidly losing altitude once more.

'Daniel,' she called, who was holding on for his life, 'See the road and the farmhouse, I'll bring us down there.' He remained mute, holding on tightly and sure he was about to die.

Fighting for control, Claudia recovered from the death spiral and, seeing a patch of open grass next to the house, pushed the control bar as far out as she could to induce a stall. The holes in the sail reduced the effectiveness of her brake manoeuvre, and they crashed into the ground with a thump, sending both them and the glider tumbling, all ending up in a tangled mess.

Winded, Claudia glanced at Daniel, who was underneath her. 'Are you alright?'

'If you could take your knees out of my face, I would be.'

'It's your lucky day, Daniel. They're not my knees.' Undoing her harness, Claudia fell on top of him before extracting herself and then uncoupling Daniel from the wrecked glider. Brushing herself off, Claudia said, 'When was the last time you've had so much fun?'

'Fun isn't the word that springs automatically to mind.'

Witnessing the crash, an elderly farmer and his wife, both in their late eighties, came from the house, calling 'Estás bien?–Are you okay?'

When they were a little closer, Daniel answered with a wry smile on his face for Claudia's benefit, 'Never better.'

Claudia added, 'No broken bones, just a little winded, and other than that, we'll both survive.'

The woman, gesturing with her hands, started to say, "Come in, come—" until she noticed the semi-automatic pistol strapped to Claudia's waist. She froze, apprehension flooding her, fearing for her life.

Following the woman's eyes, Claudia touched the gun and said, smiling, 'Policía.'

'Oh, Si,' said the woman nodding, 'Police. Please follow me.'

As they started walking towards the house, albeit for Daniel with a slight limp, Claudia spotted another Volvo XC 90, the same type of SUV the soldiers had been using, speeding down the road towards them.

Here we go again. Daniel must be a prize target!

Speaking to the couple, Claudia said, 'My friend here, he's not with the police, but an important witness in a case against the Mafia and they're chasing us.' She pointed to the approaching car and continued, 'Do you have a vehicle of some sort we can borrow?' The old man beckoned for them to follow, leading them into an ancient barn behind the house and pulled back a canvas tarpaulin covering a vintage, light earth-coloured, ex-German WWII BMW 754cc flat-twin motorbike and sidecar combination. Claudia ran her hand over the petrol tank. 'Oh, she's beautiful. Does she go?'

'Like the wind,' the woman said with a toothless grin.

Looking at Daniel, Claudia instructed, 'Okay, in you get.'

Cocking his leg over the sidecar and then trying to manoeuvre his body into the confined space, Daniel swallowed hard. 'Will this ever end?'

Claudia touched him reassuringly on the shoulder. 'Think of it as a grand adventure.'

'You're not helping,' Daniel said, abruptly.

After priming the old motorbike, Claudia moved to the side so that she could perform a full kick-start.

'I love these old bikes but, if you forget to follow-through with your kick, the bike will bite you.'

Daniel watched as she pressed the kicker until it reached a firm place and was hard to press. She then brought it back up to the top and stomped through the kicker, using her weight, not her muscles, pausing at the bottom to wait for the engine to start. After a second attempt, it sprang into life. While she was starting the bike, the elderly man retrieved two vintage helmets, giving one to Claudia as she mounted and the other to Daniel in the sidecar. Halfway through securing them, they heard of spinning wheels and a revving motor. Near the barn door was the Volvo at a perpendicular angle, trying to straighten itself before entering at speed. Calmly, Claudia finished fastening her helmet and opened the throttle of the bike, sending it racing towards the rear exit. Daniel, hands shaking, wasn't able to tie the chin strap and, within seconds of Claudia accelerating, his helmet flew off his head, accompanied by a shout of, 'Darn!'

As the motorbike combination exited the barn, Daniel turned his head and saw the Volvo entering through the front entrance. To his relief, they paid no attention to the old man and woman, speeding straight past in pursuit. The comfort, however, was short-lived as he spotted a pistol appear out of the passenger side window and he called, 'Step on it!'

Claudia guided the motorbike with its sidecar from the field onto the road, hoping to lose their pursuers in the town half a kilometre away. With no mirrors to look behind, Claudia called above the noise of the wind for Daniel to keep tabs on the following SUV.

'They're on the road, and you need to speed up. Go faster! Go faster!' he called.

The bike combination began shaking as it reached its top speed, causing Claudia to back off to a pace more comfortable for the bike.

'They're gaining on us!'

As they entered the town limits, Claudia took the first right, lifting the sidecar's wheels off the ground as she turned from the main road and into a narrow street running between buildings on the left and a tall stone wall to her right. She eased back, still travelling faster than the conditions permitted.

'I can't see them,' shouted Daniel, his voice distorted by the wind.

'That's good.'

A hundred metres later, Claudia turned left, squeezing the motorbike and sidecar between vehicles parked on both sides of the laneway without slowing. 'Can you see them now?'

'No.'

Slowing almost to a stop, Claudia eased the bike combination into a narrow pedestrian alleyway running between buildings, bouncing it down the steps, before bringing it to a halt out of sight of the main road on which they'd left.

'What now?'

'Get out,' Claudia said. 'We'll hide and then find ourselves a better set of wheels. This way.' Claudia led Daniel through the back gate of a nearby house, one with a view over the main road below, and whispered, 'Down.'

Out of sight, they watched as the Volvo SUV entered the town limits and crawled along, searching for them. Daniel felt the urge to run, his muscles flexing, and Claudia placed a steadying hand on his shoulder as she whispered, 'It's okay. They don't know where we are.' As she spoke, the Volvo stopped directly below their position. Two heavily armed men exited and stared straight up at their hideout.

How do they know where we are? Claudia muttered to herself.

Raising her pistol, Claudia opened fire, hitting one man in his leg. 'The bitch!' she heard him yell as he sent a volley of bullets back towards them.

Tapping Daniel on the shoulder, Claudia said, 'Let's go.' She slid backwards on her belly before standing and running back the way they'd come. Reaching the abandoned motorbike and sidecar, she kick-started it as Daniel climbed on board.

Rat-a-tat-tat, a burst of automatic fire came towards them.

'Hang on,' Claudia shouted as the bike lurched from side to side as Claudia bumped it up the steps, retracing their steps. At the top, she turned left, heading out of town.

'What now?'

Humour gone from her voice, Claudia said, 'Stop asking that.'

Up ahead, Claudia could see where the laneway rejoined the main road. As an escape route, it wasn't ideal; however, she had no other choice. When the Volvo turned towards them, an assault weapon pointing from its passenger side window, Claudia sighed in frustration.

'Stand up and jump when I tell you.'

'What?'

'You heard me - don't forget to roll when you hit the ground.'

Gingerly, Daniel wobbled to his feet, bracing himself by putting his hand on Claudia's shoulder. The two vehicles raced head-on towards each other.

Panicking, Daniel thought, *there's no way this will work. I'll die hitting the ground at this speed.*

Claudia eased back on the throttle and yelled, 'Now!'

'Now?' Daniel repeated in alarm; his feet welded to the spot.

'It's do or die, Daniel. The choice is yours!'

Claudia eased the speed further, and Daniel leapt. With his weight gone, she opened up the throttle before abandoning the motorbike and sidecar herself, launching it like a guided missile towards the Volvo. Claudia was pleased to be wearing the motorbike helmet when her head struck the road as she rolled, trying to wash off speed. Claudia came to a halt as the bike hit the SUV, but the impact was not as dramatic as she'd hoped. After the collision, the Volvo, now at walking pace, continued towards her. Claudia opened fire, putting three shots into the windscreen near where the driver would be. The vehicle stopped in its tracks as Claudia turned, in agony from the fall, and started hobbling up the lane toward Daniel, who, seeing her struggling, rushed towards her, his limp gone. After placing his arm under her shoulder for support, he led her up the road. He stole a glance behind to see both men, one hobbling badly, walking up the road after them. When they saw Daniel look, they smiled, one of them calling, 'You're dead!'

'I've had enough of this,' Claudia said with resolve. 'Down here.'

They turned into another pedestrian alleyway, running between the buildings. As they entered, she stopped and, from an inside jacket pocket, removed a tube of P.E.4. plastic explosives with a detonator. Sticking to the side of the building she said, 'Go!' Unaided by Daniel, Claudia moved down the laneway and turned, raising her hands in surrender, pistol in one hand, remote control hidden in the other. 'Get behind me,' she said to Daniel while shuffling backwards, trying to increase the distance between them and the explosives before the men came round the corner. As they appeared, they levelled their weapons at her.

The man with the leg injury called, 'Put your weapon down. Our beef is not with you, Claudia. If you hand him over, you're free to go.'

'Okay. I'll put my gun on the ground.' Keeping the remote concealed, Claudia bent her knees and placed the pistol on the ground in front of her before saying, 'I'll get him for you.' The mercenaries nodded. Claudia turned and faced Daniel, yelling, 'Come here.' With her back towards the men, she triggered the device.

BOOM!

The explosion sent dust and debris flying, killing their assailants instantly. Traumatised, Daniel faced Claudia as she brushed the dust caused by the blast from his clothes. She stood back, inspected her handy work and said, 'That's better. You look neat and tidy. Shall we go?' Claudia started walking, the pain in her leg easing back up the alleyway towards the rubble of the explosion.

Falling in behind her, Daniel asked shakily, 'How?'

'There's a nice Volvo parked around the corner. I hear it's only been driven to church on Sundays. You drive because I need to talk with Stephen.'

'How can you be so calm?'

'You asked me that before, and the answer is still the same. It's what I do.'

Ignoring the gathering crowd of people drawn to the commotion, Claudia and Daniel climbed into the damaged Volvo and drove out of town. Claudia tapped Stephen's number into her phone.

'Stephen, it's Claudia.'

'I know who it is,' Stephen said, his voice terse, 'You're alive then?'

'Thanks for the concern, Stephen. You must know we've experienced trouble?'

'We didn't need a spy satellite to tell us, that's for sure! All we needed was a social media account and then, along with everybody else on this planet, simply follow the reports of explosions and gunfire coming from across the Canary Islands. The Minister isn't pleased and the Spanish Government is after our blood. You even set off plastic explosives in the middle of a town!' Stephen paused before saying, his voice drooling sarcasm, 'Is there anything left of our house?'

Annoyed, Claudia responded, 'You haven't asked me about Saint Vladimir.'

'Oh, I'm sure he's fine, or you wouldn't sound so chirpy.' The phone went quiet and when Stephen spoke again, the tone of his voice had changed. Sounding pleasant, Stephen said. 'Right Claudia, as instructed, I've read you the riot act and now with that out of the way. Well done. It must have been difficult?'

Claudia shook her head in disbelief.

What just happened? You British are a weird lot.

Gathering her thoughts, Claudia said, 'MI6 leaked. They knew exactly where I was.' When Stephen didn't reply, she sighed and continued, 'What are the arrangements for Saint Vladimir? Is he to be evacuated to the UK?'

'We have a submarine stationed off the east coast waiting for you under the cover of darkness. Do you know The Triton? A large bronze sculpture of a Greek God?'

'Yes.'

'Breakwater and a sandy beach can be found at the northern end of the car park. That's where the Royal Navy will land at nine o'clock tonight to retrieve him. Will you be safe until then?'

'Yes, the fight here is over.'

'Good. The submarine is for Daniel alone. You are to find your own way back.'

'Okay. What are you going to tell the Spanish Government?'

That it was their fault, of course. We will say our intelligence sources suggest that the turmoil on the island stems from a power struggle within a violent faction known as the 'Fourth Mafia.' This unrest is a direct consequence of the vacuum created by the recent arrest of its leader in San Bartolomé de Tirajana, part of the Italian police's anti-mafia operation "Neve di Marzo" on the Canary Islands.'

'I like that,' Claudia said, 'but that happened last November.'

'You know how these crime syndicates operate, Claudia. It takes a while for the internal feuds to boil to the surface.'

'If you don't mind Stephen, after all the excitement here, and the death of John, I'd like to take a week's holiday in Barcelona on the way back to the UK.'

Stephen thought for a moment before saying, 'Time off is a good idea, but a word of caution. Soon, we are expecting Spain to introduce emergency COVID-19 measures and close its borders. They're planning to put their citizens in lockdown because infections are doubling every four days. Yesterday, over one thousand people in Italy died of the virus. Spain is trending in the same direction.'

'Are you suggesting that I might find myself stuck when the UK closes its borders?'

'At this moment, Britain is considering Sweden's herd immunity strategy, so our borders will remain open.'

'Herd immunity? Will that work?' Claudia asked.

'From China, South Korea, Singapore, Taiwan, New Zealand and Australia, to name a few, we know what does work. The growth curve needs to be flattened; reduce the effective transmission rate below one. They're achieving it through mass testing, tracking, and social distancing measures, ordering citizens to stay at home, a lockdown in other words. I predict that our failure to learn from other countries will be one of the biggest disasters of our lifetime. The gravity of the situation is crystal clear; the government here is failing to act, and the impact on the economy will be severe, like nothing we've seen since the 1929-33 Great Depression. Some countries argue that the economic impact of locking down an economy is a greater catastrophe than the number of people who will die. Only time will tell, but I think those nations who limit the spread of the COVID-19 will emerge from the crisis in better shape.'

'I didn't realise the situation was so dire. What sort of fatalities are we suggesting? Is this like the 1919 Spanish Flu pandemic which, from memory, infected a third of the world's population and killed at least fifty million people?'

Stephen took a deep breath. 'Our modelling for the UK suggests that if we keep doing what we are currently doing, fifty to sixty thousand will be dead.' Stephen hesitated. 'I've just emailed the last page of a report that was prepared for the Government by our health boffins.'

Claudia's phone beeped, as she thought, *you are taking this all rather seriously, Stephen.*

The virus follows a predictable algorithm—R0, the replication number, a measure of how many others a COVID-19 sufferer might infect. Scientists suggest it is between 2 and 6 – a wide range because of uncertainty as it's a novel virus. As a comparison, the related SARS virus has an R0 value of 1 and measles between 12 and 18. So, COVID-19 is quite infectious, more so than SARS, Ebola and Influenza but less so than Measles, Chickenpox and Mumps. From experience abroad, we can extrapolate the rate of Coronavirus deaths

Having read the message, yet not fully understood it, Claudia said, 'Enlightening Stephen, I wonder, however, if fifty to sixty thousand is such a high number if it gives us that herd immunity?'

'Fifty thousand in the first six weeks, Claudia. These are unthinkable numbers in our modern age. Our projections for the USA, who like the UK have a low testing rate, are over two hundred thousand dead within six months. Unless something changes, a vaccine, better treatments or government policy, this is only the beginni ...'

Claudia interrupted, '... but, if there is no vaccine–a distinct possibility-then a herd immunity approach would be the right one, yes?'

'That may very well be true, Claudia, but my question is, is it the right first option to accept some in your country are expendable? We know so little about the virus, whether there is a post-infection immunity and how long it lasts, for example. Our approach smacks of complacency.' Claudia remained silent, so Stephen continued, 'Early reports out of China suggest that the virus is disproportionately killing those over sixty-five with pre-existing medical conditions. It also seems to prefer men. Of those going into an ICU bed with COVID-19, the odds of coming out alive are worse than the toss of a coin.'

With a playful lilt in her voice, Claudia remarked, 'Perhaps it's a conspiracy by Millennials to wipe out their parents before they can spend their inheritance.' Stephen made a noise, akin to a reluctant laugh as Claudia continued, her tone now sombre, 'Why is a spy agency so interested in what is predominantly a health matter?'

'Foreign adversaries are behind disinformation campaigns on social media, blaming the spread of COVID-19 on 5G Network towers and even accusing Bill Gates of wanting to use a Coronavirus vaccine to microchip the population. They aim to stoke civil unrest, unsettle the economies of the West. It wouldn't take much in this anxious climate for protests to break out infiltrated by extremist groups, further inflamed by foreign agents. We could see violence spread, undermining our Western Democracies. That is very much a Security Service issue. If we experience the most significant contraction in national output and income since the Great Depression, well, we all remember what happened next: WW11. MI6, the Foreign Intelligence Service, is very interested in COVID-19. This pandemic is not only a serious and imminent threat to public health but also our national security. As a country, it's the biggest threat we have faced in a generation.'

CHAPTER 14
Montserrat Spain

Barcelona Spain

Richard Liew looked at his watch excitedly, calling to his family, 'Come along everyone, or we will be late.'

Samantha Liew glanced at Molly, their seven-year-old daughter, while packing her bag and said, 'How will we find the guide when we don't know what she looks like?'

'Roxanna told us to stand next to the Venetian Towers. That's the popular name for a pair of towers on Avinguda de la Reina Maria Cristina at its junction with Plaça d'Espanya. She wrote that there are two towers on either side of the street and that we are to stand next to the West one, near the Fundació Fòrum Ambiental. She promised we couldn't miss it; besides, I have her phone number.'

'Hold my hand Molly,' Samantha said, as they left their hotel, the Ayre Hotel Gran Via, before looking at Richard and asking, 'How far is it?'

'Honey, I chose this hotel because it's just around the corner from the meeting place. As it turned out, it was a wise choice, for Roxanna wanted to begin our tour of Montserrat earlier than planned.'

With a thrill in her voice, Molly said, pointing at two forty-seven-metre-high structures, 'Is that it?'

Richard Liew chuckled. 'I told you we were close.'

Samantha nodded. 'I can see a pedestrian crossing. Do we need to cross the road?'

Richard Liew's smile broadened. 'Not only did I choose a hotel close by, but it's also on the west side. No, we don't need to cross.'

Samantha, knowing the right thing to say, said, 'Molly, aren't we lucky to have such a clever daddy?'

Richard Liew swaggered on, absolutely in his conviction that his wife's assessment was accurate. Ahead was a woman, in her early thirties, he estimated, wearing a pink day pack, waving as she walked towards them.

'Hello, I'm Roxanna. Are you the Liew family for the trip to Montserrat?'

'Yes,' answered Molly eagerly.

'That's wonderful. Speaking directly to Richard Liew and Samantha, Roxanna continued, 'Thank you for agreeing to the change of time at such short notice. We tourist guides hear that the government's COVID-19 containment plan may force the closure of public attractions as early as this afternoon. I feared that if we didn't get up there first thing this morning, you would miss out.'

Samantha smiled, saying, 'Thank you, Roxanna, for thinking of us.'

'Yes, thank you,' Richard said, staring at Roxanna. Her hair was tucked under a blue wide-brimmed hat and with round tortoise sun glasses both partially hiding her features. She looked nothing like the woman he'd seen on the website. Regardless, he found her vaguely familiar.

Roxanna, seeing Richard looking questioningly at her, said, 'Are you ready to go?'

'I think we are,' Richard answered, before adding, 'You look different from the picture on your website'

'Oh, I'm so sorry. In all the excitement, the rush not to miss Montserrat before it closes, I neglected to say that, for safety reasons, we female tourist guides don't place our actual likenesses on the web booking site. Male guides don't have to worry about such things, but we women have to be careful that the wrong type of man doesn't choose a guide for her appearance. I hope you understand my meaning.'

Richard Liew dropped his head slightly. 'That makes absolute sense. Please excuse me for asking.'

'Not at all. I fully understand. Now, we have an amazing morning planned. I can assure you; you will see places at Montserrat and have experiences that most tourists don't. Will ...' Roxanna gestured towards Richard and Samantha's daughter, inquiring after her name.

'This is Molly, and I am Samantha.'

'Hello Samantha,' Roxanna said before facing Molly, a grin spreading across her face. 'Molly, that's a beautiful name.' Roxanna returned her focus to Richard and Samantha Liew continued, 'We'll be venturing into some tight, dark spaces. Do you think Molly will be alright?'

Molly, listening to the conversation between the adults, piped in, 'I'm not afraid, am I, daddy?'

'No, you're a big and brave girl.'

'Excellent. Are we ready?' Roxanna called, her voice full of excitement and before anyone could respond, she put her hand up in the air, saying as she strode forward, 'Follow me.'

Samantha fell in beside Roxanna with Richard following up behind, holding Molly's hand. As she walked, Roxanna spoke, 'The railway station, Plaça España, is huge with many surface entrances to the platforms which are below ground. Tourists who try to make the trip on their own to Montserrat often finding it confusing, made worse as each entrance has limited information about the lines accessible from it.' Roxanna stopped speaking and, peering behind, called to Richard and Molly, 'Come along, please keep up. You don't want to be left behind.' Looking at Samantha, she said, while increasing her stride, 'The best advice I can give you if you intend to take trips on your own is to ignore the line information displayed as you enter and use the nearest surface entrance. Once underground, look out for the sign for the track you want. Today, we want R5, which is right over there.'

'I see it,' Samantha said.

'That's good. Are your family still with us?'

Samantha glanced back and said, 'Yes.'

Roxanna raised her hand again. 'Come along, you two. We don't want to miss our train.'

Following Roxanna and Samantha onto the platform, breathless from their pace of walking, Richard Liew said, 'Is it always this quiet, the station, I mean?'

Roxanna looked about her before saying, 'No, this is very unusual. I think it's because of the Coronavirus crisis. If Montserrat is the same, you are in for an extraordinary visit because most days it's very crowded - Oh look, here comes our train now.'

The one hour and five-minute journey to Aeri de Montserrat passed quickly, and Samantha Liew was impressed at how Roxanna balanced engaging them in conversation with allowing them time to take in the scenery. As the train pulled into the station, Roxanna said, 'We are coming to my favourite part of the journey, the cable car from the bottom of Montserrat mountain to the monastery. You will be interested to know that it started running way back in 1930 and travels at a speed of 5 metres per second and a gradient of up to 45%.' Roxanna smiled as she added, 'That's my tourist guide bit said.'

'I'm interested,' replied Richard Liew.

'It's a boy thing,' Samantha added.

'For you then, Richard. We will travel 1,350 metres up the mountain.'

'I'm interested as well,' Molly said.

'A family conspiracy,' complained Samantha light-heartedly, a smile upon her face.

Like the Barcelona train station, Aeri de Montserrat was unusually quiet. As they were boarding the cable car, Roxanna observed, 'Your day just keeps getting better. We have the car to ourselves. Every other time I've been here, we have to share it with at least twenty other people and their guides.' As the suspended car left the station, Roxanna added, 'If you're not afraid of heights, the five-minute ride up the mountain is exhilarating. Putting my guide hat back on, I need to point out the River Llobregat, the village of

Monistrol, and the famous Santa Cova shrine commonly referred to as "The Holy Grotto". For those of religious persuasion, it's an important place of pilgrimage when visiting Montserrat. According to a legend, the image of the Mother of God was found at Santa Cova. It is told that, in 880, some shepherd children saw a light appear in the sky and, along with the illumination, a soulful song could be heard in the mountain. The children returned with their parents, and the vision appeared a second time, repeated for the four following Saturdays. News travelled swiftly, and the Bishop of Manresa visited the mountain. He and those accompanying him witnessed the image of the Virgin Mary in a cave. Since that time, the cave has been a site of worship. Oh, my ears just popped. Anyone else?'

'Me!' Molly said, raising her hand as the cable car arrived at the monastery.

'We're here,' Roxanna said, her tone triumphant, 'Follow me, we have a touch of climbing to do, some steps first, then it's inside.' Without stopping for a breath, she added, 'Most people wish to enter the basilica to see the Black Madonna, it's said to possess healing powers. Then the museum, which is in the same square as the basilica? I thought we would start by exploring the tunnels and hidden chambers below the monastery? Then we can do the touristy stuff, and I will give you some free time. Is that okay with you?'

'That sounds fine,' Richard Liew answered.

'Excellent, follow me,' Roxanna started heading up the steps, talking as if the family were beside her. Richard Liew heard her say something like, "Order of Saint Benedict", but didn't catch the rest. When they reached the top of the stairs, Roxanna was waiting, a torch in her hand taken from her backpack. 'This is your special day. Follow me and... do keep up.'

Inside, Roxanna led them through a series of corridors and down several flights of stairs and into a library where she said, her voice a whisper, 'Shush, follow me.' At the far end of the library, they arrived at an ornately carved wooden door. 'Close your eyes; you're not allowed to see a secret button that triggers the door. Tell me when they are closed.'

Molly was the first to say, 'My eyes are closed,' and Samantha and Richard followed.

'Okay, you can open them now.'

Looking inside, Richard Liew saw a stone corridor wide enough for two people leading to steps heading downwards.

Her voice still in a whisper, Roxanna explained what would happen inside. 'At the bottom of the stairs, we'll come to a corridor leading to another wooden door. As we pass through that, we step back in time, entering a complex built by the Romans and which pre-dates Christian times, and that's where our tour begins. You lead on Richard, and I'll close the door behind us. The stairs and corridor are well lit.'

At the bottom of the spiral staircase, Richard saw the door that Roxanna had mentioned. Molly in hand, he began walking towards it. Richard froze, and Molly screamed as the lights extinguished and the area fell into total darkness. It was pitch black, and he couldn't have seen his finger if he'd held it a centimetre from his eyes.

'Hello Sweeties', came a voice from behind as torchlight bathed the Liew family. They turned, unable to see the person holding it.

'Daddy, daddy,' Molly called in distress.

'It's alright, Molly. Everything is going to be fine.'

'Oh, Sweetie, if only that were true.'

'Richard, what's happening?' Samantha cried.

'Don't you know Sweetie? Your husband is an assassin and a Chinese spy. He kills people.'

'Richard?' Samantha said, fear decorating her voice.

'I thought you looked familiar at the station; I should have guessed you weren't Roxanna. What she said, Samantha isn't right. This woman can't be trusted.'

'Which part, Sweetie?'

Richard Liew remained silent before he said, 'What do you want, Claudia?'

Samantha gasped. 'You know her?'

'I promise you, Samantha, that I am not an assassin and I don't hurt people.'

'You're a spy!' Samantha's tone suggesting an assertion rather than a question.

'I work for the Chinese Ministry of State Security. I'm sorry, Samantha, but I'm not allowed to tell anyone, even you.'

'Oh, Richard,' Samantha said tearfully. 'What's happening to us?'

Claudia laughed, 'Sweetie, your husband killed a friend of mine, John Moss. Today is his judgement day. Your judgement day.'

'Let my family go. You have me.'

'Sweetie, how melodramatic of you.' As Claudia spoke, a red laser dot from a gun sight appeared on Molly's forehead. 'Lead on Macduff, through the door.'

'There's no need,' Richard pleaded.

'Sweetie, be on your best behaviour and Samantha and Molly may yet see daylight. I won't ask again. Lead on.'

Once the Liew family turned away from the torch, it lit the path in front of them. Reaching the door, Richard Liew opened it and went through. As he did, he contemplated taking a risk and attempting to disarm Claudia, but decided against it. Her reputation went before her; Claudia wouldn't hesitate to maim his family, or worse. He understood he was in for a slow and agonising death; somehow, he had to stop her.

'Sweetie, wait there. Now, turn to the left and take three paces. Excellent.'

With the light once more behind them, Richard Liew spotted the steel doors of a prison cell.

'The door is open, Sweetie. Now in you go!'

They complied with the instructions, and the beam of the torchlight revealed three chairs in the corner of the cell.

'Over there, Sweeties. Excellent, now sit.'

Facing the light again, Richard Liew noticed the red laser dot centred on his daughter's chest and he pleaded, 'I didn't kill John Moss.'

'No, Sweetie and I doubt you planted the bomb either, but you're as guilty by association as the person who did.'

'You don't understand, Claudia. The Ministry of State Security didn't kill John Moss. It wasn't us.'

'Sweetie, why didn't you say earlier? You can all go home.'

Samantha breathed a sigh of relief.

Richard placed a hand on her knee. 'She is being sarcastic.'

Samantha brushed his hand away, saying with malice, 'You've lied to us.'

Claudia said, laughing in a feigned evil manner, causing Molly to whimper, 'Tut, tut, tut. Sweeties, this is no time for family disputes.'

Samantha ran her hand through Molly's hair, saying, 'It's alright honey, everything will be alright.'

'Touching,' Claudia laughed. 'Richard Liew, if you would kindly stand up Sweetie. I have another cell for you.'

Samantha cried out, despair in her voice, 'No, no. Don't leave us.'

Claudia laughed again, evil dripping from her words, 'Sweeties, that was a quick family reconciliation.' Her tone turned harsh, and she commanded. 'I said, stand up Sweetie! I won't ask you again.' Richard Liew complied. 'Samantha, there is a light switch next to the door. I'll turn it on when I leave and, if your husband is cooperative, the lights will remain on. See, I am a reasonable psychopath.'

'What do you mean, cooperative?' Samantha asked.

'Sweetie, it's not wise to ask too many questions but, seeing you're not in the game, I will cut you some slack. Your husband wasn't the only person involved in John's death. I want to know how to find the others. Except for Wen Xu because I've already found him, haven't I Sweetie?'

Richard Liew stared straight into the torchlight as he said, 'If I tell you what you want, will you let them go?'

'Sweetie, let's talk about this in private. We don't want to scare your family. Now, move.'

Claudia backed out the cell door, keeping her pistol trained on Molly, then swapping it for Richard. When Richard had exited, Claudia spoke to Samantha. 'A guard is stationed outside, and there's no point in calling for help. I'm about to turn on the light, so you might want to close your eyes.'

Richard heard the door slam behind him and Claudia saying to someone, 'Put the bolt across when we are gone.'

A person he couldn't see, a man's voice replied, 'Yes, boss.'

Claudia isn't acting alone. MI6 is sanctioning this hit.

'Cover him,' Claudia said to the guard before saying to Richard Liew. 'I'm going to blindfold you. In the unlikely event of

your escape, we wouldn't want you finding your way back here...
too easily. Sweetie, I always say best to be safe than sorry.'

Except for the torchlight, the outside of the cell was in total
darkness. Richard Liew felt the blindfold slip over his eyes and a
strap was pulled tight behind his head. The thought of escape
entered his mind, but it seemed impossible, so he remained still.
Once the covering was in place, he heard the click as the lights were
switched on, a dim glow seeping through the blindfold.

'Sweetie, hands behind your back while I secure them with a
cable tie.'

He complied, after which he felt a hand slip under his arm
accompanied by Claudia's voice, which said, 'This way.' After a
short distance, he heard a door open and then shut behind them. He
was trying to map the route, memorising the steps he'd taken until
Claudia scuppered his plan.

'Sweetie, I'm going to spin you around to disorientate you. I
won't let you fall - well, not yet.'

Richard Liew felt her hands grip his shoulders before they
turned him around, slowly at first, then quickening the pace. As he
began to wobble towards the point of losing balance, the turning
stopped and the direction reversed. After a minute that seemed
longer to Richard Liew, he stopped again and felt Claudia's hands
holding him securely to prevent him from falling. She was silent for
a moment before she said, her hand slipping under his arms to guide
him, 'This way, Sweetie.'

Richard Liew estimated that they'd walked for ten minutes,
ascending and descending stone staircases, through four doors and
along a narrow stone-paved corridor where his footsteps echoed.

After going down another flight of stairs and through another door, Claudia said as she released his arm from her grip, 'Stop.' Richard heard Claudia take a couple of steps forward in front of him, followed by the sound of a door unlocking.

'Sweetie, I'm going to untie you and lead you into a cell and then, when you hear the door close, you may remove the blindfold.'

Richard Liew pleaded, 'I'll tell you whatever it is you want to know if you promise to let my family go.'

'I know you will, Sweetie.' Claudia let her statement hang in the air before adding, 'Do you know what happened when your friends captured me in Germany?'

Richard Liew was well aware of what occurred and debated denying it, then settling on the truth, said, his voice shallow, 'Yes.'

'Go on, Sweetie, tell me what happened.'

'The man you later killed in London, the one we call the dentist, Mr Yáyī. He was going to extract all your teeth without an anaesthetic.' Richard Liew dropped his head in shame as he continued, 'I don't agree with any of that.'

'It's a little late for that, don't you think?'

'You're going to torture me?'

'Sweetie, by the time I'm finished with you, even hell will seem like heaven. Sweetie, be a good boy and in you go.'

Claudia guided him forward from behind and, when her hands let go of his shoulders, he stopped and waited. She snipped the cable tie on his wrist before giving him a gentle push ahead. Standing still, Richard Liew heard a steel door close behind him with a loud thud, followed by a key being turned in the lock. He removed the blindfold, squinting. It took thirty seconds for his eyes to adjust to the light and to see that he was alone in a primitive cell. Turning, Richard checked that the peephole in the steel door was closed. Seeing that it was, he took out his mobile phone. 'Bugger!' he groaned when he discovered that there was no signal. 'That's why she didn't bother taking my cell phone from me.'

Miserable, Richard Liew sat on the bed occupying a corner of his jail. He let his face fall into his hands, and tears run freely. Five minutes later, wiping his eyes dry, he stood and started pacing the cell like a caged lion.

Think, Richard, think!

With no other means of escape possible and, in pure desperation, he tried the cell door.

It is unlocked! But I heard Claudia lock it?

Shrugging his shoulders, Richard Liew pushed the door fractionally open, listening for sounds of a guard. He knew that he would have one chance to escape.

What should I do? Try to find Samantha and Molly or look for phone reception and call for help?

While his heart said family, his head told him phone reception. Hearing nothing, Richard Liew prised open the prison door and stepped out. Taking stock, he reckoned he was deep underground in a medieval type dungeon used for holding prisoners, cells lining one side of the chamber. At both ends of the room were heavy wooden doors.

Which way should I go? Right, it's closer.

The heavy oak door with its steel ribbing creaked open, Richard Liew applying his shoulder to it to overcome its reluctance. On the far side was a vaulted chamber, a forest of columns, with a pool of water at its centre running off into the distance. Crude wiring for the electric lights which bathed the space with dull, soft light hung in loops along a jagged edged wall carved from solid rock. It was a dead end.

No, this is not the way I came in.

Not wishing to alert his captives to his escape, Richard Liew tried to close the door before making for the next exit. Its unwillingness to open only matched by its refusal to close, and he abandoned the task, leaving it ajar. Swiftly, without breaking into a run, Richard Liew rushed to the other exit, his chance of escape from the underground prison. The door opened easily and revealed a long passageway leading to a stone staircase heading upwards. Taking a deep breath, he darted down the corridor and climbed. When he reached a landing, Richard Liew had to make a quick decision: left along a narrow passageway or keep climbing.

I need a mobile signal. Keep going up.

As he climbed the next flight of stairs, he was met by the sound of voices coming down towards him. With his heart pounding in fear of capture, Richard Liew turned on the spot and retraced his steps to the landing, searching for somewhere to hide. Straining his eyes to see along the dimly lit passageway, he made out the outline of a door and what he hoped was an exit. With the voices and footsteps coming closer, Richard slipped off his shoes so his steps wouldn't make a sound as he sprinted towards the door. He made it in the nick of time and, as turned the handle to push on the opening, he glimpsed two people as they stepped off the bottom stair.

Monks! They could easily be MI6 agents in disguise.

The stakes were too high to risk calling for help, so he sneaked inside, leaving the door ajar, hoping to detect which direction the people went: down the stairs or towards him. The footsteps grew louder, as did the voices. They were coming Richard's way. As carefully as he could, Richard Liew pressed the door shut. Turning, he found he was inside an imposing Christian chapel, stone columns supporting decoratively carved arches which morphed into the ceiling. Level with the height of the arches and running the length of the chapel on either side were vaulted ornate stone windows through which rays of sunlight were entering to bathe the space in a golden glow.

I'm nearly out!

The chapel was too vast for him to hide before the monks entered, and his only hope was they were indeed men of religion, not secret agents. Richard Liew stood back and waited for the door to open, ready to accept his fate. After a minute, when nobody showed, Richard Liew breathed a heavy sigh of relief. Taking his phone from his pocket, he keyed the number of the Minister of State Security.

Damn, still no reception.

Stubbing his toe on the uneven paving of the chapel floor, Richard Liew let out an unwelcome shriek of pain. He shook his head in disbelief, followed by a wry smile.

I forgot to put on my shoes. Best fix that.

Grasping his mobile phone in one hand, Richard Liew cracked open the chapel door, listening before poking his head out to check that the coast was clear. He tentatively walked towards a stone staircase, increasing his speed with each step, until he reached the bottom stair. Abandoning his stealth, Richard ran upwards towards the surface. At the top, he found himself in a grand open space adorned by stone carvings, sculptures, and an arched door he knew led to the outside. Once through, he rechecked his phone signal. Five bars. Richard Liew, in hurried resolve, keyed the emergency contact number for the Chinese Ministry for State Security, for agents in trouble. After three rings, the phone answered.

'State Security. How can we help?'

'Code, Red Dragon. I need to speak with Chen Li.'

'Hold the line.'

Richard Liew knew that, as he waited, his whereabouts were being traced and measures were being put in place to respond to his call.

'Chen Li?'

Unsure of how long he had before his escape was noticed, Richard Liew spoke succinctly, 'This is Richard Liew. Claudia, an MI6 agent, has kidnapped my family and me. She is not acting alone. Claudia plans to kill us.'

'Slow down, Richard. Where are you?'

Montserrat Abbey Spain. Near Barcelona.

'How many of them?'

'I don't know, at least one other.'

'Are you safe?'

'I'm free, but Samantha and Molly are still captive somewhere below the monastery.'

'Okay, Richard, I want you to listen to me carefully. You need to get away from there and wait for us to arrive. We'll send a team to rescue Molly and Samantha.'

'But?'

'Richard, you will be of no benefit to us if you are being held captive.'

'Don't turn around, Sweetie.'

Richard Liew froze.

'Are you still there?' Chen Li asked.

'You have two the count of three to drop the phone, otherwise Molly is dead, one, two,...'

The phone dropped from Richard Liew's hand and onto the ground.

'Delicious, Sweetie. Now smash it with your foot.'

Richard Liew hesitated.

'I won't ask you again, Sweetie.'

Richard Liew placed his foot on the cell phone and ground it with his heel, accompanied by the sound of breaking glass.

'Turn around.'

Seething, Richard Liew turned and said, 'You won't get away with this, help is on its...'

He stopped mid-sentence.

CHAPTER 15
Isle of Lewis

'For the time being, Inspector, stay the course with your investigations into John Moss and the Crane. Let's see where it leads. What's your next step?'

'The assumption is that Charles Scott was murdered and, unless his killer came by submarine, it's near impossible to travel to and from a small island like Barra without being noticed. There were no signs of a struggle at the cottage, so it's likely Charles Scott knew his killer. My hunch is that he picked up his assassin from wherever he or she came ashore and transported them back to the cottage, or the assailant killed Charles Scott on the way to the cottage. If the murderer drove the car, someone would have seen them; travel by ferry or airline would have left passenger records and CCTV footage. A journey by small boat, light plane, or helicopter would have alerted the locals. Sir, with your permission, I would like to involve the Barra Island and Scottish police?'

'Under what guise?'

'I suggest we tell them the truth that this is a matter of national security. My cover as a detective from Scotland Yard won't cut it, not if I want their cooperation and trust, particularly after my last visit to the island.'

'You know I don't like civilians being involved. Inevitably it goes pear-shaped.'

Inspector Axel remained silent, thinking, *It's a bit late for that, Stephen.*

After a brief pause, Stephen replied, 'Okay, and we need their resources, anyway. Is there anything else?'

'Yes, there is. If the assassin had travelled by aircraft, the plane would have flown below the radar. RAF Lossiemouth in Scotland operates five Wedgetail early warning and control aircraft, always one in the air, tracking and coordinating intercepts of Russian bombers heading towards British airspace. They would have seen a low-flying aircraft, though it would be of little interest to them. I've asked them but was politely told to go away. You might be more fortunate.'

Stephen stared at Inspector Axel while he mulled over the request and then said, 'I'll see what I can do.'

Inspector Axel nodded as he said, 'I don't like coincidences, Sir, so I think, after what you have said, I would like to nose around H1 Technologies.'

Stephen hesitated before speaking, his instinct screaming that H1 Technologies was off-limits. Inspector Axel could see his reluctance. After a moment, Stephen sighed and said,

'Inspector, you need to tread carefully in your inquiries into H1 Technologies. With the increasing unpredictability of US foreign policy, Britain is eager to strengthen its defence ties with Commonwealth countries like India. The government is at a critical juncture, seeking to identify mutual defence and security opportunities. The UK Defence Minister is poised to announce the signing of a Memorandum of Understanding between the UK and India.' He will say,' *"it underpins the collaboration between our two nations, building on our defence ties, and ensuring our nations can combat emerging threats for generations to come."*

'Economics and defence, are inseparable, Inspector, they go hand in hand. H1 Technologies has connections that reach to the top of Indian leadership. The defence agreement and the 5G discussions are at a critical stage; step on the wrong toes and I might not be able to protect you. Do we understand each other, Inspector?'

'Yes.'

Stephen softened his tone as he said, 'Keep this contained, Axel. These are all politically sensitive issues.'

'As you wish, Sir.' Inspector Axel rose and turned to leave.

'Inspector. After what happened on Barra Island, I shouldn't need to remind you to be careful.'

Inverness, Scotland, UK

Chief Superintendent Macdonald, Commander for the Highland and Island Division, the most northerly police division in the United Kingdom, covering an area the size of Belgium, didn't ask Inspector Axel for an apology. Instead, he reminded him that, as part of the Counter Terrorism network, the Scottish Police worked alongside MI5 and other intelligence partners.

'In hindsight, Sir,' Inspector Axel said, 'I should have let Area Command know I was visiting Barra Island, which is why MI6 would like to work in partnership to establish what happened to Charles Scott and who brought the biological toxin A-232 or Novichok-5, to the island and into the UK.'

'I see. I take it that Charles Scott is of interest in affairs outside of the United Kingdom, or is that a matter of "need to know"?'

Inspector Axel knew Chief Superintendent Macdonald was fishing to see the breadth of his agency's cooperation and that his answer would flavour the nature of the working relationship. 'To be honest, Superintendent, we are not sure. He's linked to the murder of John Moss earlier this year in Pi-Ski, Cornwall, and did work for an Indian company based in London called H1 Technologies. The British Government is in secret negotiations with H1 to provide the UK with 5G network equipment, the high-speed backbone for the age of artificial intelligence, and this would be at the expense of the controversial Huawei, the Chinese super global information and communications technology company. I'm sure you're aware of the political sensitivities concerning Huawei. If I knew anymore, I would share it with you, Sir. There will be no "need to know" between us.'

'Thank you, Inspector. That raises my confidence. Are you working on the assumption that there is a connection between H1 Technologies and the other incidents you were telling me about?'

'I am foremost, a police officer, Sir, and I approach evidence through the lens of a detective, not a spy. When I inquire about the motive, I mean to ask who would benefit from an escalation of tension between the UK and China. Here, H1 Technologies emerge as a clear winner; they stand to profit significantly. Considering the intelligence agencies advise the UK government on the security risks posed by Huawei's involvement in the 5G network, the motive for H1 Technologies becomes all the more compelling.'

'We live in turbulent times, Inspector. May I return our discussions to the involvement with the Scottish Police? The Highland and Island Division has six territorial command areas, each with its own dedicated Area Commander. Chief Inspector Fiona Page, based at Stornoway Police Station on the Isle of Lewis, is the Area Commander for the Western Isles Division of which Barra Island is a part. We've hired a school hall in Stornoway to act as the command centre, and the investigation is to be headed by Detective Sally Mars. She will meet your flight at the Isle of Lewis airport this afternoon. Will you be staying with us for the duration?'

'No, I'll spend three days there and then leave the police work for your staff. I will investigate H1 Technologies and hope to secure an appointment with its CEO Azim Singh at his London office.'

'I see.'

The official meeting between Chief Superintendent Macdonald and Inspector Axel was over. As Inspector Axel was about to leave the Chief Superintendent's office, Macdonald said, 'If you prefer Inspector Axel, you can take the Ferry from the Ullapool Terminal to reach the Isle. It's a two-hour, thirty-minute trip and a unique experience.'

With the memory of his last ferry crossing fresh in his mind, Inspector Axel replied, 'Thank you, Chief Superintendent; I will save the experience for another time. I think that, under the circumstances, the forty-minute flight will have to suffice.'

***

Isle of Lewis

As Inspector Axel hoped, the flight from Inverness to the Isle of Lewis was more comfortable than the Barra Island ferry crossing. Detective Sally Mars was waiting at the airport when he arrived, and it wasn't until she appeared he realised he had an unconscious belief of what she would look like–and how wrong he was. What Inspector Axel hadn't expected was a woman closer to seventy than sixty and scrawny. Even hidden beneath her red puffer jacket, worn to insulate against the cold and wind, he could see her slight frame, what some people would describe as a match stick build. Unlike other older women Inspector Axel knew, Detective Mars' hair was its natural grey colour; and with its subtle layering and a slight wave, it was clear she wore her collarbone length hair in celebration of the ageing process. With a weathered face, wrinkles around her mouth, dark circles and puffiness under her eyes, Detective Mars' appearance spoke of a studied and distinguished woman, someone comfortable in their own skin. He found himself drawn to her the moment he saw her, reminiscent of a younger Olivia—or rather, how he imagined Olivia might have looked in her earlier years.

'Welcome Inspector,' Detective Mars said in a soft Scottish accent, unlike those he'd recently encountered and struggled to understand. 'I would shake your hand, but in these Coronavirus times, that's no longer appropriate. Instead, I offer you a slight bow of my head.'

'Yes, a bow of the head. I like that,' Inspector Axel replied, replicating the gesture, chuckling, 'It makes me feel like a medieval knight.'

'My car's this way, Inspector. Is this your first time on the Isle?'

'It is.' Inspector Axel hesitated before adding, 'If you would excuse my ignorance, detective. Am I on the Isle of Lewis or Harris?'

Detective Mars laughed as she said, 'Lewis and Harris are the same, although they are often referred to separately. The top bit is Lewis, and the bottom bit Harris and most of us live at the top bit; because it's flatter. We're the largest island in the Outer Hebrides.'

A grin spread across Inspector's face as he said, 'The largest Island? Which one, Lewis or Harris?'

'Inspector, I can see that you and I are going to get on swimmingly.'

It was a ten-minute drive from the airport to Stornoway, the main town of the Western Isles and the capital of Lewis and Harris. Stornoway was formed within a natural harbour, flanked by rocky headlands, and was the location of the hall that would serve as the police command centre. When they arrived, workers were busy moving in furniture and members from the police IT department were setting up computers, photocopiers and the other resources needed during the investigation. Sally Mars led Inspector Axel through the building to her makeshift office, which was in a side room. After closing the door, she asked, 'What do you think?'

'You're doing a good job. How many detectives will be at your disposal?'

'Unlike the two hundred detectives tasked with tracking those responsible for the 2018 Novichok nerve agent attack on Sergei Skripal and his daughter, Yulia Skripal, we have a team of twenty. Given our very different environments, twenty will be sufficient. They will begin arriving tomorrow.'

'Have you given any thought to how you will approach the inquiry?' Inspector Axel asked, his brow furrowing slightly.

'Barra Island differs from the City of Salisbury where the Skripal attack took place. That's to our advantage as it is tough, near impossible, I'd say, to get onto or off Barra without being noticed. We will follow the same strategy we employed during the Skripal investigation, which identified two Russian nationals—Alexander Petrov and Ruslan Boshirov—as suspects. Our approach will involve sifting through countless hours of CCTV footage, scrutinizing plane and boat arrivals, and gathering many witness statements. In addition, we will tap into the joint law enforcement initiatives currently operating in Scotland, known as Kraken and Pegasus, praised for their advanced capabilities in crime and counter-terrorism efforts. Project Kraken looks at the maritime environment, working with key stakeholders and local communities to exchange information. It provides a mechanism for reporting unusual activity or behaviour at sea or in ports. The police have been working with the fishing and leisure boat communities to identify suspicious behaviours, like people giving evasive answers to common boating questions or attempting to avoid contact with others. The unusual presence of a vessel in isolated locations, small ports or harbours, movement late at night or early in the morning– that kind of thing. If our suspect came to Barra Island by boat, someone would have spotted them.'

'Project Pegasus, as the name implies, looks at suspicious airport and aviation behaviour. Police have been visiting non-designated airfields in Scotland to engage with landowners and pilots. We encourage them to be vigilant and notify police of anything suspicious–strange attempts to hire aircraft or use airstrips, aircraft landing at unusual locations, late at night or early in the morning. Not every plane and airstrip can be monitored twenty-four hours a day, and there are tens of thousands of light aircraft, helicopters, and microlights flying all the time. We rely upon the aviation and the local community to keep us informed. Again, if our suspect flew into Barra Island, someone would have seen them.'

Inspector Axel nodded. 'MI6 may assist your aviation inquires. We have asked for access to the military radar reports from the early-warning aircraft flying out of RAF Lossiemouth. If someone was flying at low altitude, they might have seen it.'

'Yes, that will prove useful.' Detective Mars agreed.

Inspector Axel smiled before adding, 'You do know, outside of the police, nobody else would have heard of Project Kraken and Project Pegasus.'

Detective Mars chuckled. 'I think, Inspector Axel, that you are overly generous. Most police officers will not have heard of the projects either. The names do sound impressive, don't they, as if we have our finger on the pulse? Chief Superintendent Macdonald suggested I mention them to you, which I have dutifully done. Now that's out of the way. Do you have a name for this operation?'

Inspector Axel thought for a moment before saying, 'Yes, "Operation Origami".'

'That sounds perfect. You have taken it from the paper cranes that I read about in your reports. Fitting. "Operation Origami" it is. Do you have any suspects in the frame already?'

Inspector Axel raised his hand to his chin, rubbing it as he thought, and then said, 'Not exactly. However, if Catherine Hepburn, Josephine Carter, Edith Kelly or the Reverend Charlotte Foster, all from Saint Mary's Church in Pi-Ski, were to come up during your enquiry, well, then I might. Their photographs and backgrounds were in the briefing papers you were sent.'

'I take it they are not known to the police or the intelligence community?'

'Harry Carter, Josephine Carter's husband, worked for the British foreign services. Not long after he retired, while on holiday in Italy with his wife Josephine, he died in suspicious circumstances, believed pushed from a lookout. Josephine Carter was a suspect in his murder, although there was no obvious motive. After his death, MI6 discovered he was a Russian spy.'

'Did she know her husband was a spy?'

'I don't know the answer to that,' Inspector Axel hesitated and then said, 'She is a bit of a conundrum. As far as we can tell, she's not connected to the intelligence community, but she appeared to know that Claudia was an MI6 agent. That's an anomaly. My gut tells me she knows the craft, but is unlikely to be behind any of this.'

'The craft?'

'Sorry Detective, it is short for spy craft, meaning she is a secret agent or has been one.'

'I see. I'm disappointed, Inspector, that you won't be staying with us. Can I take it MI6 will send a liaison officer?'

Inspector Axel gave Detective Mars a surprised look before sighing in frustration and saying, 'Please accept my apologies, Detective; you should have been informed. MI6 is sending three agents for the duration of your inquiries. They have been instructed that you are in charge of the operation and that they are to cooperate fully with the police. The agents will facilitate your access to the MI6 databases, as I expect that those responsible are likely known to us. If you experience,' Inspector Axel paused, 'How can I put this, obstacles, please call me immediately.'

'Thank you.' Detective Sally Mars glanced at her watch. 'If we are finished here, Inspector, you have an appointment at the Stornoway Police Station with Chief Inspector Fiona Page. As it's just down the road, I thought we could walk. Then, after your meeting, I'll drop you at your accommodation, which is also nearby, one advantage of island life. Nothing is ever far away.'

'A walk will be good. Have you always lived on Lewis?'

'No, I was born on the Shetland Islands, four hundred miles from here, north and a bit to the east. I always say the Shetland Islands, but that's the name for a group of about 100 islands. I'm from Scalloway, a coastal port on an isle called Mainland, the largest of the Shetland Islands. My father was a fisherman...' Detective Mars paused as memories filled her mind. 'I left over forty-five years ago. Oh, how time flies.

'Why did you leave?'

Detective Mars smiled. 'To attend university in London, which in those days was unusual. I joined the Metropolitan Police and eventually found my way back to Scotland, ending up in Glasgow and then here. I've been on Lewis for twenty years. Except for the occasional family visits, I have not returned to Shetland.'

'Are your parents still alive?'

'No, they're long gone.' Detective Mars paused before saying, 'This may sound weird, particularly coming from a woman in her late sixties. I'm pleased to have the opportunity to collaborate with the security services, especially MI6. Through my father, I feel a deep affinity for the agency.'

'Really?' Inspector Axel said in a tone of genuine interest. 'How so?'

'Like many children, I regret not showing a greater interest in my father's war history while he was alive. Now, as I try to understand his past, I find I'm unable to match his stories with accounts found on the internet. It's difficult, near impossible, to discern what are our family historical facts from fiction. I want to believe that what he told me was true, or at least as much as I can remember.' Detective Mars studied Inspector Axel's face, seeking clues to see if he was genuinely interested in what she was telling him or being polite.

'I had the same experience with my father,' Inspector Axel said. 'I'm fascinated; please go on.'

'My father, Frank, was a fisherman in Shetland before the war and, from all accounts, he was a bit of a rogue. It wouldn't surprise me if he were involved in illegal activities like smuggling booze into Norway. Norway, like America, had a period of prohibition. By the outbreak of war in 1939, many living in Shetland were on the brink of starvation. My mother and father often talked about the hardship. The war transformed Shetland with more than 20,000 servicemen flooding the islands, thrusting it into the twentieth century. Growing up, I recall from my father's stories that he worked for Section D. He told me that, on one of their trips to Norway, they robbed a bank before returning to Shetland. I must admit that it all sounds far-fetched. Always having a good head for letters and numbers, what stuck in my mind from those childhood days was his mention of ME7. I know that Section D of MI6, along with the SIS, the Secret

Intelligence Service, became the SOE, the Special Operations Executive in the Second World War, formed by Winston Churchill, the British Prime Minister, to work behind enemy lines. World War Two records are full of stories of the Shetland Bus or Shetland Gang. Have you heard of it?'

Inspector Axel shook his head. 'No.'

'The Shetland Islands are nearer Norway than Aberdeen. When Germany invaded Norway, numerous boats escaped across to Shetland. Many of these boats, with volunteer crews, were used in hundreds of missions to Norway, providing a lifeline for Norwegians fleeing Nazi oppression and a highway for British and Norwegian SOE agents and saboteurs. Because of the near-endless daylight during the summer months, the operations had to occur in the dark of winter, travelling without lights so as not to bring attention from the Germans while crossing the treacherous waters of the North Sea.'

'My father told me he was elected skipper to captain their boat. Over the last few years of trying to uncover my father's story, I've found no mention of him on the Honour Rolls and he hasn't a military record. The Shetland Bus and its crews have been well researched and documented, however Frank is not among them. What ME7 was, I simply have no idea. Still, I want to believe what I've known is true, which is why I feel an affinity with MI6. Perhaps it's a daughter's dream, but I sense he was involved in something important.'

Taking a breath, Inspector Axel said, 'What a wonderful story. I'm sure the truth is out there somewhere if only you knew where to look. It would be a mistake to assume that his story is fictional simply because a record does not exist or has since vanished. Our generation is the last direct link to that time in the past, and you're right to feel proud, and a connection to MI6. You'll have been to the national archives, right?'

'Oh, no, only Professor Google. I feel ME7 is our family's story, and maybe that's how it should remain.'

'Perhaps?' Inspector Axel said. He hesitated, contemplating for a moment, before continuing,

'I'll tell you what I could do with your permission. When I'm back in London, I will ask one of my elves to see if we have anything in the MI6 archives about ME7. Would that be okay with you?'

'Thank you, Inspector. You're a generous man, but I think I'm nervous, a smidgen frightened of the truth. Maybe my father is not the hero I've always believed him to be.'

'Or maybe he is? Look, if we were to find no record of ME7, that still wouldn't mean he wasn't involved in clandestine activities or was any less a hero. In my book, anyone who lived through those times is a hero. If we find nothing, you are neither better nor worse off than you are now.'

Detective Mars mulled over what Inspector Axel had said. 'Why not? Okay, that would be wonderful, thank you,' and, changing the subject, she added, 'Do you have plans for dinner tonight?'

CHAPTER 16
H1 Technologies

'Mr Singh will join you shortly,' the secretary said as she led Inspector Axel into the CEO's office. 'May I get you something, a coffee perhaps?'

'No, thank you.'

The secretary acknowledged Inspector Axel's answer with a nod before departing, leaving him alone inside Azim Singh's palatial office, occupying the top floor of a modern multi-storey building of concrete and glass. Facing him was Azim Singh's expertly crafted walnut desk, positioned in front of imposing floor to ceiling glass windows that extended the width of the office, offering uninterrupted views over London's financial quarter. Azim Singh's desk was cluttered, papers, manilla folders and books strewn about, a scene more akin to a scholarly university than the abode of the CEO of a leading communications company. The desk contrasted to the rest of the office, which was obsessively tidy. To Inspector Axel's left was a vintage bookcase, lining the wall and artfully organised, seemingly out of place in such a modern space. On the opposite side of the room, in front of an abstract painting which filled most of the wall, was a leather sofa accompanied by two matching chairs.

Inspector Axel, believing reading preferences are an eye into the character of a person, walked across to examine the contents of the bookcase and running his finger along the spines, read some titles: The Time Machine by H. G. Wells, Brave New World by Aldous Huxley, A Journey to the Centre of the Earth by Jules Verne, Douglas Adams, The Hitchhiker's Guide to the Galaxy, plus one's he hadn't heard of: Road Picnic/Tale of the Troika by Boris and Arkady Strugatshy, and Genesis of the Daleks by Terrance Dicks.

Azim Singh is a man with a passion for science fiction. It's not surprising, considering many of these stories predict an avalanche of future technologies. Much of what we have today was once nothing more than the figment of these authors' imaginations.

Inspector Axel turned towards Azim Singh's desk. His personal computer was at its centre, partially buried in a pile of papers. Axel exhaled loudly and his heart sped up, blood pounding in his ears, as he considered opening Azim Singh's computer to examine his files and messages. In the movies, seemingly without fear or trepidation, a spy left alone in a target's office hacks into the villain's computer to copy incriminating evidence onto a memory stick.

That's Hollywood, and this is real life.

Inspector Axel glanced towards the office door before moving to stand behind Azim Singh's desk, facing the window under the pretence of admiring the view. He waited a moment and, when no one entered, manoeuvred himself so that he was standing behind Azim Singh's office chair, inches away from the computer. In anticipation of turning around and touching the keyboard, his stomach knotted; he was an ordinary policeman, unaccustomed to behaving like a spy.

Just do it. Claudia would.

Inspector Axel swivelled to face the desk and, as he did, the office door swung open. Azim Singh, accompanied by a woman, walked in. They hesitated when they saw where Inspector Axel was standing. Slipping his hands into his suit trouser pockets, Inspector Axel said, 'I was admiring the view. You have quite a vista.'

He glanced over his shoulder and out the window as he spoke. If they believed his story, Inspector Axel couldn't tell, but Azim Singh's response was friendly as he extended his hand and said, 'Inspector Axel, this is an unexpected pleasure. It's not often we have a visit from MI6,' chuckling as he added, 'Knowingly, at least.'

For a moment, Inspector Axel worried about the social distancing protocols, but dismissed it and came out from behind the desk to grip Azim Singh's hand firmly. 'It's a pleasure to meet you, Sir.' Turning to the woman, Inspector Axel extended his hand and added, 'Inspector Axel.'

The woman dropped her hand to her side in rebuttal to his approach, and Inspector Axel withdrew the offered hand, bowing his head instead, but the woman remained unmoved. He proffered a smile while she held him in her gaze, a hunter staring down its prey.

'You must excuse Miss Adele,' Azim Singh said. 'She is taking this Coronavirus thing seriously. Possibly we all should.' Gesturing towards the couch and chairs, he continued, 'Please take a seat. I believe you were offered a drink?'

'Yes, thank you I was, and I'm still fine.'

Azim Singh appeared younger in person than he had from the pictures seen by the Inspector in the MI6 dossiers which he'd read before his visit. They told him that Azim Singh was an Indian technology entrepreneur and businessman who founded H1 Technologies in 1998. He was a millionaire by the age of twenty-three and now a self-made billionaire with an estimated net worth of forty-billion US dollars. Azim Singh, in an MI6 report, was described as having a rare combination of intelligence, grit, and scorn. A maverick, risk-taker, and international influencer, Azim Singh boasts personal connections to the highest echelons of both Indian and UK politics. According to the file, he was a key figure through whom the British government could bolster relations with India, particularly in trade and defence. Tucked away at the bottom of the report was a nota bene (NB), meant to catch the reader's attention yet subtly concealed: "Azim Singh is prone to mood swings and unpredictable behaviour." Inspector Axel suspected this warning had been intentionally downplayed.

'Now, how might I be of assistance to the British Intelligence Service?'

'Sir, I believe when the arrangements for this meeting were made, they told you we are looking into the disappearance of one of your staff, a person by the name of Charles Scott.'

'Inspector, please call me Azim. I don't hold with the old colonial use of "Sir".'

Inspector Axel smiled in acknowledgement as he said, 'Thank you.'

'As we have thousands of staff based throughout the world, Inspector, I'm sure you appreciate I don't know them all personally, which is why I asked Miss Adele to join us.'

An interesting paradox. Azim Singh doesn't like the formality of titles, yet refers to Adele as Miss Adele. I wonder why? Perhaps it matches the contradictions I observe in his office.

Inspector Axel looked towards Adele as she removed a manila folder from her brown leather document case. She said, her voice chilly, 'I hope you understand Inspector, we can't give you access to our computer systems. What I've done instead is to print Charles Scott's HR file.' Adele passed the enclosed document to Inspector Axel and continued, 'As you will see, Charles Scott retired from H1 Technologies some time ago. I'm not sure how we can assist you.'

Azim Singh crossed his legs and, while straightening his tie, said, 'Do all missing person cases attract the attention of British Intelligence?'

'Not at all, Mr Singh. Charles Scott's disappearance came to our attention through another matter which coincided with our monitoring of the sensitive negotiations occurring between our government and foreign entities surrounding the 5G network. H1 Technologies being one of these. As he is an employee of yours...'

Adele interrupted Inspector Axel, 'Ex-employee.'

'Yes, a retired employee,' Inspector Axel said, staring at Adele, 'We want to rule out any connection. I wonder if you can help me with something? We examined Charles Scott's internet service provider's traffic data records, and it appears he was communicating regularly with H1 Technologies via email. I wonder why that might be?'

Adele shrugged her shoulders as she said, 'Perhaps he still has friends here. If you have seen his correspondence, doesn't that tell you?'

Inspector Axel ignored Adele's question; she would know that the emails were encrypted, and possibly that his computer was professionally wiped. In a voice intending to portray his confusion, Inspector Axel asked, 'The other thing I'm struggling to understand is why a retired employee would have access to your internal computer systems?'

Azim Singh interrupted, 'This is alarming, Inspector. Are you telling us you suspect Charles Scott was hacking into our company systems, trying to steal our secrets, perhaps? I'm grateful that MI6 is bringing this serious security breach to our attention, particularly during this time of sensitive negotiations with your government.'

Inspector Axel put his hand to his chin, as if considering his response, yet signalling that he was unmoved by Azim Singh's answer. He said, 'That would explain it; I suppose, industrial espionage.'

A momentary look of displeasure flashed across Azim Singh's face, quickly replaced by a warm smile, as he said. 'Inspector, this evening at my Oxford estate, I will be hosting the Indian Defence Minister, the Honourable Kumar Surest, the Indian Ambassador, along with several British senior government officials and influential business leaders. If you have no other plans, I would like to extend a warm invitation to you. Miss Adele will ensure all the necessary arrangements are made.'

Adele, with a movement of her head, acknowledged the instructions.

'Inspector,' Azim Singh continued, 'where should we send your invitation? To the MI6 office or to the place where you are staying while in London?'

'To the St Ermin's Hotel in Westminster.'

Azim Singh nodded, then glanced at Adele before standing, indicating that it was time for Inspector Axel to leave. 'If you would excuse me, I am a busy man and have another appointment to attend. Perhaps we can continue our conversation this evening?'

When Inspector Axel had safely left the room, Azim Singh said, 'Miss Adele, take care of Inspector Axel, preferably make it look like an accident or a robbery gone wrong. Use your discretion, and nothing must lead back here. Do I make myself clear?'

Adele pursed her thin lips and made to leave the room. As she reached the door, Azim Singh called, 'Our x-ray revealed that he's not armed.'

Adele scoffed, 'Typically, British. I'm never sure whether it's their arrogance or whether they are fools. Regardless, it will make the task easier.'

'Don't fail me, Miss Adele.'

***

The St Ermin's Hotel concierge greeted the Inspector as he entered the building and added, holding out a decorative gold coloured envelope, 'This has arrived for you, Sir.'

The invitation. That was quick.

Deciding whether he should drive to the reception or take the train and stay in Oxford for the night, Inspector Axel glanced at his watch, a frown appearing on his face. The concierge, noticing the Inspector's dilemma, said, 'May I assist you, Sir?'

'Perhaps. I have a function to attend in Oxford tonight. I know that it's only ninety odd kilometres away. However, with the traffic and a late finish, I'm deliberating my best options.'

'If I may be so bold, Sir, I can recommend an excellent chauffeur and a superb hotel in Oxford. You could return by train in the morning when the time constraints are less pressing. If this is your desire, I can organise it for you, Sir?'

Inspector Axel reflected for a moment before saying, 'An excellent recommendation, thank you. If you would kindly make those arrangements for me, I would be grateful.'

Dressed in a tuxedo dinner suit and wearing a white shirt with a black bow tie, Inspector Axel, carrying an overnight case, went down to the St Ermin's Hotel lobby where his driver was awaiting.

'Good evening, Sir. My name is Sebastian, and it's my pleasure to be driving you to The Old Bank Hotel in Oxford, an excellent choice, and then on to the reception. If I may, Sir?' Sebastian reached towards the bag Inspector Axel was carrying and, taking it, said, 'If you would follow me, please.'

Inspector Axel was shown to a Silver BMW 7 Series Sedan parked in front of the St Ermin's Hotel. As a police officer, he was unaccustomed to staying in the lavish lodgings provided by MI6, let alone being chauffeured in a luxury vehicle. When Inspector Axel went to open the back door himself, the driver interceded, saying, 'If you would allow me, Sir,' opening the door for him. Then, before they began their journey, Sebastian went around to the boot of the car and retrieved a 200ml bottle of French Champagne, pouring it into a glass and giving it to Inspector Axel saying, 'It's all part of the service, Sir.'

The welcoming interior of the BMW, with its high-quality materials, comfort, fading light and the effects of the laced glass of bubbly, found Inspector Axel nodding off to sleep in the back seat. He was awoken with a THUD! when the car hit a large pothole before stopping. Gazing from the side window through his sleep-filled eyes, Inspector Axel made out buildings on a farming property, a couple of old sheds, horse stables and, out of the front windscreen, an old farmhouse. 'Where are we?' He asked, his voice slurred.

Sebastian switched off the BMW's engine and swivelled in the driver's seat to face Inspector Axel and pointing a gun said, 'I hope you enjoyed your sleep, Sir. Now if you wouldn't mind getting out!'

Inspector Axel lifted both hands in a sign of mock exasperation as he said, 'You will not open the door for me? My, my, the service appears to be deteriorating.'

Sebastian grinned. 'For a condemned man, Inspector Axel, you have an unusual sense of humour. Enjoy it while you can.' Sebastian opened the driver's side door and, as he alighted, beckoned with the barrel of the gun for Inspector Axel to do likewise. The Inspector reached towards the door and cracked it open before hesitating, waiting for Sebastian to take a step towards the rear of the car. With all of his strength, the Inspector flung the door open, smashing it into Sebastian. A crunching sound heard as the edge of the door frame shattered Sebastian's jaw and struck his forehead. In an instant, Inspector Axel leapt from the car and, reaching around the door, removed the pistol from Sebastian's grip. As the half-dazed Sebastian staggered backwards, Inspector Axel administered a karate chop across the side of his neck, knocking Sebastian to the ground.

'I hope you enjoy your sleep,' Inspector Axel said, a smile creeping across his face. Believing the encounter to be over, Inspector Axel moved towards the BMW, intending to drive away. As he reached for the driver's door, three shots rang out from the direction of the farmhouse, accompanied by the sound of footsteps running towards him. Abandoning the car, Inspector Axel rushed towards an old barn, and once inside, he heard someone say, 'You go round the back, and I'll take the front.'

Now what?

Inspector Axel assessed the options: In the middle of the barn, he made out the outline of an old tractor. *That could be useful*, he said to himself. On closer inspection, the keys were in the ignition. Fingers crossed, he starting it and switched on the powerful headlights which shone directly at the person approaching from the front. The man shielded his eyes. Engaging low gear, Inspector Axel jumped off the tractor, taking cover, as the machine began creeping forward.

BANG! BANG! BANG!

A volley of shots hit the tractor as it exited the shed. Keeping out of sight, Inspector Axel manoeuvred himself, hiding beside the barn door and pushing his back hard against the wall. His hand dislodged a shovel wedged there, and miraculously he caught it before it could fall to the ground with a loud clatter. Slipping the stolen pistol into the top of his trousers, Inspector Axel grasped the shovel handle with both of his hands. Holding his breath, he waited, and as the shadow of a man appeared at the barn entrance, he swung and struck the person with such force that it caused the shovel head to ring like a bell, accompanied by a thud as a body fell to the ground.

'Are you alright?' he heard a voice call out.

Inspector Axel opened his mouth to say something provocative, then thought better of it. Carefully, he leaned the shovel against the wall and retreated into the heart of the barn, where in the gloominess, he spotted stairs leading up to a mezzanine floor, a level that was difficult to see from the ground. Fearful of being shot, he inched his way across to the stairs and scrambled up the steps, cringing at the rhythmic pattern, a drumbeat, as his feet struck the rungs as he climbed. Reaching the top, he found that the level provided storage for an assortment of discarded machinery, and scraps of metal were scattered amongst bales of hay. Now concealed in his vantage point, Inspector Axel had a view of the dimly lit space below.

Where are you?

A shard of light appeared from the rear of the barn as someone opened a door and Inspector Axel saw the vague outline of a person entering. Taking out his pistol and holding it in both hands to steady his aim, he pointed it towards the shadow. The bright beam of a torch as it swept like a radar, scanning the space before it, temporarily blinded him, forcing Inspector Axel to duck for cover. After a couple of seconds, he raised his head again and watched as the barn periodically illuminated as the torch beam swept left and right in search of its prey. From his hiding spot, Inspector Axel had a clear view of his pursuer: a heavy-set man with a pistol in one hand and the torch, held away from his body, in the other. The light angled upwards and Inspector Axel, to avoid being seen, had to duck again. Wary of attracting attention to himself, Inspector Axel put away the pistol, deciding on a silent kill instead. Patiently, he waited for the beam to finish its sweep of the mezzanine floor before raising his head again. Feeling around him, he searched for something he could use, discovering a discarded bolt hidden amongst the layer of hay covering the floor. Grasping it, he waited for the man to be directly below before throwing it to the opposite side of the shed. It hit the ground with a clang and, as the torch beam swung, zeroing in on the sound, Inspector Axel shoved forward the bale of hay he was hiding behind. It fell from the mezzanine, landing squarely on the head of his pursuer and, as the man collapsed under its weight, Inspector Axel launched himself from the loft, using his assailant as a cushion to break his fall. Quickly recovering from the drop, Inspector Axel rolled to his feet, ready to take on the attacker, but the man remained motionless, knocked unconscious. Brushing himself down to remove the hay that had attached itself to his pristine tuxedo, Inspector Axel walked briskly towards the BMW. In the background, he heard the engine noise of the tractor he'd sent forth from the barn. It was close! Turning around, he saw the outline of the machine heading towards him. The headlights were off–he'd switched them on.

Bing!

Like a rabbit, he was caught in the beam of a spotlight as the powerful headlights awoke. Removing the pistol, Inspector Axel aimed at the approaching tractor then changed his mind because, without spare ammunition, shooting blindly at the looming machine was futile.

Now what? Run!

Wanting to draw the tractor away from the BMW, Inspector Axel's only escape route, he darted to the right, heading back towards the barn. The plan, to run straight through and out of the back door then double back to the car while the tractor was still in the shed, assuming the tractor would follow him. As if reading his mind, the tractor altered course to intercept him, causing Inspector Axel to skid to a halt and make an about-face. The tractor increased its speed and turned directly towards him, intent on running him over. Inspector Axel started sprinting, glancing over his shoulder as he fled, dashed towards the farmhouse. To his dismay, he realised the tractor had slowed, shepherding the Inspector towards what he imagined would be a trap.

The house is certain death.

While running, he scanned the environment for an alternative option.

There must be something I can do.

On his left, he saw a large oak tree.

I could use that as cover.

He darted behind the tree, and peeking out, he watched as the tractor stopped, blocking his path back to the car. Behind him, he heard the farmhouse door open. He was trapped.

You are running out of options, Inspector! Your only choice is up. Not a brilliant choice at all. Not at all.

He was about to climb the tree when he realised the tractor hadn't extinguished its headlights, meaning the people coming out of the farmhouse were looking straight into the beam, making him difficult to see, whereas, for him, they would be illuminated. His assailants had made a mistake, a fatal one. Turning, Inspector Axel spotted two heavily armed men running towards him. Aiming, he dropped them, one after the other.

BANG! BANG!

Immediately after shooting and out of sight of the tractor driver, Inspector Axel scampered up the tree and shimmied along an outstretched tree limb of the ancient oak which overhung the tractor. Gun in hand, he aimed downwards, intending to kill the driver, but the seat was empty. Mouthing an expletive, he edged his way back to the truck and, perched in his crow's nest, scanned the area.

Where are you? You must be here somewhere.

At the far end of the farmyard, beyond the BMW, a set of car headlights appeared and, rather than turning towards him, turned away. He watched as the taillights vanished into the distance. Guessing that the remaining man had fled, he climbed down from the tree and walked back to the seven series BMW. After checking that the remote-control key fob was in the car, the Inspector pushed the start button and continued his journey to his hotel in Oxford and then onto the reception.

***

Oxford Reception
Azim Singh was talking with the British Secretary of Defence, Sir William James Lovegrove, when he saw Inspector Axel arrive. 'If you would excuse me for a moment, Minister,' Azim said. 'I need to speak to someone.' Azim Singh glanced about for Adele and, when their eyes met, he showed with a discrete movement of his head that he wanted to speak with her.

His tone contemptuous, Azim Singh said to Adele, 'Do you see who's arrived?'

Replying with reticence, Adele said, 'Yes.'

I should have dealt with you, Inspector, when I had the chance, Azim Singh thought, before saying,

'You assured me, Miss Adele, that he had been taken care of!'

Adele scrunched up her face, showing her displeasure at the situation, before saying, 'I believed it to be so. The hired help isn't what it used to be. I will have to deal with this myself.'

'Not here, Miss Adele.' Azim Singh said and paused before continuing. 'The Inspector has seen us and is coming over. He is grinning like a Cheshire cat. Get him a glass of Champagne.'

'Inspector Axel, I'm so glad you could join us. We were worried when you were late.'

'Thank you.'

'I've asked Miss Adele to bring you a drink. Ah, here she comes now.'

In a sweet voice, contrasting her sour look, Adele said, 'Hello, Inspector. It's a pleasure to see you again. I've brought you a glass of bubbly.' She held it out towards him as he placed his hands in his pockets.

Inspector Axel replied, his eyes narrowing, 'That's most kind of you, Miss Adele, but I've found in recent times that Champagne makes me sleepy.'

Adele withdrew the glass, downed its contents in a single gulp and said, 'Pity, Inspector. You're missing one of the great pleasures in life.'

'Come, Inspector, we will leave Miss Adele to entertain my other guests,' Azim Singh said. 'Let me introduce you to the Secretary of Defence. Do you know Sir William Lovegrove?'

Inspector Axel opened his mouth but, before he could respond, Azim Singh began walking away, beckoning Axel to follow.

'Minister,' Azim Singh said. 'Do you know Inspector Axel from MI6?' Inspector Axel recognised the Minister from TV and newspapers but had not met him.

Sir William Lovegrove was angry, and it showed in his face as he said, 'MI6! The Home Secretary didn't inform me of your presence here.' He paused as a revelation struck him before continuing, 'Ah, of course, Inspector, please accept my apology. You must be here as part of our security arrangements; it is an international affair after all.'

Before Inspector Axel could reply, Azim Singh, feigning surprise, said, 'No, not security. You didn't send MI6 to scrutinise us, Minister. Inspector Axel came to my office today asking questions, an investigation of some sort. I assumed that sent him and therefore thought it prudent to invite him tonight. As a sign of goodwill and my company's openness.'

Inspector Axel saw the displeasure drift across Sir William's face as he said, 'My apologies to you. Mr Singh. The reception is a great night for both the British and Indian Governments. If there is a misunderstanding, I will rectify it the moment I return to Whitehall and speak to my colleague, the Home Secretary.'

Smiling at Inspector Axel, Azim Singh continued, 'Thank you, Minister. On another matter, I have spoken to the Honourable

Kumar Surest, the Indian Defence Minister, and he's agreed to meet with you for an informal chat in the drawing room. If you would kindly follow me, Sir, I'll take you to him.'

'Thank you, Mr Singh, if I might have a word with...' Sir William hesitated, as if he was struggling to recall the Inspector's name.

'Inspector Axel,' Azim Singh said.

'Yes. With Inspector Axel. I will join you shortly, Mr Singh.'

'As you wish, Minister. I will wait for you at the door to the drawing room.' Pointing across the ballroom, Azim Singh continued, 'It's down the corridor and second on the left. You will see me.' He gave a slight bow of his head and left.

When Lovegrove and Axel were alone, Sir William asked, his tone exasperated, 'What in heaven's name are you doing here?'

'I was invited!'

Sir William looked about him and, satisfied they were not being overheard, snapped, 'By accepting the invitation, they have played you for a fool. Whatever has garnished the attention of MI6 will have a stop put to it, Mr Singh has seen to that. Such incompetence is why we don't have flat-footed police officers blundering about in sensitive matters of State that require the finesse of spy craft and an understanding of the subtleties of diplomacy.' The Minister paused before saying, 'Don't look surprised, Inspector. I know who you are.' After another moment of silence, Lovegrove continued. 'Strengthening the military and economic ties between the United Kingdom and India is of national importance, especially following Brexit and with China flexing her growing military and economic influence. If giving Mr Singh a slice of Britain's 5G network is a price we have to pay, then it is something we will do. Yes, Inspector, I know MI6 is sniffing about because of Mr Singh's 5G interests.'

'At the expense of the Chinese?' Inspector Axel said.

Annoyed at Inspector Axel's impertinence, Lovegrove said,

'China is Britain's fifth-largest trading partner, worth some thirty billion US dollars. Defence is more than military hardware, Inspector. Securing a free trade agreement with China, which would be welcomed by the communist country, in this post-Brexit environment is not off the cards. These are not black and white matters, Inspector Axel, something clearly, you don't understand!'

Although Inspector Axel understood the conversation with Sir William wasn't a debate, the events of the evening had loosened his tongue. When he had a chance to speak, he said, 'There are times to pursue quiet diplomacy behind the scenes. I understand Sir William. There are also moments when our concerns should be voiced, especially when urgent action is required.'

The Secretary of Defence pursed his lips in displeasure as he said, 'I doubt that the Home Secretary knows of MI6's meddling in these affairs but, by morning, he will. Whatever it is you're doing here needs to stop, as of now. Do I make myself clear?'

The word "Crystal" popped into Inspector Axel's head, but he said, instead, 'I understand, Minister.'

Sir William Lovegrove's left eye narrowed. 'Is there something that should concern us?'

'That's what I'm here to find out.'

Shaking his head in a disapproving manner, Sir William Lovegrove walked away towards where Azim Singh was standing. At that moment, Inspector Axel recalled the advice given by Stephen Walls.

Step on the wrong toes, and I might not be able to protect you. Stephen did say "might not" rather than "will not". As the old saying goes, in for a penny, in for a pound, so I might as well have a nose around while I'm here. Besides, I must discover something incriminating, or my tenure with MI6 may be short-lived.

Inspector Axel left the grand renaissance revival style ballroom with its fused classical Roman technique and renaissance aesthetics, intent on exploring upstairs. Two burly security guards, dressed in tuxedos and wearing communication earpieces, blocked his path as he approached the elegantly balustraded staircase.

'I'm sorry, Sir, you can't go upstairs.'

From his pocket, Inspector Axel removed his secret services identification card and said, 'I'm checking the security arrangements.'

The man looked at his name and said, 'Sorry Sir, we have not been told of your presence and without authorisation, I can't...'

Inspector Axel, interrupting, said, 'I know, my good man. Stephen Walls, Head of MI6, has sent me. If you would kindly ask your supervisor to call him, he will have his number. Stephen will confirm my authorisation.'

'We're with the Specialist Operations Directorate of London's Metropolitan Police. We don't have anyone from the

Security Service, working with us tonight. You may need to be patient while we inquire.'

'Please, take your time.'

I hope Stephen will back my claim, although he will be displeased. And that is an understatement.

The security officer spoke quietly into his lapel microphone, relaying the conversation he'd had with Inspector Axel. Two minutes later, Axel was climbing the stairs and, reaching the top, said to himself, 'Which way? The West Wing, I think.' He chuckled at his joke.

Behaving as if he owned the mansion, Inspector Axel walked along the corridor, opening each door and peering inside, until he came across one that caught his attention: a study, a typical one, albeit on a grander scale than the average home. It housed bookshelves stacked to the gunnels, an executive desk, chair, computer, and desk lamp. A selection of abstract artwork, like those in Azim Singh's London office, hung on the wall. In contrast, the central piece of art was of an ancient map.

I'm a spy, Inspector Axel said to himself. I have a valid reason to be here, because this is what we do. He made a bee-line for the desk to rifle through its draws and to examine anything of interest. Finding nothing, he turned his attention to the papers strewn across the top.

How can he make any sense of this mess?

After a few minutes of scanning the documents, invoices for renovations, memos from his executive, plus myriads of other mundane snippets, Inspector Axel found his eyes drawn to the slithers of bold red decorating the map hanging on the wall. Examining it, Inspector Axel read the title printed in capital letters: THE DALOGRAPHY OF SKARO.

I've never heard of it. I will have to Google the title when I return to the office. Okay, this search has been a waste of time. What next?

His musing was interrupted by the sound of the office door opening and, in the doorway, stood Adele, who said tersely, 'I thought I might find you poking about up here.'

'What can I say, Miss Adele? I'm a spy; what else would you expect?'

The chill of her demeanour froze further, and she smiled menacingly. 'I hear you won't be with us much longer?'

'Is that a threat, Miss Adele?'

'Not at all, Mr Axel. A forewarning from a friend, that's all. The Home Secretary will terminate your services with MI6.'

'Are you offering me a job, Miss Adele?'

'We have standards, Inspector Axel.'

A slight smile drifted across Inspector Axel's face as he said, 'Is there another name that accompanies Miss Adele? "Attila" perhaps?'

Adele responded with a polite smile, 'Is there another name that accompanies Inspector Axel? Clouseau perhaps?' It was a reference to the bumbling fictional character Inspector Jacques Clouseau.

'Maybe, Miss Adele, I will accept that offer of Champagne after all. I will, however, choose my glass if you don't mind because I too have standards. Shall we?' Inspector Axel said, gesturing towards the door.

***

It was one-thirty in the morning when Inspector Axel opened the door to his hotel room at The Old Bank Hotel, in the heart of Oxford, a grand old building dating back to the fourteenth century. He was looking forward to bed, and the concierge had booked him into one of the superior deluxe rooms at the front of the hotel with views on to Oxford's limestone buildings which line the High Street. Inspector Axel had exchanged it for a quieter room at the back.

Before retiring to bed Inspector, Axel checked for messages on his smartphone, something he had been avoiding after his exchange with the Minister at the reception. There were three voice messages from Stephen Walls, each one increasing in urgency, insisting that he call back immediately; the last message was timed at midnight. A further voicemail was from Detective Sally Mars, telling him they had made a breakthrough.

They can wait until the morning. No, I'll reply to Detective Mars in the morning, but Stephen Walls, I'll deal with him in person when I'm back in London. That could be an exciting meeting!

Dressed as a hotel guest, using a counterfeit master swipe card, Adele let herself in through the rear entrance to the Old Bank Hotel. Inside, she looked at her watch, which showed four in the morning, before checking her silenced pistol. It was loaded, and the safety was off. Using the stairs, Adele made her way to the second floor. From the car, she had, for the second time that night, hacked into the hotel booking system to check Inspector Axel's room number and disable the CCTV.

My, my Inspector, that would have been embarrassing, killing the wrong person. Regardless, I have you now.

Adele drifted along the corridor, stopping outside of Inspector Axel's room. She removed the pistol from inside her coat and tightened its silencer. Using the swipe card, she disabled the lock and pushed the door gently open. Light filtered in from the hallway, enough to illuminate the double bed. She aimed at the sleeping body and fired off two rounds; the bullets leaving the muzzle with a suppressed, Thud! Thud! a noise unlikely to wake the other patrons. Adele beamed as she saw the shots find their mark.

Good night, Inspector Axel.

Pulling the door closed, Adele, still smiling, unscrewed the silencer from her pistol and concealed the weapon. Returning briskly to her car, Adele whispered to herself, 'If you want a job done properly, do it yourself.'

CHAPTER 17
Snowflake

Montserrat Spain

Seething, Richard Liew turned and said, 'You won't get away with this. Help is on its...' He stopped mid-sentence. 'You're not Claudia!'

A woman of similar height and build to Claudia was directly in front of him, holding a pistol in one hand and a taser in the other. She smiled saying, 'No, that's right Mr Liew, Sweetie,' laughing, she continued. 'I'm not Claudia but, thanks to you, Chen Li and the Chinese Ministry of State Security think that I am. Even better, they believe MI6 is holding you and your family. What can I say, Mr Liew, other than... thank you, *Sweetie!*' She laughed again.

Richard Liew shook his head. 'This makes no sense, unless ... unless this entire episode has been a set-up from the start.' A look of enlightenment washed across his face, changing to one of resignation as he continued, 'It was you who killed John Moss and implicated the Chinese. And you who killed Wen Xu to incriminate Claudia and MI6? You're aiming to escalate tensions between the British and Chinese, and that will lead to conflict, precisely what you want?'

'Very perceptive, Mr Liew. My deception is a play as old as time itself and, surprisingly, it still works. Remarkably well, as it turns out.'

'Madness,' Richard Liew said. 'Even if you kill my family and me, your game won't work. The Chinese State Security Service was already suspicious and, when they find Claudia isn't here, they

...' He paused, glancing at the woman pointing the gun at him when the realisation suddenly struck. 'Claudia is coming here. That's right, isn't it?'

'I'm expecting her soon and do you know what I find so exciting, Mr Liew?'

Richard Liew remained mute, ignoring the provocative question, refusing to pander to the mysterious woman's streak of megalomania.

'When your agents arrive to eliminate Claudia, there will be quite a blood bath. She is, after all, one of the best. You will remember how she dispatched your Mr Yáyī.' A chopstick to the brain–brutal efficiency I think you'll agree.'

'Why are you doing this?'

'This isn't some B-grade movie where I miraculously reveal the plot to you, Mr Liew. Enough of...'

Richard Liew interrupted. 'Whatever they are paying you, the Chinese Government will double it. Triple it even!'

'I keep my word, Sweetie.' The woman laughed. 'Would you believe it? I'm even beginning to talk like Claudia now? Enough of this idle chatter. Pleasant dreams, Richard.' She pointed the taser at Richard Liew and fired. He fell to the ground convulsing and, using a syringe, the woman injected something into Richard Liew's arm, and he was out to the world in seconds.

***

Before arriving in Spain, Claudia had studied Montserrat Abbey from an old drawing she'd discovered that showed the layout of the tunnels and structures built in Roman times and upon which the Christian monastery now sat. She knew the route and timing of the Liew family tour beneath the mountain, and her preparations were thorough. She could draw a map of the entire complex with her eyes closed. Arriving at Monistrol de Montserrat Train Station, Claudia used the Cremallera de Montserrat rack railway to travel from the bottom of the mountain to the Montserrat Monastery. Despite her wicked intent, Claudia was relaxed on the twenty-minute journey, enjoying the surroundings as the locomotive wound its way up the side of the mountain.

Speaking to the cat hidden in the daypack she had strapped to her front, Claudia said, as she made her way to the Abbey Library,

'Come on, Snowflake, let us give Richard Liew, Samantha, and Molly a big surprise. Do you know what I thought I would do?... No, Snowflake, I suppose you don't. Well, I thought I would hide in one of the monk cells, and as they approach, the door slightly ajar so they can't see me, send you out through the crack to greet them. Can you imagine their shock? Samantha and Molly will be dumbfounded, but Richard Liew will know. Oh yes, he'll know that he's in for a lot of trouble. What's that, Snowflake? You don't think I should? Let's wait and see, shall we?'

Inside the Monastery library, Claudia had to wait three minutes until she was alone and could push the secret panel to trigger the hidden door revealing the interior. Checking her watch before entering, she had fifteen minutes before the Liew tour was about to start. Inside and following her mental map, Claudia spotted the stone spiral staircase and descended. At the bottom she began walking the length of the corridor, seeing the door which would lead to the Monastic cells. Claudia paused, a sense of unease striking her sharply. She peered about to check that she was alone. Claudia breathed out and whispered, 'Snowflake, I'm not sure if something is wrong, or it is me having second thoughts.' Standing perfectly still, she listened and, except for the sound of Snowflake purring, seemingly enjoying the ride in the daypack, nothing stirred.

I think you're jumping at shadows, Claudia.

Claudia continued walking toward the door when her spine tingled, the unquestionable feeling of someone behind her. As she prepared to swing around, a male voice, anticipating her move, broke the silence.

'I wouldn't if I were you.' The command was accompanied by the telltale dot of a red laser sight flickering on the door in front of Claudia. The message: There's a gun pointing at the middle of your back.

'Keep walking,' the voice said and, when she reached the door, Claudia heard the newcomer speak into a two-way radio. 'We're coming through.'

'Okay,' came the squeaky reply, followed by an instruction to Claudia from behind, 'Open the door and step through. Move!' Through the door was a man waiting with an assault rifle, pointing at Claudia. Using the barrel of his gun, he beckoned towards her.

'Snowflake, this is taking a nasty turn.'

'Shut up. Move, now!' said the man behind.

Stepping through the door, Claudia approached the second man, who said, 'Stop and listen carefully. Do as instructed, and you will be unharmed. Personally; I'm hoping you try something so that I can kill you; the choice is yours. Slowly, remove the day pack and place it on the ground in front of you. Any sudden moves will be your last.' Claudia did as she was instructed. 'Excellent. Next, hands up against the wall.' The man giving the instructions stepped aside, allowing Claudia to approach the wall which had been behind him. Raising her hands, she placed them on the wall. 'Spread your legs and shuffle backwards until you're leaning with your weight on your arms towards the wall.'

Claudia knew, in that position, her body would be off balance and she wouldn't be able to attack the person about to search her because she'd be dead before she'd laid a hand on him. From behind, she sensed a person approach and then felt his hands frisk her. He spoke as he worked. 'What do we have here? A Glock pistol and two clips of ammunition, two mobile phones and oh, nasty, a tube of plastic explosives.' The man stepped back from Claudia, asking his colleague, 'What's in the daypack?'

'A cat,' came the reply.

The man who had conducted the body search said, 'You've brought Snowflake.'

How does he know the cat's name? I bet the Chinese have been watching me, watching them. Now I'm in deep trouble.

Claudia heard a cell door unlocking, a bolt sliding across. A person spoke, 'Stand up straight and turn around.'

As she did, for the first time, Claudia saw both of the men together: mercenaries, she concluded. The one nearest the cell door said, 'Pick up the pack, and inside you go.' He gestured with the barrel of the gun towards the door and, speaking towards the opening, said, 'Stand back, you have company.'

'Daddy,' Claudia heard a child's voice say.

Walking toward the cell, Claudia whispered to herself, 'What's going on?'

Molly's face had disappointment written all over it as she spotted a woman enter, a tear forming in the corner of her eye as she sobbed, 'Daddy, daddy, I want my daddy.'

The plot thickens. Samantha and Molly, but no Richard Liew. How did they beat me here?

Samantha Liew, assuming the woman was another victim of the vicious Claudia, asked in a sympathetic tone, 'Who are you?'

Claudia hesitated, wondering whether she should tell the truth before deciding that there was little point in lying. 'I'm Claudia Sweetie.'

Pointing behind Claudia, Samantha said, her voice shrilled, 'I thought she was Claudia?'

Claudia swivelled on her heels and lifted her arms in astonishment as she said, 'Linda Orr... now, this is a surprise.'

Linda smiled. 'A surprise and not an unexpected pleasure?'

'Perhaps not on this occasion but ordinarily, yes.'

Linda laughed. 'Regardless, Claudia, I've missed you. What has it been, all of fifteen hours? By the way, how is the cat?'

Samantha glanced between Claudia and Linda Orr, her eyes wide as she said, 'You know each other?'

Claudia shrugged. 'What can I say? Linda is my best friend. Well, I thought she was.'

'We still are, Claudia. What's happening, all of it, is work, that's all; nothing personal and besides, I wouldn't accept a contract to kill you, anyway...'

Claudia interrupted, her question shining like a beacon in her mind. 'John Moss?'

With a note of regret, Linda said, 'I'm sorry, Claudia. I didn't enjoy doing that, but in our line of work, a contract is a contract. I know you understand that.'

'The bomb you set it could have killed me?'

'No. I was in control of the motion detector. Besides killing you would wreck the plan; we've gone to considerable lengths to keep you alive. You see, Claudia, I knew John had brought you an engagement ring, and after the concert, he would come back to the house for it. Predicting human behaviour is what we do, and he didn't disappoint.'

The engagement revelation caught Claudia off guard, and she felt a twinge of sadness.

Linda noticed immediately saying wickedly, 'You didn't know!'

Ignoring Linda, Claudia asked, 'What about the other origami crane, the one left on the church altar?'

Linda shook her head. 'I don't know what you're talking about. I only know of the one I gave to Charles Scott.'

'I didn't think so.' Claudia thought for a moment before asking, 'Wen Xu, Charles Scott on Barra Island, the shooting at Truro Cathedral, all you?'

'I've been a busy girl.'

Samantha's mouth dropped open. 'This is all a game to you, isn't it? I don't understand.'

Claudia gave Samantha a wry smile before asking Linda, 'Do they live?'

'I'm afraid not. Murdered by a madwoman they call Claudia, and I can tell you, the Chinese become annoyed.'

'The Chinese, they are on their way, I assume?'

'Yes, but mind you, Claudia, while I personally would never accept a contract on your life, I can't take responsibility for what the Chinese State Security Service does once they arrive. They have orders to kill you—shoot on sight. That said, I have every confidence in your ability.'

Claudia shrugged her shoulders as if to say, what will be will be, before saying, 'The phone you gave me in London. That's how you've been keeping tabs on me?'

Linda nodded, adding, 'Remember when you gave me the MI6 phone while you went cat burglarising?'

Claudia sighed. 'Cat burglarising. Is that a word?' She hesitated before adding, 'yes, of course, I remember. What was I thinking, trusting you?'

'Sorry, I hacked and cloned it, and we've known every move you have made. Do you know that intelligence breach you keep complaining to Stephen Walls about? Well, that was you, which is I think is quite ironic.'

Claudia shook her head. 'I can tell you one thing, Linda Orr. When this is over, you will buy the next round of drinks.'

Linda chuckled.

Claudia pondered for a moment before saying, 'I can see that this is just work and for people like us, and the "why" isn't important, but I wonder who it is you're working for?'

Linda thought for a moment. *Should I answer?* She decided, why not. 'Davros and The Firm.'

Claudia shrugged her shoulders. 'They're new ones on me. Does it pay well?' Her statement was a lie. Stephen Walls had mentioned Davros and The Firm before her mission to protect Saint Vladimir. Her conclusion, Sergey Rutskoy, the Russian Oligarch, was a member of The Firm.

'It's a flat fee plus an outcome-based bonus. Now, that's enough questioning, Claudia.' Snatching a glance at Samantha, Linda said, 'I know what you're thinking. Can I trust the real Claudia and will she help us escape?'

Linda turned her head towards Claudia. 'Have you shown Samantha and Molly what's in the day pack?'

Claudia scrunched up her face. 'Oh, that's awkward, Linda.'

'I know. I'm good like that. Open your daypack, Claudia, and let us see what pokes a furry face out?'

'Snowflake!' Molly and Samantha said in unison as Claudia took the cat from her pack.

A tear formed in the corner of Samantha's eye. 'Why?'

Linda chuckled, 'Why indeed? Claudia was coming here to kill you; she's not the sort of woman you can trust, a person with a dark past.'

Claudia interrupted, 'If Davros and The Firm thought I was going to kill them, why are you here, Linda?'

'Sadly, my friend, since meeting Max and Olivia, you've become weak, developed a conscience. We couldn't rely upon you executing them out of pure vengeance. I'm here to ensure that there's no misunderstanding. We want everyone to believe that you are a woman driven by hate, and their bodies will be proof of your anger.' Linda laughed. 'And don't expect any help from MI6, because when the Chinese State Security Service contact them, they will see from your phone trace that you've been here. Plus, we've ensured the Chinese know you hacked into the Liew's WI-FI system, which they will share with MI6 and, of course, your catnapping of poor Snowflake. Interesting evidence, you will no doubt agree. Stephen Walls will believe that you've "gone rogue" and send a team to eliminate you, while the Chinese believe you're doing this on behalf of MI6. When MI6 and the Chinese arrive, my men and I will start the gunfight between them before we bolt. What I find brilliant about the Davros plan is not only do MI6 and the Chinese fight each other, they both want you eliminated. You have no friends in this other than me. I will, of course, release you before we go and even leave you some weapons with which to defend yourself. As I say. I have every confidence in your abilities.'

Samantha, listening to the exchange, butted in, 'Won't this man Stephen Walls just tell the Chinese that Claudia's has "gone rogue" and that will end the conflict?'

Linda laughed and, speaking to Claudia, said, 'Will you tell her, or will I?'

'After you,' Claudia answered, adding. 'But I haven't "gone rogue".' The insight into her behaviour caught Claudia by surprise.

Linda was about to say, *then why are you here?* She checked herself, saying instead, 'That's the brilliance of my plan. It doesn't matter.'

Looking at Samantha, Linda said, 'To answer your question, the spy agencies spend their time lying and spreading disinformation about each other. When Stephen Walls denies complicity by blaming a rogue agent, the Chinese won't believe him and vice versa. My job is to exploit the shared suspicion between the two countries. Safe in the knowledge, people will believe whatever they wish, won't they, Claudia? Without trust, Samantha, there is no truth. Now, ladies, I've enjoyed our little chat so, if you will excuse me, I have some work to do.'

As Linda was leaving the cell, Claudia called after her, 'I'll see you at Castle, seven o'clock Saturday night for dinner, and you're paying.'

Linda turned, grinned and said, 'That's the spirit, Claudia. I'll be there with a bottle of your favourite, 1996 Dom Perignon.'

Waving a finger towards Linda, Claudia said, 'Don't over chill it.'

'I'll keep that in mind,' Linda replied as the prison door closed with a thud, accompanied by the sound of the bolt sliding across.

Samantha, facing Claudia, said, her voice raised, 'You broke into our house, stole the cat, and then spied on us. What kind of woman are you? Samantha lunged at Claudia; hands outstretched.

Claudia sidestepped, sending her tumbling to the floor. Molly burst into tears, howling as she ran to her mother before curling up on the ground with her. Samantha embraced Molly, mother and child crying in unison.'

'Enough!' Claudia yelled, incensed by the constant wailing.

Samantha stood and, after helping Molly to her feet, said, 'When the Chinese come, if you surrender, I will tell them it wasn't you who kidnapped us, then we will all be safe.'

Claudia picked up the cat and, while stroking its head, said, 'Snowflake, I can see some flaws in Samantha's plan. First, Linda is going to kill you before the Chinese arrive and second, both MI6 and the Chinese State Security Service will issue a kill on sight order against me. It wouldn't matter if the Queen of bloody Sheba herself were my witness. They will shoot first and ask questions later.' Peering at the cat, Claudia continued, 'Snowflake, the only option is for me to get both of them out of here alive, which I admit is an irony.' Lifting her head and staring at Samantha and Molly, she said, 'There is one slight problem. I have no idea how.'

Samantha started weeping again, saying, her voice a whisper, 'You're crazy, all of you are.'

Claudia felt a twinge of anger. *If they don't shut up crying, I'll kill them myself.* The anger quickly faded, and she said instead, sympathetically,

'Do you know where Richard is? We need to save daddy as well, don't we Molly?' Touching Molly gently on the head as she spoke, Claudia said, 'Snowflake and I are developing a plan and we need you to be a brave girl. Will you do that for me?'

CHAPTER 18
ME7

He'd put bedding across the marble floor of his hotel bathroom for cushioning, yet Inspector Axel still awoke from his fitful sleep with a stinging pain in the back. He sighed as he said to himself, *'I'm too old to be sleeping on the floor.'*

After dressing and slipping the stolen pistol into the top of his trousers, Inspector Axel strolled into the bedroom to remove the pillows from where he'd stuffed them, under the bed quilts to make it look as though he was sleeping there and to pack his bag for his return to London. He pulled back the curtains, and daylight filled the room as he went about his tasks. It was while removing the third pillow that Inspector Axel noticed the bullet holes. The sight caused his heart to race involuntarily, and he took a couple of deep breaths.

You were right to be careful.

Questions filled his mind. *What's going on with H1 Technologies? Do they think I know something? Whatever it is, I need to convince Stephen that something is wrong. Seriously wrong.*

Regaining his composure, Inspector Axel toyed with ringing Adele and inviting her for breakfast, until he acknowledged to himself that his bravado existed more in a fantasy world than in real life. He had little doubt; if Claudia were in his predicament, she'd do exactly that. His mobile phone interrupted his musing, and Inspector Axel glanced at the caller ID to see that it was Stephen Walls who was calling again. Inspector Axel exhaled loudly, deciding whether he should answer before letting it go through to voice mail, thinking at that moment, Stephen Walls was the last person with whom he wanted to chat.

Stick with the plan, Inspector. Talk with Detective Mars first. Besides, I want to tell her what I've discovered about ME7.

After breakfast, having spoken to Detective Mars, Inspector Axel departed, leaving the BMW 7 Series in the hotel car park and catching the train back to London.

***

MI6 Headquarters London

'Good afternoon, Inspector,' James said. 'Stephen is expecting you, go straight in.'

'Is he in a good mood?'

'Ah. The Home Secretary has been here all morning. It's not just you Inspector; there's been a major blow-up with the Chinese involving Claudia. It seems she's gone rogue, although they, the Chinese, don't believe so. Is Stephen in a good mood? In short, no.'

'Thank you, James.' Inspector Axel knocked on Stephen's door.

'Come. Ah, Inspector, please take a seat.'

Overly formal, this is not looking good. I think I'm about to be sacked.

'I have a couple of things to discuss with you, Inspector, as I'm sure you are aware. First, I warned you to tread lightly with your inquiries into Azim Singh and H1 Technologies. Last night, Sir William, you met him at the reception, rang the Home Secretary, getting him out of bed. He was displeased, and when he called me, like the Home Secretary, I was sleeping. I defended you, Inspector, as best I could, assuring him that whatever your actions, they were in the Nation's best interests. Against my better judgment, I went along with your charade of checking the security arrangements at the reception. So, tell me, Inspector, what have you discovered? I need concrete evidence, please.'

'Azim Singh is a megalomaniac orchestrating tension between the British and Chinese Security Service.'

'Is that right? I've had a phone call from spy chief Chen Li, my counterpart in the Chinese Ministry of State Security. He's accusing Claudia and, may I add MI6, of kidnapping one of their agents, Richard Liew, along with his family: Samantha, his wife, and their seven-year-old daughter, Molly. They allege MI6 is holding them captive at Montserrat Abbey in Spain. Richard Liew escaped and, before he was re-captured, told Chen Li that Claudia was going to kill them all. No amount of persuasion on my part could convince Chen Li that MI6 was not involved. The Chinese have dispatched a retrieval team with instructions to eliminate Claudia. He said that our provocative actions could lead to dire consequences. The UK is experiencing a wave of sophisticated cyber-attacks targeting British organisations across a range of sectors: government, industry, political organisations, education, health, essential services providers and operators of other critical infrastructure. These are brazened, broad-scale cyber intrusions by state actors – coming from China, we suspect. Our security experts have identified copy-paste compromises, heavy use of proof-of-concept exploit code, web shells and other tools to enable the attacks. There is no evidence yet of attempts to disrupt or destroy our network, more a demonstration of capacity, a warning of what will occur if Britain, in the eyes of China, doesn't change its course.'

'It may not be the Chinese,' Inspector Axel proffered.

'There are only a handful of countries with sophisticated cyber warfare capability, Inspector. The United States, Russia, India, Pakistan, China, Iran and North Korea. Only one of these has a current motive - China. The Home Secretary is seeking to de-escalate tensions and is resisting a strident response to the cyber-attack. He has approved a specialist team from our Gibraltar office to be sent to Spain to rescue Mr Liew and his family, and terminate our rogue agent, Claudia. The Home Secretary believes the only way we can return to the status quo is to manage this before the Chinese team arrives. We have to hand them Claudia's head on a plate.'

'If I may speak, Stephen. Claudia is not doing this. It is a setup.'

'Really, Inspector! The Chinese say Claudia is in Montserrat Spain, and our tracking tells us the same thing.'

'Sir, this is urgent, and you need to trust me. Put a stop on the Gibraltar office mission until you've heard me out.'

Stephen shook his head. 'It's too late for that now. The Home Secretary has issued the order and I couldn't reverse it even if I wanted to. However, to combat a deadly outbreak of Coronavirus, Spain has closed its borders, cancelled flights in and out of the country, closed all but its essential services and ordered its citizens to say at home. The Home Secretary believes, because of this, our team can reach Montserrat and resolve the situation before the Chinese can get their people on the ground.' Stephen hesitated, considering his words. 'What I'm saying, Inspector, is that we have some time. Not days, but certainly hours, because even our Gibraltar unit will have difficulties reaching Montserrat. Tell me what you have, and I need the full details. Don't jump to the end by telling me Azim Singh is a megalomaniac.'

'Thank you, Sir. I'll start with the investigation into the disappearance of Charles Scott from Barra Island and the use of the

Novichok Toxin, headed by Detective Sally Mars in Scotland. It is all interconnected.'

Stephen nodded.

'Detective Mars's team has sifted through hundreds of hours of CCTV footage and witness statements. The breakthrough came from Donald McIntyre, a creel fisherman, lobster and crabs, and the skipper of the Anne Rose. He reported seeing a suspicious boat in Brevig Bay, where Charles Scott lived, on the evening before his disappearance. He recalled the name: the Guiding Star, with the registration number CY-165, showing it hailed from Castlebay—his own port. Since he didn't recognise the boat, his instincts told him it was out of place. He provided the investigators with a detailed description of the vessel, adding to the mounting intrigue surrounding Scott's mysterious fate. Detective Mars and her team traced accounts of the ship to Stornoway on the Isle of Lewis, two hundred and thirty kilometres north, where harbour records record it as the Mavic B. CCTV footage from the Port of its crew proved inconclusive. Data from an RAF Airborne Early Warning and Control Systems (AWACS) plane showed a low altitude light aircraft on route to the Isle of Lewis the day the Mavic B arrived in the harbour. The team traced the aircraft departure to Hatton airstrip, located in Hatton on the East Coast of Scotland, thirty-three miles north of Aberdeen. They were able to track CCTV footage of a woman called Linda Orr arriving at Aberdeen International Airport on a flight from London. She travelled north to Hatton and we have footage of her in Stornoway an hour before the Mavic B departed from the port. Are you aware, Sir, of Linda Orr?'

'Yes, a Russian Mafia associate of Claudia's. I met her after the sinking of *Lelantos*, Monya Mogilevick's, superyacht.'

'We can place Linda Orr at Pi-Ski when John Moss was killed, in Truro on the day of the Cathedral shooting, near where Wen Xu, the Chinese agent, was brutally murdered and on Barra Island the night before Charles Scott disappeared. There are images of Linda Orr in disguise and, from a distance, she is indistinguishable from Claudia.'

Stephen Walls nodded. 'Do you know where she is now?'

'Yes, Sir. Barcelona, Spain.'

'Inspector, Chen Li told me they have evidence of Claudia breaking into Richard Liew's house, hacking into the WI-FI system and spying on the family. It's inconvenient that she is now also in Montserrat. How do you explain this?'

Inspector Axel dropped his head and rubbed his chin with his hand as he contemplated the dilemma. Staring at Stephen Walls, he said,

'I'm not suggesting that Claudia didn't want to exact revenge against those she held responsible for John's death. What I am telling you is that Linda Orr exploited the situation and has played Claudia. She, Linda Orr, is accountable for this saga, its wickedness and complexity. It has been a deliberate ploy to ensnare Claudia and the Chinese and British intelligence service.'

Stephen Walls weighed Inspector Axel's words before responding. 'Claudia and Linda may be acting in concert.'

'No,' Inspector Axel said emphatically, 'Claudia wouldn't kill John Moss, of that I am certain.'

'Do you know who Linda Orr is working for, who is pulling strings?'

Inspector Axel hesitated, an indication to Stephen that he was unsure.

'Well?'

I'm convinced, Sir, that Azim Singh of H1 Technologies, goes by the alias Davros in the criminal underworld. Davros, in a name Saint Vladimir, the man Claudia was sent to protect, mentioned.'

'You think, or you know, Inspector, which is it?'

'Circumstantial and motive, Sir. The attempts on my life that coincided with my interest in H1 Technologies, the map of Skaro, home planet of the fictional character Davros and the creator of the Daleks, hanging on Azim Singh's home office wall, and, H1 Technologies who will benefit if Huawei is excluded from Britain's 5G network. Do you know of Davros and the Daleks, Sir?'

Stephen nodded. 'Yes, now that you have made the connection.'

I believe, Stephen, we can't ignore the evidence. My fear, Sir, is Linda Orr will, in the guise of MI6, attack the Chinese agents when they arrive at Montserrat. She will do the same to our team in the guise of the State Security Service. She is provoking a firefight.'

Stephen Walls sighed as he deliberated on what he'd learned. After a minute which seemed longer, Stephen Walls said, 'There are wheels within wheels, Inspector.'

'It's deliberately complex, Sir.'

Stephen hesitated once more before saying, 'Alright, let me speak with the Home Secretary. Have James make you a drink, and I'll call you back in when I'm done.'

Twenty minutes later, Inspector Axel was summoned back into the room by Stephen Walls. As he entered, he tried to gauge Stephen's demeanour but found himself at a loss, unsure of what the MI6 Chief and Home Secretary had decided.

'These are complicated matters, Inspector. Our team from Gibraltar cannot leave the British Territory because the border is closed. I put the evidence you presented to me to the Home Secretary, and he is of the view that, because of the uncertainty surrounding Claudia's duplicity, it's unlikely he'll be able to dissuade the Chinese from their current course of action. If they secure the release of Richard Liew and cooler heads prevail, we can work towards a de-escalation of tensions by exposing what you have found. Claudia is on her own and there is nothing else I can do.'

Inspector Axel stared at Stephen, and Stephen said, 'What is it?'

'If there was something we could do, would you?'

'You know I can't give a blanket answer like that. Inspector, tell me what's on your mind?'

'We have agents on the ground who could go to Claudia's aid.'

'Who?'

'Max and Olivia are in Barcelona.' As Inspector Axel said their names, he held his breath, unsure of how Stephen would react.

His response was brisk. 'How do you know?'

'When you were speaking to the Home Secretary, I rang Monya Mogilevick, and he told me.'

Stephen pursed his lips, his voice rising with disbelief. "You called Monya Mogilevick—the very man Max was ordered to kill by the US and British governments, but chose not to? The same Monya Mogilevick who is a ruthless Russian Mafia boss and heads a brutal organisation known as the Brotherhood? The Kremlin's go to for mercenaries, cyber-attacks on the West, and God knows what else? You just happened to have his number in your phone? And you thought it was a good idea to reach out to him, believing that he—not MI6, the CIA, Mossad, or any of the other security services that shake their heads in despair at the mere mention of Max and Olivia's names—would know where they are hiding. Is that really what you're saying?"

'I wouldn't put it quite like that.'

'No! How would you put it?'

'Just hear me out, Stephen. Max and Olivia are in Barcelona, only sixty-one kilometres from Montserrat. They know about Linda, and what's more, Claudia trusts them.'

Stephen Walls interrupted, 'How do Max and Olivia know about Linda Orr?' He shook his head in disbelief. 'You spoke to them and shared national security information?' When Inspector Axel remained silent, Stephen shook his head again before continuing. 'Go on, tell me what's on your mind.'

Stephen Walls interrupted, 'How do Max and Olivia know about Linda Orr?' He shook his head in disbelief. 'You spoke to Max and Olivia and shared national security information with them?' When Inspector Axel didn't respond, he continued, 'Go on, tell me what's on your mind.'

'Max and Olivia go in and rescue Claudia and the Liew's. Then they'll take them somewhere safe while we negotiate with the

Chinese. Max and Olivia can end this, Sir. They are the only ones who can do it.'

'Barcelona is in lockdown, Inspector.'

'When has that ever stopped them?'

'True, and if Barcelona weren't in lockdown because of COVID-19, it certainly would be if Max and Olivia were let loose in the city. Inspector, they have a history of leaving a trail of destruction in their wake: the Germans, Austrians, French, American, and Italian are all still annoyed.'

'They can end this,' Inspector Axel repeated.

Looking reluctant, Stephen Walls said, 'What about access to equipment, like weapons?'

'I'm assured they will be well equipped.'

'British agents equipped by the Russian Mafia, is that what you're saying?'

'Unusual times require extraordinary measures. You know they can do this, Stephen.'

'It's out of my hands, Inspector.'

'Sir, we can't leave one of our own to the mercy of the Chinese, or anyone else for that matter.' Inspector Axel paused, then sighed. 'Sir, can I remind you of the words of Teddy Roosevelt?'

"It is not the critic who counts; not the man who points out how the strong man stumbles, or where the doer of deeds could have done them better. The credit belongs to the man who is actually in the arena, whose face is marred by dust and sweat and blood... who spends himself in a worthy cause; who at the best knows, in the end, the triumph of high

achievement, and who at the worst, if he fails, at least fails while daring greatly, so that his place shall never be with those cold and timid souls who neither know victory nor defeat".'

Stephen Walls leaned back in his chair, and the room fell silent as he contemplated the Inspector's words.

Waiting, Inspector Axel thought, *Will I disobey a direct order if Stephen says no?*

An uncomfortable silence lingered in the room until Stephen spoke. 'This operation cannot be sanctioned by MI6. The Home Secretary has made his position clear.' Inspector Axel nodded. 'Understand, Inspector, if they do this, they will be on their own.'

'Yes, Sir.'

Inspector Axel stood and prepared to leave, believing the meeting was over. 'Wait,' Stephen said, then hesitated before saying,

'Inspector, you and Teddy Roosevelt are right. To hell with it. Tell Max and Olivia to bring out Claudia, Richard, Samantha and Molly Liew. And even the cat, Snowflake. I want them all alive.'

Raising an eyebrow, Inspector Axel said, 'Snowflake?'

'Don't ask Inspector how I know.' Stephen shook his head in dismay and said, 'The Americans would send in an elite SEAL team, and we commission a couple of over bloody eighty-year-old pensioners.'

Inspector Axel smiled. 'True. Thank you, Stephen.'

'Wish Max and Olivia God's speed from me and tell them MI6 will do whatever it can to help.' Inspector Axel turned towards the door. 'One further question, Inspector. You've had people searching the archives for ME7. Where does that fit?'

'It doesn't, Sir.'

'Then what is it?'

'ME7, was the early code name for what became better known as the Shetland Bus.'

'I won't ask. Get out Inspector, before I change my mind.'

CHAPTER 19

Mobilised

'Max, wake up!'

Yawning, Max said, 'Olivia, I'm in the middle of my afternoon nap, my favourite time of the day. What's so urgent that it can't wait?'

'Sit up, you grumpy old thing and listen. I've spoken twice on the phone to Inspector Axel. Claudia is in trouble, and she needs our help.'

'When isn't Claudia in trouble?'

'Max!' Olivia exclaimed in alarm. 'How can you say that?'

'Olivia, my love, it was said in jest... in jest. I'm all ears.'

Olivia relayed the story told to her by Inspector Axel that Claudia was being held captive deep below Montserrat Abbey, a location only sixty kilometres away from where they were in Barcelona. She told him about Linda Orr, the Liew family, Snowflake, and the Chinese Ministry of State Security. 'It was when Inspector Axel mentioned Davros; I realised the attack on us in A Coruña and Claudia's predicament was part of a larger master plan.'

'Are you suggesting Davros wanted us out of the way so that we couldn't come to Claudia's aid?'

'Well, it would appear so. Inspector Axel has emailed me a map which shows a detailed layout of the monastery with its underground rooms and secrets passageways. I've printed it. Here, look at this.'

Taking it from Olivia, Max asked, 'What about MI6? Is Inspector Axel operating on his own?'

Olivia shook her head. 'No. The rescue is a sanctioned operation.'

Max huffed, 'I can believe the entire story except that Stephen Walls has authorising our mobilisation. He would rather ...' Max paused before imitating the voice from the Monty Python sketch about the four Yorkshiremen, '... dance about on our graves singing *Hallelujah.*'

'Well, Max, it goes to show how important this mission is to MI6.'

'Olivia, my love, don't make me laugh. Be realistic; they have mobilised us because Spain is in total lockdown and there's nobody else. If Stephen had any other choice, you can bet that he wouldn't be asking us. It's a sign of his desperation, nothing more.'

'Even if that is true, Max, it doesn't detract from the fact that Claudia needs us.'

'I understand that, but Spain is rife with COVID-19. If we go outside and catch it, at our age, we will die; no question, we will die!'

'I know Max,' Olivia sighed, taking a deep breath before continuing. "But even if there were no coronavirus, confronting Linda and the Chinese Secret Service would likely lead to our deaths, regardless. Is there really a difference?'

'The virus is an invisible, insidious killer, a complex, cunning and clever enemy. I'm more confident in our ability to take on the Chinese State and Davros than the Coronavirus. At least with them, we know what we are up against.' Max stood and started to walk away.

'Where are you going?'

'If we are going to save Claudia, I'll be needing my new English brolly and bowler hat, won't I?'

Olivia shook her head in disbelief. 'Didn't you throw the old thing out?'

'I put it away for a rainy day, and now it's arrived.'

Olivia shook her head again. 'And weren't you arguing that we shouldn't go out?'

Max laughed as he replied, 'Olivia, I'm the man who couldn't talk his way out of Parkour lessons. What hope do I have when it comes to saving our beloved Claudia? I've had my cathartic whine and lived up to my reputation as an old, cranky, stubborn curmudgeon. Now, all that remains is for me to change into my Superman outfit. The eccentric English Gentleman with a touch of dementia.' Max hesitated, touching his chin in thought. 'For you, my love, if we are to avoid arrest for breaching the lockdown regulations, may I suggest its time for... Lady Olivia Suzanne Elizabeth Huggins to make a comeback?'

Olivia considered for a moment before chuckling, 'Max, you're right, and I will need my Pink Parasol.'

'Excellent choice, m'lady, although I'm not sure I saw one of those in the weapons cupboard.'

'Damn! a Glock, a brolly and torch will have to suffice.'

'Good pick up, Olivia. I would have forgotten the flashlights. Come, dear, it's time to choose our weaponry from Monya's supplies. Let's see what he has.'

As had been the way throughout Max and Olivia's long and illustrious career, they indulged in jovial banter as they prepared to face what was arguably their greatest challenge. The banter eased their fear and focused their minds.

Half an hour later, they were armed and ready to leave. As Max opened the front door to wave Olivia through, he said, 'And so it begins, m'lady.'

To conceal his weapon, Max dressed in a double-breasted, long-sleeved khaki coloured trench coat with a fitted belt, which Olivia maintained was beige. On his head, he wore a black bowler hat and carried an identically coloured umbrella in his hand, doubling as a walking stick. To hide her armoury, Lady Olivia had chosen a burgundy trench coat which Max insisted was pink. Like Max, she also carried an umbrella and, for her head, she'd chosen a *beige* short-brimmed canvas bucket hat, Max asserting that it was khaki, of course.

'I assume you have a Cunning Plan?' Max said, locking the door behind him.

'Isn't that something you should have asked me already?' Before Max could answer, Olivia tapped him cheekily on the bottom with her umbrella and continued, 'Of course I have a plan. As always, it's KISS – Keep it simple, stupid. We catch a taxi to Montserrat and then do as we always have, play it by ear.'

Despite suspecting that public transport had been mostly suspended, except for essential services, and that taxis would be in short supply, Max tipped his bowler hat and said, 'After you, m'lady. Oh, and you do, of course, realise, if we come across the police or army who are patrolling the streets to enforce the lockdown, they will arrest us for being outside?'

Since the beginning of the COVID-19 pandemic, Max and Olivia had kept themselves abreast of its impact on the global population and taken seriously the warnings the virus posed, especially to older people, and adopted actions to protect themselves. They had maintained good hygiene, covered coughs and sneezes with their elbow and used hand sanitiser. Most importantly, they had stayed home, avoiding contact with anyone, having groceries and essentials home-delivered.

Leaving the house, they expected lockdown would mean fewer people on the streets, but encountering the deserted city, a ghost town that was usually the bustling metropolis of Barcelona, came as a shock. If they hadn't before appreciated the seriousness of the COVID virus, they did now.

Max went to open his mouth, and before he could speak, Olivia said, 'Don't you dare say anything because I can see that there are no cars, let alone taxis.'

'Who me?' I was only going to offer to step out into the middle of the road to see if the buses are still running.'

'Sure, you were,' Olivia said and, with a flick of her head toward the road, added, 'If that is what you were going to do – off you go then. I'll wait here.'

Max, mumbling to himself, stepped off the footpath and strolled towards the centre of the road when Olivia glimpsed an approaching police car. With no time to call out a warning, she stepped back and drifted into the shadows, hiding in the doorway of a shop. From there she had a good view of proceedings while being concealed herself. Facing in the opposite direction and leaning on his umbrella, the first Max knew of the police car was its blue flashing lights reflected in the shop windows.

Damn!

Ignoring it like a statue, he remained perfectly still.

'Señor,' Max heard a woman's voice call.

He didn't flinch.

'Señor,' the lady called, louder this time.

Turning slowly, an effort appearing to the officers to be greater than raising the Titanic, Max saw a woman in a police uniform standing next to a white and blue Peugeot 208, with the inscription "Policia" inscribed down each side. Showing little sign that he knew of any lockdown restrictions, cupping his ear with his free hand feigning deafness, Max said, 'Sorry, what is it you're saying? You must speak up.'

'Señor, you can't be out. It's not safe. You must be at home.'

Max, using an exaggerated aristocratic English accent and speaking with broken Spanish for effect, replied, 'Ah, Mi Señora - My Lady. Sorry, excuse my rudeness. I mean, my very good Lady.' Max raised the tip of his umbrella to the rim of his bowler hat, a noble salute, before snapping it back down again and giving its tip three taps on the ground. Moving his head from side to side like a scanning radar, he added resolutely, 'I am looking for London bridge. I know it's here somewhere. Perhaps you've seen it, my good Lady?'

Before the policewoman could respond, she was distracted by the sound of a woman dashing towards her while calling. 'Oh, thank you, thank you, you've found him. I've been looking for him everywhere.'

The policewoman stared confused at the flustered old lady, carrying an umbrella and dressed in a trench coat that matched the old mans, albeit a different colour.

What is going on? The policewoman thought.

'Normally, I write his name and address on his forehead in case a good person like you finds him wandering the street. Today he was too quick for me.'

Olivia noticed a look of disbelief flicker across the policewoman's face. *Was that a touch melodramatic? Maybe unbelievable too? Best I tone it down a notch.*

'When he first started running away, I would hang a lanyard around his neck with a note displaying his name and address, but he started pulling it off.' Olivia said, letting her shoulders slump, the sign of a disheartened woman. 'I'm afraid Max becomes confused these days and, with the stress from this virus thing, it's making him worse.' Looking towards her husband, Olivia summoned him in a voice tinged with both compassion and sadness. 'Come along, Max, and I'll take you home.' She held out her hand towards him, inviting him to take it.

Max beamed, apparently inspired by the sight of Olivia, and said, 'Ah m'lady, have you seen London Bridge? It's falling down, did you know?'

'Yes, Max, it's falling down.'

'Have you seen it?'

'I know where London Bridge is, and if we hurry, we can reach it before it falls down. Come along, my precious man, and I'll take you there.'

The policewoman's instincts were yelling at her; something was wrong about the scenario playing out in front of her. She gave the couple the once over, looking them up and down, disconcerted by their peculiar appearance. Had it not been for their advanced age, she would have called for backup, wondering if she was being played as a fool. *Don't be silly; they are harmless – more of a risk to themselves than to the community.*

Olivia approached the policewoman, Max in tow, stopping short to remain at the required social distance of 1.5 metres. 'My name is Lady Olivia Suzanne Elizabeth Huggins from England. May I enquire to whom I have the privilege of addressing?'

The policewoman bit her lip, trying to stop herself from laughing. Her concerns melted away with the absurdity of a geriatric calling herself "Lady Olivia Suzanne Elizabeth Huggins from England". Maintaining a straight face, she replied, 'Michelle.'

'Michelle,' Max said. 'That's such a lovely name. I once had a beautiful poodle called Michelle. Mind you, that was a long time ago now. She's dead, of course.'

The policewoman's eyes widened. *Can this get any more bizarre?*

Michelle, please excuse my husband, Max. He wasn't always like this. When we moved to your beautiful city ten years ago, can you believe it? He was different—strong-minded, witty, and thoughtful. I would attest he was an intellectual giant. But it's dementia, you see. When it flares up, if I don't keep a constant eye on him, he packs a bag and—Voom!—he's off in search of London Bridge again'

Dementia, the policewoman thought. *That explains it. I've heard that British seniors have the propensity for extreme eccentricity and when you add a dose of impaired abilities into the mix, what do you get? Two absolute crazies, that's what - lovable crazies, but crazy nonetheless.*

Michelle smiled at Max and Olivia, her demeanour softening as she said, 'How about I give you both a lift home? Now is not a good time to be out on the street, not with COVID-19 everywhere. Plus, there are hefty fines for leaving your house.'

Ignoring the comment about the fines, Olivia beamed, saying, 'Oh, would you? That's so generous. Max, did you hear that? The kind policewoman, is going to drive us to London Bridge, isn't that wonderful. Come along, and I'll take you to the police car.'

When Olivia went to move, Max remained rooted to the spot and yelled, 'I'm not going in a police car. I haven't been naughty.'

Concealed from Michelle, Olivia squeezed Max's hand hard, a message that she was displeased at his added twist. Continuing the game, she replied, 'If we get lost, who do we ask for help?'

'A police officer,' answered Max.

'London Bridge is lost, so who will know where it is?'

Max grinned in enlightenment. 'A police officer!'

'Come along then.'

When they reached the police car, Michelle opened the rear door for Max to enter. Olivia was about to follow when she turned to the policewoman and said, her tone solemn, 'Would you be a genuine love and retrieve the overnight bag Max packed when he ran away? He left it over there, in the doorway of that shop.' Olivia pointed to where she had been hiding and added, 'I would fetch it myself but, being over eighty-five years of age, I find it's too heavy for me to carry. How Max manages it, I'll never know.'

Olivia's humble request, spoken in the manner of a frail woman embarrassed by her physical decline, caused Michelle to smile, and she bit her lip to stop a tear forming in her eye. Her parents, who were in aged care, were of a similar age to this couple, and she wondered how long it would be before Lady Olivia and Max joined them in God's waiting room.

'Of course I will, Lady Olivia,' Michelle said sincerely.

Olivia waited until Michelle's back was turned and was stepping onto the footpath before she climbed behind the driver's seat of the police car, engine still running, and pulled the automatic transmission into D for drive and stamped on the accelerator. The screech of spinning wheels caused Michelle to turn. The sight of her white and blue Peugeot 208, lights flashing, left her dumbfounded as she stood on the footpath, watching it race away into the distance.

What just happened? How on earth am I going to explain this?

Taking a deep breath to steady her thumping heart, Michelle used her two-way radio, fastened to her utility belt, to call for assistance.

'Far be it from me to be a back-seat driver,' Max said. 'As we don't want to attract undue attention to ourselves because we are about to have the entire Barcelona police force and probably the Spanish army hunting us, may I suggest we switch off the flashing disco lights?'

'Max, for once in your life, you've had a good idea.' As they raced along the road, Olivia dropped her eyes, glancing at the console with its array of buttons and switches.

Which one? Eenie Meenie Miney Mo.

Olivia reached across and hit a button that she hoped would subdue the blue lights. Instead, she jumped, startled by a commotion that caused her to pull on the steering wheel, making the car swerve from side to side as the police siren sprang noisily into life. Olivia glanced in the mirror, and at Max in the back seat, expecting a sarcastic retort. Instead, he was studying his phone.

If at first you don't succeed, try, try again.

Olivia released her right hand from the steering wheel, feeling for the switches ready to try another combination, when she spotted a police car waiting at the intersection up ahead. She eased back on the accelerator to slow the vehicle as Max spoke to her from the back seat. 'Olivia, you will see an alleyway coming up on your right. I would like you to turn into it, please.'

Surprised, Olivia said, 'How do you know that?'

'While you have been pretending to be a DJ, fiddling with your lights and music, I've found a more practical use of my time, studying Google Maps on my smartphone and plotting a way to get us out of here.'

Olivia huffed. 'Well then, navigator, I'm turning left onto this side road instead.'

Confused, Max looked at his map. 'What side road? I don't see it!'

'You're viewing Barcelona in Venezuela, aren't you?'

Ignoring Olivia, Max looked over his shoulder and through the back window saying, 'I suggest, m'lady, that you step on it because the police are following us. And now there are two of them.'

'I will take that Max, as a yes. Are you are looking at Venezuela?'

'They've put their flashy things on, Olivia. Best shake a leg or this is going to be the shortest-lived rescue mission in our history.'

'You're not being helpful, Max.'

Olivia slammed her foot hard on the accelerator, and the little police car leapt forward. Three seconds later, she was forced to ease off again when, four hundred metres in front of them, another police car appeared and positioned itself across the road, blocking their path. Checking her mirror, Olivia noticed that the following cars had slowed to a crawl, driving side by side to block her retreat. They were locking them in and probably waiting for reinforcements.

Tightly packed, historic architectural multi-storey units lined either side of the street along which Max and Olivia were driving. The disturbance of wailing sirens and flashing blue lights brought the residents in lockdown out onto their balconies to see what the commotion was all about. Armed with their mobile phones, some were filming and live streaming the unfolding drama. Olivia brought their vehicle to a standstill and said, her voice betraying urgency, 'Max, are you looking at Spain yet?'

'Ye of little faith, m'lady. I'm studying the satellite images on Google Earth, and there appears to be a pedestrian walkway on our right. It runs between two buildings, and from the picture, it is too narrow for vehicles. It leads into a Cul-de-sac and then continues on the other side. If we dump the car and hoof it, we may escape before they realise what we are doing.'

'Where is it?'

'It's difficult to see from the car, but it's here.' He held his phone for her to see.

Olivia scanned outside the car again, unable to spot the laneway. She became aware of the people standing out on their balconies and said, 'Max, have you noticed that we are being watched?'

Max looked up at the units through the car window and said, 'I imagine we are the best reality TV they are likely to get during the lockdown. I suggest that when we get out, we play to the crowd. It might buy us sympathy, even help, you never know.'

'Okay, I'll follow your lead.'

With its siren still wailing and lights flashing, Max and Olivia alighted from the stolen police car, hats on their heads, umbrellas in hand. Max instructed Olivia to acknowledge their captive audience. He removed his bowler hat, bowing while turning a full circle, before returning the hat to his head. Olivia followed suit and, when she had finished, they hurried towards the laneway Max had shown on his phone. When Max and Olivia first climbed from the police car, the watching residents were deathly silent, trying to determine if the fugitives were heroes or villains. Seeing two eccentric geriatrics, they concluded that the man and woman were pensioners on the run from a nursing home lockdown and were being pursued by overzealous police. Applause broke out as they bowed to the crowd and grew into a rapture when, having replaced his bowler, Max raised his brolly in triumph as they made their escape towards the alleyway. When Olivia used her umbrella to give Max a loving smack on his bottom, the audience went wild, howling, stamping their feet and clapping. A chorus of boos aimed at the law enforcers rang out across the neighbourhood, and Max and Olivia knew the police were on foot in hot pursuit.

'There it is,' Max said, pointing at their escape route. They dashed between the old buildings and, as they emerged from the other side, a rousing ovation greeted them. Max raised his umbrella in acknowledgement before he checked behind. The foot patrol was yet to enter the laneway. 'Come on, Olivia, let's keep moving before a patrol car comes up the road and they catch us.' No sooner had Max finished the sentence than a collective gasp of apprehension rang out from the balconies above as two police cars raced into the dead-end road, one blocking the pedestrian path for which they were heading and the other closing the street.

Max and Olivia kept walking into the Cul-de-sac as Olivia said, 'Now what?'

Looking over his shoulder, Max saw three officers emerge from the alleyway and he said, his voice betraying the despondence he was feeling, 'I think our goose is cooked.'

'Quick, in here,' a male voice called out.

Looking to her left, Olivia noticed that the front door of an apartment building was slightly ajar. The police officers, anticipating what was happening, sprinted forward, trying to cut Max and Olivia off before they made it inside. They were too slow as the door slammed shut in their faces, Olivia and Max passing through moments before.

'Open up inside!' the police demanded, banging their fists against the locked door.

A man in his seventies was helping them, his smile in satisfaction at outfoxing the police, revealing his missing front teeth.

'Thank you,' Olivia said. 'How do we get out of here without being caught?'

'This way,' the man said, eyes sparkling with excitement, unable to wipe the grin from his face.

Olivia, worried about what would happen to the man when the police entered the complex, said, 'It would be best if you were to hide, Señor. We wouldn't want you getting into trouble for helping us. We would be grateful if you would point us in the right direction and then we will flee.'

'Nonsense, I won't hear of it. Follow me and I will show you the back way out, and I have something that may interest you. Can you ride electric bikes?'

'Do we ride?' Max said excitedly. 'Like the wind... providing the batteries are fully charged; otherwise, it's like we are tethered to a tree.'

To Max's annoyance, the man with the missing teeth ignored his attempt at humour, beckoning instead for them to follow him while saying as he strode, 'We mustn't dilly-dally because it won't take long for the police to find their way around the back.' A moment later he added, pointing to a storeroom while grinning to himself, 'The bikes are in here. I hope your balance is sound, no wobbles?'

Olivia smiled reassuringly, 'Wobbles, goodness gracious no. We do Parkour.'

The man with the missing teeth said in amazement, 'Isn't that where people jump off buildings and roll around on the ground?'

'That's it,' Max interrupted grumpily. 'We do the roll around on the ground bit.'

His statement made the man with the missing teeth smile, who, feeling an affinity with Max, glanced at him saying, 'Parkour, is that like having to eat your Brussels sprouts?'

'Precisely!' Max exclaimed with a chuckle.

Leaning towards Max, the man whispered in his ear so that Olivia couldn't hear, 'This is why I give you our electric bikes – please don't bring them back.' Then speaking louder, he said, 'This white one is mine and the black one, my wife's.'

'We couldn't,' Olivia said, surprised by the stranger's generosity.

'Nonsense, of course, you could,' said their saviour as he switched on the bikes, then stood next to his and continued speaking. 'They're easy to ride. I'll show you. Next to the brake lever, here is the thumb accelerator. It's the same for the black bike. This makes them go without the need to peddle, and they have a top speed of forty kilometres per hour. They are supposed to be speed restricted, but I bought the ones that allowed you to change the computer program. They go like the wind and have pedal assist.'

He opened the back door of the apartment block, instructing Max and Olivia to wheel the bikes outside. Max was surprised to see that the door opened onto a large courtyard with apartment buildings on either side. Like around the front, people were on their balconies, hoping to glimpse the escapees. They cheered as Max and Olivia appeared.

Pointing to Max and Olivia's umbrellas, the man said, 'Let me hold those for you. It will be easier for you to mount.' When they were safely seated, he returned the brollies to them, only to discover that they were a hindrance. Mr "missing front teeth", suggested that they rest their umbrellas across the bike's handlebars, tips pointing forwards, so they didn't skewer themselves. To those watching from above, Max and Oliver were reminiscent of medieval knights, but instead of horses, they had electric bikes and umbrellas in place of lances. Max and Olivia eased on the power, and their bikes moved forward to the whirring of electric motors.

'Stop right there,' a police officer called, he and his three other colleagues having inadvertently been let into the apartment block by a resident. When Max turned his head to see who was speaking, it unsettled his balance, and the bike swayed, almost unseating him.

'They're coming,' Max called to Olivia in alarm. 'It is best m'lady, that we split up and make a run for the main road.'

The spectators on their balconies let out a collective "Ooooh!" and the audience erupted in applause, their cheers ringing through the air as Olivia navigated her path with dazzling agility. She zigzagged through the maze of pursuers with the precision of a slalom skier, making sharp, quick turns that left her chasers struggling to keep up. When one of the police officers lunged at her, missed, and ended up sprawled face-first on the ground, the crowd's exhilaration nearly brought the house down, fuelling Max and Olivia's momentum. More officers poured into the courtyard, and spotting Max heading toward the road, they darted diagonally across the square, determined to cut him off.

The crowd called in unison, 'Watch out!' their voices echoing around the impromptu gladiatorial arena.

Riding using one hand, Max lifted his umbrella from the handlebars, intending to wield it as a sword and slash his way past the incoming adversaries. Unfortunately, the move inadvertently removed his thumb from the accelerator and the bike slowed. Max was confused as it began rolling to a stop.

What's happening?

The watching spectators yelled in unison, 'Pedal Max – Pedal.

Did they just use my name? No, that can't be possible!

Max pushed down with one foot after another and, with the aid of the electric pedal assist, the bike began moving forward again, but it was too late; the police officer was almost upon him. From the corner of his eye, Max saw Olivia, her lance angled towards the intercepting police officer, sweeping in to his rescue. The officer, seeing Max's wing-woman approaching at high speed, to the delight of the spectators, who began singing together in a display of public solidarity with the elderly absconders, abandoned the chase and started running away. Olivia's intervention bought the time Max needed to reactivate the electric bike's accelerator.

Using his thumb, he eased the bike back up to speed and Olivia, seeing his recovery, altered course to join him, saying, as they merged and rode in formation, 'Let's make a run for the road before we find ourselves trapped.' Max nodded his agreement as Olivia continued, 'Okay then, this calls for full throttle.'

'Full throttle!' Max exclaimed in horror.

'Keep up,' Olivia commanded and, riding side by side, they raced towards the exit of the courtyard. With only metres to go, a police car swept in, passing them on the inside, but they were too late. Max and Olivia were once more on the street.

'Stick to the footpath,' Olivia instructed.

Max nodded in agreement before stealing a look over his shoulder and saying, 'The police are shadowing us.'

Frustrated, Olivia answered, 'We have to get away because, at this rate, we are going to be hunted down and then it's over for Claudia before it's begun.' Recognising where they were, Olivia yelled excitedly, 'A shopping arcade is coming up on our right and, with bollards blocking the entrance, the police won't be able to follow us in. I'm thinking, if we ride through as fast as we can safely manage, remembering the floor will be slippery, we may be able to make it to the other side before they reach it. Perhaps we can lose them.' She stole a glance at her husband. 'We will lose them, Max.'

Were it not for the COVID-19 stay at home order, the shopping arcade would be full of people going about their frenzied business, making it impossible to transverse at speed. That day, its walkways were near-deserted. Thumbs pressed firmly against the throttles, Max and Olivia sped unimpeded through the centre and, except for a couple of hairy moments when the bike tyres lost their grip on the smooth tiled floor, they made it through to the other side without incident. Olivia's strategic advantage turned into a drawback as they exited onto one of the main retail strips. There we no residential apartments stacked with people on their balconies spurring them on. With the street deserted, there was nowhere to hide.

As they pedalled slowly along the empty road, Max said, 'This is a surreal experience. It's like a scene out of a horror movie and any moment now, a horde of zombies will appear.'

Olivia nodded. 'This year will go down in history, and I fear we haven't seen the worst of it yet. I'd like to think that countries would work together when faced with the biggest health and economic crisis of a lifetime. If they don't, the consequences will be catastrophic and, as usual, it will be the elderly, poor and disadvantaged who will suffer the most. Countries will face heart-breaking choices.'

Max and Olivia slowed their bikes before coming to a complete stop in the middle of what would ordinarily have been a busy intersection. Looking first to their left and then right, they spotted barriers in the distance, road checkpoints, put in place by the army.

Olivia pointed, saying, 'It's not just us.'

'What do you mean?'

'The roadblocks. They're to stop the free movement of the general population, not just us. There is no doubt the police will be on the lookout for us. Regardless, these are unprecedented times and, because of the countrywide lockdown, our escape is more difficult, if not impossible. Eventually we'll be apprehended, and Max, we do stand out. Not the easiest people to miss.'

'You think two eighty-eight-year-old pensioners riding electric bikes in bowler hats isn't a common sight on the streets of Barcelona? I would have thought our look is very continental.'

Ignoring her husband, Olivia deliberated, before saying, 'Somehow, we have to find a way to the other side of barriers. If we can extract ourselves from this zone, the quest will become somewhat easier, I'm sure of it.'

'I agree, Olivia. We need to be on the other side of those barriers.' Max assessed the possibilities as he saw them, speaking aloud as he pondered, 'Public transport isn't an option because, if it is running at all, there isn't much around. Passenger vehicles will be checked as they pass through the roadblocks. Um..., but a food delivery truck or maybe a hearse!' He stroked his chin with his free hand. 'Yes, they would work, although a hearse is a bit tacky.'

'No hearse, Max!'

Max exhaled loudly, rolling his eyes upwards as he said, 'Okay, but if there's a hospital nearby we could steal an ambulance. With its lights and sirens operating, we could drive through a checkpoint unchallenged.' He paused before saying, 'I must admit, m'lady, if the hearse is out, then I'm at a loss.'

Olivia smiled. 'I think we should move forward out of sight of the checkpoints.' As they cycled away from the intersection, Olivia continued, 'I like the ambulance plan. I suppose if we become desperate, we could call for one and then hijack it, although it's not my preferred option. Come on, Max – think! There must be a way to escape on foot.'

'I've got it,' Max said triumphantly, a man experiencing an epiphany as he pointed to a maintenance hole cover, the removable plate forming the lid over Barcelona's underground sewer system. 'The historic sewer networks! Its foundations were laid in medieval times and crisscross the city. There is a veritable maze of galleries, passageways, and tunnels. From down there, we can go anywhere in the city undetected. If you want a guaranteed way out of here, there's your answer.'

'You're a genius, Max, but I have one question. If it's a complex underground maze down there, is there a map, so we don't become lost?'

'We won't need a map, Olivia. The sewers follow the road network. We go in here, follow it back to the intersection we passed, turn right, travel three blocks to bring us to the other side of the checkpoint we spotted. Then, we steal a car and drive to Montserrat ourselves, and if we come across other checkpoints ...' Max took a breath, smiled and said, '... we'll have to deal with it, think on our feet if it happens. Far be it, Olivia, that I should blow my own trumpet, but I must admit, this is one super cunning and brilliant plan!'

'I'm not sure that Lady Olivia Suzanne Elizabeth Huggins from England sees herself wallowing about in excrement. Won't we come out the other side - how can I describe this politely? A little on the nose.'

Max laughed heartily before saying, 'At our age, people expect us to be incontinent and have the smell of wee, so why disappoint them?'

Olivia thought for a moment. 'I have some reservations, but I won't stand in the way of one of your *cunning plans,* Max. I'm in your hands, so lead on Sir Max of the sewer rats.'

With no traffic to contend with, Max dismounted his bike and, after lowering the stand, walked to the middle of the road, stopping beside the maintenance hole cover. When he didn't move, Olivia, assuming that he was waiting for her, left her bike and joined him, however Max remained motionless. 'Is something wrong?' she asked.

'Um, I've discovered one slight hitch to my supercalifragilisticexpialidocious plan.'

Olivia looked at him inquisitively. 'And that would be?'

'The maintenance hole cover – it's an immovable object.'

'Immoveable?'

'Yes. Even my superpowers have some limitations, and one of them is called gravity. I've thought about leveraging it up with the tips of our umbrellas, except the cover is made from solid steel, too heavy for even the finest British brolly. For a fleeting moment, I even contemplated kneeling and attempting to lift it off myself, but that would end in tears.'

Olivia, who had another idea in mind, smiled to herself, saying with a straight face. 'I see. And it's too heavy for a big, muscular man like you. If I was unkind, which I'm not, but Lady Olivia Suzanne Elizabeth Huggins from England might say, this immovable object, as you describe it, is a fundamental flaw in your otherwise brilliant plan. She might add that you've fallen at the first hurdle. Or in this case – maintenance hole.'

Max shrugged his shoulders, a grin spreading across his face. 'I suppose now you're going to tell me you have an alternative solution.'

'Indeed, I do Max. We climb onto the roof of a multi-storey building and, from that vantage point, we can assess an escape route. We then use the rooftops as our footpath to freedom. When we need to cross a road, we descend to the ground floor, in between checkpoints and barricades of course, before entering another building and taking to the skywalk again. I'd estimate that we have to transverse one or two blocks before we are free of the lockdown epicentre. I call this my atmospheric idea and, if I were a trendy young consultant, I'd charge you twenty-five thousand dollars and call it "Blue Sky Thinking" or something like that.'

'An interesting scheme, I admit. However, I also have one question. If Lady Olivia Suzanne Elizabeth Huggins from England found displeasure in going underground, how will she heave her weary body up rickety old fire escapes?'

'Ha! If God had intended Lady Olivia Suzanne Elizabeth Huggins from England to walk up rickety old fire escapes, she wouldn't have invented lifts.' Olivia gestured for Max to follow her, saying, 'Come along, Sir Max of the sewer rats.'

Back on their electric bikes, they rode away from the shopping strip and back to where residential apartments surrounded them. *This will do nicely*, Olivia said to herself, raising her hand, signalling Max to stop.

'Dismount,' she called with the authority of a cavalry officer.

Abandoning the bikes, Olivia led Max to the entrance of an apartment building. Next to the front door was a row of the intercom buttons that allow visitors to call a resident and be buzzed into the building. Olivia raised her index finger and, running it over the panel, said, as she had done in the police car, 'Eenie Meenie Miney Moe – I hope it works this time.' As her figure stopped, she pressed the button under it. Thirty seconds later, a voice on the other end of the intercom, a woman said, 'Hello?'

'Good afternoon, madam. My name is Olivia, and I'm here with my partner, Max. We are with the Ministry of Health's Coronavirus contact tracing team. I'm sure you have heard of us. Our task is to find people who have been in close contact with someone diagnosed with COVID-19 and our aim is to reduce the chances of that person inadvertently passing the virus onto family, friends and the community. We need to speak to you Madam and request that you undertake a COVID test. There's no cause for alarm, as this is a precautionary measure. Please remain in your flat; my partner and I will come to you.'

There was a humming sound followed by the click of the door remotely unlocking from inside. Olivia turned to Max, saying with a grin. 'Lady Olivia Suzanne Elizabeth Huggins from England intends to take the elevator to the roof. If you desire to climb the fire escape, far be it from me to deter you.'

'After you m'lady. I'll be right behind you.'

Olivia stopped and, looking at Max, dropped the pretence of their game and said, 'No Max, you will be right beside me as it has always been and I dream that, throughout eternity, it will always be. Come, my precious man, and one last time, let us rescue our girl.'

The roof of the apartment offered what Olivia had hoped, an unimpeded view of the checkpoints they had to avoid. The ease of moving from one rooftop to the next came as a surprise, and they breezed past the first roadblock, albeit six stories up.

'One down and one to go,' Olivia said, pointing, 'At the end of this block, we have to drop down to the ground, cross the road, and then use the buildings over there to take us past the last barrier. What could be easier?'

Following Olivia's instructions, unobserved, they crossed the street and used the same deception to gain entry to another apartment building. This time, however, there was no lift to a common area, a flat roof used for recreation and social gatherings during more normal times. Instead, they found a maintenance access ladder. Max kept his thoughts to himself.

A steep ladder. This isn't looking promising.

Climbing a ladder at any age poses its challenges, but when one is over eighty, reaching the top is like conquering Mt. Everest and just as dangerous. With their legs shaking and breathing erratic, they made the landing with its service access door. On the other side of the door, they found an observation platform, one meant to permit repairs on the ridge of a 30.26-degree pitched roof of red terracotta tiles. The checkpoint they were avoiding was on the left side of the building, halfway along the road below, three hundred metres away from where they were standing. Olivia shook her head.

How did I miss the pitched roof? She realised she hadn't. *I saw it but didn't consider the consequences. Silly girl.*

Max, standing beside Olivia, surveyed their predicament, thinking,

Even if we could walk precariously along the capping tiles – only fifteen centimetres wide – and make it past the patrol below, we would have another two hundred metres before we reach the safety of another service platform.

Straining his eyes, Max thought he could see a maintenance door, like the one they had come through.

If we could make it, it looks like we can access the building.

Peering to his right, Max noticed a row of solar cells secured to the pitched roof, running the entire length of where they were heading.

Olivia, scratching her head while taking stock of their predicament, expected Max, in the guise of wit, to make a funny observation of their current problem. Instead, he offered what she was thinking.

'Is this where our Parkour lessons come in handy?'

Olivia grinned, masking her fear. 'I told you I was a woman of vision.'

Max chuckled, 'Let it never be said otherwise. Do you want to go first or shall I?'

'This time, Max, it is I who will be right behind you. Watch that breeze, my love, because it may unsettle your balance.'

I wish you hadn't said that!

Taking a deep breath, Max pulled his bowler hat hard down on to his head so it wouldn't be blown off.

Grasping his umbrella between his two hands as he had done on the wall at Parkour to aid his balance, Max put his right foot onto the ridge, moving it from side to side to test the tile, ensuring that it was secure, before moving his other foot. Carefully, he edged forward while pushing to the back of his mind the sensation that his body was swaying side to side each time a foot was in the air. Behind him, Olivia was issuing instructions, her voice a steady stream of commands that Max struggled to ignore, though not without some difficulty.

'Remember our lessons, Max. Momentum! Momentum! Momentum! If you keep moving, the motion will assist with your balance.'

That's easy for you to say. Just wait until you're out here.

'Okay,' Max snapped, increasing his speed as he mumbled to himself, 'Whatever you do, Max, don't look down. Focus on where you're going.'

A gust of wind caught Max mid-step, and he felt his bodyweight being pushed dangerously to the left as his foot hovered mid-air, unable to find a secure grounding. He knew he was at risk of toppling from the roof with the prospect of certain death. 'Oh my goodness!'

Remember the lessons. Redirect your momentum – find the most efficient placement for your feet. Most of all - bend your knees, Max!

Letting go of his umbrella with his left hand, Max swung it out to the right, using it as a counterweight, allowing him to ground his foot on the capping. He brought the umbrella back to its resting position in front of him and held it between his two hands again. The sway of his body stopped, and he took a deep breath.

That was close.

'Are you there?' Max called to Olivia, in a voice that sounded cooler than he was feeling.

'Right behind you.'

Max opened his mouth to say *I almost fell,* but changed his mind and said instead, 'Parkour is about overcoming obstacles, one of which is gravity.'

Having witnessed the close encounter, Olivia called encouragingly, 'Keep going, Max. You are doing well.'

Edging slowly forward, Max called back, 'I hope the police don't look up, or we'll have a welcoming committee by the time we reach the other side.'

'Yes, we must be quite a sight from the groun ... Ah!'

Olivia's call of anguish was followed by the sound of her sliding out of control down the tiled roof. Max stopped, panic-stricken, dead in his tracks. He tried turning his head to look behind to see what had happened; however, the movement unsettled his balance and, for a moment, he rocked precariously, tinkering with falling himself. Max regained his poise, and the dread of falling was replaced by despair, a feeling of helplessness, knowing that Olivia had plunged to her death and that there was nothing he could do.

'Aren't you going to ask me if I'm okay?' Olivia said, an edge of panic in her tone.

From the direction of her voice, Max knew Olivia was behind him, suspended on the pitch of the roof. How far down he couldn't guess. Max called back, 'What happened?'

'I've fallen and was stopped by one of the solar cell panels, or at least that's what I think, because my toes are resting on something. I can't tell because I'm facing the roof.'

'Have you broken any bones?'

'No. I don't think so.'

Olivia felt movement under her feet. The panel was coming loose with her weight and, if it gave way, she would fall six storeys to her death. 'Max!'

'Yes.'

'My love, there's nothing you can do for me up here. Keep going and, when you get to the other side before you leave to rescue Claudia, call the fire brigade. They will come and save me.'

There was something in Olivia's voice, and it told Max that she didn't expect to survive that long and he guessed her footings were giving way. Max couldn't turn around or walk backward; all he could do was keep moving forward. What other choice did he have? As he thought about their predicament, the breeze picked up again, causing him to sway. They both could die.

What should I do? If I don't call for help right now, Olivia will fall to certain death. But if I contact the authorities, they'll arrest us, and Claudia will be lost.

Max looked to the heavens and whispered a quiet prayer, before saying quietly to himself, 'There's only one thing for it, Max, and you know it. Save Olivia or die trying.'

Max brought his feet together, shuffled clockwise and began edging his way around until he was perpendicular to the capping. From this vantage point, as he stared out over the sloping roof, he could see for the first time Olivia's perilous state. A gust of wind caught him and his body rocked. His brain supercharged, Max popped opened his umbrella and held it against the breeze, using it as a sail to stabilise and restore his balance.

That might work!

By shifting the position of the umbrella, tacking it against the wind, he was able to complete the U-turn and face back the way he had come. Retracing his steps along the ridge, Max stopped above where Olivia had fallen. While staring ahead, fearing looking down to where Olivia was stuck lest he tumble, Max said, 'Hello.'

Olivia glanced up at him. 'You're a silly but wonderfully brave man. I wonder, however, what you are expecting to do?'

'Watch this; I'm calling it my penguin shuffle.' Max started turning to face Olivia, although all she could see of him were the tips of his shoes over the ridge. Dropping his eyes, Max added, 'I can see you now.'

Oooh, that's a long way down.

'Do you have a plan?' Olivia asked as the solar cell mounting bracket gave way further.

Feigning surprise, Max said, 'Do I have a plan? Of course. Now, I want you to hold the tip of your umbrella and push the handle up towards me. I'll lower mine down and, when we have hooked the handles together, you can climb up.'

Max lowered his brolly down but, as Olivia had already surmised, it reached only to his feet.

Max mumbled, his voice betraying his annoyance. 'Well, that didn't work as I was expecting. Never fear, I have another brilliant idea.'

The solar cell moved again, and panic flowed through Olivia's body. She tried to adjust her footing, hoping to spread her weight more evenly.

Max began to shuffle back, retracing his steps before making a U-turn. Olivia's voice, betraying her desperate situation, cut through the tension. 'Where are you going now?'

Max warily lowered himself so that he was sitting, his legs on either side of the roof capping.

I hope I can get up again!

Sounding confident, Max yelled. 'Lift your brolly again.'

Once more, the umbrellas were short of each other. A creaking noise startled both of them as Olivia felt her footings give way further as a roofing tile came loose and tumbled to the ground, smashing on impact.

'Leave now, Max.' Olivia said, not wishing her beloved husband to witness her fate.

Think man, think!

Placing his umbrella on the ridge in front of him, Max untied the belt of his trench coat before slipping it from his shoulders and taking off his shoulder holster. After removing the gun, putting it in his pants, he threaded the umbrella handle through the holster and lowering it over the edge. 'Try again.'

Olivia reached up, this time hooking the bottom of the holster with her umbrella.

'Well done, my love. You can do this, Olivia. The roof pitch is shallow so, if you use the umbrellas as anchors, you'll be able to climb up.'

'I'm not sure I can, Max.'

'Of course you can, my love. What is it they unkindly say about we oldies? That we revert to being toddlers. Well then, show me how well you can crawl and scramble up the roof.'

Olivia raised her head and looked at Max as she smiled and said, 'I'm not sure I like that analogy as a motivational speech, being likened to a toddler, but that reference makes me want to come up there and smack you. Hang on tight because here I come.'

Despite his preparation, the sudden transfer of Olivia's weight to the umbrellas—her only support as she began to climb— caught Max off guard. He swayed dangerously for a moment before managing to steady himself. Olivia, her body pushed flat against the tiles, placing one hand over the other and using the brollies as her guide, began crawling up the roof. As she reached the top, Max asked her to wait while he retrieved the umbrellas and his shoulder holster, saying when it was done. 'Okay my love, I'm ready for you now.'

Had anyone been watching, they would have witnessed the last part of Olivia's ascent, an undignified affair as she arrived and mounted of the capping. By the time it was over, she and Max sat straddling the pitch of the roof, one leg hanging down each side, facing in opposite directions, back-to-back. Olivia let out an exhausted sigh as she said, 'Thank you, Max. I thought I was a goner!'

Max laughed.

'Here I am, trying to be grateful, and you find something to snicker about.' Her tone did not match Olivia's testy words as she continued, 'And what is so funny?'

'I thought we must look like a couple of beached whales. Then it occurred to me it's been many years since I've been able to rise from the floor without leaning on something. I have no idea how we're going to get up from this position. Even the authorities might need a helicopter to lift us out of here.'

Olivia smiled, 'That would be true, Max except, Lady Olivia Suzanne Elizabeth Huggins from England has a plan.'

'Oh, yes? Pray tell, my love.'

'We push against each other and stand up at the same time. Like we did on those silly team-building weekends. Who would have thought that those ridiculous trust exercises would have a use?'

Max reminded Olivia that the last team-building activity they had "been forced" to attend was thirty years ago. Regardless, on their second attempt, they were standing. It then occurred to them, with the noise they'd made, the police at the checkpoint had probably been watching. Olivia stole a glimpse, and it seemed their life-threatening deeds were going unnoticed. Max continued forward across the ridge. Olivia, rather than risking the dangerous manoeuvre of turning around, returned to the maintenance platform and started the crossing again. With great relief, they both made it to the other side without further incident, then sprang slowly in the way only an octogenarian could, down the internal stairs of the apartment, exiting unseen onto a deserted street. They breathed a collective sigh of relief, having made it past the inner circle of control points.

Handing Olivia back her umbrella and brushing dust and grime from his clothes, Max asked, 'What now, my love?'

'If my memory serves me correctly, which fortunately it does, you have a talent for stealing cars.'

'Only the older ones like us, m'lady.'

'Well then, that will have to do. Let's go shopping for a vintage vehicle, red if you can find one. I hear they are faster.'

As they walked down the empty street, Max checked over his shoulder, wanting to ensure that they were alone. Rounding the corner at the end of the road, they saw a city square with a decorative fountain at its centre. They stopped. On the far side of the fountain was a white van, its rear sliding door open and the motor running. "Ajuntament Barcelona" – Barcelona City Council, was inscribed on its side.

Dropping back to be out of sight, Max searched for the driver, saying, 'It's not an older vehicle, m'lady. However, one with keys in the ignition is always preferable, regardless of its age.' He looked about again and added, 'I can't see anyone, can you?'

Olivia shook her head while saying, 'No.'

'Okay, as quick as we can, Olivia, before the owners return.'

With umbrellas swinging out in front of them as they strode, Max and Olivia set off at a brisk pace. Two secret agents on a mission, walking with the confidence of people meant to be there. Oliver inconspicuously glanced to her left then right as they passed the fountain, observing that they were still alone, which in any other circumstance, other than a global pandemic, would have been out of the ordinary and a cause for alarm.

Where is the driver? Olivia wondered as they approached the van, before whispering to Max, 'I'll drive.'

Max nodded, changing his trajectory and moving towards the passenger side. Olivia reached the driver's door and was surprised by a man dressed in work overalls seated behind the wheel. He looked up from his smartphone, 'Hello, Olivia ...' and then glancing at the passenger side of the van, added. '... and a hearty welcome to you, Max. I've been expecting you both.'

For an instant, Olivia wondered if the man was a Chinese agent, and their goose cooked. Dismissing the thought as impossible, she said, 'My good Sir, you seem to have us at a disadvantage. Who might you be?'

Giving a slight bow of his head, the man answered, 'Pedro Cadiz, at your service.'

Max appeared from the passenger side of the van and, joining Olivia, asked, confusion written on his face. 'Pedro, how is it you know who we are?'

Holding his smartphone for them both to see, Pedro said. 'You two are all over the internet. First, you're being chased by the police with everyone out on their balconies singing encouragement to you, and then I watched in horror at your antics on the apartment roof. I honestly thought you were going to fall to your deaths. I recognised the location; it was only a matter of time before you ended up here. I'm surprised the police aren't already on the scene. But then again, they're probably more focused on handling roadblocks and apprehending you both than on watching the live feed of your escape. Regardless, you have little time—they will be here soon.

Realising that time was running out, Olivia couldn't resist asking, 'Yes, but how do you know our names?'

'You are the famed Max and Olivia of the motorbike and sidecar adventure that went viral when you were spritely eighty-five-year-olds. People are posting your past stories while this latest escapade unfolds. The horrific crash that almost cost you your lives, running away from a nursing home in Australia, your escape to the United Kingdom and then being chased across Britain by the police. All of it!'

Max smiled to himself, feeling chuffed as he remembered the people on the balconies: *they were calling my name*. The ramifications suddenly struck him. He scrunched up his face, mouthing to Olivia so that only she could see, 'Linda and the Chinese will know we are coming!' Then he thought, *Stephen Walls! He will be furious – again.*

Olivia raised her eyebrows, acknowledging Max, while Pedro kept talking, unaware of their private conversation. 'It's all right here on my phone. Many of the comments cite you as spies; secret agents like Ja ... Ja. What is his name again? Oh, that's right, Jason Bourne.' He hesitated for a second, unable to think of a famous female spy and not wanting to exclude Olivia, added 'Jason Bourne and Wonder Woman.'

'Was Wonder Woman a spy?' Max asked, chuckling.

Olivia growled at Max for his comment, saying sternly, 'Max!'

Olivia, stroking her chin, suggesting she was contemplating her words, before saying. 'We still are Pedro.'

Pedro examined Olivia, a puzzled look drifting across his face as a smile lightened his expression.

Olivia continued, 'We are secret agents, and we're on perhaps our most dangerous mission yet – a rescue operation. We mustn't get caught by the police, and we need your help.'

Pedro chuckled, then it morphed into full-blown laughter as he reflected on the absurdity of Olivia's comment. He believed they were on the run from a care facility, trying to escape the lockdown. 'Seriously!' he said. 'I can believe that you were both once involved in espionage, and it's a privilege to meet such famous people. Even if you are... no disrespect intended Max and Olivia, ex-spies. At your age, it isn't plausible for you to still be involved in active missions.' He paused before saying, 'If you are spies, where are the guns?' Imitating an American accent, he added. 'Are you packing?'

Olivia gave a slight nod of her head and unbuckled her trench coat, revealing her right shoulder and the pistol holstered there.

'Oh, my goodness!' Pedro said, his mouth hanging open but, before he could make another utterance, Olivia changed hands and, opening the coat on the other side, revealed another pistol secured in a shoulder holster. Pedro's attention drifted to Max, who was holding a Glock in the palm of his hand.

Olivia said, smiling, 'Satisfied?'

Pedro nodded, lowering his head as he said, 'I'm sorry. How rude of me. I must have sounded patronising.' He took a deep breath, paused for a moment before adding, 'Excuse me for asking, but aren't spies meant to be incognito – not draw unwanted attention to themselves?'

Olivia shrugged her shoulders. 'Ordinarily, yes. Wouldn't you agree with me, Max?' She glanced at Max, and he knew from her tone that it was his turn to make up the story.

'Ordinarily,' Max repeated, buying time as he pondered what to say next. 'Yes, you're referring to the grey man or woman, a person who moves around the periphery of our awareness, an essential skill for any spy. That applies only to the young ones, anyone under eighty, that is.' Max snatched a glance at Olivia, indicating that it was her turn to continue.

'Yes. As you age, Pedro, eccentricity and being noticed becomes a disguise in its self. You didn't believe that we were spies, did you? That proves our masquerade worked.'

Pedro was far from convinced.

Olivia touched him lightly on the arm and said, 'We need your help.'

With a hint of nervousness in his voice, Pedro asked, 'How do I know your good spies and not the bad kind? I will not commit treason.'

Olivia gave Pedro a reassuring smile while spreading her arms, a sign of transparency as she said, 'Look at us, Pedro. Do we appear the black-hatted type? No, we're the good guys, and if you drive us to Montserrat, I will tell you about our mission to rescue a kidnapped couple and their seven-year-old daughter from the clutches of the sinister Linda Orr and ruthless agents of the Chinese State Security.'

'And their cat,' Max added.

'They have a cat?' Pedro said in a tone of confusion.

Olivia nodded as she said, 'Snowflake is its name. Now drive, my good man, for I feel you have an important part to play in your nation's security.' Olivia raised a finger to her lips and continued, 'What we will tell you is top secret. When this is over, you will appear to have been abducted by two crazy seniors, Max and Olivia. Only you and your government will know the truth, and it's a truth that can never be shared. Are you with us, Pedro?'

'I'm with you,' Pedro said triumphantly before turning his mind to smuggling Max and Olivia to Montserrat, saying. 'You will both have to hide in the back of the van because we have several checkpoints to make it through.'

A look of concern passed over Max's face, and he asked. 'Will that be difficult?'

Smiling, Pedro held an official-looking piece of paper aloft as he said, 'Not with one of these it won't. An essential worker travel pass.'

'Time for you to go; you've served me well,' Max said, taking off his bowler hat and then holding it like a Frisbee.

Pedro, seeing what Max was about to do, asked, 'If you are going to throw it away, would you mind if I kept your English hat as a souvenir?'

'Sure.'

CHAPTER 20
The Rescue

For Max and Olivia, the trip from Barcelona to Montserrat was bumpy and uncomfortable in the back of the Council van. During the journey, they meticulously studied the Abbey plans sent by Inspector Axel, on which he'd highlighted old dungeons built below what was once a Roman temple to worship the God Venus, a good as any to begin their search for Claudia. The map highlighted the long-forgotten service tunnels, passages built inside the complex for the movement of goods. They were hidden pathways which Max and Olivia hoped to exploit during their daring rescue. The entry into the tunnels system was a chapel, one story below the monastery's ground floor, and a secret door behind the altar, its entrance camouflaged as a stone arch opened by engaging a hidden mechanism embedded in the architecture. Once inside the passageway, they would travel underground, eventually reaching the dungeon complex further below. Olivia called to Pedro from the back of the van, asking him how long it would be before they arrived at Montserrat.

'We're about ten minutes away. Where would you like to be dropped?'

'How well do you know Montserrat Abbey?'

'I've been a few times, as it's one place we take overseas visitors. Very popular it is, too.'

'You know where the museum is?' Olivia asked.

'Yes.'

'Excellent. There's a door below an arched stained-glass window, close to the entrance to the museum. Do you know it?'

Pedro replied, his voice peppered with alarm, 'Oh yes, I know it. It's on the main road - right out front! I thought that you'd sneak in via a back entrance or arrive disguised as a pizza deliverer, like in the movies, or something that meant you're not seen, stopped or, worse, killed.'

Olivia's voice oozing with calm said, 'Ordinarily Pedro, a surprise is essential but, with what you told us about our current notoriety, our adversaries will expect us. If I were them, I'd want us inside where we could be easily cornered and contained. Neither Max nor I expect any resistance getting inside. Once there, well, it becomes a different story.'

'That makes sense,' Pedro called from the cab.

Olivia continued, 'Once you've dropped us off, drive two or three kilometres away and wait for our call. If all goes to plan, you will have a full load for the return trip to Barcelona.'

'And if it doesn't?'

'Let's not think about that, Pedro.'

As they reached the outskirts of Montserrat, no one spoke until Pedro called, 'I can see the entrance.' His heart pounding with a mixture of fear and apprehension, he slowed the van before coming to a halt. His legs were like lead weights as he moved to extract himself from the van and open the sliding door for Max and Olivia to disembark.

'Aren't you taking your umbrella?' Max asked Olivia, noticing that she was leaving the van without it.

'I thought yours would suffice.'

Max breathed out heavily before replying, 'I'd be more comfortable if you carried yours as a backup.'

Olivia was uncertain, but complied. 'Alright, that sounds sensible.' As she stepped down, she reminded Pedro, repeating, 'Remember, park two or three kilometres away and await our call, please.'

The door below the arched stained-glass window opened easily onto a narrow passageway that Max and Olivia followed to the edge of the main hall. From their vantage point, they spotted a stone staircase twenty metres away on the opposite side of the room, leading to the level below. Uneven light filtered through the stained-glass windows above, permitting them to scan the wide-open space in search of a trap. The silence jangled Olivia's nerves, and she said, 'I don't like it, Max, we'll be too exposed. They'll mow us down if we try to cross – there must be another way?'

Max studied the map in the dim light before saying, 'Nothing has changed since the last time we looked. My love, regretfully, this is our lot! If you want a more positive spin: once we are down those stairs, our options improve.' He reached inside his trench coat and took out his pistol and, with more confidence than he was feeling, said, 'I'll go first. You stay here and cover me and when I make it to the other side, I'll do the same for you.'

Unsure but with no alternatives on offer, Olivia replied as Max was about to step out, 'Okay, but this is one of those occasions where I wish we could still run.'

Max chuckled and, as he took his first stride, said, 'I'm not even sure I remember how. Once, my love, we moved with speed, and now it's with dignity.' Clear of the hiding place, Max strolled forward, moving his weapon in a sweeping arch as he began making his way across no-man's land. His tactics were to take the shortest route and head directly across the hall, stealth his friend. The plan shattered when, each time his foot struck the floor, its impact echoed, filling the otherwise silent chamber with reverberation, causing him to cringe with each stride. Max was surprised when he made it to the other side unscathed and he unconsciously brushed himself down as if surviving an epic journey, a man walking across the Sahara Desert or conquering some other insurmountable obstacle. Turning, he beckoned for Olivia to follow and, as she began her marathon, he gazed across the area, the barrel of his gun following his eyes.

When Olivia arrived safely, Max said, as though he'd never thought otherwise, 'That wasn't so bad.'

His newfound confidence was short-lived as Olivia whispered, 'They are funnelling us into their web.'

Wanting to remain positive, Max jested, 'Ah, yes, m'lady, but little do they know that is precisely what we want them to think.'

'We do?' Olivia said, feigning surprise.

'No, but shush. Don't tell them that.'

Olivia shook her head, pretending dismay. 'Come on Max, according to our map, the Chapel is down the stairs and then we turn right on the landing.'

With their weapons at the ready, they carefully approached the stairs beginning their descent. As in the apartment building, Max found the going challenging, resorting to his umbrella as a walking stick to steady himself. In the apartment building, the carpeted stairwell had absorbed the sound of the tip of his umbrella hitting the ground. On the stone staircase of Montserrat, the Tap-Tap-Tap noise sounded as if Long John Silver, the peg-leg pirate from Robert Louis Stevenson's Treasure Island, was descending. Every few runs, the tapping would stop as Max swivelled his head and shoulders to see if they were alone, only to start up again, a signal to anyone waiting that they were continuing their downward journey. If Max's stereophonic movement perturbed Olivia, she kept her thoughts to herself, only speaking when they reached the landing. 'The Chapel's this way.'

On any other occasion, opening the Chapel door to reveal its architectural splendour would have taken their breaths away but not on this occasion. Instead, Max and Olivia felt a mixture of relief tinged with apprehension, believing they'd only made it this far because that's what Linda Orr wanted. They feared they were entering the lion's den. Max, alert to his wife's concerns, said reassuringly, 'The monastery is a labyrinth and Linda can't patrol all the entry and exit points.' He wasn't sure if he believed himself as they lingered in the doorway, straining their ears for signs of a trap inside. Finally, Max whispered, 'The Chapel is deathly silent.'

Olivia raised her eyebrows as she said, causing Max to shrug, 'My love, perhaps you could have chosen a word other than "deathly".' She gave him a tap on the bottom with her umbrella before saying, 'Come on, there is no point in lingering any longer. Shall we walk boldly down the Nave to the Apse behind the altar or keep to the Aisle and use the columns as cover?'

Pondering, Max said, 'It's always good to have a plan. I say we've been lucky so far, so let's stay closer to the Aisle and weave in and out the columns.'

Young nimbler agents would have sprinted, guns drawn and dashed from column to column, ready to shoot it out with their enemy. For the venerable that wasn't an option, so as Olivia stepped over the threshold, she said to Max, 'A menacing pace is what's needed.'

'Aye, aye Captain, a menacing pace it is.'

They set off, lingering at each of the massive columns, as much to catch their breaths as to take cover. When passing a substantial architectural feature on the fortress-like wall, they didn't spot the person hiding there, not until a male voice spoke, 'Don't either of you move a muscle and do not turn around!'

Max and Olivia froze.

'It's your lucky day because the boss has instructed me to ensure that you are delivered to her alive. Do exactly as I say, and you will be unharmed. I hope we understand each other?' Unbeknown to Max and Olivia, the statement was untrue, intended to encourage their compliance.

'We do,' Max and Olivia said in unison.

'Make no mistake, Max and Olivia, I will not underestimate your cunningness or skills. Despite appearances to the contrary, your reputation suggests that you are both extremely dangerous. One wrong move and I will not hesitate to kill you, whatever my orders. Now, toss your guns away.'

Max and Olivia obeyed, and the sound of the weapons striking the stone floor reverberated throughout the chapel.

'Okay. Turn around slowly, keeping your hands where I can see them.'

Max and Olivia turned to face an athletically built man in his mid-forties, wearing a black short-sleeved T-shirt, bone coloured cargo pants and pointing a high-powered assault rifle at them. His sidearm was a HK45s, Heckler and Koch, a semi-automatic pistol. To Max and Olivia, he resembled a mercenary, similar to the men they'd encountered in A Coruña. Probably part of the same team, they both thought.

'Drop the umbrellas.'

Olivia immediately did, but Max hesitated and said, 'My balance, it isn't what it once was, and I need the brolly to help me stand.'

'This isn't a debate, Max. Besides, I watched the live streaming of you walking across the ridge of a roof. Your balance was exemplary, wouldn't you agree? Now, I won't ask you again. Drop it, and if the tip leaves the ground, even a whisker, you're as dead as a Dodo.'

Max released his grip, and the umbrella tumbled to the ground with a crash.

A smirk drifted across the mercenary's face. 'A good decision, Max. Now, very slowly, Max, I want you to remove your trench coat and drop it.' As Max's overcoat slumped in a heap on the ground, the mercenary turned to Olivia. 'And now you.'

She followed suit.

'Looky here! Olivia is like an American gangster, a weapon for each shoulder. Using two fingers so that I can see you, I want you to remove the weapon and let it fall to the ground.'

Olivia followed the instructions.

'Boot it away from you.'

Olivia tried to comply but, after two attempts, when the pistol moved only a couple of centimetres, and she wobbled unsteadily on one leg, the mercenary said, his voice dripping with impatience, 'That will do.'

He weighed up Max and Olivia's appearance, his eyes telling him that in front of him were a couple of doddering old fools and he felt sure the frailty wasn't a façade, however, he knew they were lethal. It seemed, for this old couple, what you saw wasn't what you got.

'You don't know me, but you met my brother in A Coruña, and one of you killed him, shot him dead in the back of a van. The boss may want you alive, but I have other plans for you. In memory of my brother, I will shoot you both, and I think ...' He paused as he swung the barrel of the gun towards Olivia, '... I will start with you.'

Max cleared his throat, attracting the mercenary's attention before saying, 'To be fair, my good man, your brother was trying to kill us. We acted only in self-defence. If you are killing us because of a directive, well, that is understandable. Retribution seems hypocritical, considering the space we each play in.'

'Are you trying to tell me that losing my brother was just *bad luck*?'

Olivia, her voice lowered, said, 'Well, Max, that went well.'

The mercenary shook his head in disbelief. 'If dying laughing is what you wish to do, I will be happy to oblige. I know better than to play your stupid games.'

Max saw tension flexing in the mercenary's trigger figure. He wasn't sure why he was trying to stall; he hadn't a plan in place, and no one was coming to their rescue. Regardless, he said, 'Don't we get a last wish?'

Pointing the gun directly at Olivia, the mercenary's face remained emotionless, the resolve of an executioner as he squeezed the trigger saying, 'No ...'

BANG!

Death was instantaneous as a bullet struck the mercenary in the chest, sending him tumbling backwards to the floor. Max and Olivia froze to the spot, both perplexed and shocked by what had occurred. After ten seconds had passed, they glanced at each other, having expected the unseen person who'd killed the mercenary to issue instructions. In the silence, it was Olivia who spoke first, 'Where did that come from?'

Breathing a heavy sigh of relief, Max answered. 'I believe it came from somewhere behind us and my guess, the front of the church, using the altar as cover. It's all speculation, mind you, Olivia. What I know is, whoever fired is an excellent marksman because the bullet passed so close to us, I felt it's bow-wave as it flew by.'

'Could it have been Claudia?' Olivia asked.

Moving for the first time since the shot rang out, Max turned and scanned the direction of the mystery shooter before saying, 'I doubt it, because if that were the case, she'd be with us now. Whoever this was wanted to remain hidden and has vanished, but it would seem we have an ally on our quest, a guardian angel lurking in the shadows, which I can only describe as interesting.'

'Interesting isn't the word that springs to my mind, Max. A miracle is more fitting, especially considering our religious location. Let's keep moving before another assassin confronts us, and if our angel does have wings, this time we might be on our own.'

Olivia began salvaging their discarded items, passing Max his pistol and then the umbrella but not his coat. Her eyes close to the floor, Olivia spotted the mercenary was wearing an earpiece, meaning that he was carrying a two-way radio. 'That will come in handy,' she said while moving the body and removing it. Max, unable to see what she was doing, gave Olivia a confused look.

'This,' she said, holding the radio up for him to see before securing it to herself, placing the headphones in her ear while adding, 'Let's do it.'

Max stood his ground. 'What about our coats?'

'I think we should discard them because they've served their purpose and may hinder us from here on in.'

'Have they indeed? What about the flashlights in the pockets?'

'Max, you see, you didn't forget. Those people who unkindly say that you are going senile have it wrong. Congratulations, you just passed the memory test that I set you.'

Max smiled as Olivia groaned with the aches and pains of an older woman as she began to bend down once more.

'Wait,' Max said, and then used the handle of his umbrella to hook Olivia's coat. Removing the torch, he handed it to her and repeated the process for his jacket. Feeling smug, Max gestured with his arm towards the front of the church and, giving a slight bow of his head, said, 'After you, m'lady.'

Something caught Max's eye as they approached the altar. 'Well, I never. I thought she retired a long time ago.'

Olivia looked at him with surprise, saying, 'What is it?'

From on top of the altar, Max retrieved an origami crane and held it for Olivia to see. 'The Crane is here and that, my dear, is who saved our lives' He shook his head, 'I wonder why?'

'She?' Olivia said, her voice laden with surprise. 'You know the identity of the Crane?'

'Sort of, though I've never laid eyes on her. However, we have spoken. Twice, as a matter of fact, and the last time was' - Max hesitated as he tried to recall the occasion, '... it would have to be twenty-five, perhaps even thirty years ago. That would make the Crane somewhere in her sixties, if not seventy by now.'

'You've never told me this before.'

'No, I don't suppose I have. Both times followed one of her executions in the circumstances not dissimilar to what has occurred here today. I would discover the body and next to it, there would be an origami crane. As I looked about for the assassin, a voice spoke to me from the shadows, telling me to *relax, "Max, you are not my target today"*. We chatted for a couple of minutes and then she would say *"until next time"*. Then, as if by magic, the crane would disappear. I vividly remember my heart in my throat, knowing that if I were the target, I would be dead for sure. The Crane always was unstoppable. I probably didn't tell you because it's one of those encounters that you push from your mind. I wonder what she's doing here and why help us? It's a puzzle, Olivia.'

Olivia held her hand out towards Max as she said, 'Can I take a look?' Max passed her the origami crane and Olivia turned it over in her hand, noticing what looked like writing. 'Look at this; it might be a message.'

Max nodded his agreement.

Olivia carefully unfolded the work of origami, not wanting to damage it. 'It's not writing, Max, but a drawing. It looks like a map.' She held it for Max to see and he placed the Crane's drawing next to the monastery plans that Inspector Axel had provided.

'It's a map, all right.' Max said. 'Those two crosses: one is in the dungeons where we are heading, the other is in another underground complex. The Crane is telling us that our hostages are in two separate locations, which is both good and bad. Good, because we made the right decision making for the dungeons and bad, as this job has become a lot harder.'

'Where do you think the Crane went after she shot the mercenary?'

Max considered the question and, pointing towards the stone arch that topped the two-figure statue columns of the Virgin Mary holding the baby Jesus behind the altar, said. 'It has to be the same place we're heading.'

'I think you are right.'

'Olivia, my love, you know what to do.'

Following the instructions Inspector Axel had given her, Olivia simultaneously pressed the open hand of the Virgin Mary on each column. A panel, the size of an enormous fist, appeared to the right of the arch, springing open with a *plop*.

'Well done,' Max whispered, wondering why he'd suddenly started whispering.

Olivia unconsciously followed Max and whispered, 'According to Inspector Axel, the trigger mechanism is about a metre inside the panel, and all we have to do is pull on it, and it will unlock the secret door.' Using the torch, she peered inside the hole. 'It looks a long way back. I hope this is going to work.' Poking the handle of the umbrella inside as a hook, she reached in and began fishing for the mechanism. 'It's out of my grasp. Maybe you have a longer arm.'

'Maybe? Try leaning in and pressing your shoulder up against the opening. That should give you maximum reach.'

Olivia followed Max's advice and, with her arm at full stretch, she moved it about, searching for the catch by feel. She let out a sigh of relief as she said, 'I've got it.'

'Well done, Olivia. Didn't I say an umbrella would do the job?' Max smiled at his ingeniousness while pushing against the centre of the arch, causing the secret door to the passageway behind to open silently. Switching on his flashlight and stepping over the threshold, Max said, 'I still marvel at the architectural genius of incorporating these secret entrances and passageways into the building, although this one is rather tight, barely wide enough for us to fit.'

'People weren't as big as they are now,' Olivia said.

'Or as tall. Watch your head!'

When they were both inside, Olivia pulled the door closed, whispering, 'Lead on, Max.'

After two hundred metres of twists and turns, the passageway came to a narrow stone staircase. Max, lowering his torch, could see that it spiralled steeply downwards, and the steps were barely the width of his shoe. He realised how dangerous and slippery it was and hesitated.

How on earth am I going to make it down there without breaking my neck?

Olivia, sensing Max's apprehension, suggested that he rest his shoulder against the wall as he descended, leaning against it to steady his balance. Hesitantly, Max took his first step, knowing that a slip would be fatal. When his foot landed on the first run, the toe of his shoe hung over the edge, causing him to rock back and forth. He breathed out slowly and said, 'I'm sorry, Olivia, I can't do it. Help me back up and then you will have to go on without me.'

'You're a silly old fool sometimes, Max. If it's too steep, narrow, and slippery for you, what makes you think I will make it?' She thought for a moment before musing aloud, 'There has to be a way because the Crane did it.'

Max gave a half-hearted laugh. 'Cranes have wings. Besides, when we were her age, this wouldn't have been an obstacle at all.'

'That is so true,' Olivia lamented. 'Everything changed the day we turned eighty. But, be as it may, there is no going back and we have to find a way over this hurdle, or down as it is in this case.

Overcoming obstacles, Max, is what we've always done, and we may have lost our agility but not our inspiration.'

Max let his body weight transfer from his shoulder to the tunnel wall, hoping that it would prevent him from tumbling forward. After a moment he said, 'Remember the roof when I said old people are like toddlers, and you've got to crawl. That got me thinking: how would a baby tackle these steps?'

Olivia laughed, recognising where Max was taking the logic, and said, 'On their backsides, of course, scooting down one step at a time.'

'Exactly! And like many of the challenges we elderly farts face in old age, it won't be dignified, so we should feel quite at home. Olivia, I promise never to tell anyone if you promise to.'

'It's a deal.'

Max lowered his bottom to the stone floor and, putting his feet on the step below, using his hands, he bumped his backside to the next step and repeated the process on his way to the bottom. Olivia followed him and said, 'You know, Max? It may be true that we end up where we started, although a toddler would giggle with each bump but, for me, it's like sitting on a hot poker pushing through to the top of my head, and if I wore dentures, they'd be knocked right out of my mouth. This is one of those occasions where it would pay to be a...' Olivia broke into the rock band Queen's song, "Fat Bottom Girls". As Olivia hoped, her ranting distracted Max from the difficulties he was experiencing. Other than a slight pain in the bum, they both made it unscathed to the bottom of the stairs. Max, with the aid of the wall and his umbrella, stood and brushed himself down, a ritual aimed at restoring his pride rather than cleaning away the dust and grime.

'Are you ready?' he said, as if nothing had happened.

'Lead on,' Olivia replied, equally nonchalant.

On the lower level, the tunnel was more extensive than it had been above. Max and Olivia followed it to reach a T-junction, a solid wall facing them. Max whispered to Olivia that, according to the plans, the dungeon was on the far side; the secret entrance with a peephole was to their right. When they arrived, Max looked through the spyhole. 'I can see three of them.' He waited, then wondered why Olivia hadn't responded until she pointed to the earpiece she was wearing, showing she was listening in on a conversation.

'What are they saying?' Max asked.

'A woman is speaking – possibly Linda. She is telling someone that they are a man down and that *we* are heading for the dungeons.' Olivia paused as she listened to the rest of the conversation before adding, 'She's told them to lock the doors and shoot anyone who tries to enter. Should I say something to them?'

Max smiled as he said, 'Absolutely.'

In a mysterious, haunting tone, Olivia said into the radio. 'It's too late to lock the doors because we are already amongst you. I will make this offer only once. If you put your weapons down, Max and I will let you live.'

Max, watching their reaction through the peephole, whispered, 'That has their attention. They are strutting up and down like peacocks, waving their guns about and checking the perimeter. Hang on. Oh dear; sadly, my love, they are laughing at us.'

Olivia huffed, 'Are they indeed.'

Max raised his firearm and aimed it through the peephole. 'I can take them one at a time from here.'

Olivia shook her head; this was not what she wanted.

'Wait, Max. We mustn't default to killing unless it's an absolute necessity. There has to be an alternative. Look, do you see the switch there, next to the secret door trigger? I reckon it controls the lights inside the dungeon.'

Max peered at her and said, 'Go on.'

'What if, when one of the mercenaries wanders near our secret door, we plunge the place into darkness, open the entrance, knock him unconscious, and drag him back in here before switching the lights back on? That would give them quite a shock, one of them vanishing into thin air.'

Max exhaled as he considered the scheme. 'Only if we can carry it off with speed.'

They had to wait only thirty seconds before one mercenary propped himself in front of the secret passage. Working in unison, they extinguished the lights, opened the secret door, hooked the man with the handles of their umbrellas, and dragged him backwards, off-balance, into the tunnel. Olivia knocked him unconscious with the butt of her pistol while Max closed the entrance and restored the lights. In little more than the blink of an eye, one of their crew had disappeared, leaving two mercenaries inside the dungeon.

Olivia spoke into the two-way radio, her voice displaying a ghoulish quality as she recited the title of an Agatha Christie crime novel, 'And Then There Were None.'

'One down, two to go,' Max said, his voice triumphant, guessing that Olivia had a plan for disarming the others. He added in jest, safe in the knowledge she would reject his idea. 'Can I shoot them now?'

'No, Max. This time, when we dim the lights, I want you to go inside and convince them to surrender.'

Max looked at Olivia, his eyes wide open as he said, 'Seriously?'

'I'll be covering you from here, and if the mercenaries don't comply, I'll protect you.'

'That's your plan?' When Olivia remained silent, a smile forming, he added, 'I knew I should have kept my bowler hat. A little theatre, even if it makes one look silly, would have helped unsettle my opponents.' As Max spoke the words, his mind was racing.

Theatre? Now there's an idea.

Olivia removed her hat and held it towards Max. 'Here, take mine.'

'Ha, I said silly, not ridiculous.'

'They are game words from a man who is about to rely on my Annie Oakley skills. What did I do with my glasses?'

'Ha, ha. Okay, once more into the valley of death.'

Olivia plunged the dungeon into darkness and, five seconds later, when the light returned, the two mercenaries were surprised to see Max, an older man, leaning on an umbrella, standing three metres from them. He shot them a menacing glare, prompting them to level their rifles at him. His sudden appearance and unusual posture weren't overtly threatening, yet there was an undeniable intimidation in the air. Maintaining his gaze, Max said, taking them by surprise, 'I know what you're thinking. Did he fire six shots or only five? Well, to tell you the truth, in all this excitement, I've kinda lost track myself.' Lifting his umbrella off the floor for them to see, he said, 'Being as this is a 44 Magnum, the most powerful handgun in the world, which would blow your head clean off, you've got to ask yourself one question: Do I feel lucky? Well, do you, punk?'

The mercenaries looked at Max first with confusion and then with a mix of disbelief and contempt. Max smiled, ignoring their countenance as he said, 'That's my Clint Eastward impression, from Dirty Harry.'

The mercenaries shook their heads, and one of them said, 'Never heard of it.'

'Pity, I've practised those lines for years for a moment such as this. How about this instead and this time it is from me? Gentleman, it is over. If you wish to live to fight another day, I suggest you lay down your arms and surrender.'

'Are you nuts old-timer?'

Max tapped the tip of his umbrella against the floor, pausing to choose his words carefully. 'It would be unwise to underestimate this old timer. Let me remind you of what happened to your associates in A Coruña when they crossed Max and Oliva. And here in Montserrat, two of your colleagues have already paid a steep price. My good wife, Olivia, believes there has been enough bloodshed, and she has asked me to deliver this ultimatum. Gentlemen, you have lost this battle. It's time to release the prisoners and assume their place.'

The mercenary closest to Max looked nervously about the space before saying, 'Where's Olivia?'

Max smiled in delight as he lifted his umbrella and levelled it at them. 'Exactly. Do I feel lucky? Well, do you, punk?'

The mercenaries stole a glance at each other.

'Olivia has you in her sights. The choice is simple: surrender or die. I will count to three. One, two ...'

'Okay, we surrender,' one mercenary said.

Max grinned. 'Jolly good show. If you would kindly let the prisoners out.'

One mercenary began opening the cell door, saying as he did, 'We only have Richard Liew here.'

When the door was open, Max pointed with his umbrella for the guards to go inside. He followed.

Expecting the worst, Richard Liew's face was grim as he moved from the corner of his cell to see who was coming in. Like a salute, Max raised the tip of his umbrella to his forehead and said,

'Mr Liew, I'm Sir Max, of the British Secret Service, and I'm here to rescue you. If you would kindly relieve these gentlemen of their weapons and come this way.'

Richard Liew remained rooted to the spot, amazed that an old man, an ancient man, armed with nothing but an umbrella, had freed him. *This scene is ridiculous,* he whispered to himself.

'Please, Sir, time is of the essence.'

Richard Liew followed Max's instructions.

With the mercenaries secured, Olivia lowered her pistol and, unseen by Richard Liew, came out from the secret passage, gently closing the door behind her. Upon noticing her presence, Max said, 'Mr Liew, allow me to introduce my wife, Olivia.'

Olivia raised her umbrella in a gesture of greeting. Richard, seeing an old woman, holding an umbrella and wearing a silly hat, shook his head from side to side as he said, 'Look, I don't understand any of this and don't have the time nor patience for whatever stupidity is going on right now. My daughter and wife are in danger and it's up to me to save them.'

'Very noble of you,' Max said, adding, 'You mustn't forget Snowflake - your cat!'

Keeping an assault rifle and pistol that he'd taken from his jailers and discarding the other weapons, Richard Liew started running towards one exit. Max raised his arms in exasperation and called out after him, 'Where are you going?'

'Someone has to save Molly and Samantha.'

Richard Liew vanished before Max and Olivia could tell him they had a way of reaching his family without risking an armed confrontation. Seconds after Richard fled through the door, they heard the sounds of automatic weapons fire. Olivia was the first to speak. 'What just happened?'

Max shrugged, his voice betraying his annoyance. 'The act of an impetuous young person, I suppose. Racing off half-cocked and without thinking.'

'I think, my dear Max, you're being overly generous,' she said. 'When Richard Liew looked at us, he judged us solely on our appearance—two elderly people—and assumed that, because of our age, we were pathetic, incompetent, and a burden. To him, we were merely obstacles to be discarded in his quest to save his family, completely overlooking the fact that it was we who had saved him. It's disappointing, but that's how life is when one reaches a ripe old age.'

'I fear, my love, it has always been thus Let's hope our Richard Liew is as good as he believes himself to be because, from the sounds of what's happening out there, he will need to be.'

'Max, I'm annoyed!'

'I know, my love, so am I. Let's find our Claudia and worry about Richard Liew later.'

It was not to be so, for no sooner had Max finished speaking than the door burst open and Richard Liew, firing his weapon in retreat, reappeared. Slamming the heavy door closed, he locked it while calling out, distress resonating in his voice, 'Take cover, they're coming through.' He dived away in time to avoid being hit as bullets ripped through the door, leaving a pattern of holes in their wake. Rolling away and then rising to his feet, Richard Liew, panting for breath, said, 'What are we going to do now?' He pointed to the heavy oak door with its steel ribbing on the other side of the space, adding, 'That's a dead end. We are trapped.'

Max smiled, 'Mr Liew, you left in such a hurry that I'm not sure you have been properly introduced to my good wife, Lady Olivia Suzanne Elizabeth Huggins from England.'

Another burst of machine-gun fire ripped into the door.

'They're coming through,' Richard Liew repeated hurriedly, ignoring Max and focusing on the door.

Increasing his tone and authority, Max said again. 'You left in such a hurry that I'm not sure you have been properly introduced to my good wife, Lady Olivia Suzanne Elizabeth Huggins from England.'

WHAM! WHAM!

The mercenaries were bashing down the door.

As more gunshots rang out, Richard Liew turned to face Max, shaking his head in disbelief before catching himself. A flicker of civility surfaced within him; instead of responding defiantly, he offered a slight bow of his head. 'It's a pleasure to meet you, Lady Olivia Suzanne Elizabeth Huggins. I humbly apologise for my earlier rudeness. The gravity of the situation overshadowed my manners, and that was unintentional. I assure you, I'm truly sorry. Without the gallantry of both of you, I would still be behind bars.'

WHAM!

The door shook on its hinges and Richard Liew knew that in any moment the mercenaries would be through.

Olivia smiled, 'That's quite alright, young man.'

Interrupting, Max said, 'Would you m'lady?'

'Most certainly.'

To Richard Liew's astonishment, Olivia triggered the mechanism, and the entrance to the secret passage revealed itself. Olivia waited for Max to enter before following herself. She paused and looked back at Richard Liew, who was still watching in amazement.

'Are you coming?'

'Yes. How?..'

'Hurry up Richard, because they are coming through, as you observed yourself.' As Richard reached her, Olivia pointed with her umbrella at the unconscious guard on the floor. 'There is a small housekeeping matter. Would you be so kind as to drag the mercenary from here? Oh, and Richard, dispose of him away from the entrance. We wouldn't want to show where we've gone.'

WHAM!

When Richard Liew was out of earshot, Olivia said to Max, 'Your castigation of the young man was rather harsh. I don't deny that I was offended and said as much, however, I wonder how silly and humiliated we will feel if forced to transverse another set of steps on our bottoms while in Richard Liew's company?'

'You think I was a little over the top?'

'Hubris Max, hubris! I shared my discontent with *you*, but sometimes we have to cop these things on the chin.'

Max dropped his head a touch in acknowledgement of the reprimand and said, 'John 8:7, my love. Let anyone who is without sin cast the first stone.'

CHAPTER 21
Snowflake

Linda Orr commanded angrily, 'Break it down.'

WHAM! WHAM!

The mercenaries slammed into the entrance to the dungeon.

'Shoot at the hinges, blow the bloody thing off the wall,' Linda barked but, after a volley of shots rang out, the door remained in place, and she continued with, 'Hit it again and don't fail this time.'

WHAM! WHAM!

The solid medieval wooden door, which had stood for hundreds of years, gave way to the onslaught, falling to the ground. Weapons at the ready, the troops burst into the dungeon to secure the space. In a matter of seconds, without a single shot fired, it was all over, and Linda heard the team leader call, 'Clear.'

Clear! How can that be?

Linda was furious as she stormed into the dungeon. Except for the unconscious guard on the floor, the room was empty. She barked,

'Check the cell.' As the door opened, Linda Orr's wrath boiled over, and she struggled to contain her anger. Instead of Richard Liew, two of her team exited, and she fought the urge to shoot them for incompetence. The mercenaries waited sheepishly for Linda to speak. Linda took a few moments to regain her composure, after which she snapped, 'What happened?'

'Um, Max and Olivia got the drop on us.'

'Two old coots got the drop on you, did they? And how was that?'

'One moment, there were three of us. The lights went out, and we lost one. It happened again and, the next thing we know, they were here in the room. We secured both entrances as you had instructed.'

Linda scanned the room. 'We have rats in the walls; there must be in a secret passageway that leads in and out of here. How did those old buggers know of its location?'

We should have dealt with you in A Coruña. Now I'll teach you to mess with me, you old farts.

Speaking into the radio, knowing that Max and Olivia would be listening, Linda said. 'Delta team, do you copy?'

'Yes boss,' came a crackled reply.

'You have unwanted company on the way. Like rats, they are travelling by hidden routes inside the walls. Kill the prisoners, all of them, including the child. Then fall back to the designated assembly point *alfa two*. Listen to me carefully, Delta team.' Linda slowed her speech, talking steadily to ensure that her instructions were understood. 'Under no circumstances are you to engage *any* of the prisoners or the incoming bogies in conversation. They are all experts in weasel words. If you hesitate for even a microsecond, you will be dead. Claudia, Max, and Olivia are like no opponent you've encountered before. Shoot the prisoners on sight and Max and Olivia if you spot them. Have I made myself clear?'

'Yes, boss.'

***

As Max and Olivia navigated the tunnel system on their way to rescue Claudia, Samantha, and Molly, they seized the

396

opportunity to share what they knew about Davros and his intricate web of deception. They explained how Linda Orr had been used in Claudia's guise to fuel tensions between the British and Chinese security agencies. Olivia was in the midst of responding to Richard's question when she suddenly halted, raising a finger to her ear to signal that she was listening to a transmission.

'What's happening?' Max asked.

Wearing a forlorn expression, Olivia said, 'I'm sorry, Richard, Linda has just ordered the execution of the prisoners.'

'Molly?'

'All of them.'

'If I run, maybe I can make it there in time.'

Olivia knew that wasn't realistic, but she unfolded the map and, pointing to it, said, 'We are at this junction and here is where we are heading. See how the tunnel zigzags like a maze, and we have two main passageways to transit. Even if you found your way, it would take at least ten minutes. I'm sorry, Richard, run if you will, but the distance is too great. Truly I'm sorry.'

'They will pay for this!'

Olivia placed a steadying hand on Richard Liew's arm, saying, 'Now isn't the time to contemplate revenge, as it will cloud your judgement. A clear mind is required if you are to escape from here alive. As callous as this sounds, for the moment that needs to be your focus.' Olivia removed her hand as Richard Liew nodded his head slowly. Max interjected.

'You forget one thing.' They both looked at him as he continued, 'Claudia is with your family and she is one formidable opponent and a wonderful ally when on your side. I don't want to get your hopes up because whatever happens will happen long before we arrive. Regardless, we should take our time, proceed with caution and make it there safely.'

Richard Liew struggled against his instincts, which urged him to run rather than stay with Max and Olivia, who seemed to navigate the tunnels at a snail's pace. By the time they finally arrived, he could taste blood in his mouth from where he had bitten his lip to suppress his frustration at their slow progress. Deep down, however, he understood that Max and Olivia were moving as quickly as they could; the effects of their aging were undeniable.

'Wait!' Olivia said as Richard Liew reached for a trigger mechanism to open the secret door. 'Max, take a look.'

Max pulled back the cover of the peephole.

'What do you see?'

It looks like the mercenaries have carried out the executions and left for the assembly point.

'Nothing, the place is empty,' he said, not wishing to expose his thoughts.

Olivia shuffled past Richard Liew and triggered the latch, causing the secret door to swing open. As she peered inside, she noted that the space was distinct from the dungeons, resembling what might have once been accommodations for monks or nuns. Six individual rooms lined the passageway. Max said he thought the cells had once served as spaces for devotion and worship. Whatever their original purpose, they had become a prison. Turning to Richard, Olivia placed her hand on his arm. "Do you know which cell it is?"

Richard pointed to the first steel door next to the main entrance. 'I'm sure it's that one.'

'You should wait here and let Max and I go. It's for the best.'

Richard thought for a moment, before reluctantly agreeing.

'Good man.' As she left the tunnel, Olivia added, 'Keep the exit open because it's only accessible from the inside.'

Richard nodded his understanding.

With a massive sense of foreboding, Olivia and Max made their way to the cell, expecting the worst. Olivia was about to slide the bolt back when something on the ground caught her attention. It was another origami crane. Immediately, a warm glow of expectation swept over her as she picked it up for Max to see. 'The Crane.'

CLUNK!

With the door unlocked, Olivia pushed it open, narrowly dodging Claudia's fist as it shot out from inside the cell at the speed of a rattlesnake.

'That was close,' Olivia said. 'Max and I were expecting a warmer greeting from you, Claudia. Perhaps even a hug.'

'Olivia!' Claudia called, a mixture of surprise and delight punctuating her voice. 'I'm sorry, I didn't mean to...'

'Daddy, Daddy?' The cry of a hopeful Molly interrupted Claudia, the child's voice booming out from inside the cell to echo around the chamber.

Running towards the cell door, Richard Liew called, his voice emotional, 'I'm here. Molly, I'm here.'

Claudia and Olivia stepped aside as Richard Liew, standing at the entrance to the prison, saw his daughter holding her mother's hand, staring back at him. Samantha let go of Molly's grip, and Molly sprinted to her father, who swept her up in his arms in one flowing motion before kissing her gently on the cheek.

'I so sorry,' he wept as he hugged her tightly. Putting his daughter down, he reached out towards Samantha, who remained frozen to the spot, her emotions a mixture of relief, love, and anger. After a few seconds, she walked towards her husband, and they embraced. Richard whispered into her ear, 'I love you and promise, when this is over, I will leave the security service. I never want to hurt you and Molly. I'm so, so sorry.'

'Daddy, Daddy, Snowflake is here!'

Richard Liew looked at Max and Olivia in bewilderment, who both said in unison, 'Don't ask.'

Olivia turned to Claudia and opened her hand, revealing the origami crane. Astonishment swept across Claudia's face. 'The Crane is here?'

Olivia nodded. 'Yes, and this is the second time today that she's stepped in to help. In this instance, she's saved all of your lives. Linda ordered the guards to—' She paused, suddenly aware that Molly was listening intently.

Claudia took the crane from Olivia's hand, examining it. 'She? You keep saying *she?*'

Max nodded, then told Claudia what he'd explained to Olivia earlier.

'Well, she also tried to warn me that John was going to be killed.' Claudia paused, realising that Max and Olivia hadn't heard of John Moss and their relationship.

Olivia smiled and, touching Claudia reassuringly on the arm, said, 'We know, dear. Inspector Axel told us everything.'

A look of surprise crossed Claudia's face. 'Max, you said the Crane is a woman, and you've spoken to her a couple of times. She's probably in her sixties by now.' Enlightenment flickered in

Claudia's eyes, a spark she tried to conceal, but it was too late—Max and Olivia had already noticed the shift in her demeanour. They exchanged glances, and Olivia asked, 'Do you know who she is?'

Claudia smiled. 'I think I might.'

Max grinned, tilting his head slightly to one side. 'Do you now! We won't ask. Not right away.'

Claudia replied with a slight shrug of her shoulders, an apology of sorts, adding, 'Well, maybe. I have a couple of choices.'

Olivia watched the interplay between two people that she loved and said kindly, 'There will be time for idle chatter later. In the meantime, we should put our heads together and come up with an escape plan.'

Claudia looked at Olivia, a puzzled look sweeping across her face. 'Can't we go out the way you came in?'

Should I tell the truth? In a rush to be with Molly and Samantha, Richard closed off that option?

Olivia glanced at Max and, with a tiny movement of her head, spoke a thousand words to her lifelong partner, who replied secretly,

The truth will only serve to attribute blame.

Olivia responded with a blink of her eye before saying, knowing the others were listening, 'The way we came in is no longer an option because Linda knows the route. She would corner us in those narrow passages.'

Claudia understood that Olivia had her reasons for lying, accepting the statement without question. She glanced around the space and said, 'Alright then, we'll have to find another way out.'

'Is there another secret passage?' Richard Liew asked.

'Not on the map we have,' Olivia responded. 'Unless... Claudia, can I have a look at the origami crane?'

Claudia passed the folded paper to Olivia.

Smiling as she unwrapped it, Olivia said, while holding the paper to the light for a more unobstructed view of the image. 'The Crane has helped us again. As best I can make out, according to this drawing, there's a secret service shaft.' Olivia looked around the room. 'It's just past the end of the last cell.' Olivia moved the paper closer to her, then further away, trying to read what it said. 'Without my glasses, the writing is too small for me to read. Claudia, what do you think it is saying?'

'Um, that is small. There's a steel shackle in the wall which must be turned to the left and then pushed all the way in. That will open the entrance.'

Olivia began to walk away while the others waited for Molly to fetch Snowflake before following. As Olivia reached the fifth cell, its door was ajar. Inside, strewn on the ground like discarded packaging, redundant weapons beside them, and surrounded by a pool of bright red blood, were the dead bodies of the mercenaries tasked to kill Claudia, Molly and Samantha. Olivia had to think quickly; there was no time to close the door before Molly arrived, and she did not want the child to witness the carnage. Olivia popped open her umbrella, using its canopy to shield the view from Molly, but not the others who could gaze over the top. When they had passed, Olivia folded her umbrella and respectfully closed the door, whispering to herself, 'Such a tragic waste of life,' even though she knew that the men would have slain their targets without compunction.

May you rest in peace, she whispered.

Richard Liew, wanting to make amends, was the first to reach the shackle, and he grasped the ring in his hand, lifting it and turning it to the left, but it refused to budge. Claudia, imitating the move with her hands, said in frustration, 'Try loosening it by giving it a good solid shake.' Privately, she thought, *stand aside and let me have a go.*

Using both hands and his body weight in tandem, Richard Liew pulled and twisted the ring to the left with all his strength. On his third attempt, the mechanism snapped clean off. A sense of foreboding swept through the party. For a moment, no one spoke. Richard Liew knew that this was the second time he'd failed, and that he was putting his family's life in jeopardy, along with everyone else. For Samantha's sake, wanting to sound in control, he said with phoney authority, 'With the weapons we have and ones from the cell back there, we can fight our way out!'

Claudia nodded in agreement. Not wanting the hopelessness of the situation to take hold, she took a moment to gather her thoughts before saying, 'You're right, Richard. Our only option is to fight. If you give me a moment, I'll go fetch the guns from back there.'

Max and Olivia watched the interaction taking place between Richard Liew and Claudia, people seeking atonement for different reasons.

A minute later, Claudia returned carrying two automatic assault rifles, spare magazines, and sidearms.

'If I were them,' Claudia said firmly, looking at Richard Liew as she spoke, 'I would ambush us ...'

'Excuse me,' interrupted Samantha angrily, 'Would you mind making your plans out of earshot of this seven-year-old girl? What world do you people live in? Yes, Richard, you too. That woman

...' Samantha pointed at Claudia as she continued, '... she broke into our house, spied on us, stole the cat for God's sake, and then came here intent on slitting our throats. Oh, my goodness, sorry, Molly.' Samantha's voice rose in pitch, a woman on the verge of hysteria as she shrieked, 'Now look at you Richard, comrades in arms casually discussing how you're... How you're ...'

Olivia repeated the gesture she'd done with Richard and Claudia and touched Samantha on the arm, whispering, 'It's okay, we understand.'

Samantha dropped her head, and Olivia motioned with her eyes to Claudia, for her and Richard to continue their conversation elsewhere.

'I want to show you something,' Claudia said to Richard Liew while leading him away. When they stopped, out of earshot of the others, Richard said, 'What were you saying about an ambush?'

'We know Linda has regrouped her forces and by now will be aware we are alive. We know nothing about her strength, or whether she will come for us or expect us to make a run for it. I'm going for the later and, if I were her, I'd set up an ambush on the far side of the ornately carved door in the library, the one we have to funnel through to exit. She'll wait until we're inside, in the kill zone from her point of view, before opening fire using a linear ambush technique. Of course, she could choose an L-shaped attack with automatic weapons shooting down the long leg of the L. I doubt that she'll use that tactic. What I know is, with her losses mounting, Linda won't risk her troops getting caught in their crossfire. She will set up the flank on our left or right as we enter the library.' Claudia paused and took a deep breath as she mused before continuing. 'Richard, ideally, we want to return fire, manoeuvre against her flank, pushing our way through while protecting the others. Once behind Linda's crew, we'll have the advantage. She will wait until we all pass through the door then open fire. We risk being caught in a turkey shoot before we can counter.'

Richard Liew pondered on their predicament before he said, 'How about we choose a direction before we enter? By that I mean, the moment the door is open, rather than going straight ahead, you break, say to the right, and we follow you. We either punch our way through the ambush or make it safely to the wall of the library. It's a win in either case and we can use the cover of the bookcases to reach the opposite side.'

Claudia smiled to herself. Richard may have been an excellent spy, but he wasn't a military tactician.

'The problem is that if we guess wrong, Linda pins us to the library wall – no-win Richard. The only option is for Max and me to clear the room as you walk in front of Samantha and Molly, Olivia bringing up the rear, heading straight up the centre. As long as it's not an L-shaped ambush, that is our best chance of success. I can promise you one thing, Richard. Max and I will lay down one hell of a firestorm. We'll create an impenetrable barrier of bullets so that you and your family can escape.'

Richard Liew's face twisted, uncertainty clear, as he said, 'Are you sure? Is Max the right choice for this?'

'There is no greater person I would willingly go into battle with.'

'Look, Claudia, I don't dispute that Max was once a great man; however, those times are behind him. To push through the ambush will require speed and agility. I watched them in the service tunnel ...' Richard paused and shrugged as he continued, 'I don't want to sound disrespectful, but Molly as a toddler could move faster. Neither Max nor Olivia has the speed or agility they once had—a fate I know awaits us all. Yet they compensate admirably for their declining physical abilities with sharp wit and quirky props like silly hats and umbrellas. Don't get me wrong, Claudia; it serves them well, and they've proven to be formidable opponents—there's no denying that. But in a firefight? I think not. I have my family to consider.'

Claudia rubbed her chin, a smile drifting across her face. 'Time has changed them – an inescapable truth – but, if you want proof that their abilities are greater than they have ever been, well, look around you.' Richard Liew screwed up his face in confusion as Claudia continued, 'If it weren't for their wit and props, as you call them, we wouldn't be having this conversation at all. We, including Molly and Samantha, would be in lying in the bloodied cell rather than the mercenaries.'

'Wasn't that the Crane?'

'Perhaps, but then we would still be locked in the cell.' Claudia hesitated before saying, 'You're focusing on one small part of Max and Olivia, but you need to see the complete picture.'

Meanwhile, Max, Olivia, Samantha, Molly and Snowflake were considering the problem of the broken trigger mechanism, though Snowflake was contributing little. It was a comment of Samantha's that caused a cascade of neurons to fire in Olivia's mind. Olivia repeated Samantha's question.

'Where does the air come from?' Olivia rubbed her chin. 'When they built this place, if there were only one entry and one exit point, it would have been easy in medieval days for an attacker to cut off the air supply.' She took a deep breath – smelling the air. 'Even down here, the atmosphere is fresh. The air is circulating, and it has to be coming from somewhere.'

Surveying the surroundings, Olivia scanned the chamber for the source of the air, chuckling silently to herself when she spotted it.

How did I miss that?

The size of a small piece of airline hand luggage, above and to the right of the entrance to the secret passage, was an air vent. Pointing at the outlet, Olivia said, 'Samantha, you're brilliant.'

'I am?'

'Absolutely. It was you who asked the obvious question. Where does the air come from? Well, Samantha, right here.' Olivia weighed up the size of the opening before adding, 'Is Claudia slight enough to fit through, do you think?'

Samantha looked at the outlet and then at Olivia. Sorry, 'I'm not following.'

Olivia smiled saying warmly. 'The vent shaft may have a branch line that feeds air into the passage on the other side of that door, the one we have difficulty opening. If Claudia can fit, she might be able to crawl through and drop down into our tunnel, opening the door from the other side. It's worth a shot.'

Max and Samantha moved closer, studying the opening. Together, they shook their heads. 'It's too narrow,' Max said, and with his words, the feeling of optimism faded.

'I could,' Molly said. 'Snowflake and I could fit inside easily.'

Samantha smiled lovingly at her daughter as she said, 'Molly, you're so wonderfully brave...'

Molly interrupted, 'And Snowflake.'

'Yes, and Snowflake. Your father will never allow it. What would happen if you become stuck?'

'I won't Mummy, I promise. If it gets too tight, I will stop and crawl out backwards. Won't we Snowflake. Snowflake says, yes.'

Samantha laughed nervously, before saying, her voice tinged with anxiety, 'You are truly brave but, I'm sorry, neither you nor Snowflake are crawling down a dangerous tunnel.'

'I am not three any more, Mummy,' A pout developed on Molly's lips as she added, 'I know nasty men are waiting on the other side of the door to shoot and kill us because Daddy is a spy. I saw those dead men on the floor in the room we walked by. Snowflake and I can do this. We have to do this Mummy, and you have to let us.'

Max, listening to the exchange, looked at Samantha. 'Samantha, even if Molly can't find her way out of the vent into the secret tunnel, she could follow it to the surface and freedom. I know that this is like nothing you've ever experienced, but sometimes we must weigh the lesser of two evils. Where do you think Molly will be the safest? If you are in any doubt, just remember the monk's cell we walked past.' Max paused and shrugged his shoulders before continuing, 'It may be a moot point because we don't know if Molly will fit.' He hesitated, unsure if he should say the words on his mind. 'Samantha, we won't find out unless we try.'

Samantha, feeling overwhelmed and out of her depth, considered the options. In her mind, she saw the brutal carnage; the mercenaries slain in the cell, and remembered Linda Orr's sadistic threats. She sighed to herself, knowing that despite the dangers, Max was right: the ventilation shaft was the safest place for Molly. She exhaled as she said, 'How will she see in there?'

Giving Samantha a reassuring look, Max held out his flashlight.

With hesitation written all over her face, not knowing what, or if, there was a right decision, Samantha said, 'Okay.'

With Samantha and Max watching, Olivia explained to Molly what they needed her to do, emphasising each point to ensure the child understood. She stressed that if Molly couldn't find an exit into their tunnel, she must keep going until she reached the surface, where she should stay hidden and call for help. To aid her, Olivia handed Molly her mobile phone, which had Pedro's number—the man who had driven them from Barcelona to Montserrat—programmed as a contact. Once she finished, Olivia used a gentle tone and asked Molly to repeat everything she had been told.

When Molly had finished, Olivia grinned. 'You and Snowflake are going to make one super team. I think, everyone, that we are ready. Let's do it.'

'Hang on,' Samantha said, her voice betraying her surprise. 'Aren't we going to consult Richard and *that* Claudia first?'

Olivia gestured toward Richard, who was buried deep in conversation with Claudia, saying, 'They still seem to be focused on a bloody gunfight.'

'Daddy still thinks I'm a baby,' Molly said. 'I'm not, and I can do this Mummy.'

Seizing the opportunity, acting before Samantha had second thoughts, Max handed Molly his torch. 'You're a big brave girl, Molly, and this is a magical quest of great importance to us all.'

He turned to Samantha, instructing her to lift Molly so that she could clamber into the vent. Samantha gave her daughter a gentle kiss on the top of her head, then grabbed her around the waist and hoisted her up onto the lip of the shaft entrance. Molly turned on the flashlight, putting it down inside and then asked for Snowflake. She placed Snowflake alongside the lamp, took a deep breath and, without saying goodbye, heaved herself in. Within seconds, all that Samantha could see of her beloved child were the heels of her shoes, which quickly vanished. She swallowed a couple of times to stop herself from crying.

Dreaming that Snowflake would guide and protect her on their secret mission, Molly pulled herself into the narrow, claustrophobic vent. The cat would nuzzle against her face, saying with his purrs, *'Come on Molly, I've been waiting for you,'* before raising his tail and leading Molly into the depth of the scary labyrinth. Instead, Molly witnessed a cat that wanted to be anywhere else but the narrow passageway. Not for a moment had Molly imagined that she'd have to push Snowflake further inside the vent. Unable to be annoyed, Molly said, speaking softly despite her racing heart, 'Don't be scared, Snowflake, I'll look after you.'

The beam of the flashlight lit up the narrow passage, which, after ten meters, curved to the left and then out of sight. Giving Snowflake an encouraging shove with her head, Molly crawled forward, screaming out in alarm as a sticky spider's web wrapped itself around her face, covering her eyes and mouth. She wiped it away, having to repeat the process several times before removing all the ticklish remnants. Edging her way forward, Molly lost sight of Snowflake as she manoeuvred around the first corner, followed by a series of twists and turns. When the shaft straightened again, Snowflake was still nowhere to be seen.

'Snowflake, Snowflake, where are you?'

In the distance, Molly's beam of light revealed the narrowing of the passageway, followed by a solid wall of rock. At that point, the tunnel became a vertical ventilation shaft leading to the surface and the end of her quest. Molly's anxiety rose as she thought about how difficult it would be to reverse, but she was distracted, remembering that Snowflake was missing.

'Snowflake. Snowflake, where are you?'

The ventilation shaft remained spookily empty - devoid of feline sounds.

'You're a naughty cat!' snapped Molly as she started crawling forward in search of her pet. Her rescue mission slowed as the passageway narrowed and it became difficult to force herself forward, the walls pressing against her shoulders. Unperturbed, Molly pressed on, her mind focused and forgetting that she may become wedged.

'Snowflake, where are you? You're in lots of trouble when I find you.'

The walls pushed harder against her, making crawling difficult, and Molly groaned as she edged forward.

'Snowflake!' she exclaimed on spotting the cat's furry face as it appeared in front of her before disappearing again.

'Come back here, you very naughty cat!'

Unseen by Molly, until she reached it, was Snowflake, standing at an opening that fed air into the getaway tunnel, the one she was sent to find.

'You're a clever Snowflake after all,' Molly said while hanging her head over the edge and looking down into the escape route. 'Snowflake, that's a long way down and, if I go over, head-first, I will hurt myself. I don't think I can do it.'

Snowflake pushed past Molly to re-enter the ventilation tunnel and cat walked toward the solid wall and the hidden vertical shaft. Molly called angrily, 'Where are you going now, you naughty cat?' and started crawling after Snowflake. Snowflake stopped, then pushed back past Molly again before returning to the opening and jumping down. Feet first this time, Molly backed into the gap, lowering herself down into the secret passageway.

'Okay, Snowflake, so you're a clever cat after all!'

***

Back at the monks' cells, Claudia was in conversation with Richard Liew. 'I've done this before, fighting my way out of a tight situation. Success is about being bold, aggressive and driving forward regardless of the opposition. Once we are inside the library, there will be no turning back. With each kill, we will take the mercenary's weapons and ammunition, using their corpses as cover if we have to. Max and Olivia may not have lightning speed, and they may lack agility; however, they make up for it with relentless momentum and audacious courage. People fighting for their survival can overcome the most confronting odds.' Claudia paused before saying, her tone serious. 'Between you and me, Richard, the odds are against us, but if we want to live, there is no other option. Do you agree?'

'Yes.'

Claudia sighed before saying, 'Let's break the news to the others.'

Samantha, watching Claudia and Richard approaching, said, while keeping the sarcasm from her voice, 'What's your plan?'

Richard's expression suggested regret, and he looked pathetic to Samantha as he told her what he and Claudia had discussed. Samantha, speaking in a tone with which Richard was familiar, implying that she was unimpressed, hands planted firmly on her hips, said, 'Is that the best you can come up with?'

'I'm sorry?' was all Richard could manage.

Samantha, daggers as eyes, glanced from Richard to Claudia and said, 'While you and that catnapping she-devil shoot it out at God knows what cost, the rest of us are heading this way.'

Samantha pointed towards Olivia and Molly, who were standing next to the open secret door.

A look of astonishment washed across Richard Liew's face as he said, 'How?'

Samantha replied, her words clipped. 'Molly did it, and I can tell you this, Richard Liew. She has more brains than the two of you put together.'

Max and Olivia snatched a glance at Claudia, who was trying to maintain a straight face. When Samantha looked away, Claudia, remembering what Linda once said about her, mouthed, '*The taming of the Shrew.*'

Max shook his head, whispering, 'Claudia, you and Richard both deserve this.'

CHAPTER 22
Freedom

'Where are we?' Samantha asked.

Standing behind her, Max answered, 'Santa Cova de Montserrat: it's a hillside cave on Montserrat where the Virgin of Montserrat was traditionally hidden during the Moorish invasions and later discovered by shepherds in 880. Its discovery made Montserrat into a pilgrimage destination and led to the founding of the Santa Maria de Montserrat Abbey.'

Samantha staring out over the vast valley below, enjoying the fresh air and sunshine after they had escaped from deep inside the mountain, replied, 'We saw it this morning from the cable car. How do you know that's where we are? Have you been here before?'

Raising his hands, though Samantha couldn't see them, Max laughed. 'I confess; I didn't have a clue, but I have phone reception again, so I put our location into a search engine. Wikipedia was insightful, don't you think? I thought I sounded quite the oracle!'

Olivia mocked, 'Well then, Oracle, how do we reach Barcelona from here?'

'That's easy, my love. We call Pedro Cadiz and then walk up the path to meet him. It will take about twenty minutes, or so this map app tells me. However, there are a couple of minor problems – hurdles if you like. The path will lead us back to the Monastery and it is steep, which will make it hard going for you and me. On the plus side, because Linda is expecting us to break out, most of her resources will be deployed inside. Hopefully, just as Pedro dropped us off, he should be able to make the pickup with no trouble or fuss. We will be gone before they even know we are missing.'

Olivia studied the terrain and path. 'Max, it looks like he can drive down and pick us up? It would be quicker and easier for us.'

Max held his phone so that Olivia could see and shrugged his shoulders. 'Without the local knowledge of someone who works here, it's impossible to tell from the app whether this is just a walking track, which the tourist articles suggest. I figure it's best to be safe than sorry. Besides, the Monastery will be easier for Pedro. He can stay out of sight until the last moment, then swoop in for our rescue.'

The rendezvous was set for thirty minutes at the Monastery of Santa Cova Funicular, the cable car station. Like a military patrol, as the party moved out, Claudia took point, walking several meters in front of everyone, alert for an attack, while Richard Liew was last, protecting their rear. Molly, wearing Claudia's daypack with Snowflake riding in it, held Max's hand and gently pulled him up the side of the mountain, uttering words of encouragement as he tackled the steep slope.

You can do it, Max. One foot after another.

Olivia and Samantha were walking together and as they climbed, Samantha confided in Olivia.

'When we're back in London, I'm going to tell Richard that he either leaves the Chinese Ministry of State Security or Molly and I will leave him. I'm so angry, Olivia. I feel betrayed. All of this time, Richard has been lying to me and, if Claudia is right, he's an accomplice to murder, killing people – how can I love a man like that? A spy!' Samantha stopped, realising what she'd said. 'Oh, I'm sorry, Olivia. I didn't mean to imply anything about you and Max. I can see that you're different.' Samantha stole a look at Olivia, who was struggling to walk up the incline. She offered Olivia her arm, and it was gratefully accepted.

'I will have to leave him!' Samantha continued, letting her exclamation hanging in the air.

Olivia kept her counsel, causing Samantha to peer at her again. Olivia's lips were pursed and Samantha was confused by the expression, asking, 'After what he's done, do you think I should stay with him? Our daughter could have died.'

'My dear, I am a little short of breath at the moment and I'm worried that a brief answer to a complicated situation may be misinterpreted and hinder you in this unenviable position you find yourself in.'

'Olivia, I need to know what you think. I'll try not to overreact. Please, Olivia!'

Olivia took a deep breath and said, 'In countries like the United Kingdom, the United States and Australia, people in jobs like Richard, Claudia, Max and myself, can walk away without ...' Olivia hesitated, seeking the right word, '... significant consequences. You will recall the poisoning, or should I say the attempted assassination of Sergei Skripal, a former Russian spy and double agent – possibly the murderer of Alexander Litvinenko a former officer of the Russian Federal Security Service (FSB) with Polonium-210. Both occurred on British soil.' Samantha nodded but remained mute as Olivia continued, 'Some countries treat an untimely exit from the secret services as disloyalty. If leaving involves the defection to an opposing spy agency, it's treason. Oh, my dear ...' Olivia wheezed, her words interrupted as she gasped for air, '... we might have to rest for a second.'

'Wait here Olivia,' Samantha said, before running ahead and calling to Claudia, who turned around.

'Olivia needs to catch her breath.'

'Okay.'

With her automatic weapon at the ready, Claudia took up a defensive position to the right of the path, a guardian angel watching over her flock. A few minutes later, Olivia waved she was ready to proceed.

'Shall I retake your arm?' Samantha asked Olivia kindly.

'Let me try this last bit on my own, at least to start with.' As they moved off, Oliva said, 'Where was I?' Oh, yes. Spending time, though it was out of your control, with Claudia, Max and me will be looked upon suspiciously, my dear, particularly if Richard said he wanted to leave the service. China, at this point in its history, is more likely to behave like the Soviet Union of old than Britain. My advice, for what it's worth Samantha, is that now is not the time for Richard to be considering a career change, or for you to be expressing unhappiness. I understand that, unlike Max and myself, Richard's livelihood as a spy is not a working partnership with you. However, and I steal these words from a film: "Are you still an effective team?" For the time being, my dear, any disquiet you feel must be a private matter. Samantha, I know this is difficult to understand, but when this saga is over, for a while, your life will not be your own. You need to behave as if someone is watching you, listening to everything you say. It's crucial that they perceive you as a cohesive team—you're a supportive wife in a happy marriage. Never mention Claudia, Max, or me, and under no circumstances should you suggest Richard consider leaving the service. Your life must convey the illusion of returning to how it once was.'

Samantha stared at Olivia for a moment before she said, 'There must be somewhere Richard and I can talk freely?'

'Perhaps while swimming naked on top of a mountain and only then if you can arrange that without raising suspicion.' Olivia took a gasp of air. 'Though it's not as bad as that, but I think you get my drift.'

'If I have to play happy families, what about in the bedroom? Will they be listening and watching that as well?'

Olivia stopped using the umbrella as a walking stick and put her hand on Samantha's arm, saying in a lowered voice, 'In keeping with my movie analogies dear, do you remember the film, "When Harry Met Sally", the moment where Meg Ryan's character fakes an orgasm in the middle of a New York deli?' Samantha nodded as Olivia continued, 'You want Richard's handlers to think *I'll have what she's having.*'

The bluntness of Olivia's answer took Samantha by surprise, especially coming from a woman who was over eighty. Regaining her composure, Samantha asked, 'How long will I have to live like this?'

'Two years or even longer, until everyone's satisfied that you're an effective team.'

'And if I can't do it. Are you saying we will all be killed?'

Olivia took another deep breath, struggling to walk and talk at the same time. She said, 'Look, we've almost made it to the station.' She hesitated; 'Samantha, nobody can be a hundred percent sure. If you're not an effective team, nothing may happen. More likely, however, the next time Richard travels to China, he will be arrested on trumped-up treason charges, or simply disappear. It could happen to both of you, even Molly. I'm not telling this to scare you, far from it dear, but for you to understand your predicament. For the sake of two years, you and Molly can have a full and free life. Richard too, if that's what you want.'

Samantha's eyes filled with water as she said. 'It's worse than I thought.' After a moment's silence, she added. 'Why is it you and Max are not like the others?'

Olivia wanted to say something inspirational, an assertion that would instil hope but settled on, 'In many ways, Max and I are no different, which is why I understand the rules, the uncomfortable truth.'

Claudia raised her hand, telling the party to stop. She signalled for Max to join her. Letting go of Molly's hand, Max whispered, 'Thank you, Molly. Your help was greatly appreciated.'

'Snowflake also helped.'

'And thank you, Snowflake.'

When Max had joined her, Claudia told the others that she and Max were going to check that Pedro was waiting and the coast was clear.

A white van was idling at the rendezvous point. 'Is that Pedro?' Claudia asked. 'I don't want to get too close, in case it's a trap.'

From a distance, Max peered through the van's side window. He saw a man wearing an English bowler seated behind the steering wheel. He smiled and nodded to Claudia. 'That's our Pedro.'

Claudia signalled to the others to move up while sending Max ahead to open the van's rear door, ready to load quickly and for a fast getaway.

***

'Boss,' called a mercenary, as he ran into the library, 'They are at the Funicular station.' Linda Orr shook her head in dismay, snapping, 'If we'd killed those meddling old farts, none of this would be happening.' Staring at her soldiers, she commanded, shouting, 'Well, what are you waiting for? STOP THEM!'

***

Claudia signalled to the others, all the while keeping a watchful eye and her rifle on the monastery's exits, to make a dash for the van. There was movement and Claudia didn't hesitate, opening fire before she saw the first of the mercenaries appear. Samantha stopped in their tracks at the sound of Claudia's weapon.

Olivia commanded, 'Keep moving,' as automatic gunfire came from the Abbey. The ferocious sounds of weapons discharging caused Samantha to stay frozen in her tracks, until Olivia linked arms with her, giving her a gentle pull while saying, 'We have to keep moving, dear.'

'What about Molly?'

'It's alright; Max has her.'

The escape scene became chaotic, overpowered by the deafening noise of battle and the pungent smell of cordite swirling in the air. Richard came up behind his stationary wife and snapped, 'You have to keep moving, Samantha. Max and Molly are already in the van and are waiting for you.' He gave Samantha a nudge and, when she started moving with Olivia on her arm, he left to join Claudia, firing at the mercenaries as he advanced.

'That man,' snarled Samantha.

'That was love, my dear. See, now he goes to put his body between you and mercenaries.'

Claudia, seeing Richard approaching, called above the gunshots. 'Are they all in the van?'

Richard glanced over his shoulder. Olivia and Samantha were climbing inside. 'Yes.'

'Okay, I'll cover you, then you do the same for me.'

Rat-a-tat-tat–rat-a-tat-tat.

With the sound of Claudia's gunfire ringing in his ears, Richard broke cover and sprinted toward the van. As he reached it, he dropped to the ground, shielding himself from the barrage of fire, and called back for cover.

'Withdraw!'

Claudia retreated, firing as she ran. Jumping in the back of the van she called, 'Everybody on the floor... Pedro, drive as if your life depends on it, because it does.' As they lay prostrate, a volley of bullets tore through the side of the van, whistling over their heads. Pedro accelerated, and the van lurched forward as it gathered speed. In a matter of seconds, they were out of range. Claudia let out a loud sigh of relief. 'You can all sit up now.'

'Are we safe?' Samantha asked.

'It's over, Max answered. 'You're safe.'

Olivia smiled when she saw Samantha place her arm around Richard's shoulder and squeeze him affectionately.

Max, sitting next to Olivia, found her hand, and clasping it lovingly, said, 'We made it.'

'That we did, my love.'

Claudia's eyes were drawn to Molly, who was tenderly cuddling Snowflake as only a child could. When Molly joined her parents, Claudia's eyes found Max and Olivia, who were sitting hand in hand, and the euphoria Claudia felt after the escape faded. Lost deep in her thoughts, the tender kiss on the cheek caught her by surprise. Molly smiled, kissing her again before throwing her arms around Claudia and hugging her warmly. Claudia joined in the embrace, whispering to the child, 'Thank you.'

Snowflake said you weren't going to hurt us and that she wants to be your best friend forever

'I would like that very much.' A tear formed, and Claudia let it trickle down her cheek.

***

Inside the monastery, a mercenary reporting to Linda Orr said, 'Sorry boss, they got away.'

Linda pursed her lips, saying, 'Do you have any idea what a bottle of Rose Gold Methuselah costs?'

With a surprised voice, the mercenary answered, 'No, boss.'

'Well, you'll find out because it's coming out of your pay.'

CHAPTER 23
London

'Welcome home Claudia,' James said as she entered his outer office. 'Stephen and Inspector Axel are expecting you.'

'Thank you, James.'

'Tea? English Breakfast?'

'That would be most kind of you, James.'

As was her way, Claudia knocked on the door before opening it. Inside, Stephen and Inspector Axel were seated, and they rose to their feet. They smiled warmly. To Claudia, the greeting appeared genuine. Stephen gestured towards a vacant chair while saying, 'It's good to have you home, Claudia.'

'Thank you. It's good to be home.'

As they regained their seats, Claudia taking the vacant one. Inspector Axel asked, 'How are Max and Olivia?'

'They were in good spirits, but Max had a niggling cough and a temperature. I was surprised when Stephen suggested they remain in Spain. When I left, there were unthinkable numbers of people, the elderly in particular, dying of COVID-19 every day. Yesterday the fatality rate exceeded one thousand again. Surely Britain, with its National Health Service, would be a safer place for them to see out the pandemic?'

There was a knock on the door which paused the conversation. James entered, 'Excuse me, Sir. I have a cup of tea for Claudia. Would anyone else like a refill while I am here?'

When Stephen and the Inspector declined, James left.

Stephen looked at Claudia. 'The pandemic is one item Inspector Axel and I were discussing before you arrived, though perhaps lamenting would be a better description.' Stephen hesitated, considering his words. 'I seem to recall having this discussion with you over the phone before you left for Spain. Unfortunately, our R-value remains too high. Pandora's box is well and truly open and Britain is in for a difficult time. Max and Olivia are safest in Spain; besides travel is too dangerous.'

Claudia nodded.

'I fear, Claudia,' Stephen said, his voice heavy with concern. 'We will all be affected by this virus in one way or another. We'll bring Max and Olivia home as soon as Spain relaxes its lockdown rules, before the inevitable second wave hits. By then, I hope Britain will be better prepared.'

Claudia nodded.

Inspector Axel sighed. 'In a genuine disaster, fault is rarely simple. The contagious nature of the virus makes containment difficult for even the most proactive of countries.'

There was a pause in the conversation before Stephen asked, 'How was the handover with Chen Li?'

Claudia stared at Stephen, then raised her hands in exasperation. 'You might have told me that Britain had back flipped over allowing Huawei into its 5G network and that you're drawing up plans to strip out existing Huawei gear by the end of the year. Chen Li stopped short of calling it an act of war, but his language was provocative. He was blunt, telling me that there would be consequences. Stephen, you know it was Davros and H1 Technologies and not the Chinese who were behind the recent tensions. The outcome is what Davros wanted. We've played into his hands.'

Stephen considered his answer for a moment before saying, 'As you know, GCHQ has, for some time, advised the Government against even limited use of Huawei equipment but they approved its use in January. They did not want a dispute with China at the same time as the Brexit negotiations were happening in Europe. That broader geopolitical game has changed, with China imposing national security laws on Hong Kong and enforcing sterilisation on Uighurs and other minorities to curb the Muslim population. This has altered our government's perspective. What China sees as its internal affairs, we perceive as gross and egregious human rights abuse and yet another example of its aggression and wish to dominate world affairs.'

'So, what of Davros?'

The Government's priority, post-Brexit and responding to an increasingly assertive China, is to strengthen its military and economic ties with India. We have satellite imagery in the remote reaches of the Himalayas, on the disputed border between China and India. China is employing the same tactics it used in the South China Sea, incrementally extending its influence. This behaviour is strengthening the emerging Indo-British alliance, which makes the government hesitant to take action against Davros or H1 Technologies at this critical moment, fearful of jeopardising its relations with India.'

'Even if that means signing contracts with H1 Technologies?'

'Yes,' Stephen raised an eyebrow and tilted his head to one side as he said, 'Although I needn't remind you, Claudia, government priorities can change.'

'And what about Adele?' Claudia asked. 'She tried to kill Inspector Axel?'

'The Inspector and I both agree that what occurred is an occupational hazard. Now, if I may ask you another question, Claudia. The Crane. Why the help in Montserrat and the warning in Pi-Ski?'

Claudia shrugged her shoulders. 'I can only guess it was because of Linda; the Crane, not appreciating an impersonator.'

'I see.' Stephen let the silence hang in the air before saying. 'Which means the Crane is one member of the St Mary's Parish Council?'

Claudia pondered her response. *What should she say?* 'That does seem like a logical conclusion, Stephen, but I can't say for certain which one it is.'

Stephen pursed his lips. 'Couldn't or wouldn't?'

Claudia looked at Inspector Axel. 'Perhaps the Inspector's insights are wiser than mine.'

Inspector Axel finished the remains of his coffee and, placing his cup down on the table, said, 'Sorry, Stephen, the Crane could be any of them.'

Annoyance present in his voice, Stephen asked, 'Any, Inspector?'

'Well, yes. The legacy of the Crane could pass from mother to daughter, so it could even be the Vicar.'

Claudia bit her lip, trying to stop herself from smiling.

Stephen shook his head. 'Why do I feel you are both being deliberately misleading? For the time being, at least, I will accept that you have your reasons.' After a moment's silence, Stephen continued, 'Okay, let's move on. How is the Liew family after their ordeal?'

Claudia smiled as she remembered what Olivia had told her and said, 'They're an effective team.'

Stephen and Inspector Axel glanced at each other, the subtlety of the message flying over their heads.

Claudia felt a sense of satisfaction watching her colleagues' puzzlement. Suppressing a grin, she asked, 'How is Daniel Tinkov? Did he make it safely to the UK?'

Stephen nodded. 'Yes, thanks to you. He's still with us for the time being and, when he's moved, even I won't know of his new identity. What we learned from Daniel Tinkov and the information you gathered from Linda Orr has awakened the security service to the threat posed by The Firm and The Seven. We are slowly unravelling the identities of the seven. Hopefully, this will lead us to the Principal, the head of this new organisation. We know Sergey Rutskoy is Jasper, and that Azim Singh is Davros. There is also an avatar called Cosy Bear, who the actual individual is, we don't yet know. However, we assume that he, or she, has links to the Russian Intelligence Services hacking group, Cozy Bear.' Stephen paused. He gave Claudia an inquisitorial look before asking. 'Your ex-boyfriend, the Russian Mafia Boss, Monya; is he the avatar Cosy Bear, perhaps?'

Claudia chuckled. 'Were the hackers successful in securing the information about ongoing COVID-19 vaccine research?'

The question caught Stephen by surprise, which showed in the tone of his voice as he said, 'No.'

'Well, that's your answer.'

Stephen shifted uncomfortably in his seat before saying, 'Identifying the person calling themselves The Principal and the remaining members of The Firm is a priority. Taking down Jasper was a victory, but there's more to be done.'

Claudia, thinking of Davros, muttered, 'When it suits you!'

'Indeed Claudia,' Stephen replied, a smile creeping across his face. 'I recall you like ancient proverbs. What is it they say? *The enemy of my enemy is my friend.*'

'Indeed, Stephen. Did you find Charles Scott from Barra Island, Inspector?'

Inspector Axel shook his head. 'No, and we can only assume that he's dead. Perhaps you could ask Linda Orr when you see her this evening?'

Oh, they know I'm seeing Linda. Now, that's interesting.

'Yes, I can do that for you, Inspector. When I was at Montserrat, Linda promised me a drink, and she's paying.'

'Did she indeed,' Stephen said. 'At The Windsor Castle I understand. I take it you won't be lending her your phone again!'

Claudia raised her hands, a sign of defeat, as she chuckled and said, 'What can I say other than sorry?'

Stephen nodded. 'Under the circumstances, Claudia, allowing for the murder of John, your apology is accepted.' Stephen breathed out slowly, 'I must ask Claudia, what are your intentions for Linda?'

Claudia thought for a moment before answering.

Two octogenarians, Saint Vladimir, seven-year-old Molly, Snowflake the cat, and a man called John Moss had left their mark in ways that meant her life had forever changed.

'To savour a glass of Rose Gold Methuselah–anything else is a decision for MI6.'

'Indeed, it is Claudia. Indeed, it is.'

THE END

MOLLY'S UNICORN STORY:
WRITTEN BY: CHARLEE ROBERTS, AGED NINE-YEARS.

One foggy day there was a mysterious village of Unicorns and Pegasus in all shapes and sizes and colours. One was called Frostys. She had a BFF named Snowflake. Snowflake had a BFF named Flora. Flora had a BFF called Brownie. One day a girl named Molly was flying through the air in a helicopter. She saw Frostys and thought, what a beautiful unicorn. So, she landed in her helicopter nearby and found four Unicorns standing there. 'Hi, my name is Molly, what's yours?' she asked them.

'My name is Frostys, my name is Snowflake, my name is Flora, and my name is Brownie,' said each of the Unicorns.

'Would you like to be friends?' Molly asked.

'Yes please,' they all said. 'Will you come home with us and play.

As they were now all friends, Molly decided to write the Unicorns a special poem; quite a few.

Dear Unicorns ever so kind

One day I would like to find

The loveliest friend

But in the end

If I can't, I don't mind.

Unicorns all glamorous and amazing

With braids all through their shiny hair

They love to eat sparkling cupcakes

Mythical creatures are everywhere.

Dear lovely Unicorns oh so sweet,

I would love to give you a treat,

So, tell me what you like, and

I'll get out my bike

And ride down the street.

Unicorn with a shining horn,

Dancing on the lawn,

Said hi to a fawn,

Then suddenly its eyes were drawn,

To something in the lawn.

One day at 8:30 in the morning, Molly carried the poems to the unicorn's house in the mysterious village and knocked on the door. No response. So, she reached into her pocket and pulled out a key. The Unicorns had given her a spare key to their apartment. She put it in, twisted the lock...but there was no one home!

Maybe I'm not their friend anymore, she thought. *Maybe I said something wrong. Maybe they don't like me so they ran away*. Her brain was going 100 kilometres an hour.

She spent the whole afternoon trying to think of a reason that the Unicorns would leave.

***

Now Molly's mum was home from work and was cooking dinner. Tonight, it was Spaghetti, Bolognese.

Finally, they were at the table when there came a knock at the door. Molly's Mum gave Molly a secret nod so that meant she could answer it. You would not believe who it was. Frostys, Snowflake, Flora and Brownie were all waiting behind the door. They were covered in fairy floss. For some reason, when Molly's Mum saw them, she opened her mouth so wide that the spaghetti fell out.

'Mum these are my new friends,' Molly said, picking fairy floss off Frostys.

'They can't stay here!!!' cried Mum.

'Yes, they can. It's just for tonight,' Molly said, passing Mum a piece of fairy floss.

'Fine,' grumbled Mum.

Molly gave them the rest of her spaghetti, as they told her about where they had been. 'It was magical,' Brownie said.

'Yes,' said Snowflake and it was lucky we got out before the rain.

'We went to a magical circus,' said Frostys.

'That is why we are covered in fairy floss,' said Flora.'

'I would love to go to a magical circus,' said Molly and gave each Unicorn one of the poems she had written.

'It's a shame we don't know how to get humans there,' sighed Snowflake. 'These are lovely poems by the way,' she added, to keep Molly's mind off the magical circus.

'Thank you,' said Molly. I have considered being a poet one day, but she was still sad about the magical circus.

Flora came up with an idea. 'How about we describe everything to you, and you can imagine you're there.'

'That would be lovely', replied Molly and she imagined lush blue skies, chocolate rivers, and flying in her helicopter and seeing the magical circus in a field beside a mysterious village.

LOVE LETTER FROM DRESDEN

MARK A. BIGGS

WWII love letters tell of romance and tragedy

Moving her mother into a nursing home, Jacinta discovers a bundle of old love letters setting her on a journey of discovery. What unfolds is a touching story of lost but enduring love, a tale of death and heartbreak. But sometimes the truth is best undisturbed.

"With the winds of time, love letters drift from our lives, taking their secrets with them".

OPERATION UNDERPANTS

Book #1 Max & Olivia Series

MARK A. BIGGS

Growing old is peculiar to the individual

Unceremoniously dumped in a retirement home by their children, international spies Max and Olivia languish, forgotten and waiting to die. After finding a secret message in the newspaper, they must escape and travel to the UK with the fate of London and much of the world hanging in the balance.

CLAUDIA

Book #2 Max & Olivia Series

MARK A. BIGGS

The adventures of our eccentric old spies, Max & Olivia continue in the exciting sequel to Operation Underpants. *Claudia* is an uplifting story full of danger, fear, good vs evil, never being too old, never giving up hope, and having ultimate faith in others.

Feared assassin Claudia doesn't kill Max but takes him with her - putting her at war with herself and a past she hoped to forget. Meanwhile, Olivia must escape the watchful eye of MI6 to track her beloved husband Max across Europe, leaving in her wake a delicious trail of chaos.

OPERATION OBE

Book #3 Max & Olivia Series

MARK A. BIGGS

Novichok Nerve Agent, Gutenberg Bible, Russian Oligarch

Max & Olivia face their greatest challenge

Living their remaining days onboard the Queen Mary 2, Max and Olivia are suddenly dragged back into the world of international espionage and an undeclared war with Russia.

A story of adventure, humour and love set against the happenings of the world today.

Operation Snowflake

Book #6 Max & Olivia Series

Mark A. Biggs

Till death us do part

Operation Snowflake brings an end to the delightful six-part Max and Olivia series. In this story, Olivia and Max must prevent the forced rendition of Samantha, her eight-year-old daughter Molly and Snowflake the cat, from Britain to Beijing. Tensions between the United Kingdom and China run high, as a British aircraft carrier strike group prepares to sail through the South China Sea.

This is a story for everyone, a story for a lifetime.